WELCOME TO KAMINI

GUERNICA WORLD EDITIONS 39

WELCOME TO KAMINI

Don Engebretson

GUERNICA
World
EDITIONS

TORONTO—CHICAGO—BUFFALO—LANCASTER (U.K.)
2021

Michael Mirolla, general editor
Scott Walker, editor
Interior design: Jill Ronsley, suneditwrite.com
Cover design: Errol F. Richardson
from royalty free images in the public domain.

Guernica Editions Inc.
287 Templemead Drive, Hamilton (ON), Canada L8W 2W4
2250 Military Road, Tonawanda, N.Y. 14150-6000 U.S.A.
www.guernicaeditions.com

Distributors:
Independent Publishers Group (IPG)
600 North Pulaski Road, Chicago IL 60624
University of Toronto Press Distribution (UTP)
5201 Dufferin Street, Toronto (ON), Canada M3H 5T8
Gazelle Book Services, White Cross Mills
High Town, Lancaster LA1 4XS U.K.

First edition.

Legal Deposit—Third Quarter
Library of Congress Catalog Card Number: 2021937480
Library and Archives Canada Cataloguing in Publication
Title: Welcome to Kamini / Don Engebretson.
Names: Engebretson, Don, 1955- author.
Series: Guernica world editions ; 39.
Description: Series statement: Guernica world editions ; 39
Identifiers: Canadiana (print) 20210141689 | Canadiana (ebook)
20210141700 | ISBN 9781771836609 (softcover) | ISBN 9781771836616
(EPUB) | ISBN 9781771836623 (Kindle)
Subjects: LCGFT: Novels.
Classification: LCC PS3605.N44 W45 2021 | DDC 813/.6—dc23

In Memoriam

Dave Schneider
Minaki, Ontario

Carpenter • Guide • Bush Pilot
Husband • Father • Friend

A Few Words from the Author

Not so long ago, in a simpler time, the Hudson's Bay Corporation—the oldest corporation in North America—had stores in small Canadian towns. Canadian readers will know that it no longer does, but in this novel, the town of Kamini still has one. That's because I used to buy candy and comic books there, and I miss it.

As an American author writing a novel set in both Canada and the US, the subtle spelling differences between certain words shared by Canadians and Americans caused me fits in the early drafts. In Canada, one buys a *licence*; in America, a *license*. Additional words in the book with two spellings include favour/favor, harbour/harbor, metre/meter, colour/color, neighbour/neighbor and no doubt several more I can't recall at the moment.

I had to take a stand, and opted to use American spellings throughout, even when the word is spoken by a Canadian character. I feared that some American readers might think they'd caught a typo. I did let Gribber say "grey" one time (grey/gray), but he put his foot down. You don't mess around with Gribber.

As for juggling the differences between the two country's systems for weights and measures (Metric in Canada, Customary Units with a dash of Imperial Units in the US), I did the best I could, until finally throwing up my hands and making it a running gag.

To every people the land is given on condition.
Perceived or not, there is a Covenant,
beyond the constitution, beyond sovereign guarantee,
beyond the nation's sweetest dreams of itself.

—Leonard Cohen

Chapter 1

Two figures pushed off from the dock in a canoe after sunset. Embarking on their mischief in the evening provided grand benefits beyond the cover of darkness.

They lived in Kamini and knew that evening in the Ontario bush is infused with sound and scent. On still nights, when the sprawling miles of water flowing through the wilderness turn to glass, the ghostly wails of loons echo for miles. When the wind persists, soft rhythmic clapping of waves along jagged granite shores adds a soothing, seductive cadence. Crisp notes of pine, spruce and fir spice the air. These mingle with the musky odor of damp ancient soil to concoct a bracing, primordial bouquet. Sweet yet earthy, the robust scent permanently perfumes the souls of those who enter, and stay.

This spring night, under a slender crescent moon, the surface of the great river lay still. After landing on the opposite shore, the two paddlers crept silently into the bush. Walking fully upright for more than a few steps was no option. Crouching and at times scrambling on hands and knees where thinning tree branches offered the only passage, they advanced swiftly through the rising, erratic forest floor toward their destination. Seventy yards from shore they reached the crest of the slope. Here the trees halted as a broad patch of smooth granite emerged from beneath them, covered sporadically by tufted grasses growing only where crevices harbored thin deposits of soil. Lying on their stomachs and rising on elbows, they had a clear view of the activity in the clearing below.

Two halogen lights rose on stands, illuminating the area from a narrow dock ramp to a late-model Chevy pickup backed up to a folding table. The low, dull strumming of a gasoline generator came from a slumping shoreline shack nestled into the bush just outside the lighted area. Tied to the dock was the battered, twenty-foot commercial fishing boat christened *Keeper* and owned by Andriy Karpenko. For the past twelve years, Karpenko had possessed the only commercial fishing license for the thirty-eight mile stretch of the Winnipeg River flowing from Lake of the Woods to Kamini then on to the Blackdog Dam.

The two watched in silence as the portly Karpenko, dressed in rubber boots and frayed coveralls, carried a large plastic bin from the hold of *Keeper* up the ramp. The big Ukrainian walked slowly and grunted as he slid the bin up onto the table. He removed the lid and then removed fish, grabbing one in each hand by a gill, and quickly stacked them lengthwise in two coolers. The delicate herringbone pattern of each fish's scales shimmered gold under the lights. When only four inches of space remained in each cooler, Karpenko slit open a bag of cubed ice and poured it over the fish before snapping closed the lids. He slid the coolers into the truck bed and returned to the boat.

One of the observers, a slender man whose age was difficult to discern as he blended in with the shadows, turned his head to whisper to his companion. "I counted twenty in the bin. Six and seven pounders. Big walnuts."

His companion didn't respond. Karpenko reappeared on the dock, carrying another bin toward shore. He set it on the table, removed the lid and began unloading more fish.

Rising higher to get a better look, the soft moonlight revealed the second observer was a woman, her long, dark hair framing a sharp-featured face of exotic beauty. "Some of them are eight," she whispered.

"What do you want to do?" the man asked. "Roar down there and confront him? Or should we wait for adult supervision?"

The woman gave a subtle shake of her head. The two watched silently for another minute as Karpenko repeated the process, loading the golden fish from the second bin into more coolers.

Without sound or signal, the woman began to crawl backward toward the edge of the dense tree line. The man did the same. When safely out of sight, they rose, turned and vanished into the bush.

Chapter 2

So now it's six-forty, Russell Dean thought as he wheeled his black BMW M5 from the garage at his home in Lake Forest. Should he follow the lakeshore into Chicago, to arrive at his downtown office by eight? The route took forty-five minutes six years ago, when he and Cheryl bought their grand, Lake Michigan shoreline house. Now, with spring road projects and increase in rush hour traffic, it could take twice that long.

Might as well bite the bullet and head west to I-94, he decided. Stretches of it will creep but he'd avoid the bump-and-grind of garbage and delivery trucks, the delays from police cars and ambulances racing to the scene of the crime and the infuriating pedestrian traffic from inner city denizens jamming the crosswalks between dozens of downtown blocks.

Merging onto the interstate, the massive Chicago skyline and its iconic Willis Tower came into view. The tower always sparked in Russell the memory of the first time he saw it as a ten-year-old, back when it was the tallest building in the world. His parents loaded him and his sister into the station wagon and left their farm near Kaweena to experience the wonders of the big city. Before his family entered the tower to admire the view from the top, he stared up at the building's 1,453 feet and for the first time in his life felt like an alien creature.

Now his firm had over four thousand square feet of expensive, well-appointed office space in that very tower. It had been famous as the Sears Tower before Sears moved out in the mid-nineties and eventually filed for bankruptcy. While racing past slower traffic, Russell pinpointed the reason for the once-mammoth company's demise: Its leaders had been unable to predict the future.

Russell ignored the horn beeps and blasts from drivers annoyed by his aggressive driving. Annoyance in others was based solely on their perception. He was a swift and assured driver in a superb automobile. He knew he created no danger as he blew around them. "Asshole!" one man shouted, having rolled down his window after briefly catching up to the BMW during a slow-down. Russell turned his head and gave the angry man a gentle smile.

Inside the Willis Tower underground parking garage he eased the BMW into his reserved stall and took the elevator to the 70th floor, making a mental note to send a stern email to the garage supervisor. Employees were to wipe down his vehicle with a barely damp chamois each day to remove any bit of dirt. Twice recently they missed a spot.

Russell smiled broadly when he exited the elevator and said good morning to Tyrell, the impeccably groomed and sharply dressed guard seated behind the curving Brazilian ipe wood security kiosk. "Good morning to you, sir," Tyrell said as Russell strode to the oak double doors of Samuels Dean Advertising.

Jessica, the firm's young receptionist, greeted him as he entered and glanced at her computer screen. "You have a ten o'clock conference call with Mr. Samuels and the folks at ESPN, and lunch at twelve thirty with Bill Carter."

"Lovely Jessica, thank you. Plus, I'm leaving on a well-deserved vacation right after lunch, don't forget."

"Yes, of course! And I have absolutely no details about what you'll be doing on *that*," Jessica said, a flash to her green eyes. "Have fun in Canada. Ontario, isn't it?"

Flirting with the boss, Russell thought. Approved. He winked in reply and headed to his office. Ten would work. He would have two hours to review the newest batch of ESPN radio, television and electronic media ad copy before the call.

He shut his office door behind him, hung his tailored Tom Ford suit coat in his closet and poured a cup of coffee from the carafe delivered by an intern only minutes earlier.

Russell glanced at his desk. Aside from his iMac Pro Xeon with its massive screen and a cordless phone set, the folder

containing the ad copy was the only thing on it. Three weeks ago
he had placed the framed photo of Cheryl face down in a drawer
of the bureau centered along twenty feet of floor-to-ceiling glass
that gave his office its commanding view of downtown, the Art
Institute, Grant Park and Lake Michigan.

Russell sat, loosened his tie and reached for the file holding
the copy. All advertising copy written by associates was printed
on paper, as he requested. He found reading copy on a computer
screen added a level of deception to the writing. Words on paper
didn't lie. Russell opened the folder and read the subject title across
the first page: ESPN+ Fishing Fantasy :30 Copy to be Read by
ESPN Radio Hosts. He shuddered. ESPN recently had launched
their new video-streaming app, ESPN+. Promotions included an
all-expense paid Florida offshore fishing "experience" to one new
subscriber. It was hackneyed—the winner would spend two days
in a bobbing boat on the ocean, fishing, drinking and probably
throwing up with a couple of B-list retired pro ballplayers—but it
was in the works and announced prior to Samuels Dean winning
the coveted account last month.

He glanced at the name of the copywriter: Adam Corby,
one of the firm's newer hires. The Stanford kid. Russell placed
his iPhone in front of him, pulled up the stopwatch and tapped
"Start." Assuming his radio announcer voice, he began reading
aloud:

"Fantasy baseball gets a new spin when one lucky ESPN Plus
subscriber will have their fishing fantasy dreams turned into reality—three nights deluxe hotel accommodations and two full days
of fabulous fishing off Florida's Gulf Coast. Joined by your shipmates, former baseball greats Herb Costello of the Miami Marlins
and Minnesota Twin Jorge Perez, by day you'll cruise the Gulf
Coast's crystal blue waters in search of trophy fish, then by night
enjoy the lavish hospitality of the Ritz-Carlton Sarasota. Register
to win by downloading the ESPN Plus app on your smartphone,
then get ready to pack your pole and take home some lifetime
experiences courtesy of ESPN!"

Russell tapped STOP on the stopwatch and muttered a favored obscenity. The copy was hopeless. Worthless. Comically so. He glanced at the time on the stopwatch: 31.15 seconds, read at a galloping pace. In addition to being absolute crap, it was one second too long. Now he would have to call in Corby, tear him apart, then see if there was any hope of putting him back together. He buzzed Marilyn, the senior admin he shared with his partner and asked to see Adam Corby. Twenty seconds later Corby knocked and entered.

"Ah, good morning, Adam. Please, sit down." Russell motioned toward two plush leather chairs facing his desk. "I need to speak to you about the ESPN radio copy."

Corby—blond, vaguely handsome in a California surfer-dude way—selected a chair and sat. "Do you think it's alright, sir?"

"No, Adam, it's not." Russell paused. Be a mentor, he reminded himself. Take it easy on the kid. You once were a young advertising copywriter fresh out of college wearing a cheap JC Penney suit. Control yourself. Try to teach, not torch. "Adam, you must be able to recognize clichés," Russell said calmly. "'Turning your dreams into reality' is perhaps the most over-used advertising phrase of all time. It isn't original. Are you under the impression you created the phrase? That it's never before been used?"

"Well ..." Corby said, his face flushing red. "I ... I may have heard it, somewhere, maybe."

"Somewhere, maybe? It's been around at least fifty years. Watch any low-budget television ad for any siding and replacement window company in Chicago, or any shit-kicker town in America, for that matter," Russell added, his voice rising, "and the fat and balding owner, the same schmuck who wrote the ad and stars in it, will look into the camera at the close and tell you his company will help turn your fucking dreams into your fucking realities."

Corby swallowed air, unable to speak.

"'Deluxe hotel accommodations'?" Russell said, looking up from the copy. "What, you didn't know how to spell 'luxurious'? Good thing, that would have stunk also."

Corby, near cross-eyed, stared at a vague point just above his crotch.

Russell continued to scan the copy. "You state in your lead that the fishing takes place on the Gulf Coast then in the next sentence repeat the information. Why write 'by day you'll cruise the Gulf Coast's crystal blue waters' when we already know where we are? When saying 'by day you'll cruise crystal blue waters' paints the same picture only cleaner? It also shortens the ad length by a second, so the announcer doesn't have a fucking coronary trying to spit this crap out in thirty seconds."

Corby was shrinking in size now, his unfocused eyes losing the glint of life as his breathing slowed to that of a mammal in hibernation.

"'Pack your pole'?" Russell said, chuckling. "As in fishing pole? Is that what they're called? When deep sea fishing, one uses a long, slender bamboo device, is that it? From the tip of which is affixed what, a bit of cotton string? With a safety pin hook? The term, Adam, is fishing *rod*, and it makes no sense for the winner to pack one unless he's one in perhaps five thousand Americans who indeed owns a deep-sea fishing rod. When you're on a charter fishing boat, the rods—and the reels, for that matter—are supplied."

The young Stanford graduate began unconsciously shaking his knees rapidly together and apart, an adolescent ADHD habit previously eradicated by drug and behavioral therapy when he was twelve.

"Then in your close you write, 'Take home some lifetime experiences.' Never use the word 'some' to describe quantity. It defines nothing and is the dullest word in the English language. Note also your close ends on the word 'experiences.' A lifeless dud. What would you prefer, Adam, 'some lifetime experiences,' or the experience of a lifetime? How about, 'Take home the experience of a lifetime, courtesy of ESPN?' Rather a more attractive offer, wouldn't you agree?"

Russell stood, which Corby, despite his torpid state, recognized as signaling the end to the meeting.

"Adam, it's about simple, clear communication, writing in such a way that the mind of the person hearing the ad receives and processes the information exactly as designed without having to think about it."

Corby nodded too eagerly, like a bobble head doll. "I see, sir. That's all ... a big help. I'll get to work right away on a rewrite."

"Wonderful. Take ten minutes, really tune it."

Corby stood up, almost, a few seconds passing before his legs resumed normal function. He started unsteadily toward the door.

"Oh, Adam, one last thing." Corby turned. Russell smiled. "I liked 'shipmates.' Yeah, it's a boat, not a ship, but ... calling the ballplayers your shipmates, that was good."

Chapter 3

"I call this meeting of the Kamini Clown Tonsil to order," Lou LeBlanc said, banging a loose fist on the sagging plastic conference table before him. He had not garbled his words. LeBlanc always called the Town Council the Clown Tonsil, ever since garbling his words at the start of a meeting seven years ago. He glanced at the cracked screen of his cell phone: nine twenty-six a.m. He had called the meeting for nine, meaning most members of the six-person council, including LeBlanc, found their way to the outside of the clapboard Kamini Community Center by around nine fifteen. There, some smoked and all chatted while waiting for the rest to arrive.

"Let the record show the meeting started late."

"Noted," said Faith Pearson, a petite, baking- and fishing-crazed high school English teacher serving a life sentence as Town Council secretary. She gave a brief scratch to a yellow legal pad.

The burly LeBlanc wore a tattered Kamini Lodge fishing cap, jeans and faded lumberman's shirt and sported a ragged, salt-and-pepper beard. He adjusted his large metal-frame glasses.

"Thank you for coming on such short notice. First and only item of business: the activities of one Andriy Karpenko." He glanced at the lone council member not seated in a metal folding chair facing him. "Gribber, why don't you tell everyone what you told me last night?"

John Dogrib slipped from his perch on the edge of a pool table and walked toward the front of the room. Just over six feet tall and lean, dressed in faded green warm-up pants and a black t-shirt, his slow amble couldn't disguise that his long legs and broad shoulders belonged to a man of athletic prowess. Though the white silk-screened letters running down the side of each pant leg were long ago dismissed by age and laundering, their dim outline remained: Dartmouth.

Earlier that morning he had stood at his bathroom mirror and cut his full head of thick, long black hair short for summer. Wielding scissors and a scalpel-sharp filleting knife, he deftly achieved a feathered, punk rock look. His face was splendid sculpture, broad cheekbones, softly curved nose, full lips and dimpled, square chin. Large, dark brown eyes proved rich complimentary contrast to his almond-colored skin. Even under the fluorescent lighting of the Community Center, his age would have been difficult to discern. An Ojibwe of the Wabaseemoong Independent Nations, at a glance he could pass for thirty. Only when staring directly into his eyes did one see an older man.

Gribber approached the table and turned slowly to address his fellow council members. What flew from his mouth was a deep voice spraying a rapid-fire barrage of clipped words disguised as buckshot. "So two weeks ago when the spring whitefish season started, I noticed Karp had set his nets in the usual spots, Mine Bay, Big Sand. He gets up every morning to bilge out *Keeper* if it isn't already at the bottom of the drink, motors out and harvests the fish in the afternoon. He resets his nets, heads back to his shack, ices 'em up, delivers them to the wholesalers in Miskwa and is home in time for cocktails and a fashionably late supper.

"Last week I brought an early party up to Roughrock, three yahoo firemen from Milwaukee. See if I could possibly convince one of them to keep from getting hung up long enough to somehow snag a walleye and cease their endless blathering about steelhead fishing on Lake Michigan. By noon that storm was coming in, so rather than land and build the fire for shore lunch on the rock point so I could watch it wash into the river like last time, I headed for the grassy spot under the oaks in that little bay at the end of the narrows.

"Coming in I passed a gill net. Almost ran over it because the floats weren't orange, they were grey. Blended right in with the chop. So I figured one of the locals was engaging in a little illegal walleye harvesting, and I wouldn't put it past any of you, or a better chance that ol' Andriy was expanding his product line to the crooks at the Miskwa fish wholesalers. Because no whitefish worth its girth is going to be swimming out of a tiny bay in the narrows in spring."

Some in attendance nodded while all understood his reasoning. Whitefish schooled in large, shallow bays near deep water in late August, congregating in great numbers before beginning their fall spawning ritual. This was why the fall commercial netting season was a lucrative one for licensed fishermen such as Karpenko. The two-week spring season was a recent add-on by the Ontario Ministry. Adult whitefish moved quickly from these large bays into deep waters after ice-out, making netting viable for a brief period.

"The firemen headed home the next day—fifty dollar tip for four days, cheap bastards—so I shot down to Roughrock in the afternoon, except no nets. Maybe Karp's pitching for walleye in different spots, so I checked the small bays and channels with current, but no dice. So I call Jammer and for the next few days he and I take turns late afternoons watching for Karp to head back to his landing in Pistol Lake, parking in Mullock's boathouse near the entrance so he wouldn't see our boats. Mullock and his current mistress don't sneak down and open the cottage until early July, after Marnie's been off from teaching long enough to get safely back on the sauce and start driving Mullock nuts."

"Damn it, Grib," LeBlanc said. "Get to it."

"First couple days, *Keeper* swings by and heads into Pistol around five coming from the north, meaning he's returning from Big Sand or Mine Bay—spring whitefish territory. Next day, on my watch, no *Keeper*. Seven, eight o'clock, sun getting low, still no *Keeper*. I figure, terrific, he's broken down somewhere and dropped anchor for the night, sipping his vodka and swapping one-liners with the loons. Then ten minutes to nine I hear her motoring up the west channel from Roughrock. So I figure every three days he's setting nets for walleye early morning down there, harvesting and removing the nets in evening when there's less boat traffic and chance of being seen.

"If he keeps that schedule—we all know he's a stubborn, clockwork Ukrainian, of course he keeps that schedule—yesterday was a walleye day. Jammer had to fly some guests up to the Big North outpost on Otter and spend the night, so I asked Annie if she'd join me for some late night espionage. She has eyes like an eagle and in case anything went sideways, she's good in a fight." Gribber proceeded to recount what he and his friend Annie Chase observed while spying on Andriy Karpenko's landing the night before.

"You sure they were walleyes?" Gordon "Gang" Green, general manager of the town's Hudson's Bay store, asked. Corporate had transferred him, kicking and screaming, to the tiny Kamini outpost from the large Regina store for a two-year rotation fourteen years ago. "How could you see? You must have been way out in the bay, so Karp wouldn't hear you coming in."

"Foolish mortals. We drove my steed into Pistol towing Annie's canoe, parked at the campground docks, then paddled across the marsh at the base of Billings Point. Crawled through the bush to the top of the bluff looking down on Karp's landing. He'd set lights. We had a clear view from fifteen meters while he unloaded the fish."

LeBlanc lifted his cap to scratch his head. "You know, this is starting to make sense. It was four years ago the Ministry approved the damn spring whitefish season, and Karp started coming down in May. I remember he told me the first year the harvest was hardly worth his time and boat gas, he was only making a few bucks. If he started netting walleyes after that—three years of netting, especially big females, could explain the drop in the walleye population."

The slump in walleye fishing the past several years—small but noticeable—was of great concern to the 147 year-round residents of Kamini. The local resorts attracted their share of musky, northern pike and smallmouth bass aficionados, but walleye was the game fish of choice for many of the nearly three thousand Canadian, American and European anglers who descended on the town between June and September each year.

"We'll need evidence for the Ministry—photos, video, something tangible," Dave Burtnyk, the round-faced, jovial owner of the town's lone bait shop, said. "They won't send an officer from Thunder Bay to investigate otherwise."

"Yeah, and even with proof, that could be a month from now," added Kim Anderson, co-owner with husband Bruce of Great North Lodge, one of four fishing and hunting camps scattered across the vast islands and mainland of the Winnipeg River around Kamini. The fifth tourist destination, and main lifeblood of the town, was the famous "Jewel of the North," the massive Kamini Lodge. "Look how long it takes the Ministry to fix the road every time it washes out. We're two minutes away from the start of tourist season, most of us are booked full, and the road's been out for four days."

"Two days from now, Sunday, could be the last time Karp double dips," Gribber said. "His season ends soon. We want evidence, we may need to pay him a little visit Sunday night before he takes off until fall."

LeBlanc spoke sternly to his friend. "Gribber, I want to go on record as saying I have no idea what you intend to do, would not condone it if I knew, and speaking for the Council, I implore you not to take action of any kind. That said, please inform the Council of your plan at your earliest convenience. All in favor, say 'Aye.'"

"Aye," the Council members said.

"Noted," chirped Faith Pearson, without moving her pen.

Chapter 4

At nine fifty-five, Russell's iMac chimed to life and the conferencing screen appeared. His partner, Dan Samuels, was live in the upper left of four video frames.

"Good morning, killer," Samuels said. "We'll be joined by Jack Pattridge and Alan Rowe in Bristol. They have a few comments on the new campaign. Doubt we'll need to get into any great detail. You still on schedule to take off this afternoon?"

"Debatable. I've made it through half the new ad copy. All of it needs work. Same old problem. We're hiring the top kids with shiny marketing degrees from the best colleges, and none of them can write."

"You could dump it all on Caroline." Caroline Klein was the firm's talented senior VP.

"No, she's up to her ears with Grain Berry and Ikea. Which reminds me, if I hear that Grain Berry cereal jingle one more time, I'm going to shoot myself."

"Sign of a great jingle," his partner said, chuckling. "Gets stuck in your head and keeps you up at night."

"Keeping me up at night is one thing. Keeping me up at night contemplating suicide is quite another."

Russell's computer chimed twice, and the faces of the two ESPN marketing directors appeared on his screen. The meeting proceeded in breezy fashion until Pattridge, ESPN senior head of marketing, raised concern about the new advertising campaign's overall lack of "edginess," saying: "It's slick, I see how the parts fit together, but it's all fun and games. At ESPN, we don't shy away from controversy."

15

"No, you don't, which is one reason why your television ratings have slipped and membership is down," Russell said. Staring only at Pattridge on his computer screen, he didn't notice his partner raise his eyebrows in alarm. "Fun and games is an apt description of what ESPN should be about, what it used to be about, back when your network became the most successful startup in cable history. 'Controversy' today is a synonym for 'political,' and if there's one thing Americans are sick of, it's politics. You're covering protests and boycotts and gender equality issues like the news stations. My advice to your network is the same I give our clients in the entertainment industry. Stay out of it."

Silence hung for several seconds until Samuels cut through it. "I think what Russell is saying is that instilling the fun factor back into the marketing, and lessening the distractions, will serve your network best."

"I guess we'll just have to wait and see," Pattridge said. "We're willing to hold judgment until the final ratings at the end of the year. I just hope we selected the right agency after all."

"That, I'm not worried about," Samuels said. The four men signed off with awkward goodbyes. Seconds later, Samuels strode briskly into Russell's office. "Jesus Christ, what's gotten into you? Snapping at a client? Having to be right all the time? I know the divorce and … the other thing are weighing on you, but I'm worried it's affecting your work."

"Relax, Dan. You read the three-year contract we signed with ESPN. Pattridge couldn't fire us if he caught me screwing his wife. You also know everything I said in the meeting is true. It's better they get their minds straight about the new direction now, rather than later."

"I suppose. I've never doubted you before and, well, look at us," Samuels said, admiring the view from Russell's office that matched his own. "I guess it's good timing for a two-week vacation. God knows you haven't taken one in years. Where you headed again? Canada someplace?"

"A tiny town on a river in Northwest Ontario that for some

reason has this grand resort in it, The Kamini Lodge. You remember it from the ad campaign? Built in the nineteen twenties,
breathtaking. Golf course, tennis, fishing, spa, gourmet dining.
I rented a shoreline cabin. The weather start of June should be
sunny, seventies, no bugs—perfect golfing weather. Don't know
much about the fishing, but that's never been my thing."

"You flying?"

"Nowhere to fly to, unless I want to charter a floatplane, and
you know how I hate small planes. Going to run up there in my
new pickup. There's a gravel road into the town." Russell smiled
at his partner. "Relax, Daniel. Give me two weeks away from the
grist mill, and I promise I'll come back a new man."

"I know you will," Samuels said with a nod as he turned and
left the office.

Russell immediately called his attorney, Bill Carter, to cancel
his lunch meeting, telling Carter's secretary to have Bill call him
tomorrow. He hung up and closed his eyes. He wanted to get
the latest update on the divorce proceedings from Bill at lunch,
head straight home, pack and be on the road by three. It was a
seven-hour drive to Minneapolis, then another eleven to Kamini.
He'd made a motel reservation in someplace named Cloquet,
Minnesota, two hours north of the Twin Cities, to break the trip
roughly in half. Editing the ESPN copy, and in some cases starting from scratch, meant he would instead be at the office into the
evening.

Russell rose and crossed his office. He pushed a spot on the
center oak panel of the wall, and with a click the hidden door to
his elegant private bathroom swung open. After splashing cold
water on his face, he bent at the waist, placed both hands on the
edge of the marble sink and stared at his reflection in the mirror.
Russell recognized the act as a dramatic effect, a cliché, a tired old
bit from a thousand movies. He did it anyway. A touch of theat-
rics was called for.

Russell smiled at what he saw. Wavy mane of black hair,
deep blue eyes, broad shoulders and six-foot three-inch height.

Ruggedly handsome, more so at forty than ever before. He reflected deeper on the man in the mirror.

His entire life had been about controlling his environment.
Precision. Order. Knowing best. It had served him well. Escaping
the farm and rejecting the life sentence of humble, meaningless
agrarian toil so cheerfully embraced by his parents. Climbing to
the top of his class at Northwestern, landing a job straight out of
college at top-ranked Frankel & Company, his quick emergence
as the golden wunderkind of Chicago advertising. The national
spotlight, awards, bonuses, prestige. Then came the offer of a part-
nership with Dan when Dan left Frankel to start the new agency.
The astonishing growth of Samuels Dean, the lavish parties, exotic
travel, marrying Cheryl. The five hundred thousand-dollar annual
income while in his thirties. Instead of life becoming tougher it
had become easier.

It was all so perfect. So why did it feel so far from perfect?
What's gotten into me, he asked himself, failing to recognize the
more astute question: What's gone out of me? Russell stepped
back from the mirror and closed his eyes. So, what was the point
to this exercise? What was the root of his problem?

The answer came so clearly that his eyes shot open. No one
in his life was authentic. Dan Samuels wasn't authentic. He was
a five-faced chameleon, a grand schmoozer, a highly polished
sixty-year-old snake oil salesman who told people exactly what
they wanted to hear. Neither was Jessica. She was a twenty-
something programmed product of other people's opinions,
bouncing from vegan to gluten-free to organic diets depending
on whatever she'd read in last week's *Cosmo*. That he hired her
because she was the most attractive of eight equally qualified
women applying for the receptionist position would never in her
lifetime occur to her.

The restaurant maître d's and waiters at the expensive Chicago
eateries where he was known, who fawned over him and Cheryl
to maximize their tips, they weren't real people. His acquaintances
in the industry, at the club, Cheryl's friends—none added value to

his life. Not even Cheryl, Russell realized, was authentic. They'd met eleven years ago after the new agency landed the Life Time Fitness account. She worked in the Life Time marketing department and led him on tours of the company's high-end workout salons sprinkled across the affluent suburbs of Minneapolis and St. Paul. Young, smart, beautiful and, of course, fit, their whirlwind long-distance romance concluded in marriage only seven months later.

Russell's mind traced back to the beginning of tension between them, while buying the large lakefront home five years into their marriage. The ensuing periods of her pleading, awkward silences, tears. Their lavish lifestyle didn't come without his sacrifice, constant travel and sixty- to seventy-hour workweeks. He'd always been faithful, and lord knows he'd been put to the test. Women were drawn to him. That was no fault of his. Now, instead of gratitude, she wanted a divorce. People didn't make sense.

Russell walked back into his office and stared out the plate glass. The only truth, the only honesty, the only sanity he could sense in the world existed in the few inches of air surrounding him. Gazing at the city from inside the Willis Tower, he felt as much an alien creature as when he was ten years old and gazing at the tower from the outside. *A break*, he thought. Yes, it was perfect timing. A two-week break from the suffocating, vast array of imbeciles currently upsetting his immaculately planned and precisely ordered life.

When Russell returned to his desk, he clicked the small JPEG in the corner of his monitor. The colorful photo oozed out and blossomed to fill the enormous screen. He remembered ten years ago when he first saw it. Samuels Dean had picked up a simple job designing and implementing the Midwestern US advertising campaign for the Ontario Ministry of Tourism. The process began with the Ministry sending what seemed like every photo ever taken of the Ontario wilderness. He and staffers sorted through them for hours, trying to find ten suitable images for the campaign and most important, the essential money shot to be

featured in print and television ads, online, and the cover of the
tourism brochures. That photo stared back at him now.

It was, by simplest description, a photo of a building. Yet there
was quite a bit more to it than that. Shot from a plane, the photo
showed the entirety of a massive, stone and timber Ontario wilderness castle. Enormous, chiseled blocks of bluish-gray granite
formed the foundation and structural support columns rising
thirty feet in the air. Large, red-stained cedar logs ran horizon-
tally between the evenly spaced stone columns. Halfway up, the
log work ended as the design transitioned into a white stucco and
timber Tudor style, highlighted by three central dormers. The
steep roof, its peak towering fifty feet above the ground, was shingled in dark green cedar shakes. At each end of the rectangular
structure, the building dropped in height and extended further,
long wings similar in appearance jutting out at forty-five degree
angles front and rear.

As impressive in the photo was the view of the wilderness
territory surrounding the castle. Brilliant blue water edged by
sloping granite shorelines curled around on both sides. The water expanded into a swirling maze of channels, bays, points and
evergreen-covered islands before bleeding off the top of the
image.

Russell found the photo mesmerizing. His gaze fell to the
simple calligraphy centered at the bottom:

Kamini Lodge
The Jewel of the North

Russell Dean knew a great advertising photo when he saw
one. He knew better than most the principles behind marketing,
the power of images and words, how to create advertising that
influenced minds and dictated actions. He knew how to make and
invest money, how to gain the respect of his peers, even how to
make a woman fall in love with him, if only for a while. However,
he did not yet recognize that life—some say by an intangible,

supreme creative force—has a curious way of evolving, not in the direction dictated by the participant but along myriad potential pathways well beyond one's control. Some may lead to a future of quiet (or loud) desperation, others to unsettling and tragic ends, while still others—if one is proven worthy—to shining moments of graceful deliverance.

Above all, he did not recognize when something was calling to him.

Chapter 5

Gribber expertly landed his boat in a tight spot at the Miskwa municipal dock, a deft maneuver achieved by factoring in the approach line, speed, engine angle and timing of the precise moment to shift the motor from neutral into reverse. When mastered, a boat magically halts its forward movement and slides sideways to gently kiss the dock. Gribber's boat was a seventeen-foot Lund powered by a sixty-horsepower Yamaha outboard motor he bought new eight days after arriving in Kamini. It took him one week to dispel his assumption that he was only passing through.

His passenger, Daryl "Jammer" Mackay, adjusted his ragged fishing cap and swept his shoulder-length, almost blonde hair behind his ears and stood. He offered no compliment for Gribber's landing. Jammer could land a boat of any size or horsepower as gracefully, equipped with a tiller or steering wheel, as could Faith Pearson, Lou LeBlanc, Annie Chase, town patriarch Frank Dobbs, or any eight-year-old kid in Kamini. In the Ontario bush, boats replaced cars. Nearly half the residents of Kamini owned only a boat, or two. If disregarding seaworthiness, owning three boats was not uncommon, with one in the water and two of various sizes and vintages perched on crumbling Styrofoam blocks in their side yards.

"So, Canadian Tire, anyplace else?" Jammer asked as he deftly jumped from the boat and tied the bow rope with a quick daisy chain knot.

"Nope, should have everything we need. Fifty bucks from the community fund, I suppose I'm owed a few bucks for gas. And for your stalwart assistance, maybe lunch at Kung Pow's. Sweet and sour chicken balls for both of us."

"God no," Jammer said. "Last time I ate at Kung Pow's, I went after a gig and had the sweet and sour chicken balls. Didn't make it back to my boat before puking. Dyed my Vans orange."

"And your boat? Did you spew in your boat as well?"

"Yeah, I think I did."

"Nearly correct. I was with you. And we took my boat."

Jammer thought intently before speaking. "Yeah, I guess you're right."

Jammer was lead guitarist for the on-again, off-again rock band Chesterfield Potato he'd founded with various Miskwa musician friends. The musician pool was shallow; they had difficulty finding and retaining drummers. He came to Kamini from Winnipeg, Manitoba as an infant. His parents were cottagers, the term for residents who owned the seventy or so summer cottages dotting the islands and mainland shores within eight miles of the town. After graduating high school ten years ago, Jammer spent his summer at the family cottage. When summer left, he remained, moving into a houseboat he had begun building the previous summer. With a knack for carpentry, he found immediate employment repairing cottages and building docks and decks. Bruce Anderson taught Jammer how to fly and sold him an old, single-engine floatplane.

Gribber and Jammer's eighteen-mile boat journey from Kamini to Miskwa, a tourist and paper mill town, took forty-five minutes. That was the average time if the driver knew the most direct route, an important factor. The Winnipeg River was not a river in the standard sense of a flowing waterway with one channel and two opposing banks. It flowed north out of the Lake of the Woods, an enormous, wilderness maze of channels, bays and islands which originated in northern Minnesota. The name changed from Lake of the Woods to the Winnipeg River at Miskwa, but the complex configuration of the stunningly gorgeous river system continued.

Different parts of the river up and downstream from Kamini were given names for reference purposes. Pistol Lake, Gunn Lake, Roughrock Lake, Little Sand and Big Sand Lakes were not lakes, per se; they were sections of the river, often immense, intricate bays billowing off the multiple main channels and filled with their own assortment of channels, bays and islands. Roughrock and Pistol Narrows, Myrtle Rapids, The Big Stretch, The Dalles were distinct sections where the river narrowed, broadened, or split along its nearly forty-mile journey through the Ontario wilderness.

Tourists launched their boats and became lost all the time. Attempting to navigate down a main channel in hope of getting from Point A to Point B could involve boating for miles along a half-mile-wide, picturesque stretch of the river only to zoom around a bend to abrupt discovery of a dead-end bay. Even with a topographic map, the desired route could quickly become confused in the mind of the boater. Is that island directly ahead this island on the map? Or is it the next one? Or maybe the one just passed?

From the dock, Gribber and Jammer walked five blocks to Canadian Tire, a box store chain selling everything a home or cottage owner might need. They grabbed a cart and began filling their shopping list: a gallon of kerosene, sixteen pairs of black cotton socks, light gauge wire, fireworks. Passing electrical materials, Jammer picked out a four-foot length of metal conduit. "Hey Grib, what about getting a bunch of these? Wouldn't burn."

"Jam, jeez, didn't you ever see the movie *Frankenstein*? The black and white original, with Boris Karloff? That's the mood I'm trying to achieve. It's all in the details, my good man."

Checking out, the two agreed lunch wasn't vital, so they returned to Gribber's boat. "Guiding tomorrow?" Jammer asked as they untied and climbed in.

"Just a half-day, musky party of two, Minnesotans who need to be on the road by one. Good thing, I need to see Frank when we get back. By tomorrow afternoon, I'll have a number of peculiar projects to tend to at Morning Wood."

Jammer didn't bother to ask.

Gribber dropped off Jammer at his houseboat, then drove the short distance to Town Bay and docked at Kamini Marina. Along with the Holst Point Pub and the Community Center, the marina served as one of the town's social hubs. It boasted a small convenience store, boat and motor repair shop, and the only gasoline pump in town. Gibber walked the quarter-mile of gravel roads from the marina to the small, weather-beaten home of Frank Dobbs. He found Dobbs sitting on his front porch.

In his seventies, slender and spry, Dobbs's full head of silver hair swirled around his deeply lined face. The distinct twinkle in his hazel eyes hinted at high intelligence. Comb his hair and put him in a finely tailored suit, and he could pass for a high-ranking senior politician or corporate CEO. When Gribber arrived, Dobbs was sipping coffee, smoking a cigarette and reading a two day-old copy of the Toronto *Globe and Mail*. Two days was the soonest major newspapers wended their way to Kamini. "Oh, for fuck's sake," Dobbs said, looking up. "I didn't do it."

"News flash, Frank. There are these things called computers, and this other thing called the Internet. Combined, you get the news of the world as it happens, instead of having to wait forty-eight hours."

"You know, I had a computer once," Dobbs said, folding his paper and placing it on the rusted TV tray next to his Adirondack chair. He leaned forward, his eyes brightening like those of a child thrilled to tell a story to adults. "In the early nineties one showed up on my lab desk at the college. A great, rounded, blue thing. Looked like the hood ornament to a space ship."

"An Apple 'egg.'"

"Egg shmegg. First thing I did was take it apart, of course. Not much to removing the plastic outer shell. And do you know what I found inside?"

"A little label reading, 'Removing Shell Invalidates Warranty'?"

"No." Dobbs glanced quickly right and left. "Fairies. Little blue and pink fairies, flying around a suspended orb of white light like moths around a Coleman camping lantern. Even as a scientist, there are things I don't need to know."

The story of how Dobbs came to live in Kamini was different from the rest, the same as the rest. Early in his career he attended a convention of the Canadian Association of Physicists held at the Kamini Lodge. After the convention he returned to the town for long weekends every chance he could, including in winter. After only a few visits, he no longer paid for his lodging. Enamored by his endearing and childlike albeit salty demeanor, "hosting Frank" was the term used by townspeople who invited him for weekend visits. His first act upon retiring a decade ago was to purchase a year-round home in Kamini.

"I need to build a stereo system for my boat," Gribber said.

"Why the hell? You hardly need music to woo female Lodge guests out of their swimsuits after squiring them up to Big Sand Beach."

"One-time use, Sunday night. Need to blast a song real loud, so it's heard above the sound of the motor from at least a mile away."

"Pretty simple. You need a deep-cycle marine battery, a car radio amplifier, battery powered mixer, RCA stereo cables, contact switches, twelve volt power switch, some alligator clips, speaker cables and speakers, of course. I assume you'll want to play the music off your cell phone?"

"That's what I was hoping."

"The little mixer I have has an input for a phone. I have two, two hundred amp speakers you can borrow. Use one of your marine batteries, fully charged. Car radio amplifier, I imagine you can lift one from any of the junkers over at Red House Johnson's, if he's semi-sober and you bring him a mickey of rye. Or pinch it when he's passed out. I should have everything else you need in my shop. One warning. At seven-point-five-amp-hours for the battery, this contraption is only going to blast your song around seventeen minutes before you're out of juice."

"That should be plenty. Can we go back to your shop and take a look?"

"Certainly," Dobbs said, rising from his chair. "But I have to ask. This wouldn't have anything to do with a certain Andriy Karpenko, would it? I've been hearing things."

Gribber feigned puzzlement. "Andriy who?"

Chapter 6

The alarm on Russell Dean's iPhone broke his slumber at six on Saturday morning with the chorus from Queen's "We Are the Champions." He quickly showered, shaved and dressed in the travel outfit he'd laid out the night before: L.L. Bean canvas deck shoes, tailored khaki pants, blue long-sleeve Polo shirt and cream Ralph Lauren jacket, topped off with his pink gold Cle de Cartier watch. He hauled his computer bag and a small cooler out to his new, metallic red Ford F250 pickup truck standing sentry in the center of his five-car garage. His golf clubs, garment bag, large Eddie Bauer duffel bag and matching tote were already in the truck's bed beneath the black roll-top cover. Climbing up into the driver's seat, Russell was reminded of how high the big truck rode. It was his first truck, and he liked being able to look down at people in cars. It had certain advantages to merely blowing by them in the BMW. He tromped on the gas pedal of the glistening red beast and headed for the freeway. Finally, he was on his way.

Russell had remained at the office until ten the night before. The ESPN marketing campaign to be launched on Monday was complete, honed, perfect. He'd neglected to cancel his hotel room in Cloquet, but at ninety bucks, why bother? Leaving on Saturday morning instead of Friday afternoon he would make more miles before nightfall and had booked a room for the night farther north, at a resort in Orr, Minnesota. He had attempted to call the Kamini Lodge to inform them of his delay, after discovering their website lacked any options for amending reservations. Upon dialing the number, he further was surprised to hear the message, "We're sorry, but the phone number you have dialed is either not in service or the system is experiencing technical problems." Good grief!

After leaving Madison, Wisconsin in his rearview mirror, Russell picked up his phone to again try calling Kamini Lodge. Instead, it rang in his hand.

"Russell Dean here."

"Good morning, Mr. Dean," the female voice at the other end said. "So good to reach you. I'm calling from Kamini Lodge with a few items concerning your arrival later today."

"Yes, very good, I've been trying to reach you as well. I'm afraid I've had a delay and won't be checking in until tomorrow. I attempted to change my reservation on your website, to use the term loosely. Also tried phoning but couldn't get through. A bit frustrating."

"My apologies, Mr. Dean. Two nights ago a storm knocked out power and phone service to the town for a day, even the landlines. So, you'll be checking in tomorrow, Sunday?"

"Yes, I should be arriving in Kamini around three." Russell liked her distinctive voice, rich and deep for a woman. Quite sultry, and spiced with the lovely Canadian accent that Russell observed gave Canadians of any ilk a bit of an upper-class air.

"Thank you, I've changed the reservation. You of course won't be charged for tonight since you had difficulties reaching us, and we can extend your stay an extra day to Saturday, the fifteenth, if you'd like?"

"Yes, let's do that."

"Very good, although, a heads-up. You will need to move from your cabin into a room in the main Lodge for your final night."

"Oh, come on," Russell said. "That's pretty inconvenient. I booked a private, lakeshore cabin for two weeks. Certainly the incoming guests can be given a room for one lousy night?"

"Which seems to me would be an equal inconvenience to them," she replied smoothly. "I'm trying to remember. Were they delayed a day, or was that you?"

Russell was taken aback by the jab. "Now look, I just don't like the idea of having to load up everything and move out the morning of my final day. I'm quite capable of paying for whatever inconvenience you think I'm causing."

"I assure you, Mr. Dean, it's not the slightest inconvenience to me. It's the conveniences of all the guests involved I need to consider. Let me look." The phone went silent as the woman penciled Russell's name and a room number onto a page in the reservation book lying open on her desk. "There, I've just reserved a nice main Lodge room for your final night on our computerized registration program, to use the term loosely."

"Oh, all right." Russell couldn't get anywhere with this woman. "Can you at least make it a suite? Or the largest room available?"

"Mr. Dean, please keep in mind that the Lodge was built in 1927. All rooms in the main lodge are the same rustic, charming, log construction. We don't offer suites or rooms of various sizes. I'm sure you'll enjoy the room immensely."

Russell huffed a short breath.

"Now, on to one more item of importance," the woman said. "The Kamini road from Miskwa is currently out of service, washed out halfway between the two towns. The unfortunate result of recent spring thunderstorms, I'm afraid. Latest word is the road will be open in two to three days."

"Marvelous! So, for the final leg, one does what? Hike? Swim?"

"Certainly not!" the woman said cheerfully. "We have two launches operating between Kamini and Miskwa to transport our guests to and from the Lodge until the road is reopened. A launch leaves Miskwa from Miller's Landing approximately every three hours, meaning tomorrow you'll be able to catch the launch either at two or five p.m. As a Lodge guest, you may park at the adjacent marina for no charge."

"And how long does this illustrious boat ride take?"

"Just under two-and-a-half hours."

"Oh, terrific! I'm not sure I can make Miskwa by two tomorrow, meaning after an eighteen-hour drive followed by a two-and-half hour boat ride, I'll be checking into your esteemed, glorious Lodge around eight o'clock at night. Exactly the pristine start to a long-awaited vacation I was hoping for!"

The woman paused before she spoke.

"Mr. Dean, if while in the launch you make an effort to feel the river," she began softly, "breathe in the air, listen for the sounds coming from the forest, observe the landscape as it envelopes you … you may find your boat journey the start of a quite magnificent vacation. I want you to understand that you are coming to a remarkably beautiful place, not just the Lodge but the surrounding wilderness as well. There's even more to discover than these physical attributes. Some people find Kamini to be far beyond relaxing. It can be restorative, transcendent … even magical. I sincerely wish you a most pleasant stay." She hung up without saying goodbye.

The abrupt end to the conversation took Russell by surprise. He wasn't used to being dismissed. Had she given her name? He didn't think so. That alluring, hypnotic voice. Her soothing, enticing words. He drove nearly a mile before realizing he was still holding the silent phone to his ear.

Chapter 7

After driving through the rolling hills of Wisconsin, Russell was unimpressed by the flat farmland of Minnesota. It resembled the featureless mile after mile surrounding the Kaweena, Illinois of his childhood. His phone rang as he approached the unremarkable St. Paul skyline. It was Bill Carter, his attorney.

"What's the word, Bill?"

"Things look good. Everything has been filed, all is in order. Cheryl's attorney is pulling some ticky-tack crap, but it's nothing to worry about."

"How long are we looking at before this is over?"

"I sent word of your vacation dates. You'll both appear before the judge in two weeks or so, whenever it's scheduled. The judge will order the selling of the house, which is pretty standard. No kids, so that … um … simplifies things. Cheryl is asking for half, excluding your stake in the firm, which we could bat away if she tries."

Russell winced. Losing half his net worth in cash, investments and property would be a blow. Still, at over eight million dollars, it wouldn't be debilitating. Thank god he'd invested aggressively since his first paycheck. He'd recover.

"If anything else comes up, I'll call you," Carter said. "You'll have cell service wherever it is you're going?"

"I assume so. There is Internet. If you have trouble reaching me, shoot me an email."

"Will do. Hang in there."

Russell tightly gripped the steering wheel. It was happening. His wife was divorcing him, and he couldn't stop it. From a beautiful wife and baby on the way to divorce in only two years. As he drove the interstate freeway through the featureless land, Russell's mind was free to roam. How had he felt when Cheryl told him she was pregnant? It made him happy. He told her that of course they had the means to hire nannies. He'd see to it she received all the help and support she needed. When she miscarried, he took a day off work to be with her.

Then there was the matter of the Foundation to sort out. After they married, Cheryl no longer needed to work. At first she seemed happy donating her time and his money to Chicago charitable causes. She soon approached him and Dan about the firm starting a charity focusing on aiding at-risk youth. They immediately agreed. Cheryl was named Executive Director, and attractive suburban office space was rented. As the Samuels Dean Charitable Foundation and its marquee program, Upward Youth, grew, Cheryl proved terrific at running the Foundation. Better yet, it proved terrific for the Samuels Dean brand name. He hoped she would remain as Executive Director. As for the divorce, the only answer was to get it behind him.

Russell ate the turkey wrap and apple he'd packed in the cooler. His boredom with the flat Minnesota countryside on either side of the Interstate increased. And where were these alleged ten thousand lakes? In two hundred miles he'd passed perhaps six.

Just south of Duluth, Russell exited onto the two-lane state highway taking him north to the Ontario border. It was here that he began to notice subtle changes in the landscape. Mile by mile the farmlands, with their displays of emerging spring crops Russell could identify with only a peripheral glance, began to diminish. First sprinklings, then swaths, then swarms of trees began taking over—birch, pine, spruce, hemlock—flooding the open spaces from afar to create tall corridors of dense green foliage lining both sides of the road.

The further he advanced into northern Minnesota, the more water came into play. Driving through Cloquet, Russell crossed a lengthy bridge over a broad river and was startled by the view.

Running swiftly through the center of town, the river burst with whitewater across its boulder-filled width, nearly escaping its banks with the addition of spring rains. Compared to the static one- and two-story buildings lining its shores, the river was wildly alive, stunningly unchanged by the merely cosmetic bricks-and-mortar additions of human civilization. He was struck by the fact that the river appeared to belong while the buildings didn't.

In early evening, Russell noticed yet another change in topography. Small outcroppings of gray granite began to nip at the ditches beside the highway, sometimes streaming backward to merge into larger outcroppings filtering off into the forest. As he continued northward, the outcroppings grew into eight- to ten-foot rounded bluffs of the same brutish material. Looming monoliths colored varying hues of gray, tan and pink jutted from the ground as if escaping ancient burial.

Russell stopped for dinner in the small town of Cook. When he climbed from his truck in the parking lot of a Subway restaurant, he was immediately struck by something he couldn't at first put his finger on. It was the air, or rather ... its scent. Clean, certainly, but spiced with tones of pine and the pleasant, earthy smell of composting vegetation. His thoughts turned toward his childhood on his family's farm, which Russell found curious, unaware as he was of the connection between the olfactory bulb in the nose to areas in the brain that persistently retain both memories and emotions.

Suddenly, he recalled being a boy and shoveling dark brown compost from the wire bin in the corner of his back yard into a wheelbarrow. It was spring. He wheeled it to the sunny center of the yard—an act that required his full strength and attention—then dumped the load in his mother's large, soon-to-be-planted vegetable garden. It had been one of his childhood chores on the farm. He enjoyed it, he recalled now, using a bow rake to carefully "paint" the tired, gray soil in the garden bed with the fresh, brown compost, carefully noting his progress until the entire plot was covered evenly, perfectly, with the dark, nutrient-rich material.

Russell walked into the Subway unmindful of his earlier concerns. He paid for his seven-dollar meal with a twenty and told the teenage girl at the counter to keep the change. The sun was low on the horizon when he resumed his journey, sending shimmering gold sparks across the blue-gray water of the numerous lakes he passed on either side. Increasingly, stretches of shoreline were defined not by trees and soil sloping gently to water's edge but by rounded granite deposits similar to those along the highway.

An hour later, Russell entered the small town of Orr. He spotted the neon sign for Mailer's Pelican Lake Resort, pulled into the parking lot and eased his F250 into a spot between two other beefy pickup trucks. He was again invigorated by the crisp smell of the air when he opened the door.

A half-dozen fishing boats on trailers were lined up with military precision on one side of the lot, ready for early-morning hookup and getaway by owners not yet to their final destinations. Drawn by their commanding presence, Russell walked over to take a look. Most were sleek aluminum boats from sixteen to eighteen feet long, as attractively painted and detailed as racecars. Several were fiberglass, with equally sexy finishes of silver-flecked black and metallic red. The outboard motors mounted to the boats' sterns were sleek sculptures in themselves, their stylish, sweeping fiberglass cowls emblazoned with bold graphics for Mercury, Yamaha and Evinrude. Russell noted that only two of the boats had steering wheels. The rest sported tillers, long steering and throttle handles emerging from the base of the engine cowls. Even sitting on their trailers, all the boats projected speed and power. He'd never done much boating. There was no opportunity growing up on the farm or after moving to Chicago. A few times he'd taken over the wheel of Dan Samuels's twenty-five-foot Hacker Craft inboard on Lake Michigan, but that was it. He might have to give boats a try.

Russell checked in at the resort office and headed with his tote bag to his room in one of a dozen cabins. The room was sparse at best: well-worn carpeting, thin twin bed, old tube TV, microwave-size refrigerator, no microwave, no coffee maker. Still, he had no thought to complain. The room retained the fresh, woodsy scent of the outdoors.

Approaching the cabin, he had caught a glimpse through pine branches of an enormous, glistening lake below. The sun was beginning to set, and he felt an urge to investigate. Pathways from the rear of each cabin joined at the start of a timber staircase leading down a steep stone bluff to a long, wood slip dock extending out into the lake. A third of the way down the dock, a man with a fishing rod was casting an enormous lure parallel to the shoreline.

"How's the fishing?" Russell asked.

"Opening day of the walleye season was very good, a bit cold, but lots of fish in the lake."

The man appeared to be somewhere in his seventies and while slender, was not frail. Studying the lake surface with the lure hanging from the rod tip, he glanced to check Russell's exact whereabouts before smoothly rotating at the waist. He clasped the rod with both hands and accelerated it forward as if it were a baseball bat. The reel whirred softly as the lure soared in an arc a long distance before landing with a muffled splash.

"You use that thing to catch walleyes?" Russell asked.

"Oh hell no," the man said with a chuckle. "This is an old musky rig. Five-foot rod, casting reel, forty-pound line. I'm throwing one of my old Suicks, a wood lure that careens just below the surface like a drunken, defenseless baitfish." And then added, in a kindly tone: "Doesn't sound like you do much fishing."

"I must confess I haven't. But I'm just starting my vacation. Might have to give it a try." Russell was only being friendly. Why someone would waste hours trying to catch a fish made no sense to him.

"Well, no time like the present," the man said as he finished the retrieve and offered the rod to Russell.

"Oh, heavens, not now. I wouldn't be able to do that."

"Then here, watch, I'll show you. Right hand on the handle like this. Thumb on the line drum, light pressure as you cast the lure.

This keeps the line from running out faster than the lure is pulling it, causing what you call a backlash. Left hand about five inches below the right. That's why the handle is so long. I'll start you with a sidearm cast. Always check behind you to make sure you're not going to hook something on your backswing. Push this button here to unlock the reel, bring the rod back, a little turn at the waist, and rotate your shoulders like a golf swing. Whip the rod forward and lighten the thumb pressure as the lure shoots out. Here, watch."

Demonstrating at half speed, the man cast the lure out around twenty feet into the water.

"Your turn," he said, handing Russell the rod after retrieving the lure. "Now, hold it like I said and keep your thumb on the line after you unlock the reel."

Russell grasped the rod awkwardly at first, but when he held it as instructed, the ergonomics of the design took over. The rod and reel felt good in his hand, perfectly weighted. He glanced behind him to check for obstructions, pushed the button, swung the rod back then smoothly forward. The lure arced gracefully outward and splashed down about the same distance away as his instructor's previous cast.

"Not bad!" the man said. "A natural. Keep your rod tip a little lower in your windup for the next one. You ever see Rod Carew swing a bat? Cocked it flat behind him, with just a little uppercut swing, smooth and easy."

Russell wanted to see if he could cast farther, at least the distance he'd seen the man attain prior. He repeated the process with greater length to his wind up and more speed forward. The lure shot out in a lazy arc, landing not quite as far out as the man's longest casts but a great deal further than Russell's first.

"Excellent! You're a fast learner."

Russell began retrieving the lure by quickly turning the reel handle.

"Slow down your retrieve. Give the lure some movement, random, short jerks of the rod tip. Stop reeling for a few seconds, then start it up again."

Russell looked at him and had to smile at how happy the old man seemed just to be standing and watching another person cast. Russell did as he was told.

"I'm not going to catch anything, am I?"

"Oh hell no. You can catch a musky along damn near any shore on the lake, and sunset is a good time for it, but this shoreline gets pounded by fishermen every day. There's big fish around, but you're not going catch a musky on the second cast of your life."

No sooner had the man spoken than he took a sharp breath.

"Follow!" he exclaimed.

"What?" Russell said, alarmed by the excitement in the man's voice.

"Look two feet behind the lure. You see the V in the surface of the water, heading right for us?"

"I can't see the lure, I don't know where it is!"

"Then look twenty feet out. See the V? See it?"

Russell looked carefully and saw a sinister V-shape on the surface. Something moving was displacing water, large enough to create a small wake, and it indeed was headed straight for them.

"What is it?"

"A musky, following your lure! Interested but wary. When you have about eighteen inches of line left, stick the tip of the rod in the water and do a figure eight."

Russell finally glimpsed the approaching lure, veering sideways one way then the other a foot below the surface. He couldn't comprehend the man's instructions, much less put them into action. As he reeled the lure to the dock, he left it in the water where it floated slowly upward. Two feet behind the lure, illuminated by the rays of the setting sun penetrating the clear, emerald green water, Russell saw the fish suspended just below the surface. It was enormous, he thought, transfixed by the sight. A long, metallic submarine, motionless except for the slightest curling of two sets of crimson fins protruding low on each side of its body. Its black eyes were locked on the rising lure. Neither man spoke. After a few more seconds the musky gave a short, quick jerk of its head and curled gracefully onto its side, exposing it broad, silvery flank. Slowly flapping its crimson tail, it righted itself as it dove deeper in the direction from which it came, cruising smoothly down toward the lake bottom before disappearing from sight.

"Holy shit! That thing was huge!"

"Oh, just a pup," the man said with a smile. "Thirty-six inches or so. Probably a little male. Don't get me wrong, would have given you a nice tussle if it had hit at the end there."

"Sorry about goofing that up. The figure eight thing threw me. You're saying there are muskies bigger than that one?"

"The females are the big ones. Same with walleyes. The biggest muskies will run fifty to fifty-six inches and can weigh fifty-some pounds. Upwards to sixty if she's a fatty. There's a fight you'll remember, whether you win it or not."

Russell took a few steps backward to process what he had seen and allow his heart rate to stabilize. Gazing out across the lake, for the first time he noticed the final stages of a brilliant sunset. A few lines of thin clouds near the horizon glowed in hues of rose pink and yellow, reflecting the rays of the sun as it dipped below the far tree line. The water on the glass-calm lake picked up the reflection from the clouds, sending a luminous, pink-and-yellow mosaic carpet across the surface. For a moment, Russell was mesmerized by this physical manifestation of serenity—until he remembered the fish. "So, that fish. Still out there, I assume." Russell handed the rod back to the man. "You better take another whack at it."

"Oh, he's around, but muskies are smart. Probably curious about what was causing the vibrations from my earlier casts. But he didn't like the looks of something. I'd have to go up to the office and get a different lure. Even then, he won't be interested in any strange contraption clanking around this dock for the rest of the night." The man turned and looked out across the colorful water. "Besides, watching a follow, then seeing a pretty musky just sitting there, calculating a strike before veering back into the deep—in some ways it's just as nice as catching one."

"I'm sorry, I didn't ask your name. You've been so kind. I'm Russell." He extended his hand.

"Ralph," the man said, shaking it. "Ralph Mailer. I own this joint. Staying with us for long?"

"No, only tonight. Just passing through."

"Sorry to hear. Your room alright?"

"My room is lovely, thank you."

"Well, I doubt that very much, but thanks. Where you headed?"

"On my way to Kamini, Ontario."

Mailer's eyes perked up. "Oh my, that's gorgeous country. Been to Kamini many times. Used to drive up there with buddies in the summer when I was in high school. Camp out in Big Sand. Terrific fishing, good walleye water and some of the biggest muskies in the world. Wanted to move there for good, except I'm an American, couldn't swing it. Wound up back here, taking over this operation from my folks. I still sneak up to Kamini to fish in the fall, now that my kids are taking over from me. Where you staying?"

"Kamini Lodge."

"Well good for you, doing it up right. Say, if you want to learn how to fish, when you get up there, you ask for John Dogrib. People call him Gribber. He's the head fishing guide at Kamini Lodge. Indian fella, best guide in Northwest Ontario. He'll be booked up, but see if you can get him to take you out for a fish. Plus, if you're single, Gribber's a good guy to hang out with. The ladies find him to be a man of, uh, whatcha call it … certain charms."

"I'll hope to meet him," Russell said, mildly intrigued. "Thanks again for the lesson, Ralph. I really enjoyed tonight."

Russell took off his watch as he climbed into bed and placed it on the table beside his phone and the television remote. He reached for the remote but was interrupted by a deep yawn. As if a switch had been thrown, he felt the cozy call for sleep settle over him. He fumbled for his phone and saw it was after ten. He tapped the clock and set an alarm for five-thirty. It would be a seven-hour drive to Miskwa. If he started early, he could make the two o'clock launch.

Russell rolled onto his side and pulled up the thin covers. He tucked one hand under the stiff foam pillow and dove into peaceful sleep.

Chapter 8

G ribber awoke just before sunrise on Sunday, as he did each morning unaided by an alarm. He threw on his bathrobe and walked down to the dock. Seated with legs crossed, he meditated to the sunrise and returned to his cottage in a particularly festive mood. Today would be fun.

As head guide for Kamini Lodge, Gribber received a text at the end of each day from the other guides detailing how many fish their guests caught. If a guide and his party did poorly, Gribber would text back suggested fishing spots and techniques for the next day. If the party was down to their last one or two days and had encountered poor fishing overall, he might take over as their guide. Such was the case today. He would be guiding three wealthy oilmen from Oklahoma while their wives played golf and visited the Lodge's spa.

Showtime.

American fishermen and women were the most enamored by their perceived privilege of being guided through a vast Canadian river system by a real "Indian guide," and occasionally Gribber couldn't help but play off their well-intentioned prejudice. Instead of his usual flannel shirt, after donning jeans and work boots he reached for his costume buckskin pullover. It was his go-to article of ersatz native clothing, purchased from a tourist shop in Miskwa. Though made from deer hide, any semblance to traditional Ojibwe attire—and occasions on which such attire could be worn—ended there. Still, the minimal, nonsensical beadwork and fringe strips were sufficient decorative details to trigger the preconceptions of native dress in the minds of tourists.

The shirt worked like magic. If asked by his party where they were going to fish, his standard reply, "The wind will tell us where to fish," would bring a reverent nodding of heads. It also held the ring of truth: A strong wind often blew surface water containing schools of minnows toward shorelines downwind, attracting more feeding fish to these choppy shores than to those leeward.

Gribber also might suggest his fishing party learn a secret Ojibwe phrase to bring them luck before dropping their lines. Always thrilled to do so, his eager students would repeat after Gribber each enchanting word:

> *Niwii* (na-wee)
> *wewebanaabii* (way-way-bon-ah-bee)
> *mitaakwazheyaan* (ma-tah-kwuh-ZHAY-yon)

"Shout it to the heavens!" Gribber would implore them after they mastered the phrase.

"Niwii-wewebanaabii mitaakwazheyaan!" they would shout in unison.

Delighted, each would head home able to say, "It is a good day to fish naked" in Ojibwe.

His guests were, of course, unaware that their bush-town Indian guide was fluent in English, French and Ojibwe and held a bachelor's degree in philosophy from Dartmouth College. The shtick nearly always resulted in a particularly hefty tip from well-to-do white Lodge guests at the conclusion of his services.

Grabbing sunglasses and a breakfast bar, Gribber headed out the back door to his weary-but-unbeaten 1964 Rambler station wagon parked behind the cottage. He dropped the tailgate and did a quick inventory of the items in back. The eight torches fashioned the day before were tied in a bundle, their long handles made from slender spruce trunks he'd cut on his property. Two pairs of black cotton socks pulled down full length then rolled back up formed a rounded wad of absorbent material held tight with a wrapping of wire on one end of each torch. He noted one gallon of kerosene, a metal pail, six Roman candles, an LED pen-light, a case containing his fully charged camcorder, and a jar of black Halloween face paint. Check. Gribber slammed shut the tailgate, took out his cell phone and called Annie Chase.

She picked up immediately. "Ooh, as excited as a little boy waking up on Christmas morning, eh?"

"More so. Just heading to the Lodge. I should get back here by quarter to six, enough time to rig my boat for music and ex-plosives. I've done all the prep. Hooked up the electronics on the dock yesterday and did a sound check. Works like a charm."

"Would I be able to guess your choice of music to serenade our surprise special guest? Rush? Ramones? Neil crooning 'Rockin' in the Free World?'"

"Nothing that unrefined. When you hear it, you'll get it and probably smirk."

"Can't wait. I have the day off. Going to do more planting in my garden and work on the new outhouse. Then I'll clean up, change—wait'll you see—and swing by Morning Wood at eight-fifteen to grab your boat."

"Perfect. The others will be arriving the same time. I'll show you how to work the sound system, then you head out in my steed. The rest of us will load into two vehicles, get into position at the campgrounds, and wait for your text. Afterward, everyone can come back here for cocktails and the beating of chests."

"That's my favorite part," Annie said. "That and the cocktails."

Gribber stashed the phone in his jeans and walked down the pathway to his dock on Gunn Lake. He headed north in his boat, veering left at the main channel leading to Kamini Lodge. Time to meet the new fishing party, the oilmen. They were staying for five days at the Lodge, and for the first four hadn't much luck fish-ing. He would take them out on this final day, which was ideal for his Indian guide routine.

Any longer than one day with the same group, it was too hard to keep it up.

Chapter 9

When Russell's eyes popped open, he didn't immediately recognize where he was. All he knew was that he felt terrific, thoroughly rested and alert. It was as if his consciousness had been cleansed, his brain given a reboot. Images from the previous night—Ralph, the fish, the lake, the sunset—came to him, and he sat up in bed excited about the day ahead.

Had his alarm gone off? Even with the curtains drawn, it seemed awfully light in his room. He reached for his cell phone and was at first perplexed by its black screen. What time was it? He picked up his watch from the table. Eight twenty! How was that possible? Finally, it dawned on him his phone had died overnight. He'd never thought to charge it in the truck and didn't notice its charge level when setting the alarm. This was a first! Never in his life had he screwed up an alarm.

Russell leaped from bed, washed his face, brushed his teeth and threw on deodorant. Shaving would have to wait. Two minutes later, with tires spinning on gravel, he shot out onto the two-lane highway. He glanced at his watch as he plugged in his phone. Eight-thirty. Good lord, he'd slept for ten hours. When was the last time he'd done that? Ever? Russell did some calculations. He would miss the two o'clock launch out of Miskwa and would have to hang around until five waiting for the second launch. Hopefully Miskwa had one decent restaurant.

At least he no longer was in a heated rush to get to Miller's Landing by two. The sun was already high in the east and casting its warmth across a cloudless sky. He decided to stop in the next town for coffee and some form of breakfast. Except the next town never came. For one hundred and sixty uninterrupted miles, Russell weaved through the dense northern wilderness until finally arriving in International Falls, Minnesota and the border crossing into Ontario. The highway led directly through the eight-block downtown. Famished and craving caffeine, Russell pulled into a gas station convenience store and filled his tank. Gas was fiendishly expensive in Canada, he'd heard. He bought coffee and a breakfast sandwich and returned to his truck.

He followed the "TO CANADA" signs as two lanes merged into one approaching a long concrete bridge. "Rainy River" read the sign at its entrance. Traffic slowed to a crawl, enabling Russell to look out his passenger window and study the river from above as the line of vehicles crept along the narrow bridge. This water was starkly different from the water in Pelican Lake the evening before. Flowing swiftly between harsh, cliff-lined shores, it was alive. The strong current roiled the surface across every inch of its wide expanse. Large pools of dark water pushed upward from deep below, rippling the blue surface water like the rounded ceilings of mushroom clouds. Whirlpools of various sizes formed, danced erratically across the surface, then disappeared. *Dangerous water*, Russell thought, and a quite powerful symbol of the line he was crossing into a foreign land.

At the end of the bridge the lanes split and led to five, evenly spaced Canadian Customs kiosks. Russell pulled up to one and handed his passport to the uniformed Customs agent. She swiped his passport into her computer, stared at the result, and asked a few simple questions about his visit. She handed back his passport, apparently satisfied with his answers. "Welcome to Canada," she said with a smile. "Have a nice time."

Driving through Fort Frances, the Canadian town across the Rainy River from International Falls, Russell turned onto a highway headed east that after forty miles would intersect a highway headed north. From there, Kamini was just over two hundred miles away. What Russell did not realize was that his route traversed the entire length of the Canadian Lake of the Woods. Nor was he aware that he was journeying deeper into the Canadian Shield, an immense area of exposed Precambrian stone forming the ancient geological core of North America. Extending from northern Ontario through the province then east across Canada to the Atlantic Ocean, its southern fringe lapped northern Minnesota, the Great Lakes Region and upstate New York.

Nowhere was it as beautiful, bold and unbridled as in Northwest Ontario. The dense forests of birch and evergreens interrupted by granite outcroppings that Russell had seen in northern Minnesota expanded enormously in scale as he drove. Whenever the highway rose and crossed a bridge, the immense Lake of the Woods delivered a stunning impact. The panorama of the lake's brilliant blue waters flowing around a dozen islands stretched for several miles on each side. Shorelines were dominated by Shield granite. Rounded ribbons of stone curved gently to water's edge but elsewhere burst straight up as jagged thirty- to fifty-foot cliffs. Increasingly, the narrow, snaking highway was lined with towering stone bluffs. It was as if the earth were going back in time, taking over, protecting itself from ephemeral intruders by revealing its ancient, impenetrable stone armor.

Russell stopped for coffee at Gill's Trading Post in the small waterside town of Sioux Narrows. He took in the idyllic view as he strolled back to his truck. A long dock, its wood bleached light gray from the sun, extended from shore into the large bay. Tied to it were a floatplane, several small fishing boats and a cedar strip canoe. A small island of pink granite burst with billowy white pines, matching the theme of the mainland shoreline curving off toward a larger body of water far in the distance. There wasn't a human in sight. Russell felt as he had when he awoke: cleansed, renewed and something else. He lived in Chicago, one of the largest cities in the US. Yet somehow, in this sparsely populated wilderness, the facets of his life there seemed curiously diminished in scale.

An hour later, Russell shut down his truck at Miller's Landing on the outskirts of Miskwa.

Chapter 10

The landing wasn't much more than a narrow asphalt road disappearing into the water along a stretch of gravel shoreline. Next to the road sat a one-story galvanized metal structure with a faded sign on the roof reading "Marina." A deck with two gas pumps ran along the shore, connected via wood ramps to a series of floating docks.

Russell glanced at his watch as he pulled open the door to the marina. Four o'clock on the nose. He hadn't felt compelled to speed or become impatient looking for places to pass the logging trucks, campers and various vehicles towing boats that he'd trailed during much of the drive. He'd still made it with time to spare.

The interior of the marina smelled faintly of motor oil and strongly of cigarette smoke. Behind the counter, a hefty middle-aged man wearing jeans and a blue, oil-stained mechanic's shirt with the embroidered name patch "Earl" sat at a desk smoking and leafing through a marine parts catalogue. He looked up as Russell approached.

"What can I do ya for?" the man said tonelessly.

"I'm staying at Kamini Lodge. Here to catch the five o'clock launch," Russell said. "Is it running on time?"

"Doing purdy good today. Oughta be here 'pert near on time." Earl grabbed a booklet and pen from his desk, rose and opened the booklet on the counter. "Gimme your car make, plate number and check-out date. Don't accept liability for vehicles in the lot, but it's lit at night."

"Sounds like a deal." Russell jotted down the information. "How far is Kamini, anyway?"

"Oh, she's about eighteen miles by water. Forty minutes or so. We're on the Winnipeg River side of town, you don't gotsa weave around the Miskwa peninsula from Lake of the Woods. It's fifty kilometers by land. Takes about the same time, but the Kamini road's washed out."

"So I hear." Russell almost added, hence my need for the launch, but didn't. He was intrigued by something Earl had said. "Why is distance by water defined in miles, but distance by road defined in kilometers?"

Earl stared at Russell as if pondering infinity. "Beats the hell outta me."

"Eighteen miles by water doesn't seem very far. How can the Lodge launch take over two hours?"

"Cuz it putts. Both launches are from the forties. Full up, they got a top speed of maybe seven mile an hour."

The words concerning the launch ride spoken over the phone by the woman from Kamini Lodge yesterday morning came back to Russell. In his mind, he again heard her sultry, distinctive voice. Enjoy the journey, she advised. Still, impatient after his long drive, the thought of waiting another hour for the launch irked him. He noticed a sign on the wall: Boat Rentals Available.

"Earl, what does it cost to rent a boat?"

"Depends on the size. Standard fishing boat, sixteen-footer, two hundred-ten dollars a day."

Not bad, Russell thought. He could be at the Lodge in less than an hour. When the road reopens, he could return the boat and pick up his truck. Having the truck in Kamini would be far more convenient when it came time to return home, not to mention removing the expensive new vehicle from harm's way in the obviously unsecured parking lot above. "Fine, I'd like to do that."

"All the rentals are out. Give me a few minutes, I'll go drop one in for ya." Earl pulled a sheet from a drawer. "Fill this out, and I'll be back."

As Russell completed the rental form, he heard the sound of an engine grow louder. He stepped outside and watched Earl drive a tractor backing an aluminum boat on a trailer down the launch. The boat was hardly of the caliber Russell had seen the evening before in the parking lot in Orr. Several dings and pronounced dents were visible in the hull. The paint was scratched and faded, as was the large decal reading "Miller's Landing Rental" adorning the side. Duct tape covered portions of the vinyl driver's seat, the tape as tattered as the seat.

It took twenty minutes for Earl to launch the boat, drive to the dock, fill the gas tank and put away the tractor and trailer. Back in the marina, Earl looked over the rental agreement as Russell handed him his credit card.

"Ya been on the river before? Know the way to Kamini?"

"I haven't. I figured it was fairly straightforward."

"Should buy a map. Just to be safe, eh?"

Earl reached under the counter and withdrew a large map of the Winnipeg River system from Miskwa to Kamini. He unfolded it on the counter and placed an oil-stained finger on a point near the bottom.

"Here's us. Pulling out from the dock, head straight toward the dip in the tree line of the farthest horizon ya see. That's the channel into the main river. One of 'em, anyway. After that, ya go here, here, here, here, here and here," Earl said, tracing the serpentine route with his finger. "It's downstream all the way. So a red boy ya keep to your left, a green boy to your right."

"Boy?" Russell asked. Earl had pronounced the word "buoy" as it is pronounced in Canada.

"Them colored posts what stick outta the water. They mark reefs. All the main channels to Kamini will have boys. Ya get too far off the channels, not so much."

That was a relief. When Earl unfolded the map, Russell had been startled by the enormous size and complexity of the river and a bit intimidated by the intricate route to Kamini so swiftly traced by Earl's finger. Now he knew he could handle this. Stick with the "boys." He signed the slip for the boat rental and map and thanked Earl for his assistance.

"Gas tank's full. Ya won't even burn half a tank to Kamini. River flows north. The Lodge is just past the railroad bridge. That's the only spot 'tween here and there where the river narrows to a single channel. Life jackets are in a compartment in the bow, never dumb to put one on."

After unloading his gear, Russell parked in the lot, walked back and stepped gingerly into the boat. He was glad Earl had not assisted him with his gear and wasn't hovering over him now.

A key fastened to a small plastic float protruded from the base of the tiller steering arm. It all seemed simple enough. He had operated all manner of machinery on the farm, from the combine and tractor to the skid steer and ATV. Russell turned the key and the thirty-horsepower Mercury outboard motor started up with a smoky belch. Midway up the tiller was a shift handle. Russell untied the boat, sat down in the swivel driver's seat and shifted the handle toward the bow. The boat putted smoothly forward. To experiment with speed, Russell twisted the rubber grip on the end of the tiller handle. The engine growled louder, and the boat moved faster. Same as an ATV throttle, he noted. Turning the boat was as simple as swinging the tiller arm right or left. Piece of cake.

Russell twisted the throttle wide open, and the boat zoomed forward, its bow rising until it achieved plane, then smoothly dropped down to lightly kiss the water at full speed. He picked out the dip in the trees Earl had referenced and made a beeline for it. Though distance on water was hard to gauge, it looked about a mile away.

He was racing across the water! Compared to driving the enormous, lumbering Hacker Craft along the shorelines of Lake Michigan, Russell found driving the light aluminum boat far more exhilarating. Sitting much closer to the water surface, the sensation of speed was fantastic, as was the feel of the water when he began weaving the boat in a series of long, graceful curves. Skipping across small waves created by squalls produced rapid-fire vibrations and a light tap-tap-tap chatter from the hull. This must be what screaming down a mountain in a bob-sled feels like!

Russell took his left hand off the tiller to glance at his watch. The engine rotated slowly to the left, then sharply, causing the boat to veer violently in the opposite direction. Nearly thrown overboard, Russell frantically reclaimed his grip on the tiller. He brought the boat back under control, his heart racing. Mental note: Don't take your hand off the tiller. He took a deep breath. If that were the most perilous event of his journey, he'd take it.

Other boats were on the broad expanse of water, some running parallel to his route, others crisscrossing his path. He spotted a stately, wooden passenger vessel approaching. The Kamini Lodge launch, he surmised. As the launch cruised past, most of the dozen or so passengers waved. Russell waved back and, without removing his grasp on the tiller, looked at his watch. Five eighteen. The launch easily would take another ten minutes to travel to the landing. After the unloading and loading of new passengers, it wouldn't begin the return journey much before six. He'd made the right call by renting the boat.

The sight of the launch again brought to mind his phone conversation with the mystery woman at the Lodge. What were the odds her physical appearance even remotely matched her sexy voice? Slim to none, he supposed. Still, soon after Cheryl informed him that she was filing for divorce, it had occurred to Russell that, for all intents and purposes, he was single again. He'd even purchased condoms for the trip, the first time since high school. The woman probably worked at the front desk. Be interesting to check out the face matching the voice.

The dip in the tree line Russell was aiming for grew closer. It was a channel between two granite points. He slowed down, cruised between the points and shifted into neutral. He took the map from his jacket pocket to study his next move. Glancing at the shoreline, he saw the current continued to carry the boat downstream. He made another note to himself: Stick with the current.

The river expanded into large clusters of islands ahead. The map didn't dictate any particular route through them, but once past, Russell could see that the main waterway curved to the left. More islands and channels followed, and his route included several sharp swings to the right. Eventually, the route led to a stretch where the shorelines of one branch of the river narrowed to form two slender channels. He recalled seeing Earl's finger tracing down them. The stretch, approximately halfway between Miskwa and Kamini, was named on the map: The Dalles.

Russell accelerated to full speed, the warm wind blasting his face, the bracing scent flooding his senses. He spotted a green buoy straight ahead, turned slightly and zoomed past. Though not abundant, the buoys seemed easy enough to spot every few miles. The number of cottages dwindled to none, and he realized he was leaving the inhabited portion of the river. Weaving past pine-topped islands, the wilderness welcomed him like a friendly embrace.

Russell broke into an open stretch and saw a widening expanse of water branching off to his left, marked with both a red and a green buoy. He veered toward it, shot between the buoys and proceeded down the broad channel. Small bays appeared sporadically on either side. Several contained mounded log beaver dens. In another, a female mallard duck led a paddling procession of ducklings. Toward the center of one bay, he spotted two stilt-legged blue herons standing motionless near shore.

Russell couldn't escape the feeling that this leg of his journey was taking a long time. He'd grown up on a farm and needn't look at his watch. Glancing at the sun's proximity to the horizon he knew it was approaching six o'clock. As the channel slowly narrowed, and after what was beginning to feel like a long time, Russell swept around yet another granite point and was perplexed by the view which unfolded before him. He had arrived at the entrance to a lovely, cliff-lined, duck-filled, dead-end bay.

Chapter 11

Annie Chase knew from the height of the sun that it was quitting time. Six o'clock, give or take, and she needed to be at Gribber's by eight-fifteen. She slipped on safety glasses and with one smooth pass of her circular saw cut the line she'd marked on the sheet of plywood. Ah, the final cut, the roof section, for her new outhouse. Installation of the roof would have to wait until tomorrow.

It had been a productive day. In the morning she'd finished planting her raised vegetable garden beds running along her sunny river shoreline. Dozens of tomato, pepper, zucchini, squash and herb plants were mulched and watered in. When one added the vast assortment of vegetables already planted from seed, her summer and fall harvests amounted to literally bushels of produce for her, friends, the Kamini Lodge kitchen and the food bank in Miskwa.

Her love for gardening grew while studying in England during her junior year at Queen's University. Arthur and Margaret, the delightful couple in whose home she stayed during her summer semester at The London School of Economics and Political Science, owned a weekend cottage outside Tewkesbury in the Cotswalds. There, Margaret was a mad and fastidious gardener, devoted to her collection of heirloom tea roses, blousy perennial gardens and wildly colorful window boxes. Arthur, a retired professor at the college, was a vegetable man. Annie spent most of her time with Arthur. She thought flowers were pretty and smelled nice but marveled at coaxing a seed into a living fountain of fresh food.

After graduating Queens, Annie accepted a government position as policy analyst with the Canadian Department of Finance in Ottawa. Her excitement about living in the nation's capital and determination to have even a small impact in government quickly turned sour. Ottawa in 2006 was a man's world, and in the eyes of a young, well-educated woman, an old-fashioned, bum-patting, chauvinistic one at that.

Annie never wore much makeup or saw a reason for exploiting her physicality. Her facial qualities stemmed from a wholly haphazard luck of the draw, as do anyone's. A dashing French Canadian great-great-grandfather brought home to Halifax a beautiful woman from India he squired while a sailor for the East India Trading Company. Their marriage and children multiplied by the English, Irish and French bloodlines blended through the following generations resulted in her dark-eyed, fair-skinned, all-Canadian beauty.

As she entered her teenage years Annie sensed she wasn't plain but didn't think much more of it than that. Her freshman year at Queens she was sitting at her gate in the Toronto airport waiting to board her flight home to Calgary for Christmas. A man approached and handed her his card. He told her he was a scout for the top modeling agency in Canada and that she must take his card and promise to call his office. His agency had launched the careers of dozens of Canada's top female fashion models, including several whom had achieved international "stardom." Perhaps she didn't realize it, but from the moment he saw her he knew she was destined to turn the international modeling world upside down. She had the perfect height, body style and unique facial beauty to make a fortune as a fashion model.

Annie refused his card and asked him to please go away. When he persisted, she rose to her imposing six-foot height—the man had fibbed somewhat, she possessed quite a more statuesque figure than was in vogue for fashion models at the time—looked down at the shorter man and told him if he didn't leave her alone she'd break him in half.

She quit her job in Ottawa after eight months and returned to live with her parents in Calgary. She quickly found employment with an international banking and investment corporation. Two weeks into her new career, her male boss asked her in a casual, upbeat manner if she ever considered wearing skirts more often and a bit more makeup.

By early spring she told her parents she needed some time off, at least a summer away from cities, governments, big businesses and the men who ran them. They agreed.

Most Canadians are aware of the more picturesque regions of their enormous country. Northwest Ontario certainly makes everyone's list. Annie knew it was a land of vast forests, lakes, rivers and sparsely populated resort towns always in desperate need of summer workers. Planning her life and imposing her will on its course had so far led only to disappointment. She decided to let pure chance dictate her next path.

Her father dug up an Ontario road map. Annie unfolded it on the kitchen table and centered the western half of the enormous province in front of her. She announced that the town closest to her finger would be her summer residency come May. Closing her eyes, she twirled her finger twice in the air and placed it on the map.

She opened her eyes and announced, "Miskwa." Only when removing her finger did she find it had landed smack dab on a tiny dot labeled Kamini.

Eleven years ago in May, Annie Chase, carrying a backpack and suitcase, stepped from the passenger train during its thrice-weekly stop at the clapboard Kamini depot. She found immediate employment waitressing at the Kamini Lodge, living in the large, two-story staff quarters tucked into a patch of woods just off the first tee of the golf course.

When fall ended and the Lodge closed for winter, she remained, moving into the comfortable small home of Faith Pearson, a recently divorced schoolteacher with whom she had become friends. Two years later she bought an old mainland cottage and began fixing it up.

Inside her cottage, Annie bent over and brushed her long hair to remove any sawdust from her afternoon of carpentry. She took a shower, slipped on a robe, walked to the kitchen and pulled some leftover beef stew from the fridge. While it warmed in the microwave, she began assembling the clothing and accessories for tonight's costume.

She knew she had some hockey shoulder pads around here someplace.

Chapter 12

After processing the fact that he had cruised a great distance into a dead-end bay, Russell turned his boat around and drove full speed in the opposite direction. He was getting hungry, and the temperature was dropping as the sun sank lower. Another layer of clothing beneath his jacket would be nice. Russell was certain that he would recognize the two buoys marking his errant departure from the correct route, and he spotted them ahead after twenty minutes. From his new viewpoint, he could see a broad channel in the distance curving to the right and displaying more islands. He passed between the two buoys, slipped the engine into neutral and took out his map.

Looking at the map did not offer Russell the solace for which he hoped, despite his twice-completed traverse of an extraordinarily long and ultimately finite branch of the river fresh in his mind. He realized that the bird's eye view of a map depicting a complex river system was nearly indecipherable when one was positioned flat on the water and gazing at the same features. He studied a long bay on the map that, after curving off a major waterway, appeared to wander for at least seven miles based on the map's scale ruler, but was it the culprit? Or had he boated down a similar dead end branch of the river he saw curling left further downstream from Miskwa?

Russell was so deep in concentration that he didn't hear the sound of the outboard motor until the boat appeared through a channel fifty yards in front of him. A boat! Flag it down and he could ask directions. Russell threw his boat into gear and raced after the white rooster tail of water flying from the boat's stern.

The boat headed into a maze of islands with Russell in frantic pursuit. His hopes for situational salvation lasted only a minute. He realized he wasn't gaining. The boat he was chasing was faster than his. If only one of the two fishermen would turn and look back, so he could signal them. They didn't.

Russell again slowed his boat and pulled out the map. Not more than thirty yards on his right was a small, nearly round island. A long, narrow island was just ahead. Gazing across the expanse of water to his left, he saw a pronounced point extending straight out from shore before curling downstream at the tip. He studied the map, trying to locate these three distinct shapes. Russell realized it was hopeless after a few increasingly frantic minutes. He checked the time. Just past seven. He'd been on the water for over ninety minutes. *Rein it all in*, Russell told himself. *Stay calm. Be smart. Force the situation back under your control.* He knew the river flowed north to a single channel at Kamini. Regardless of how convoluted the route, the river must eventually deliver him there.

Russell forged ahead, aware he hadn't yet encountered the stretch where the river split into two narrow channels. It had to be coming up. The river appeared to be working itself northeast, the long jag to the right he'd noted on the map prior to the two channels. That was a good sign.

He passed a green buoy several miles later. Continuing on and curving between several islands, Russell slowed his boat as he approached a red buoy in the center of the channel. Past it, on his left, what he was certain was mainland shoreline extended outward to within twenty feet of a small island. On the other side of the island, the shoreline did nearly the same. The two channels! Flushed with relief, Russell headed for the nearest one. He noticed a strong current come back into play. Stick with the current, he reminded himself. He slowed further. The current carried him swiftly through the narrow channel and delivered his boat to the start of a long, gently curving stretch of the river.

He again took out the map and successfully located the area

marked "The Dalles." The map showed numerous places ahead where twisting, lengthy bays splintered off to the right, but there appeared to be no long, confounding bays interrupting the left shoreline all the way into town. Stick with the left-hand shoreline and he could arrive at the Lodge in as little as twenty minutes. Russell fired the boat to full speed, freed from his concern—his astonishment—that he possibly could have erred in judgment by eschewing the Lodge launch. He had instead overcome all obstacles in pursuit of his goal. Racing across the water, he again reveled in the robust scent and sublime beauty of the landscape. As always, he was the victor.

The broad channel began swinging to the left in a series of gentle jogs. A good sign, as Russell knew from the map the river would start angling to the northwest a few miles upstream from town. His keen sense of direction was one lone gift he acknowledged from a rural upbringing. When asked for directions when walking in downtown Chicago, he enjoyed the uncomprehending stares from tourists as he instructed them to walk north, then turn west in three blocks.

Russell spotted a green buoy and a log cottage with an aluminum boathouse ahead. No doubt he was back on track and entering the periphery of Kamini. The broad channel he was navigating split just before the boathouse, the wider stretch veering to the left. Judging from the tree line, the channel continuing ahead narrowed harshly in perhaps another mile. Russell reminded himself that keeping to the left-hand shoreline was the foolproof way to remain on course for Kamini. *Fool me once*, he thought.

That no additional buoys or cottages appeared as Russell cruised for numerous miles down the center of the broad channel did not register alarm in his mind, so resolute was he that his deliverance was at hand. As the light of the early evening sky softened, he noticed a faint red light high in the distance. The top of a cell tower, further evidence he was nearing Kamini.

When the channel ended this time, it did so without narrowing. Russell cruised around a bend, and to his complete astonishment the left and right shorelines curved swiftly toward each other to meet as a single, impregnable shore. His heart registered a pronounced beat. The channel *must* continue through at some point! He slowed and drove toward the long, perpendicular shoreline. As he came within ten yards, he turned and trolled its length. The flat expanse beyond the shoreline consisted principally of low marshland ringed in forest. There was no channel through it.

He slipped the boat into neutral and pulled his cell phone from his jacket pocket. It showed three bars. It also showed the time: seven forty-four. Should he call 911? Call the number and tell whoever answered what? That he was lost somewhere on the Winnipeg River, with the further obligatory statement that he couldn't tell them where he was? Was 911 even the emergency number in Canada?

Head back to the entrance to the bay, Russell decided. To hell with the map. Turn left and continue down the river. It must lead to Kamini. Still holding his cell phone in his right hand, he angrily twisted the throttle wide open, veered away from shore and sped out of the bay.

At the moment the bow lowered and the boat reached full speed there was a booming thud. The floor at Russell's feet jolted as if punched by a giant stone fist from beneath. The engine rocked violently forward on its stern mount, filling the air with an ear-shattering roar that startled Russell so horrifically, both his arms instinctively flew upward. As they did so, he tossed his cell phone over his shoulder and into the water as smoothly as if that had been his intention.

The boat coasted to a stop. As quickly as it had reared forward, the motor bounced down to its normal position, still screaming at full throttle. Russell was jarred nearly from his seat. Trembling, he put his hand on the tiller throttle and brought the motor down to idle. His mind had gone completely blank. The simple thoughts coming slowly to him now did so in single file, as if the first ever to arrive. He had hit something. Not something, a reef. Barely below the surface. Not marked by a buoy. Not marked by a buoy because he was far off the main channel.

He shifted the engine into neutral, then reverse. The action had no effect. He shifted the motor back into forward, this time twisting the throttle open. Though the motor growled louder, the boat remained motionless. Russell took several deep breaths while his heart resumed normal function and the shaking of his arms ceased. He scanned the horizon for the red light atop the cell tower. Because he was departing the bay closer to the dense forest lining the shore, the tree line loomed higher. He felt a quick needle jab of panic as he failed to find the red light. Wait, there! He glimpsed the light ducking in and out from behind the tips of the forest.

Russell turned off the motor, grabbed a paddle and began paddling toward the direction of the tower. In only a minute the bow gently scraped the sloping granite shore. He stepped gingerly from the boat, pulled it further up and tied the bow rope to a small boulder. Turning to face the dense forest, Russell had the direction toward the cell tower locked firmly in his mind's eye. If there was a cell tower there was a road running past it. Get to the road and this unfortunate misadventure would finally come to an end.

He knew that once he was in the dense forest, the light from the tower would be impossible to see. It would be nice to have his cell phone with its compass feature. He could have marked the exact direction to the tower from the water to help him stay on course while hiking. He also would be able to phone the Kamini Lodge to send someone to pick him up once he was standing on a road with the cell tower as his pick-up point. *Wishful thinking*, Russell thought, rare on his part, and as always, unhelpful. He could do this without his cell phone. Growing up on a farm, he accurately could judge distances on land, how far to the water tower in town, how far to the neighbor's barn across the fields, how far to the windmill on the corner of his family's immense property. The cell tower was only about a mile away.

With these assurances firmly in mind, Russell raised his hands in front of his face to ward off tree branches, lowered his head and stepped into the bush.

Chapter 13

"Kamini Time" was both a phrase firmly established in local lore and an ancestral mindset prevalent with year-round residents and Kamini businesses. The recalibration of expectation was cheerfully adopted by members of the seasonal workforce and, somewhat grudgingly, by summer cottagers. Fussy and impatient cottage owners, steeped in their city ways where a service call scheduled for Tuesday afternoon meant Tuesday afternoon, were forced either to modify their mindset to Kamini Time or harbor increasing levels of disappointment. Eventually most recognized it was better for their mental health to convert an estimate of a two-day boat repair to five, promise of an early July start to a cottage re-roofing job to the end of the month, and a vital propane delivery to a few hours before they ran out. It could take as many as five summers for new cottage owners to successfully complete the transition. Some never did.

There were only three exceptions to Kamini Time: Fishing guides were never late for work; Dave Burtnyk's bait shop was open at six every morning, seven days a week; and if a duty or event was of supreme importance to the residents of Kamini, they arrived on time at the very latest.

Gribber had asked those volunteering to assist with the evening's festivities to arrive at his place at eight-fifteen. At eight-twelve, two vehicles pulled into the clearing behind his cottage and parked on each side of his Rambler wagon. Lou LeBlanc, Dave Burtnyk, Faith Pearson, Bruce Anderson, Wolfgang Graf and Gord Fanson poured out.

Gribber was prepared for them. After returning home from guiding, he first had installed the sound system and fireworks into his boat. Then he stripped, bathed in the frigid river, toweled himself dry on the dock and walked up to his cottage. Standing naked in his bedroom, he spoke aloud a prayer to Gizhe Manidoo, the Creator.

Naadamawishig manidoog Giiwedinong, Waabanong,
Zhaawaanong miinawa
Ningaabil'anong
ji-nitaaniigaaneyaan
miinawa ganawendamawag giigooyag

Spirits of the North, East, South
and West
help me to lead well
and protect the fish

Gribber went to his dresser and removed several neatly folded articles of buckskin clothing he'd purchased from native clothes makers over the years and laid them on his bed. He tied a thick, braided deerskin belt around his waist. He donned a breechcloth by pulling the long, rectangular piece of tanned deerskin under the belt front and rear, snug to his groin, each end hanging down over the belt to just above his knees. He put on buckskin leggings— tube-like pant legs running from hip to ankle, held up by deerskin straps tied to the belt. Four-inch fringe dangled down each side. Colorful beadwork panels ran from knee to the ankle: red, yellow, blue, white and green beads in an intricate floral design. The pucker-toe moccasins he slipped on also featured striking accents of colorful beadwork and fringe.

The buckskin shirt he donned last was made with far greater attention to detail than the costume pullover shirt he occasionally wore to impress his fishing guests. In lieu of buttons, it was held closed in front by tying narrow deerskin strips adorning each side.

The tie strips emerged from the center of four inch-wide panels of black cotton running vertically down the front. Intricate embroidery depicting sturgeon, whitefish and pike honored Gribber's Ojibwe clan, the Giigoonh, or fish clan.

After dressing, he went into his kitchen to prepare his face paint. Gribber and his students at the reservation school, assisted by tribal elders, had researched and duplicated the traditional methods for making face and body paint worn for over ten thousand years by the Ojibwe of the region. Each year he and his students concocted body paints in every primary color and myriad hues in between by mixing various natural materials— animal blood, wood ash, red clay, pulverized minerals, berries, moss, animal excrement, plant roots, leaves and flowers being the primary—and suspending them in a liquid binder base of hot water and animal fat.

Turns out, you can freeze the stuff. Gribber had removed three Tupperware containers of one hundred percent organic Ojibwe face paint from his freezer before leaving for work. Now thawed, all it required was a brisk stirring. Gribber quickly whisked the paint in each container—it had the consistency of mayonnaise—until the vibrant colors reemerged. He took the three containers into his bathroom and stood before the medicine cabinet mirror.

Face paint was worn by warriors when heading into battle for a variety of reasons. The colors and symbols painted on the face reflected the warriors' skill, courage and combat history. A prime reason for painting the face, however, was to scare the bejeebers out of your enemy.

Selecting the first of three broad watercolor brushes, Gribber began by painting from the side of his nose straight back across the closed lid of his right eye, from the edge of the eyebrow to the top of his cheekbone. This created a wide, curving band of silvery blue surrounding the eye. The paint's pigment was derived from blueberries, duck manure, aster flowers and pulverized azurite found in the abandoned copper mining pits skirting nearby

Lake Vermillion. Blue signified confidence and wisdom. Gribber liked the silvery tone to his brand of blue for an additional reason: It glowed eerily in the moonlight.

Pigments from pulverized iron deposits, beets, native raspberry and bloodroot plants formed the basis for the next paint. Combined, the result was a paint of rich red color. Red face paint meant the wearer was at war and further symbolized energy, strength, power and blood. Gribber used it to cover the entire rest of his face in a blood-red mask.

It took only a few minutes for the first layer of paint to dry. He chose blue paint to accent the area beneath his mouth, painting a broad vertical line from the center of his lower lip to his chin, then two matching diagonal lines from each corner of his mouth to the center of each jawbone.

Black is the other war color, symbolizing strength and victory and made from a mixture of oak ash, mashed black nodes from poplar bark and the skin of ripened chokeberries. Gribber dipped a brush into the third Tupperware container and under his left eye painted a bold black line across his cheek. The deep black color leaped menacingly from its rich red backdrop.

Gribber returned to his bedroom and donned his final article of clothing: a simple headband he tied in a knot at the back of his head. He heard the scrunch of tires on gravel signaling that the other warriors had arrived.

"Welcome, Earthlings," Gribber said to the assembly in his kitchen. "It's a marvelous night for a moondance."

They heard the sound of a boat slowing as it approached his dock. "That's Annie. Just need to check in with her, then I'll be right with you."

"At your service," LeBlanc said.

Gribber saw Annie surveying the exotic additions to his boat as he descended the path to the dock. Two tall stereo speakers were mounted with metal brackets to each end of the front bench seat. Wires ran from each speaker back to a shallow plywood box next to the swivel driver seat. The open box housed a marine battery, small four-channel mixer, Gribber's cell phone, power switch and additional electronic accouterments, all wired together and neatly secured with screws and brackets. Two plastic buckets filled with sand were centered on the floor in the bow, each containing three Roman candle fireworks buried halfway.

Annie looked up when she sensed Gribber approaching. "Now there's the man I fell in love with."

"The real me, you had no choice. You look like awfully sweet musky bait yourself." Gribber went over the simple workings of the sound system. Flip on the power switch, tap the Music icon on his cell phone, select Songs, and play the one titled "Ride."

"Got it," Annie said. "From the size of those speakers, bet I can start the music from a mile out, so Karp will hear it before he hears the boat or sees the bow light."

"Exactly." Gribber handed Annie a disposable lighter. "After you start the music, troll slow and light two of the Roman Candles. Then rinse and repeat as you swing around the point into Karp's bay. Fire the last two as you pull up to his dock."

Annie confirmed his instructions with a nod. "I'll text Lou's phone when *Keeper* swings by Mullock's. From there it should take Karp fifteen minutes to land at his dock, then another, oh, twenty to back his pickup down, set up the lights and table, and start unloading his boat. So, thirty-five minutes, give or take."

"Should give us ample time," Gribber said. "It'll be dark enough we can watch from the crest of the hill without being seen. When Karp does see us, I think he'll also see his days as a commercial fisherman are over."

"Heavens, a big, stubborn Ukrainian. What possibly could go wrong?" Annie deadpanned. She stepped into Gribber's boat and headed out toward the entrance to Pistol Lake.

Gribber walked up to his house and addressed the six people huddled in his kitchen. "Wolf, you take Gord and Faith in your pickup. Lou, Dave, Bruce, ride with me in Ramble. I want ears pricked, heads on swivels, loins securely girded. Excelsior!"

"Huzzah!" the group shouted in unison. The three arriving with beers in their hands drained them and tossed the empty cans into Gribber's recycling bin.

"Hey Grib, where's Jammer?" Anderson asked as the group headed for the door. "He didn't want to be in on this?"

"Jam's on special assignment. We'll meet him at the scene of the crime. I need to grab something quick. Be right there."

Alone atop the dresser in Gribber's bedroom sat a slender box made from cedar strips. He opened the lid and removed the bald eagle feather inside. Sixteen inches long, the large, brilliant white feather transitioned midway to a lustrous black. He had received the feather six years prior in a ceremony performed by the chief of the Blackdog Ojibwe tribe. Sacred tobacco was burned, and the feather presented to him as both a material symbol and the spiritual embodiment of love, gratitude and respect.

To the Ojibwe, eagle feathers reflect a great power, for the eagle was chosen by the Creator to be leader of all birds, able to fly higher and see farther than any. Eagles were anointed as messengers (angels, if you will) from the Creator to all its children—every living thing—and from every living thing back to the Creator. Eagles carried messages in the form of thoughts, not in their talons but within the essence of their true being, to and from those possessing the spirit consciousness.

The recipient of an eagle feather presented in this manner must create a safe home for it. Gribber handcrafted the cedar box for that purpose. The keeper of the feather also must feed it, keeping it spiritually nourished by wearing the feather at powwows and other sacred ceremonies, so it retains energy to strengthen and guide the mind and soul. Removing the feather from the box alerts the Creator that its owner is humbly asking for protection, guidance and courage. Gribber knew he couldn't place the feather in his headband this evening. Wearing one's feather was reserved for sacred activities, and busting a poacher didn't cut it. Having it close by, however, afforded the same benefits.

Gribber got into his car and placed his eagle feather on the dashboard. The others climbed into Gribber's car and Wolf Graf's pickup.

With the Ram pickup in the lead, the two vehicles drove the four kilometers to Pistol Lake campgrounds and parked in a grassy area running along the water's edge. Only a few kilometers further, past the cell tower, was the long gravel road running through the bush to Andriy Karpenko's boat landing.

"Lou, what's the time?" Gribber asked.

"Eight-thirty on the nose."

"Watch for the text from Annie."

The entourage congregated at the rear of Graf's pickup. An open case of beer sat on the tailgate and several hands dove in. Gribber gave a sharp tongue whistle and addressed the group. "And now if you all would join me at the rear of Ramble, I have something for each of you. After that we wait for Annie's text. When it comes, we'll load back into the vehicles and take off, so to the piss-tanks among you, don't forget to pee."

Chapter 14

At first Russell found the bush nearly impenetrable. It was beginning to get dark and the darkness intensified the deeper he stumbled up the rising grade away from the shoreline. It soon became apparent that the thick swaths of evergreen trees growing impossibly close together would create lengthy detours around his perceived route to the cell tower. After only a few minutes of halting progress, he further discovered that fallen evergreens presented an equally confounding, waist-high barricade. They were as forbidding as barbed wire, held aloft by dense branches circling 360 degrees around their trunks.

Dead standing trees presented a different hazard. Soon into his journey one jagged branch tore the sleeve of his lightweight jacket. Another jabbed his cheek when he turned abruptly. He constantly needed to protect his eyes by snapping off the countless dead branches in his path, and his hands soon developed small cuts and abrasions as he relentlessly plowed forward. When spotting sporadic, narrow lanes through the forest on either side, Russell had to judge if veering ten feet off course to what only hinted at a prolonged open space was better than shielding his face with his hands and pushing straight ahead through the interlocking tips of branches before him.

He discovered that crouching low and even crawling on hands and knees was necessary to squeeze through the densest sections of the forest. Burrowing on all fours under the branches and across the damp forest floor soon played hell with his khakis. He felt his pants moisten at the knees and saw them becoming more stained each time he was forced into the position.

As Russell battled through the bush, there were instances where the trees thinned and he made decent progress with only minor alterations to his course. Except the grade of the slope could change so quickly. One minute he was hiking swiftly and the next using his hands to grasp at boulder outcroppings and tree trunks in an arduous effort to scale a steep, slippery stretch. Or not. As soon as he would gain some assurance by his progress, he would encounter the imposing face of a tall, granite bluff thoroughly blocking his ascent. His only option was to hike around it.

Focusing on the branches in front of him as he weaved back and forth, Russell twice stumbled over small boulders emerging from the ground. The third time, he stumbled and fell, his right knee crashing hard into the top of the boulder. Grimacing, he rolled to a sitting position. He immediately felt moisture from the forest floor wicking through the seat of his pants and boxer shorts. Russell examined the pant leg and detected a tear at the knee. He stood and dropped his pants. As the soft moonlight gently massaged the forest floor, he bent over for a closer look. He watched as the portion of his knee now covered by torn and pulverized skin started to bead with blood.

This was turning into madness. A foreboding, dark sense took hold as the depth of Russell's peril became apparent. He was losing control of the situation. It was dark, and he was alone in the untamed Ontario wilderness. Could it be possible he was hiking not toward a road but deeper into an immense forest? He could head back, find the shore, find his boat, shiver there through the night, paddle out of the bay in the morning—it would be for miles—and hope to be found by another boater.

Russell hitched up his pants and took several deep breaths. Well, if he had been captivated by the scent of the wilderness air earlier in his journey, he certainly had a corner on the market now. *Close your eyes*, came a command. *Stand here for a minute. Breathe. Stop thinking, and sense the pathway through the problem.*

He closed his eyes. For the first time he became keenly aware of the clear, rising and falling calls of invisible songbirds.

Some calls were simple, three to five notes, while others rose and swirled like syncopated jazz riffs. Focusing on the calls, Russell breathed in deeply through his nose. The spicy aroma of evergreen needles, damp moss and all other elements of the forest wafted into his head and lungs then expanded like a full-body wasabi sushi rush. A shimmering sense of peaceful calm percolated through him.

Russell's eyes snapped open and his decision was clear. Only strenuous hiking was keeping him warm. He realized that he had been sweating for some time, the smell of dank perspiration rising from him. His knee hurt, but it was not badly damaged. He certainly had traveled close to a mile since abandoning his boat. The thought came to him to start looking for the red light of the cell tower. It would be high overhead as he drew nearer. Knee throbbing, he dropped into a crouch and continued onward into the deepening darkness.

Less than a quarter-mile away, Gribber applied black Halloween face paint to the last person huddled around the rear of his station wagon. He kept it simple, using his finger to lay a thick black line of paint under the eyes of each member of his increasingly boisterous band of vigilantes. When finished, they looked like undersized pro football linemen. He tossed the jar of paint onto his front seat.

Ten minutes later LeBlanc's cell phone chirped. "It's Annie," he said. "*Keeper* just passed by Mullock's boathouse on its way into Pistol."

"You heard the man," Gribber called to the group. "We're moving out in two minutes."

In the bush across the Kamini road from the campgrounds, Russell gratefully encountered a long stretch of grassy meadow skirting a narrow pond. The terrain was flat, and though the sun had set, he was relieved by how much brighter the evening became having escaped the dense forest. He could make out precise details of the land and dull colors from flowers dancing across the meadow. He looked up toward the sky now decorated with a rising crescent moon. Off to his left he saw the red light of the cell tower looming high overhead.

Russell broke into a brisk, limping walk toward the tower, veering closer to the edge of the pond. There the meadow turned to marsh. In stride, first his left foot then his right sank into ankle-deep mud. When he pulled out his left foot, his canvas deck shoe remained ensconced in the oozing muck. Russell placed his soaked, sock-covered foot gingerly behind him, squatted, reached forward and thrust his hand into the black, water-filled hole. As he pulled out the shoe, a foul sulfur smell wafted to his nostrils.

He managed somehow to pull out his right foot from the deep slime while retaining its shoe, though his sock and pant cuff were drenched in black, acrid mud. He gingerly stepped backward onto firmer ground, poured the water from his stinking, blackened shoe and put it back on. Staying away from the edge of the pond, he took a more circuitous route around it toward the cell tower.

As Russell entered the wall of evergreen trees marking the end of the meadow, he glimpsed a head-high, tan horizontal line flirting in the distance. He advanced a few more feet and realized that he was looking at the surface of an elevated gravel road. He blew out a long breath of relief. He'd done it. His theory about the road had been correct. Russell was triumphant. He rushed through the remaining narrow strip of forest and flung his right hand at the final stout bough from a red pine looming out at head height. Pushing it away, it slipped over his fingertips and sprung back, whipping him forcibly in the face.

Russell dropped to his knees. He had closed his eyes a split second before being walloped by the branch, but his right eye seared with pain. He placed the fingers of one hand over the eye and pressed on it to help relieve the discomfort.

After half a minute he removed his hand. Looking at it through his open left eye he saw the fingerprints of his middle three fingers defined in blood. Russell crawled on hands and knees across the final patch of forest and rose slowly to his feet in a soggy, six-foot-deep ditch running alongside the Kamini road.

He flickered his right eye open and was relieved to find he could see from it. It felt much better to keep it closed.

He could hear a low thrumming inside his head and wondered if the blow from the branch had been more serious than he thought. No. Not from inside his head. The sound he heard was coming from his right. It was a sound he knew from his boyhood on the farm ... the sound of tires on a gravel road. He turned and saw headlights coming down a hill.

Russell limped across the ditch toward the road's angled stone foundation. Large chunks of granite had been graded as base material to fill the marshy low stretch where he emerged. He began crawling frantically up the stone slope, but the big pickup zoomed past before he could reach the road surface. Gasping for air he gave out an exhausted cry and slumped onto his stomach.

Then he saw the glare from a second set of headlights. Russell crawled ferociously with both hands while driving with his legs. He launched himself up the final feet of stone, flinging his right arm in the air as the second vehicle roared past. His chest landed hard on the jagged granite as his chin struck the gravel edge of the road.

Dave Burtnyk hollered from the back seat of Gribber's wagon. "Grib, stop! I saw something!"

Gribber took his foot off the gas pedal.

"You start seeing things again, Burtkiss, we're going to have to get you back on your meds."

"No, back there, on the side of the road, a guy's arm. I'm serious." Gribber hit the brakes and brought the wagon to a halt.

"Which side?"

"Your side. Somebody crawling up from the ditch."

Gribber put the wagon into reverse and drove backward fifty feet. He stomped on the brakes and jumped out. Further down the road he saw a man climb to the road surface and stand unsteadily. Gribber trotted briskly toward him.

Russell limped toward the taillights of the stopped vehicle. Thank god someone in the car had seen his desperate wave. He was alive, and about to be rescued. A figure had exited the driver's door and was fast approaching. The figure was tall and slender, but its clothing was indiscernible.

As the figure drew nearer, its body suddenly vanished into the road and surrounding wilderness itself.

Russell stopped walking and stared as wide-eyed as a one-eyed person can at the horrific sight of a garishly colored head floating toward him in the moonlight. The skin around the mouth and one eye of the monster's head glowed a silvery blue, while the rest of its demon face was covered in blood, save for an oozing black scar beneath the other eye.

Russell's every muscle locked with fear. *I must be hallucinating*, he thought. He had taken an uppercut blow to the chin from the road. Only when the creature stopped and stood in the moonlight before him was Russell able to discern that its body magically had reappeared and was clothed. Moccasins, leggings, tanned leather, beadwork, headband all flashed through his mind in a bolt of recognition. This was no hallucination. He was standing face to face with an actual Indian spirit.

The spirit spoke. "What's up, doc?"

Chapter 15

Burtnyk, Anderson and LeBlanc exited the car and joined Gribber in front of Russell. "Our boy might need a second here, fellas," Gribber said.

Russell's head began to clear as he took several deep breaths and stared at the normal faces of the three other men. Reality returned to his consciousness like the slow descent of maple syrup over a stack of pancakes. The men indeed were his rescuers. One of them was an Indian—or Native American, aboriginal, first person, whatever they were supposed to be called—who for some reason was dressed and painted in his native way.

Gribber smiled. "Sorry if I startled you, sport. My name's John Dogrib. Everyone calls me Gribber. What's yours?"

"Dogrib," Russell repeated dully. He knew that name from somewhere ... from Ralph Mailer, at the resort in Orr. "John Dogrib, the fishing guide?"

Burtnyk, Anderson and LeBlanc gave anguished groans as a delighted Gribber wheeled to face them. Curling a leg behind him, he curtsied. "What have I always told you, boys? You have a celebrity in your midst, famous the world over. Or famous at least as far away as"—he turned and stared back at Russell—"Chicago, Illinois."

Russell's thought process had not remotely cleared enough to realize Gribber had marked him from his Illinois accent, aided by an educated guess and a bit of luck. Who was this sorcerer? "Name is Russell Dean, from ... Chicago. Rented a boat in Miskwa ... staying at the Lodge ... got lost on my way to Kamini. I hit something, broke the boat ... paddled to shore ... hiked through the woods toward the cell tower."

"You know, the Lodge has a passenger launch from Miskwa," LeBlanc said. "Still, that's impressive. That's some tough, steep bush to the east of here down to the river. Looks like you lost some battles, but won the war."

"Russ, hold out your arm," Gribber said.

"It's Russell," he said out of habit, extending his left arm.

Gribber rolled back the tattered cuff of Russell's filthy jacket and stopped. "Hold out an arm that doesn't have a ten thousand-dollar French watch on it."

Russell held out his other arm.

Gribber rolled back the cuff and placed one hand lightly around his wrist while placing the back of his other hand against Russell's forehead. He stared into Russell's open left eye. "Your pulse is good and there's some warmth to your skin. Your pupil looks normal. Them are some blue peepers you got there. Looks like you took a branch to one. Keep it closed. You feel dizzy at all? Weak? Nauseated?"

"No. My eye hurts but I can see out of it. I banged my knee on a rock. I'm hungry, but that's my fault."

"Well, Rusty, I have good news and bad news," Gribber said as he withdrew his hands. "The good news is you're not in shock, plus you damn near made it to Kamini. The Lodge is only five kilometers down the road. The bad news, we're late for a very important date. Our mission isn't far from here and shouldn't take long. You can tag along with us, and when we're finished, I'll drive you to the Lodge."

"Oh please. I've been through hell. I just want to get to the Lodge. Take me there now."

Russell's plea was met with silence.

"I'll pay you, anything, any amount," Russell said. Instinctively he reached for his wallet. Flashing a crisp, one hundred-dollar bill was his intention. His wallet was in his computer bag in the boat.

"Sorry, Russco, that isn't how it works up here," Gribber said. "Guess I didn't make myself clear. What we have to do can't wait. You can. Come with us to my car. You can sit and rest while we take care of our business."

As he limped toward the illuminated taillights of Gribber's Rambler station wagon, Russell noticed the word spelled out in raised chrome letters across the tailgate of the late model vehicle. The final letter of the manufacturer's name had either fallen or been pried off. RAMBLE, it read.

Gribber directed Russell into the front passenger seat while the others piled into the back. "Let's clean some of the dirt from your scrapes and take a quick look at that eye." Gribber leaned in front of Russell, popped open the glove box, and removed a packet of sanitary wipes and a first aid kit. "Face me, close both eyes and keep them closed until I tell you." Gribber removed a wet wipe and cleaned Russell's bruised right eye then explored the area around the eyebrow with his fingers. "Pretty good scrape on the eyebrow. You'll sport a nice bruise by morning, but it doesn't need stitches. The bleeding has stopped. I have a big adhesive patch that will cover the eye, that way you won't have to concentrate on keeping it closed. Let it heal for awhile in case the cornea's scratched."

"I guess if you say so."

Gribber tore open the pouch holding the large round patch and removed its backing. He placed the patch over Russell's eye, covering the entire area from his eyebrow to the top of his cheek. Then he grabbed the jar of black face paint, unscrewed the lid, dipped his finger and painted the beige-colored patch jet black. "Just pressing on it so it adheres," he told Russell.

"That feels good."

In the back seat, Bruce Anderson bit his sleeve to keep from laughing.

Gribber took out a second wipe. "Going to clean some of the grit from the rest of your face. You have a few scrapes, nothing serious. Keep that other eye closed."

Gribber washed off the dirt, pinesap and bits of blood from the small cuts scattered across Russell's face. With a quick swipe of his finger he painted a thick black line under Russell's other eye.

"OK, all done. You can open your eye."

Russell did as instructed. "How do I look?"

"Much better," Burtnyk said with a snort.

Gribber started Ramble and spun the tires to get to the next rendezvous point quickly. After a minute he pulled off onto a narrow gravel road slicing through the dense bush. The road headed downhill in a series of dips until bottoming out at the start of a long uphill grade.

Halfway up the hill were the taillights of Wolf Graf's pickup parked off to the side in a slender shoulder of meadow. Gribber pulled in behind the truck. "You can wait here, Russ, although you're certainly welcome to join us for a torchlight parade," he said to his front seat passenger. "Don't slam the doors," he said to the three in the back.

Wolf Graf, Gord Fanson and Faith Pearson climbed out of the pickup and walked to the rear of Ramble. Gribber opened the tailgate and removed items from the back. Holding the slender penlight in his mouth, he placed the empty metal pail on the ground and filled it with kerosene. He turned off the flashlight and began handing out torches.

"Who's that in your front seat?" Graf asked.

"A long story, I'm sure," Gribber said. "Wealthy American refugee we found on the side of the road. He's seeking asylum."

"That's a first," Pearson said. "Wealthy Americans never go through with their threats to move here."

Gribber handed Fanson the camcorder case. Fanson had been a film student at Carleton University in Ottawa prior to arriving in Kamini on a summer employment lark four years ago.

"You're our cinematographer tonight. Whip that out when we get down to Karp's truck."

Gribber picked up the pail of kerosene and led the group up the gravel road past Graf's pickup.

Faith Pearson heard footsteps scraping gravel behind her, turned, and drew a sharp breath. Russell had quietly exited Ramble and was hobbling quickly to catch up. "Creaking criminy, you gave me a scare!" she said to him.

"I certainly didn't mean to. Gribber, wait up. I want to go with you."

"You sure?"

"Yes."

"Why?"

"I don't know."

"Good enough." Gribber sprinted to Ramble, grabbed a torch, raced back and handed it to Russell.

"I always bring a spare to these things, just in case. That knee OK?"

"Fine. Keeping it moving is better than sitting and letting it tighten up," Russell said as they resumed their march up the hill. "What the hell's going on, anyway?"

"Paying a visit to a poacher. No rough stuff, just need to catch him in the act, collect the evidence and convince him his commercial fishing career has come to an end."

As they approached the crest of the hill, Gribber told the group to hold, handed the pail of kerosene to Russell, and trotted ahead. He veered left to the tree line and moved stealthily until he could peer down the final short stretch of road to Andriy Karpenko's landing.

They had not arrived early.

The generator was running, the lights were on, and the Chevy pickup was backed up to the table. A number of coolers already were closed and in the pickup's bed. Several empty bins were stacked beside the table. Karpenko was on the dock, stepping into *Keeper*. He entered the cabin at the front of the boat. The cabin light was on. Through the tall glass windows, Gribber saw him pick up a bottle, remove the cap, pour clear liquid into a glass, and down the shot in one gulp. Karpenko walked to the rear of the boat and knelt beside the open double doors to the hold. He lifted out a plastic bin and placed it on the floor. He stood, picked up the bin—Gribber was just close enough to hear him grunt above the soft strumming of the generator—and slid it over the gunwale onto the dock.

Beyond the dock, the gray-black water and tan granite shoreline of the large, tonsil-shaped bay glowed under the emerging stars and moonlight. Extending out from the terraced bluffs along one side of the landing—from where Gribber and Annie Chase had spied on Karpenko—the shoreline ended in a narrow point. The glistening water curved around the point and into the main body of Pistol Lake.

Wafting from somewhere on the other side of the point, Gribber could make out the sound of violins in a series of rising crescendos, followed by an evenly paced series of popping sounds. Seconds later fireworks exploded blue, gold and red above the tree line at the base of the point.

Gribber ran back to the others. He retrieved the pail of kerosene from Russell and placed it on the ground. "Everyone line up, walk by the pail and soak your torch. Chop chop," he said in a hushed tone. One by one the torches were dipped in kerosene.

Gribber led the group to the crest of the hill where they stood in darkness looking down the road to the lighted area less than thirty yards away. Swirling orchestral music grew louder as it wafted across the water. Karpenko was standing on the dock in front of a large blue bin with his back to them, staring out into the bay.

The second round of fireworks burst in the air just off the tip of the point.

"That's our signal," Gribber said. "Light 'em up."

Chapter 16

Less than an hour earlier, standing at the steering column of *Keeper* as he rounded the point into his bay, Andriy Karpenko had burst into song. His deep, guttural voice clanked precariously around the notes of "Vesnivka," a traditional Ukrainian folk song heralding spring. It had been a very good day. As a reward, he took a bottle of vodka and shot glass from a cabinet beneath the steering wheel, filled the glass, and drank.

Karpenko was still singing when he climbed onto the dock and tied up. Rising early to set his gill nets in distant Roughrock every three days had been worth it. This morning at sunrise, he had gambled by setting his largest-size gill net in the center of a channel above a stretch of rapids. The gamble was that only the gills of very large fish would become snared in the net. Smaller walleyes—perfectly saleable to certain buyers in Miskwa—could swim unabated through the grid of large squares. Set a smaller size net, however, and schools of large walleyes would nose into the net only to swim underneath or around it. The gamble had paid off handsomely. Karpenko returned to find the net flush with enormous, ten- to twelve-pound walleyes. In *Keeper*'s hold were four large tubs of walleye, together weighing over six hundred pounds.

The illegality of harvesting walleye with gill nets on the Winnipeg River was merely a nuisance to Karpenko. Ascending the dock ramp, he thought once again about how stupid the Ontario Ministry conservation laws were, like the wimpy Canadians in general, dictating where in the province and how many pounds of walleye could be netted commercially each year.

There were plenty of walleye in this river and always would be.

It was a good thing for him that a few of the Miskwa whole-salers felt the same way. After they acquired the fish they could distribute it across Canada, the States and anywhere in the world. All they had to do was forge a simple origin certificate. After de-livering his catch late tonight—driving halfway down the Kamini road to the washed-out section where a buyer in a truck would be waiting on the other side—Karpenko would drive away with over two thousand bucks in his pocket. Not bad for a long day's work. The short spring whitefish season had again been profitable.

Now humming the folk tune, Karpenko walked briskly up the gravel road to the garage. He started the rust-covered Chevy pickup inside and backed it down the road to the landing. He dropped the tailgate, grabbed the feet of two halogen light stands and set them up on each side of the clearing. The insulated coolers, including two containing bagged ice he'd bought at the marina that afternoon, had slid all the way to the front of the bed when he braked for a deer on his way back. Huffing, he climbed unsteadily into the truck bed and pulled them toward the tailgate.

His twelve-gauge, double-barrel shotgun, sheathed in a de-caying canvas case, also had slid forward. He kept the gun loaded, the butt end at the tailgate with the flap open so he could quickly pull it if he spotted a duck or goose sitting in a back roads pond. He put the gun back where he liked it before heading to the shoreline shack and starting the generator beside it.

This would be his final night sleeping inside the decrepit, spi-der-infested shack. And his final day of having to piss and shit in the bush, at least until he returned to Kamini in the fall. Tomorrow he would be on his way to his far more lavish trailer home in Flin Flon. Since emigrating to Canada from Ukraine and acquiring his commercial fishing license, Karpenko had made a decent living, first in northern Manitoba then Northwest Ontario. Acquiring the whitefish license for the Winnipeg River twelve years ago had been a prudent move. Now fifty-five years old, he would need to work for only another five years to be eligible for Canadian

Pension Plan payments. He could afford to retire, supplemented by his savings.

A plastic table set at the tailgate of his truck and the clearing illuminated by the halogen lamps, Karpenko knelt on the floor of *Keeper* and swung open the double doors to the hold. He lifted the first bin with a grunt. This would be work. He decided that he would have a shot of vodka after emptying the cargo from each of the four bins into the insulated coolers. This was a night to celebrate.

Two emptied bins and two vodka shots later, Karpenko slid the third container of walleye across the gunwale onto the dock and stopped to rest. His ears perked up. What was that strange sound far in the distance? The buzzing of an immense swarm of mosquitoes? Couldn't be. Probably the squeaking rumble of a train passing through the bush. No, it wasn't a train, it was … music. Violins, like in an orchestra. Karpenko caught the shimmer of fireworks out of the corner of his eye. Damn cottager kids. Home from college for the summer with nothing better to do than play loud music, get drunk and stoned, and blow off fireworks while cruising in their rich parents' pontoon boats.

The music grew louder as Karpenko lugged the third bin up the dock. Now he could hear deep-throated trombones blaring a simple, rising melody over the violins. It sounded like a stern march. The music grew louder still, brightening as trumpets joined in to repeat the pounding melody. The sound of the increasingly frenetic march echoed off the stone shorelines of the bay.

Karpenko put down the bin at the start of the ramp and turned to face the water. Another round of fireworks exploded, this time off the end of the point. The green-and-red bow light of a boat appeared, moving fast and headed straight for his dock. No longer muffled by the dense forest, the swirling, sinister orchestral music boomed across the water directly toward him. He could see the figure of a lone driver in the back of the boat. This was not a late-night fisherman come to cast or troll the bay. He didn't know who it was, but this was a bad time for a visitor.

Karpenko quickly returned to *Keeper*. He stumbled to his knees and slammed closed the doors to the hold containing the final bin. Climbing unsteadily out of the boat, he veered back down the dock, focused on the large blue bin resting on the ramp. He snatched it to his protruding belly and lugged it toward shore. Looking up, he stopped in his tracks.

A silent mob of people with torches was coming down his gravel road. They already were past his garage and marching directly toward his truck. Karpenko carried the bin to the table and with a hard shove sent it sliding across the tailgate into the pickup bed. He flung the table away, slammed shut the tailgate, and lurched to the front of the truck to face the approaching mob.

Cymbals crashed at near deafening volume behind him, accented by machine gun bursts of explosions as more colorful fireworks filled the sky. In the flickering light from the torches, Karpenko could make out the close-mouthed, grim faces of the townspeople, slashes of glossy black paint under their eyes. As they closed to within ten feet, a crouching figure carrying a torch shot through the middle of the pack and rose as it flew the final feet toward him, thrusting its blood-covered face into his.

Karpenko shrieked and fell backward against the hood of his truck. "Goddamn it, Gribber, just what the fuck are you doing?" he shouted in his stern Ukrainian accent. He leaned forward off the truck and stood. "Painted like that, and here with this mob! You scared me half to death."

The maddening music blaring from the boat softened as it segued to flutes and piccolos dancing around a counter melody. The group fanned out around Karpenko.

"Just concerned about your whitefish catch today, Andriy, that's all," LeBlanc said in a friendly tone. "Worried maybe they were a little sick. Jaundiced. You know, turning yellow."

"Or gold," Graf said.

"My whitefish are fine," Karpenko said, growling. "And they're mine, same as this property. All of you are trespassing and had better leave right now."

"Or what?" Burtnyk asked.

"Or you will be sorry."

"We don't leave until we see what's in the bins," Gribber said. He dropped his torch and began walking around the passenger side of the truck. Karpenko spun and lurched quickly along the other side, meeting Gribber at the tailgate.

"I'm going to see what's in that bin, Andriy."

"No, you're not." Karpenko thrust both palms into Gribber's chest and shoved him away from the truck. He reached over the tailgate, grabbed the butt of his shotgun, drew it from its case and wheeled around. Holding the gun at waist level, Karpenko aimed it at Gribber.

The others had followed the two men around to the rear of the truck. They saw the gun and took a step back. Gribber took a step forward. Lou LeBlanc snatched Russell's flaming torch from his hand, tossed it on the gravel by the dock ramp, placed his arm across Russell's chest and backed him into the darkness outside the glare of the lights. "No one saw this coming," LeBlanc whispered. "Stay put over here while we talk him down."

Standing in the darkness, Russell watched the bizarre drama unfold.

The music blaring from the boat—a classical piece he vaguely recognized but couldn't name—reverted back to its full orchestral intensity and began building to its climax. The driver of the boat had docked and was walking swiftly toward the ramp. Outlined in the moonlight, the curving shape of the tall figure left no doubt the driver was a woman. She stepped from the ramp onto shore, her forceful gait matching the beat of the pounding music. Without breaking stride she reached down and picked up Russell's burning torch. Marching into the halo of light her features became fully illuminated.

Russell gazed at the most astonishingly beautiful woman he had ever seen.

Under the lights her long auburn hair, piled high in swirls atop her head, glinted in rich hues of red, brunette and black. Two bone-white ceramic chopsticks formed an X through the swirls rising from the back. Her lush eyebrows arched gracefully below her forehead, extending just past the edges of her large, dark, oval eyes. Red face paint slashed under each eye accented high cheekbones, her cheeks curving gently inward along each side of her sharp, slender nose. Sweeping jawlines met at a softly squared chin beneath the curling full lips of her mouth.

Over a black leotard she wore a blue-and-gold football jersey, cut off so it draped over her breasts and hung to her midriff. Battered white shoulder pads were strapped on over the jersey. Flowing upward from a pair of black, steel-toed work boots, gold yoga pants wrapped her long, sculpted legs until disappearing beneath a red-and-black plaid miniskirt. A wide black leather belt perforated with silver studs hung at an angle off her hips.

The woman held the torch high over her head as she waded through the crowd. All except Gribber were still inching backward, silenced by the appearance of the shotgun. As she strode forward and came to a halt beside Gribber, the symphony ended as crashing cymbals accented the booming final note. Despite the soft purring of the generator and seeming incongruity of the phrase, silence actually can be deafening.

Annie Chase broke the spell. "Andriy, if you fire those two shells you'd better put one in me, because if you don't, I will burn you where you stand."

Karpenko had begun sweeping the shotgun side to side to keep the crowd circling the rear of his truck at bay. "You all need to leave," he said. "You have no business being here."

"You're not going to shoot anyone," Graf said. "Gribber and Annie saw you packing up walleyes the other night. We know what you're up to, Andriy. Put the gun down."

"I'll shoot your German ass, that I assure you," Karpenko spat. "A few walleyes. I do no harm. There are plenty of them in the river. All of you, you catch them all summer. You keep some and eat them. What I do is no different from you."

Gribber moved slowly toward Karpenko, who stopped waving

the gun and leveled it squarely at Gribber's stomach. The Ojibwe warrior continued to step forward. "Here's the difference," Gribber said calmly. "All of us catch and eat the fish in accordance with human law, mindful of the daily limits, releasing the larger fish, ensuring the population remains healthy. My people understand that a fish may serve as food, a sacrifice prescribed by the Creator, just as the minnows the fish eat serve as their food. But only as we honor and insure their abundance. We are all part of the same circle."

Karpenko gripped the shotgun tighter and stood still as a statue. Gribber took a final step, creasing his buckskin shirt as he pressed his taut stomach firmly against the shotgun's muzzle. Hands at his sides he leaned forward at the waist and pressed his face to within a foot of Karpenko's. "You see, Andriy, when it comes to me, you are ignorant of one supremely important fact." Gribber's voice softened to a whisper. "I am Giigoonh, fish clan of the Anishinaabe. The walleyes you have been illegally netting and killing are my relatives."

Karpenko closed his eyes and bowed his head as his mouth curled into a grimace. Slumping, he lowered the shotgun and held it dangling from one hand. He lifted his head to face Gribber, tears wetting the corners of his eyes as his chest heaved. Karpenko convulsed into sobs. "I didn't mean to ... the whitefish, they ... I couldn't ... I'm sorry."

Gribber took the shotgun from Karpenko's limp hand and passed it behind him to Annie. "Your boat, your shack, your garage, this land, they belong to the Ministry now," Gribber said. "The only thing for you to do is leave. Go live in your truck at the campgrounds until the road reopens."

Karpenko wiped his eyes with the back of his hand and trudged slowly toward the cab of his pickup. Wolf Graf dropped the tailgate, jumped into the bed and slid the bin and coolers toward the rear. Gribber removed the lid from the bin to reveal its cargo of large, golden walleyes. "You getting this?" he asked Fanson, who was moving in closer with the camcorder to his eye.

"Got all of it so far. Next I'll get photos with my phone."

Jammer Mackay, who seemingly had arrived from nowhere, stepped from the shadows to help unload the coolers. Annie leaned the shotgun against one of the light stands and put her arms around Gribber. "Excellent choice of music, Biidaapiwinini," she said. "Even if it was lost on Karp. He wouldn't know Wagner's Ride of the Valkyries were he seated alone for a private performance by the Winnipeg Symphony Orchestra."

"My little nod to Coppola," Gribber said. "Even if only you and I get it. And allow me a final note of gratitude for your excellent eagle eyes the other night." Annie kissed Gribber on the cheek then began collecting torches, piling them in a stack on the sandy shoreline until they burned out.

Russell stepped from the darkness as if in a trance, which he was, having reverted back to the mentally confused state he possessed when first encountering Gribber on the Kamini road. Eye blinking, he stopped and stood on the edge of the gravel near the driver door of the truck as Karpenko climbed in.

Karpenko turned the key, and the Chevy's engine coughed to life. The stark reality of his situation struck. He would be arrested by the RCMP in Flin Flon. He would be fined and could go to jail. He had lost everything. His remorse dissolved as his stubborn nature, fueled by the vodka, returned with a boozy vengeance. He emerged from the truck and turned to face the group one final time. "I'm sick and tired of this stupid little bush town and all you crazy people anyway!" he shouted. "You can all go to hell!"

Climbing back into his truck, Karpenko took his first good look at the stranger with twigs and pinesap matted in his wild black hair, wearing a pirate's eye patch, torn, blood-stained clothing and stinking, mud-soaked shoes who was staring at him like a bemused zombie. "And who the fuck are *you?*" he bellowed as he slammed the door, threw the truck into gear and sped away up the hill.

Gribber gave assignments to each of the townspeople under his command. "Dave and Bruce, check *Keeper* for more bins. Lou and Wolf, hike up the hill and bring the vehicles down. Wolf, we'll load the fish into the back of your truck. Annie and Faith, start unloading the fish from the bins into coolers and ice them down."

"I checked the refrigerator space at the Lodge, we should have plenty," Annie called out as she and Faith began organizing the coolers. "At least the fish won't go to waste. The guides can clean them tomorrow then we'll donate them to the Miskwa food bank. They have freezers."

"Jammer, check the torches, make sure they're out and stick them in the front of my boat."

"Got it, Grib. I'll stick my bike in your boat too."

Gribber glanced around to locate Russell. He had seen LeBlanc wisely usher him to safety when Karpenko drew his shotgun. Gribber spotted Russell standing alone on the edge of the lighted area.

Russell's newest basic problems this evening were breathing and standing upright. His heart was beating at such a furious rate that he could barely gasp enough air, and his knees kept going weak. These curious and far from lethal symptoms began the moment the woman arriving by boat entered the light. Upon seeing her face, Russell was struck by the amorous thunderbolt, its voltage crackling even higher when he heard her speak, for her voice was unmistakable. It belonged to the woman who phoned him from the Lodge the day before.

Gribber sensed something a tad amiss in Russell's demeanor as he approached. "You OK there, Rusty?"

Russell emerged dully from his feverish trance, struggling to combat the effects induced by the intoxicating serum with which Cupid, God of Desire, tips his arrows. He turned his head slowly, blinked his eye at Gribber and attempted speech. "Who's ..." he began, but could form no additional words.

"Who's ... on first? I don't know."

"No ... Who's the ..." Again, Russell could only pause.

"Who's the boss? You're the boss, Russco. You are the *boss*."

"No, the … the woman …" Russell stammered. He raised his arm stiffly and pointed in the general direction where Faith and Annie were loading fish from bins into coolers. They glanced up and eyed him suspiciously.

"Which one, the little slip of a thing on the right? Faith Pearson. Teaches high school English in Miskwa. Well read, sharp as a new treble hook and witty as hell. She's thirty-eight, divorced, homeowner, bakes, owns an eighteen-foot, wide hull G3 with a ninety horsepower, four-stroke Yammi decked out with full electronics. A real catch."

"No," Russell said, edging a few more degrees out of his daze. "The other woman."

"Oh, you mean the tall one who looks like an unpaid extra from a Mad Max movie? That mutt? Now there's a pail of gasoline looking for matches. That woman, my good man, is the assistant general manager of the Kamini Lodge. That's Annie. Annie Chase."

Chapter 17

Gribber ushered the quaking shell of Russell into the front seat of Ramble then helped the others finish up. They loaded the coolers of fish into Graf's truck, switched off the generator and tossed the lights and table along the side of the shack. Jammer stowed his mountain bike and the torches in Gribber's boat.

"Well, quite a production," Annie said to Gribber. "You still know how to show a girl a good time. Jam and I will take your boat, but I'm going to have him drop me off at home. I need to get to work early. It's going to be a madhouse tomorrow. And who's your new friend, the pirate?"

"A guest of yours. Russell Dean from Chicago. Rented a boat at Miller's Landing, smacked the motor on the reef at the end of Lost Bay. We found him on the road after he'd crashed through the bush. I told him I'd drop him off at the Lodge, but I'm going to recommend he stay at my place tonight. He needs a beer, and a meal, and sleep. He doesn't have his luggage with him anyway."

"Huh. I wonder how the hell he wound up in Lost Bay? Must have gone through Myrtle instead of The Dalles. You know men. Probably didn't buy a map. Anyway, I told Wolf where to bring the fish. The night staff will have carts to help load it into the Lodge cooler."

"You are perfection as always." Gribber kissed Annie on the forehead. "Jam, nice work, I can only assume. I'll see you at Morning Wood."

On his way past Graf's pickup, Gribber popped open one of the coolers, swept away the ice and removed a walleye. He opened Ramble's tail door and tossed in the fish. Lou LeBlanc, Faith

Pearson and Dave Burtnyk were already in the back seat. Russell had resumed a vague semblance of brain function and was being lectured by Pearson. "Your first time driving a boat and it never occurred to you to put on a lifejacket," she said, scolding Russell as Gribber turned the key. "It tears our hearts out when tourists drown up here. It's so bad for business. It can be days before we recover."

Gribber wanted to speak to Russell, but he didn't want to interrupt Faith.

"I'll admit we locals don't wear life jackets much during the day, but we know boats and the river. And we put them on at night. If nothing else, as a courtesy—it makes it so much easier to find the body."

"Faith, I need to talk to our man here for a second," Gribber said. "Russ, I can drop you at the Lodge, but the dining room closes at nine on Sundays. The only food will be in the lounge, and the only meal option is a cheeseburger you'll taste for a week. Your luggage is in your boat. Why don't you stay in my spare bedroom tonight? I can whip up something for you to eat."

"Food," Russell said.

"Food it is."

As they entered Gribber's cottage, everyone kicked off their shoes, which Russell did gratefully.

"Beer's in the fridge," Gribber said. "Russco, you want a beer?"

"I would kill for a beer."

"Someone get our guest a beer. Community bottle of rye in the cupboard if anyone wants. Take your drinks and head for the veranda."

In his bedroom, Gribber offered a silent prayer of thanks as he returned his eagle feather to its cedar box home.

Burtnyk handed Russell an ice-cold Molson and led him through an eclectically furnished central living area defined by a massive boulder fireplace centered on one wall. Rustic barn wood shelves stuffed with books ran floor to ceiling on both sides. Passing through they arrived at a screened veranda running the length of the cottage facing the moonlit river.

Russell dropped into a wicker pine log chair while the others dispersed among a disparate collection of rustic chairs and an antique quilted chesterfield.

"Let's change that bandage," Gribber said to Russell, deftly peeling the black patch from his eye and crumbling it in his palm.

Russell blinked the wounded eye open. "You know, I think it's OK. Yeah. The bandage helped. I can see fine."

"Outstanding. I'll start fixing you a meal. Walleye doesn't take long."

Gribber ducked into the bathroom, removed his headband, and washed the war paint from his face. In the kitchen, he put a large cast iron skillet on the stove and placed the giant walleye on a large cutting board. With three effortless sweeps of a filleting knife, one enormous, pristine fillet emerged. He flipped the walleye on its other side and produced a second fillet in a matter of seconds. Filleting a fish was a mindless task for a man who had done it since childhood. He sliced one fillet in half and set it aside before cutting the remaining half and the entire second fillet into bite-size cubes. As he seasoned the fish for the pan, his mind settled on Russell. Poor guy. He'd seen that look before. Annie had that effect on men. Good luck, Rusty.

Gribber heard the rumble of Graf's big Ram truck, and in a few seconds Wolf Graf, Gord Fanson and Bruce Anderson entered the kitchen.

"Welcome. You know the drill," Gribber said. "Grab a drink and head to the veranda. Walleye appies coming in a minute."

Graf, a strapping and gregarious German, owned Roughrock Resort, a year-round hunting and fishing resort near the Blackdog dam. He surprised Gribber with a bear hug, then put both hands on Gribber's shoulders and stared at him with his electric blue eyes. "That was quite a brave thing you did back there, my friend," Graf said, smiling. "You must have some German in you, way back somewhere, to have balls like that, no?"

"Pretty certain that's not the case. I've simply found it's wise to choose the right times to show bravery. Now grab a beer, take one for our American guest, and get your Teutonic bum out to the veranda."

The latecomers introduced themselves to Russell and joined in on the boisterous discussion concerning the details of his adventure.

"But I made it through The Dalles!" Russell said. On his empty stomach, the first strong beer he gulped down was working wonders on his fragile psyche. He gratefully accepted another from Graf. "From there all I had to do was keep left all the way to the Kamini Lodge."

"This narrow channel you went through, was it maybe a hundred and fifty meters long?" Burtnyk asked.

"Sorry, I can't do meters. We tried it in the US back in the eighties, but it didn't take."

"Five hundred feet," LeBlanc said. "Cliffs along most of it, strong current, the main channel maybe thirty feet wide the whole way."

"No. The current picked up, and I went past a little island that split a narrow channel into two."

In unison, everyone on the veranda said: "Myrtle Rapids."

"You were close," Faith said. "You hung a left about a mile before The Dalles. Went down Myrtle Rapids instead. Not much of a rapids unless the water's high. Then you weaved through the back door channels. That's how you wound up in Gunn Lake."

"Keeping to the left as you entered Gunn led you right into Lost Bay," LeBlanc said. "It stretches for miles. I know the reef you hit and exactly where your boat is."

"Well, I'm glad someone does," Russell said with a laugh. "I suppose I'll have to pay for an expensive repair."

"Maybe not," Fanson said. "If you hit the reef on your way out, it rises gradually. Most of Miller's rental boats have older motors. Probably just sheared a pin."

The sound of a boat pulling up to Gribber's dock filtered into the veranda.

"There's Annie and Jammer," Faith said.

The mention of Annie Chase triggered renewed heart palpitations in Russell. She would be standing in the door to this veranda? In the same room as he? Coming in, meeting him, sitting down? In his mind he went over their phone conversation from the day before. Had he been rude to her? No, he didn't think so. Well, yes, he had been. He'd start with a sincere apology, then work in how he was a partner in a major Chicago advertising firm. Blame his insolence on his complex responsibilities at the office, his heavy workload. His impending divorce. Yes. For god's sake mention the divorce. He was available. Then the thought of what he must look and certainly smell like crashed down on him.

Jammer Mackay came solo through the veranda screen door.

"Annie not with you?" Faith asked.

"No, I dropped her off. Says she's tired from planting her garden, working on the outhouse and tonight's fun. Has to get up early."

Russell's brain, heart and loins ricocheted in unison to a fresh locale midway between disappointment and relief.

Faith introduced Jammer to Russell, and recapped Russell's evening adventure.

"Cool," Jammer said with a nod. He headed toward the kitchen to get a beer.

The sweet, smoky scent of fresh, egg-battered walleye frying hot in a little peanut oil and ample butter greeted Jammer as he entered the kitchen to find Gribber standing at the stove. Gribber turned and gave him a wink.

"I did it just like you told me," Jammer said, grinning as he opened the fridge to grab a beer. "Biked over to Karp's landing. Got there at eight thirty. Stashed my bike in the bush on the far side of his shack and hung out waiting for *Keeper* to dock. After Karp brought his truck down and got all set up, I peeked around the corner until I saw him walking toward the dock. I snuck over to his truck and hid behind it, waited until I saw him kneel down to unlatch the doors to the hold. Then I reached into the bed and grabbed his shotgun, slipped it out of its case and removed the shells. Put it back in the case and in the truck bed right where he'd left it. I was back hiding in the bush before he'd even picked up the first bin and carried it to the dock."

Jammer reached into his jeans pocket and removed two twelve-gauge shotgun shells. "You want 'em, or can I keep 'em? I use a twelve-gauge for ducks in the fall. Shells is expensive."

"You keep them," Gribber said with a gentle pat of his hand to Jammer's cheek. "As a token of my literally undying appreciation."

Chapter 18

Russell could see it was a gigantic musky, no doubt a female, many times larger than the musky that had warily studied his lure by the dock on Pelican Lake. It was evening, just before sunset. The fish was in shallow water, circling in a round area of sandy bottom near a gently sloping granite shore. Its mottled, greenish-silver body sporting vibrant crimson fins and tail appeared like the only colorized object in a black and white movie. The fish repeatedly dove upward out of the water, violently thrashing its head back and forth while airborne before crashing down, only to circle and fling itself into the air again. Each time it erupted through the water's surface, it shook its head less forcibly. Each time several more seconds lapsed before it again flew upward from water into air.

It was weakening.

The bald eagle watched the spectacle with interest from its perch atop a white pine several miles away before gliding over. Circling the musky from above, the eagle could make no sense of its wild thrashings so curled its wings and dropped down to watch from shore. It was very old. Its brilliant white head swiveled smoothly left and right like a doll's as it checked for predators before again turning its attention to the musky's strange dance. Russell could tell the eagle was a male from the deep tone of its thoughts.

That is a foolish dance for a musky, thought the eagle.

But then I have done something foolish indeed, the musky replied. Earlier this evening I ate a shiny fish that fluttered down in front of me. It looked like nothing I had seen before.

Then why did you eat it?

Because I am the largest musky in these waters and ruler of all things beneath its surface. I am old and wise and never eat the false fish that splash into the water from the sky and swim so poorly back toward the floating shadow creatures.

But it seems this time you indeed ate something that was not food from the Creator.

I said I did something foolish. It surprised me when it splashed on the surface like a frightened duckling that makes such a fine meal. Then when it flashed color like the scales of a tasty young perch I did not think. I swished my beautiful large tail and opened wide my huge mouth and struck it.

And now it is in your stomach and will kill you because it will not disappear into you I suppose.

No it is hard and strange and stuck in my throat. It will kill me because I cannot eat anything while it is there. If I cannot jump into your world and shake it free I will starve and die after two more periods of darkness. My belly will bloat and I will float to the surface to be eaten by the gulls until you eagles notice the gulls and arrive to scare them away. Then you will eat me.

It is a shame to eat you if this is not the natural time for your spirit to move forward. You are a very large musky. I can fit my head deep into your mouth. Swim toward me where I stand. With a slap of your tail you can slide your head out of the water and rest it on shore. Then open your mouth and I will try to pull out the strange fish with my beak.

But if I do as you say my head will be out of water resting on land at your feet and with a hop you will sink your talons into my brain and kill me. So either way I will die.

If I wanted to kill you and eat you—and you would be a feast for many eagles from now until the next light—I would have done so as I circled over you. I could not lift you from the water but I could have sunk my talons into your head while you did your foolish dance then flap my long wings and tow your huge body to shore to be eaten. That I could have done. But this despair that grips you is not becoming of such a wise old musky. You have heard me say I do not wish to harm you if this is not the time when your spirit is meant to move forward.

I know now you are speaking truth. Step back and I will slide my head onto shore.

Flapping its tail, the musky swam up the sloping shore until its head emerged from the water and rested on the dry, pink-flaked granite. The fish opened its mouth. The eagle hopped forward. Its head and neck disappeared deep down the musky's throat. With a jerk, the eagle pulled back its head. In its curving golden beak was a flat rectangular object Russell could not quite make out.

I do not mean to poke fun at a sister who has been so close to the spirit stage but every fish that emerges into spirit will float to the surface and I will see it no matter how far away. I have returned to soar over these waters as they turn from white to blue for more cycles of the sun and moon than you have spent swimming below and must say to you, this does not look like any kind of fish I have seen.

I will say only once more that I was foolish. Now I have learned two things. I must be careful to eat only what is supplied by the Creator.

And what is the second thing?

That the eagle is indeed the wisest creature and so serves as messenger for the Creator. And now you should take the strange fish in your talons and fly far out over the big water and drop it where the water is so deep no fish will find it.

But then a foolish fish that is hungry because it has not learned that the Creator does not supply food across broad deep waters might see it fluttering down and eat it again. I will grasp it in my talons and fly along this shoreline until I find a crevice where I can drop the strange fish so that it cannot find the river.

Again, eagle, you prove me your wisdom.

The enormous fish began wriggling its body. It slipped backward from the granite shore into the water. When fully immersed, it turned and with a tremendous slap of its tail swam powerfully forward, causing a V-shaped tidal wave tumbling so high in each direction it shook the granite shore on which Russell stood.

"Daylight in the swamp," Gribber said. He shook Russell's shoulder a second time, then placed both hands under the metal bed frame, lifted it six inches, and dropped it. "You wanna dance, Rusty, you gotta pay the band."

Chapter 19

Russell awakened from his vision and stared at Gribber standing beside his bed. It was still dark outside. Gribber flipped on the bedside light. He was dressed in a sun-faded chamois shirt, blue jeans and work boots. A leather sheath holding a filleting knife with an exquisitely carved oak handle hung from his belt. Russell saw Gribber yesterday evening on the veranda after he'd washed off his war paint, but now dressed in regular clothing he again looked like a completely different person. "I had the craziest dream."

Gribber's piercing brown eyes sharpened with interest. "Tell me about it."

"I was standing on a granite shore. A huge musky, a female, was in trouble. She had to be five feet long. An eagle landed to try to help her. They were talking to each other, and I could hear them talk."

"Hear them talk, or hear them think?"

"Hear them think, I guess. Something was wrong with the musky. It was going to die. The eagle helped her. I ... I don't remember how."

"A muskrat didn't sidle by and enter into the conversation, did it? I'm not being funny."

"No, no muskrat. Just the eagle and the fish."

"Many animals—musky, bear, otter, the eagle and others—are a part of the genealogy of my people. Their spirits teach us many things ... can teach all humans many things."

"I just wish I could remember more," Russell said, shaking his head. "It's like so many dreams. You wake up and it's vivid, but the more you try to remember, the quicker it slips away."

"Perhaps some dreams do not slip away. Perhaps they slip deep inside us. Don't dwell on it. If the dream has meaning, it will come to you, even if the dream is gone."

"What time is it?" Russell asked.

"Four-thirty. I told you last night we'd need to rise early to get your boat and luggage. If you blew out the bottom end of the motor on the reef, we'll have to tow it to the marina. If it runs, we can drive both boats to the Lodge. I have to be to work by six-thirty, so we need to move. I have coffee, scrambled eggs and bacon ready. That is, if you're hungry. You put away enough walleye and corn last night to feed half the town."

Russell remembered the meal Gribber had served him: a huge, nearly square fillet of walleye circled by warm cream corn. Faith Pearson leaned over and suggested he smear a little dollop of corn on each morsel of golden brown walleye as he cut the delicate fish with his fork. The feast nearly rendered him comatose with delight.

"Washing it down with two more beers helped usher you toward sleepy time also," Gribber said.

Russell gave Gribber a soft smile at having his thoughts concluded by the comment. "Without question the finest meal I have eaten in my life," he said, rising from bed.

Gribber returned to the kitchen while Russell headed to the bathroom. Last night before bed, Gribber had brought him there, presented him with a new toothbrush, told him to hop in the shower and that real men shared deodorant. Staring at his face in the bathroom mirror for the first time since arriving in Canada had been an alarming experience. He'd winced at the sight of the bruise above his right eye but chuckled at the broad stroke of black paint under his left. As with the meal, the hot shower had been pure bliss.

Russell thought about the dream while he washed his battered face. Every morning since high school, he had shaved. He often would shave his dark whisker growth a second time before squiring his beautiful Cheryl out for a glamorous evening event in Chicago. But this morning he wouldn't, and not because he wanted to be quick for Gribber's sake. He decided not to shave because staring in the mirror, for the first time in his life, he liked the look of his unshaved face.

Gribber dug out an old pair of hiking boots, gray sweatpants and frayed lumberjack shirt that sort of fit Russell. After slamming down bacon and eggs—*my god, my appetite up here*, thought Russell—the two men walked down the pine needle path toward the dock. They passed a narrow horizontal sign nailed to the barren trunk of a jack pine. Russell stopped to look back at the sign and saw it was a strip of plywood painted white and framed with slender paper birch trunks. Stout lengths of red dogwood stem were used to create block capital letters neatly attached to the plywood with finishing nails.

The rustic sign read: MORNING WOOD.

"I like the name of your cottage," Russell said.

"Every old cottage needs a name," Gribber replied from the dock.

The sun had not quite risen but daylight was dispersing the darkness like a breeze through smoke. Gribber sat down on one side of the dock and extended his arm toward the other. Russell understood that Gribber meant for him to sit down also.

"When a guest, your parents taught you to acknowledge and thank your host?" Gribber asked.

"Yes."

"You live in suburban Chicago and work downtown, I assume?"

"Yes."

"Then you've forgotten how to see, and worse, to listen. Sit and watch the sunrise with me. Don't think about what you are seeing. Clear your mind of thought. As the sun appears, close your eyes. Listen closely to the sounds around you. Let the wilderness speak. Then listen farther, deeper. People know they can be reading a book then look up to see hills or forest far away. Most don't know they can listen the same way."

Russell sat down and gazed across the large expanse of Gunn Lake. He focused on the emerging soft yellow orb as the distant shoreline began to glow orange-red. He closed his eyes and listened. First, he heard the gentle, pulsing wind rustling the shoreline poplar leaves. Then heard the intricate, lilting birdcalls whispered from the woods. From down the shore came a soft "glump" sound as a smallmouth bass rose from its rocky lair to take a minnow from a school scurrying along the water's surface. Slipping deeper into a tranquil state, Russell heard the squeaks and squawks of seagulls as they dipped and danced around a barren rock island two hundred yards offshore. As Russell breathed in the sweetly pungent wilderness air, his consciousness merged with the natural symphony of sounds.

Time did not stand still; in the true conscious state, time dissolves, exposed as an illusion.

Gribber opened his eyes, took in a deep breath through his nose and turned to observe his peculiar new acquaintance. He gave Russell a few more minutes before rising to untie his boat. The soft rattle of the steel ring securing the rope startled Russell back to the dock. He looked at Gribber, the question, What just happened? in his eyes. Gribber stifled a chuckle. "I always recommend that people get up just before sunrise for as long as they are lucky enough to be in Kamini."

As the two men cruised into Gunn Lake in Gribber's boat, Russell's head darted uncontrollably from water, to land, to sky. He had never felt so acutely aware of his surroundings. Both sight and sound seemed amplified. No, not amplified … distilled. He relished the luxury of being a boat passenger versus the angst consuming him while driving a boat the day before. Russell was free to fully absorb the vivid splendor of the Ontario wilderness, the sunlight warming his face.

They passed an aluminum boathouse and log cottage. Gribber curved past a green buoy and aimed the boat down the middle of the wide channel branching off to their right. "Hey, I've been here before!" Russell shouted.

"Yes, you have."

Fifteen minutes later they arrived at the end of Lost Bay. Russell spotted his boat on shore, thirty yards up from the broad, terminating shoreline he trolled along the evening before. Gribber slowed, put the motor in neutral and pointed at the water. "There it is," he said.

Russell looked into the water and saw a rippling, dark green shape looming up like a sea monster from the bottom of the bay. The algae-covered reef kept rising until its bald, rounded peak nearly broke the surface. A long, slender line where the algae had been scraped from the granite ran from several feet deep to the top of the reef.

"Wow," Russell said. "Not marked by a buoy because it's so far off the channel, I suppose."

"Yeah, but there's dozens of rocks and reefs not marked on the river, even some near shore along main channels. The Ministry marks those where there's regular boat traffic but doesn't have the budget to maintain buoys off every rock you can hit. Plus it's an economic incentive program. Tourists smashing up their motors on reefs keep the Kamini mechanics busy. You need to learn the unmarked reefs and rocks."

"I shall keep that in mind."

"At least this one now has a name," Gribber said, looking at Russell. "Pirate's Reef."

Russell looked back at him quizzically.

Gribber circled the reef and cruised toward Russell's boat on shore. Just before his boat glided alongside, he cut the motor and hit a toggle switch on the tiller arm causing the motor to tilt forward out of the water.

"I wondered what that switch on my tiller did," Russell said.

"You didn't toggle up your motor as you paddled to shore, but where you landed it was deep enough you didn't need to. Not always the case. But I can see the lower end is intact. It's an older Merc. Has a shear pin instead of a torsional bush prop."

The bow of Gribber's boat gently scraped the sloping granite shore. Gribber opened a small toolbox and removed pliers and a shear pin. He stepped into Russell's boat and toggled up the motor until the propeller was out of the water. Leaning over, he removed the cotter pin holding a black cone-shaped nob on the end of the prop. He pulled off the prop, replaced the broken shear pin with a new one, then replaced the prop, black nob and cotter pin. Gripper picked up the plastic, twenty-litre gas tank on the floor but immediately dropped it. "Your boat is ready to roll except you have about two drops of gas left. Good thing you hit Pirate's Reef. You would have made it only another hundred feet out of the bay. Saved you some paddling. Hand me that red gas tank and funnel in my bow compartment."

Russell watched as Gribber poured some gas into his empty tank. "So am I the most idiotic American tourist you've encountered in Kamini? Please say I'm at least average. I'll pay you for the gas."

"Oh, the stories I could tell you," Gribber said as he finished pouring the fuel. "You're not even close to the dumbest. As for the gas, what goes around comes around." He exited Russell's boat near the bow. "I need to pee."

"Me too," Russell said, stepping from one boat into the other then onto shore. "Coffee ran right through me."

Gribber walked a few feet into the bush and unzipped his fly. Russell continued down the granite shore to give them some privacy. He glanced out across the water and noticed that the algae-covered boulders forming the river bottom transitioned to a rounded area of sand. Suddenly his entire body tingled as if infused with a form of ethereal energy, and a pulsing, profound sense of déjà vu flooded his mind.

"It was here," he said, staring at the water.

"What was here?" Gribber asked, looking up from watching his urine stream.

"The five-foot musky. Leaping out of the water. Talking to the eagle." Russell closed his eyes. "And I just can't remember. Can't remember what it was all about."

Gribber finished his business and came over to where Russell was standing. He put his hand on Russell's shoulder, not sure what to say. "That's a big one," he said finally. "Sixty inches. The musky

Canadian record is fifty-eight. Once in a blue moon, one of us will tape a fifty-six incher before releasing it, but five feet … I don't think they grow that big up here. Although I suppose there could be a queen musky of the river out there somewhere."

Russell felt compelled to walk further along the shore toward where the pink-flaked granite ended, replaced by small boulders emerging from slender patches of sand. Approaching the end of the granite portion, he looked down and stopped. "My god." At his feet was a two-foot long crevice filled with stagnant water. Russell reached into the water and plucked out his cell phone. He held it up to show Gribber. "How the hell did this get here?" he hollered.

"What … is that yours?" Gribber hollered back.

"Sure is. I was holding it in my right hand when I hit the reef, and it flew out. I just assumed it landed in the water." Russell looked out toward Pirate's Reef. He saw a dark underwater shadow off to the left near the boats. "The reef has to be twenty yards from here, or whatever the distance is in meters."

"Canadians do yards—and feet, and miles," Gribber said as he joined Russell. He gazed out at the reef. "Twenty yards seems about right."

"My arm flew up awfully fast when the motor hit. I threw the phone backward over my shoulder, but don't see how it possibly traveled this far."

"Maybe perfect trajectory. Plus, it's flat. Could have landed close and skipped to shore, a fluky thing."

"I suppose. Doesn't matter, I guess. Anyway, it's toast. I'll use it as a paperweight. I need to get into Miskwa and buy a new phone. I can't exist for two weeks without one. On the way here I decided to keep the boat, but I need to go to Miller's Landing and get my truck."

"There's a phone store in Miskwa. Open until eight on Mondays. Word is the road will be open this afternoon. You have a pickup?"

"Yeah."

"Pickups are handy to have around. Go pee, then I'll escort you into Kamini. I can't wait for you to see the Lodge. At some point, you should probably get started on your vacation."

Chapter 20

Gribber told Russell to put on a lifejacket and wear it whenever he was driving his boat until further notice. With Gribber leading the way, the two boats traveled swiftly out of Lost Bay then arced through Gunn Lake under a brilliant blue morning sky.

With no need to navigate, Russell was able to think freely and what he thought about was Annie Chase. The striking image of her standing under the lights at the landing, this tall, powerful, otherworldly being, holding a torch for god's sake, was etched so immaculately in his mind that were he a painter he could have painted it down to each single eyelash on her impossibly beautiful face.

They passed numerous cottages, old and new, some tucked into bays on the mainland, others rising on timber posts from rocky island shorelines. The channel narrowed and the large Town Bay appeared on their left, clustered with shoreline docks and cottages. The two-story, red-roofed Kamini Marina sat near the center of the bay fronted by a series of slip docks. Fanning the bay higher up from shore, small, colorfully painted houses dotted the gently rising granite bluffs.

Past the bay they curved around a wide granite point stretching far into the channel. Russell noted it contained a sprawling, one-story log structure that appeared to be a fine old fishing lodge. The channel merged with another past the point to form a single channel with cottages on both shores. As the channel narrowed, Gribber and Russell passed under a formidable, steel-girder railway bridge. Russell was transfixed by the view beyond. The river blossomed open to reveal a swirling vista of islands, granite points, bluffs and billowing evergreen trees spanning out across the large expanse of dark blue water. He felt as if he'd seen this view before.

So hypnotized by the scenery was Russell that it took a moment for him to notice Gribber was veering toward an array of docks protruding from shore. Turning to follow he spotted the towering, steeply angled, green-shingled roof of the Kamini Lodge rising above the shoreline. Gribber parked at a dock reserved for employees' boats. Russell slowed and followed. He had never landed a boat and on his first attempt did so poorly. With a helpless shrug of his shoulders, he cut the motor as his boat approached the end of the dock at a forty-five degree angle.

"We'll work on that," Gribber said, grasping the bow with both hands to keep it from banging into the dock and pulling it parallel. "A few lessons and landing a boat'll be just like falling off a horse." He knelt beside the stern. "Tie up a boat first at the stern. Keeps it tight to the dock. A daisy chain knot is fine unless it's really windy." Gribber grabbed the boat's rear rope and with a flurry of fingers resembling a sleight-of-hand magic trick, a tight succession of loops emerged from the metal ring secured to the dock. "Then toss out the bumpers, which this crap boat doesn't have, then tie the bow."

Gribber handed Russell the bow rope and taught him the daisy chain knot. Russell was not nearly as fast or fluid with the movements but the knot sufficed.

"Danny," Gribber shouted to a blond teenager standing at the small log courier station on shore.

The young man dressed in khaki trousers and green Henley shirt embroidered with the Lodge logo trotted down from his post.

"This is Mr. Dean. He'll be staying in one of the cabins. Take care of him, please."

"Yes sir. Welcome to the Kamini Lodge, Mr. Dean." The bellhop—courier, in Canada—began removing the golf bag and luggage from Russell's boat.

"I have to check in at the guide shack up top and meet my new fishing party," Gribber said. "Danny will take your clubs to the pro shop and your luggage to your cabin. You, my friend, can head up to the main Lodge and check in."

"So your job involves boating across this amazing water and fishing all day?" Russell asked.

"An arduous folly filled with mystery and witchcraft. Going to take my party up river to the Dalles, hit a few spots on the way while the walleyes are still biting. By noon, the fishing slows down. I'll rendezvous with a few other guides and we'll cook the guests a shore lunch. In the afternoon, if my boatload wants to keep after walleye, I have to think of the best shorelines where when we troll the sun is on my face. I usually try to talk my party into casting for smallmouth and snakes in the afternoon."

"Snakes?"

"Northern pike. Slimy, stinky, tasteless in both flavor and judgment. They'll hit a cigarette butt if someone tosses one in. But the tourists think it's just the grandest thing to catch one, particularly Americans from the south. And they do grow large. Fight like hell."

Russell couldn't help but chuckle. Asking Gribber a question was like opening a present. "Gribber, you are the most fascinating person I've met."

"Well, you need to get out more. About your truck. I mean your phone. I get back around five-thirty. If you want, I can drive you to Miller's Landing. You can pick up your truck then follow me into Miskwa so you can buy a new phone. All I ask is that we make a stop near the phone store and pick up some bags of concrete mix. I'm working on a project and need a lot more bags than I can carry in Ramble."

"Of course. Happy to. I can't possibly repay your kindness after all you've done for me."

"We have almost two weeks. I'll think of something. Let's head up to the Lodge."

The two men ascended a long flight of wood stairs leading

to a wide pathway of finely crushed granite which sloped gently up the rise. As they approached the crest, the entire façade of the grand Kamini Lodge came into view. Russell stopped to absorb the scene: the sprawling, mammoth granite-and-timber wilderness castle he had stared at on his computer screen for ten years. "That is simply magnificent," he said.

"Built by the railroad in 1927 to encourage passenger travel across Canada," Gribber said. "Quite a playground for wealthy Canadians and Americans in the thirties and forties. The Gilbert Watson Orchestra, Guy Lombardo and the Royal Canadians, even Tommy Dorsey and his band all played the ballroom. Queen Elizabeth stayed here during a goodwill train trip across Canada in the fifties. Was only supposed to be one night but stayed another because Prince Philip didn't want to leave. They skipped Regina instead. A lot of famous Canadian actors have stayed here, Glenn Ford, Raymond Burr, Christopher Plummer, Katherine DeMille and her husband, Anthony Quinn. Hume Cronin caught a musky off the dock. American actors too, Cary Grant, Ernest Borgnine."

The one-room guide station stood nearby, built of the same log construction as the Lodge. Chatting guests were coming in and out, animated in anticipation of the day's fishing despite the early hour.

"I have to go to work," Gribber said. "Meet you back here at five-thirty. Go explore."

Russell gazed ahead at the wide stone steps and white double doors of the Lodge. He would not be making his grand entrance dressed in the stylish, wealthy casual attire he had planned. Instead, he could pass for one of the guides. Would he encounter Annie Chase inside? Was this the right time to introduce himself? *Could* he introduce himself? The very thought of being in her presence caused his hands to sweat and light heart palpitations.

Scaling the steps to the Lodge veranda he caught a glimpse of the mammoth rotunda interior through the windows. He still wasn't prepared for the sight that unfolded before him when he crossed the threshold of the entrance. The Lodge rotunda measured sixty feet wide by one hundred-twenty long. The same towering granite support columns and dark red, stained cedar logs comprising the building's exterior were main features of the cavernous interior. Across from the large entrance doors stood a twenty-foot-wide granite block wall rising thirty feet into the air. An enormous fireplace with curving stone hearth was centered in the wall. On a protruding stone shelf above the fireplace rested a large, intricately detailed model of an eighteenth century British man o' war. Curving above the ship, antique muskets, swords and shields were mounted to the stone.

High overhead, massive peeled and varnished cedar logs formed the arching trusses anchored to the top of each stone column, supporting the roof. Russell accurately estimated that the run of matching cedar logs set end-to-end to form the spine at the peak were fifty feet above the floor. Black wrought iron chandeliers suspended on black chains, each made from three hoops diminishing in size as one rose above the other, held yellow, candle-like bulbs and were spaced evenly throughout.

The immense rotunda floor was made of narrow strips of varnished red oak. Long runs of oriental carpet ran along the room's perimeter, down the center and crossed front to back at three evenly spaced junctures, framing seating areas arranged with burnt red and dark green antique leather chesterfields, matching chairs and oak side tables. The broad checkerboard pattern of elegantly furnished spaces included one containing an antique writing desk and two with oak tables and chair settings for card and board games.

Large windows along the rear wall on each side of the fireplace offered views of curving flowerbeds flowing down toward an immaculate white sand swimming beach with lifeguard tower. Docks containing kayaks, canoes, paddle and sailboards for guest use extended from each end of the beach. Beyond the shoreline, the Winnipeg River flowed northward through the serene wilderness landscape of granite and forest.

Centered on the wall at one end was the hotel front desk. As Russell approached, he could see that the long wing angling off to the left was the dining room, already murmuring with early breakfast diners. He glimpsed through the dining room windows one of the golf course's curving greens. The wing to the right appeared to be guest rooms.

Checking in was perfunctory. Russell was in cabin eight, his luggage was already there, and his golf clubs were tagged and sitting in the pro shop. While Grace, the cheerful front desk clerk, ran his credit card, Russell turned to look down the broad length of the remarkable room. At the other end the large wing angling away to the left was the ballroom, built to match the style of the rotunda in only slightly smaller scale. The long center wing contained more guest rooms. The wing angling to the right was no doubt the lounge; Russell could see a portion of a lengthy oak bar. A large snooker table, bristle dartboard and shuffleboard table were also visible, as was a service door at the far end.

The door opened and through it emerged Annie Chase. She was carrying a clipboard and dressed in a 1940s vintage, off-white, light wool pantsuit, black silk blouse and black, wedge-heel shoes. The double-breasted jacket was either carefully tailored to hug her body from shoulders to waist before widening at the hips or she was inordinately lucky in its purchase. Her auburn hair swept down well past her shoulders and swayed gently as she walked. Just before entering the rotunda, she stopped to smile and confer with a uniformed young woman vacuuming the lounge floor.

Russell's heart did not skip a beat; it added several. As he stared at Annie from across the rotunda his every thought dropped from his mind like marbles off the edge of a table.

"Right this way, sir," the young female courier said.

Russell turned to face her, unable to grasp the context of her statement. Then the fact he was in Canada and had just checked into his cabin at the Kamini Lodge came back to him. He followed the courier down the near corridor of rooms and through the exit door at the end. A wood stairway led to a gravel path winding toward shore.

The eight private cabins were located down the shoreline from the beach, already lively with courageous early morning swimmers and couples heading out from the dock in kayaks and canoes. Russell's cabin was at the far end. Similar to the others, it featured a stone foundation, log walls and cedar shingle roof. The courier opened the rear door and showed Russell the two bedrooms and bathroom before leading him into the cozy front living room. It featured rustic furnishings, the front entrance and a large picture window overlooking the river.

Russell tipped her twenty dollars and sat down on the sofa affording a framed view of the river and distant shores. He was exhilarated, though something felt strange. On vacations with Cheryl early in their marriage he visited exotic places around the globe, always keenly aware of his status as a tourist. For reasons unknown, he didn't feel like a tourist here, or that he was on vacation.

His mind jumbled by the crazy juxtaposition of last night's battle with the bush, the bizarre events at the landing, his strange dream and nearly as strange sunrise meditation, Russell was not quite able to recognize that he felt at home. He attempted to sort his thoughts, but they were unwillingly thrust aside by the image of Annie Chase dressed so impeccably and walking toward him through the lounge.

He bowed his head and cradled his face in his sweating palms. It was three minutes before his breathing and heart rate settled to the point he felt it safe to stand.

Chapter 21

Lydia White had set her mind on becoming a marine biologist specializing in orca whales at age eight, when at a friend's sleepover she viewed the movie *Free Willie*. From that moment forward, saving whales became her all-consuming passion.

Not that oceans could be found anywhere near her home in Transcona, Manitoba, a fading blue-collar railroad town mildly resuscitated as the city of Winnipeg, to its west, expanded gradually to claim it as a suburb. Nor were her prospects of acceptance to any of Canada's fine universities offering degrees in oceanography encouraging as she graduated high school, an earnest but average student with little proclivity toward the natural sciences. Her options for collegiate advancement dwindled to the few her hard-working parents could afford, leading her to University College of the North in The Pas, Manitoba, a small town 375 miles north of Winnipeg.

The college's student population included many indigenous Cree from across the vast region. Lydia made close friends from the surrounding Cross Lake, Norway House and Opaskwayak First Nation reservations. Their calm and assured demeanor helped her focus her mind and blossom as a student.

The Cree view of nature and ecology as something not separate from the individual but rather an origin, extension and reflection of a person's true being—similar to the view of the Ojibwe and other native tribes—appealed to Lydia. We are forever connected to the land, one Cree friend explained to her. Even thinking of oneself as a "nature lover" or espousing an "appreciation" of wilderness displayed the ignorant, silly sentimentality of narrow, limited Anglo-European thought.

The fine and devoted faculty at the college nurtured Lydia's desire for ecological knowledge, and in two years she received her diploma in Natural Resources Management Technology. She would play no part in ensuring the safety of Canada's inland whale population, but was resolute in her burning desire to save the planet from the severely narrow-minded. Meaning, she realized upon her return to Transcona, damn near everyone.

Her studies set her up for immediate employment with companies in the billion-dollar Canadian forestry industry supplying wood and paper products to the world. That the industry provided thousands of jobs, played an important role in Canadian exports and incorporated conservation practices to minimize environmental impact from harvesting a renewable resource offered her no solace. The fact the whole thing started with cutting down a tree was far too egregious an act for Lydia to accept. "It's like I'd be cutting my own arm off!" she explained to her perplexed parents.

Lydia applied for the position of Conservation Officer with both the Manitoba and Ontario Ministry of Natural Resources and Forestry, and she soon received a phone call from the Ontario Ministry in Peterborough. The Northwest Region office in Thunder Bay was hiring. How soon could she be there for an interview?

The answer to that question is seven years ago.

After six months of classroom and in-the-field training, Lydia became the newest of eighty-seven Conservation Officers serving Northwest Ontario. From the beginning she loved every aspect of her job, from collecting and analyzing water samples to monitoring fish populations to surveying forest tracts to make sure the harvesting and reforestation of trees was done in accordance with provincial and federal mandates. What she loved most, however, was investigating violations of fish and game laws, as this entailed the bottom-line payback of busting poachers. Conservation

Offices received full law-enforcement training, could investigate and analyze crime scenes, lift fingerprints, serve warrants and arrest people. They carried side arms.

Returning to her desk on this Monday morning at the Ministry's regional office in Thunder Bay after five days in the field, the first email Lydia clicked in the Report a Poacher public mailbox was titled URGENT and sent at 4:45 a.m. from a John Dogrib in Kamini. Her pulse quickened while she read his email and looked at the attached photos. Watching the brief video of bins of walleye in the back of a pickup and the hold of a boat further whetted her appetite.

Lydia printed out the email and photos and marched into the office of her superior, Jim Eastwood. "Here's one for me, sir. Just came in. The good citizens of Kamini caught the commercial fisherman netting walleyes. They ran him out of town last night. Looks like the scumbag is headed home to Flin Flon. The sooner I get to Kamini and wrap the investigation, the sooner we can have him picked up. It appears there's a commercial vessel and some property involved."

Eastwood scanned the email and began studying the photos. As he did so, he wistfully reviewed in his mind the career of the twenty-seven-year-old, now somewhat veteran Conservation Officer who stood, glowing with excitement, before him. Since her first day of training, Lydia had shown to be a driven and devoted student. Her record in the field was exemplary. She consistently took assignments that few in the department wanted, such as the five-day stint in Peawanuck from which she had just returned. The Ministry received word of a leaking underground gasoline storage tank at the lone filling station in the town, a tiny Cree community over a thousand kilometers north and accessible only by floatplane. Few officers want to spend two days in transit and three days in Peawanuck. Lydia volunteered.

Not that everything about Lydia was perfect. Eastwood recognized having her out solo in the field was preferable to having her in the office, working on projects and reports at her desk. To state that Lydia was resolute in her views was to put it mildly. She drove more than a few of her fellow officers nuts.

Every officer knew not to smoke in Lydia's presence, particularly in the field. Fieldwork often involved camping in tents and sitting around a campfire with fellow officers after a long day spent monitoring invasive plant species. Sitting around a campfire might entail drinking a beer and enjoying a cigarette by those so inclined. Unless their team included Lydia, that is, where officers soon learned that sneaking a smoke like a schoolchild was preferable to facing her lectures and frosty ire.

Campfires in general were a problem to Lydia. Her proposal to the Ministry that campfires in Ontario be banned due to the risk of starting forest fires and their contribution to climate change from the unnecessary burning of wood was ignored without comment.

As was her suggestion to ban recreational and commercial fishing in the province.

Then there was the refrigerator contamination episode. Lydia, a vegan, complained that other officers' food, particularly dairy products and meat, had the potential to contaminate her lunches and snacks as they were stored together in the office's sole refrigerator. Her request for a second small refrigerator for her private use was dismissed due to lack of funds. Instead, store your fruits, grains and nuts in airtight plastic containers, Eastwood suggested.

This proved an unacceptable solution to Lydia, who boycotted all plastic products. She brought her lunch to the office each day in unvarnished wood bowls swathed in frayed cotton towels bound with string. Well, let's make sure the other officers use plastic containers when storing their food with yours, Eastwood countered. This solution only resulted in a lecture from Lydia concerning the certain contamination of her food from BPAs and other toxic chemicals emitted by plastics that cause cancer, birth defects, disrupt endocrines and impair immunities. Eastwood finally purchased a small, used refrigerator on his dime to end the food storage wars.

Then there was the difficulty with her uniform, specifically her shirts, but that was hardly Lydia's fault. Conservation Officers wore uniforms similar to those of police officers except olive green in color. After measurements were taken, providing pants for Lydia posed no problem. Lydia was shapely but fit at five feet-three inches tall. Eastwood was aware she supplemented her footwear with lifts to add an additional inch to her height, but that was not against regulation.

Finding shirts that fit her comfortably was another matter. The first shirts ordered as part of her uniform were women's size medium, based on Lydia's height and weight of one hundred forty pounds. While properly tapered at the waist, each shirt stretched as taut as a drumhead across her bosom. The size large shirts somewhat reduced the strain on the buttons but left swales of material billowing about her waist after the shirt was tucked into her trousers. Lydia's plea for an expense per diem to have her three uniform shirts professionally tailored was immediately granted.

Eastwood studied the final photograph from Gribber and looked up to address his officer. Lydia's long, straight black hair was pulled tight in a ponytail. Her pale blue eyes shimmered with excitement, and he could see she was stifling a smile. She was an attractive young woman, and he knew her overall physical appearance was at times a hindrance to her in the field. Although lord help a person with a fish or ten beyond the limit, or man, woman or group hunting any creature out of season who were tracked and confronted by Officer White. Her caseload and annual arrest total were the highest in the department. Despite the baggage, he could use more officers like her.

"Looks like a perfect fit," Eastwood said. "You don't want any time off, though, eh? I don't recall the last time you asked for a vacation." He tossed this out as part of their established skit. Lydia never took time off.

"What can I say, sir? My work isn't work. I'm just so impressed the members of the Kamini community were so diligent. Kamini's only a six-hour drive. Just a couple of things on my desk. I could leave after lunch."

"Then do it. The Ministry of Health has accommodations in town you can use, a trailer just up the road from the post office. A room in front serves as the nursing station. Kamini used to have a full-time nurse until, well, you know. Now a nurse drives in from Miskwa three days a week but doesn't stay overnight. Ever been there?"

"No, but I've done work out of Miskwa, of course. I believe we have a Ministry boat docked at the Miskwa OPP."

"We do. And if memory serves me, we haven't done any monitoring of anglers on the Winnipeg River the last couple years. When you're done investigating the poaching, maybe you should stay, grab the boat and patrol the fishing for a week or so. I'd send another officer to assist you."

"Perfect." Lydia knew that cruising the river stopping anglers to check that all had fishing licenses and to inspect their boats' live wells was a mandated two-person job.

"Pack for two weeks. I'll call down to the garage and reserve a vehicle for you. Key to the boat will be with the OPP. I'll make some calls and find out who has a key to that trailer." Eastwood handed the printouts back to Lydia. "I see Mr. Dogrib gives his phone number in the email. Meet with him and take it from there."

"Will do, sir." It was irrelevant to their conversation that based on his last name, she knew John Dogrib was indigenous. "I can't wait to meet him."

After lunch, Lydia White loaded two large duffel bags filled with clothes and equipment into the back of a green- and yellow-striped Chevrolet Tahoe emblazoned with the shield logo of the Ontario Ministry of Natural Resources and Forestry. She was elated as she headed out on the drive from Thunder Bay to Kamini. After leaving Eastwood's office she had phoned Mr. Dogrib. He was extremely gracious. They were set to meet later tonight.

She had a good feeling about this one.

Chapter 22

Russell spent much of the morning at his laptop answering emails. He forced his vexing infatuation with Annie Chase to the back of his mind, where it flickered like a loose light bulb.

Seated in a comfortable wicker chair on the front deck of the cottage and inhaling the scenery before him, the electronic messages and images he viewed on his computer screen appeared otherworldly and trivial. Four were from his partner, Dan Samuels, mostly inspired by Samuels's inability to reach him on his cell phone last night or first thing this morning. Russell responded to the few matters of business and explained his phone had been stolen en route. Staring at the lie, he deleted it and said he'd somehow managed to lose his phone. In his third attempt, he confessed he'd stupidly dropped his phone into the water during the boat trip to Kamini. He would be replacing it later in the day and would email his new phone number if it changed. There was an email from Caroline Klein with a few questions concerning the Ikea account that Russell answered in seconds and some junk mail.

The final email was from Cheryl. The two had not communicated since the last time they saw each other nearly a month ago. Russell had arrived home from New York at around nine in the evening. As he fixed himself a drink in the living room, Cheryl told him, without emotion, that she was filing for divorce. She said that it wasn't fair to ask him to move out since both owned the house and she was the one initiating the separation. She was spending the night at her friend Jennifer's, who had invited her to stay until the proceedings were settled and the house sold. Thinking back, Russell had only vague memories of his response.

He knew he hadn't become angry. He remembered feeling like a hidden observer, an eavesdropper in an adjacent room, as Cheryl calmly told him she no longer wanted to be his wife. A foggy numbness had descended over him. Well, he had been blindsided, after all.

Russell looked at the subject title of her email—Foundation's Future—and hesitated. Divorce lawyers discouraged email communication between spouses during the legal proceedings. Couples divorcing and mad at each other often said things in emails that came back to bite them in the settlement. He wasn't angry with Cheryl and hoped she wasn't angry with him. He clicked on it.

> *Dear Russell,*
>
> *Moving forward I'm uncertain about continuing as head of the Samuels Dean Charitable Foundation. I haven't spoken to Dan but assume both you and he wish to sustain it. Would you feel uncomfortable were I to continue as Executive Director? The Foundation does such tremendous good work and helps so many families, I don't want our divorce to impact or diminish its future effectiveness. I'm very willing to remain. However, if you feel this is not in the Foundation's best interest, I have several excellent candidates in mind to serve as my replacement.*
>
> *Please let me know your thoughts.*
>
> *Cheryl*

Russell replied that of course he and Dan wanted her to remain. He was on vacation in Canada until June 15 and hoped they could meet to discuss the Foundation upon his return. If she preferred not to meet in person, he was happy to communicate about Foundation matters via email. After clicking Send, he read Cheryl's email again. It was so like her, he realized. Thoughtful, kind, unselfish.

Russell decided to spend the rest of the morning exploring the Lodge and its grounds. If he ran into Ms. Chase he would introduce himself, offer an eloquent apology for his rudeness on the phone and suggest he perhaps could make up for it by buying her a drink in the lounge when she got off work.

In the bedroom he had selected as his—it featured a queen bed versus two singles in the other—Russell changed out of the clothes Gribber had loaned him. He opted for the sole pair of jeans he'd packed over the two pairs of neatly pressed khaki pants similar to the pair destroyed during his odyssey in the bush. He brushed past the Polo shirts and put on a dark green L.L. Bean chamois shirt Cheryl had given him for Christmas a few years ago. Having ruined his canvas deck shoes, his footwear options were limited to his golf shoes and a pair of tonal-brown Berluti oxfords. The expensive shoes looked splendid with the tailored sport coat, pinstripe shirt and tweed trousers he'd packed as evening attire, but ridiculous with jeans. He laced up the weathered hiking boots from Gribber, despite the fact they were at least one size too small. Russell was about to exit the cabin's rear door when he heard a knock at the front. Housekeeping already?

He opened the door and stood face-to-face with Annie Chase. Dressed in the elegant pantsuit, her lush auburn hair framing her impeccable face, she looked like a Hollywood starlet from the black-and-white film noir era. "Mr. Dean, hello, I'm Annie, the assistant manager here at the Lodge. Just wanted to pop by to see how you were settling in."

So abrupt and unexpected was her appearance that for a second Russell's heart, palms, brainwaves and other physiological orders were caught off guard and able to maintain normal function. The clock was immediately set ticking, however. "Ms. Chase!" Russell said too loudly. "Won't you come in!" No, stupid thing to say! She might find that uncomfortable—rapist! Go for a walk! Outside it's warm and sunny. "Or we go outside. Rummy!" he blurted. The excited neurons rocketing across his brain's ill-prepared synapses had caused the words "warm" and "sunny" to meld into one. The word sounded wrong to him, but he couldn't put his finger on it.

A bemused smile crossed Annie's face as she took a few steps back to allow Russell to step onto the deck. As he did so, he stiffly swung both hands behind him then brought them forward into a clap, the first time ever in his life he had performed the movement. "Looks like a gorgeous day. Sunny, I think I was trying to say."

"The coming week is supposed to be lovely, yes," Annie said, "although forecasts are questionable up here. The weather can change on a dime. Just wanted to make sure you're all right. I understand your boat journey from Miskwa to Kamini was a bit of an adventure. And being thrust into the scene at Pistol Lake last night was not something we would choose for our guests."

"Renting a boat instead of taking the launch as you advised, then getting lost on the river … that was my fault." Russell focused on each word as he spoke it. Breathe, damn it, breathe. "The confrontation with your poacher, that part was … extraordinary. I'm actually glad I was present. That's a vacation memory that will last a lifetime." Russell began to relax somewhat, with the exception of not knowing what to do with his hands.

"Well, thank you for being such a trooper. I also wanted to let you know we're sending both launches to Miller's Landing at one this afternoon for guests who want to retrieve their vehicles. The road is being repaired as we speak and should be open by three."

"Gribber mentioned that to me this morning. He's kindly offered to drive me to Miller's Landing to pick up my truck later this afternoon. I need to buy a few things in Miskwa, then haul some bags of concrete mix he needs for something."

"That you're primed for more adventures with Mr. Dogrib is all the assurance I need that you've fully recovered from your somewhat harrowing start. Very nice to meet you, Mr. Dean. We're delighted to have you as our guest." She turned to leave.

"Please, call me Russell. And I did want to say … on the phone the other day … I'm sorry we got off on the wrong foot."

Annie turned back to face him, tilted her head, raised one eyebrow, smiled demurely and said nothing. It took a moment for Russell to realize she was waiting. Gazing directly into her eyes he noted they were dark amber. What to say next finally hit him. "No, that isn't right. *I* got off on the wrong foot. And I'm deeply sorry."

Annie smiled, a natural, effortless smile. "Thank you, Russell. Your kind apology accepted. We'll think nothing more of it."

"Are you going back to the main Lodge?" Russell asked on impulse. "I was just heading up. Wanted to poke around a bit before lunch. It's such an amazing structure."

"I am, and would be delighted to give you a private tour. Shall we?"

They stepped from the deck and walked side-by-side along a gravel pathway leading to the beach then up to the Lodge. As Annie assumed the role of tour guide, Russell nodded appropriately and asked questions he felt pertinent. The white sand beach was natural; deposits of sand appeared along shorelines throughout the river system. Over sixty rail cars of dirt from a farm in Manitoba were hauled in to create the golf course and landscaping throughout the peninsula on which the Lodge stood. An army of Swedish log cutters, Scottish stonemasons and English gardeners lived in tents onsite spring through fall for two years during construction.

The tour continued inside the Lodge, Annie noting the origin and history behind the myriad antiques—paintings, full suits of armor, muskets, swords, several exquisite grandfather clocks—accenting the halls and corridors throughout the historic building. She pointed out to Russell the different varieties of enormous fish mounted to varnished wood plaques that hung on the walls of the rotunda and lounge: walleye, northern pike, bass and musky. Russell asked several pointed questions about their size and habitat while marveling at the alluring, colorful specimens, some of the fish curving upward as if ready to strike. Annie knew the answers and mentioned that she liked to fish.

Annie led Russell to the entrance to the grand dining room, and before excusing herself introduced him to a well-dressed couple of his approximate age who were awaiting seating. Noting that he was alone, the Barneys immediately invited him to join them for lunch, and Russell realized how this smoothly had been her intention. While engaged in lively conversation with the Toronto couple about their city, Chicago, business, golf, travel and the wonders of the Northwest Ontario wilderness, Russell enjoyed a savory lunch of lemon garlic chicken and wild rice soup.

All told, he was ecstatic. He had met and conversed with Annie Chase. The ice had been broken. All he needed was a chance to spend time with her alone. There was only one nagging annoyance to what had otherwise turned out to be a marvelous day.

He wanted to go fishing.

Chapter 23

After lunch the thought dawned on Russell to check in at the pro shop and set a time for a round of golf, but he walked to the docks instead. Standing on any dock or shoreline, the clear, flowing water infused the piney wilderness scent with an additional fresh note, like the smell after rain. He stepped into his boat and put on his lifejacket. Newly aware of the precious contents of his boat's gas tank, he untied—the daisy chain knots magically disappeared simply by pulling the loose end of each rope—and headed out under the railway bridge, around the point with the old fishing lodge and into Town Bay.

Russell approached the marina and was relieved to see a long, unoccupied stretch of dock near the gas pump. As he putted in nearly parallel with the dock, the thought hit him to slip the boat into reverse to halt its momentum. Then a farm instinct kicked in and he turned the engine so that the reverse thrust pulled the stern of the boat tight to the dock for a perfect landing.

The teenage gas boy tied up the boat while Russell set his gas tank on the dock. "Fill it?" the boy asked.

"Yes, please. Do you sell fishing licenses? Rods and reels?"

"We sell licenses, but if you want gear, head over to Dave's," the boy said, giving an up nod in the direction of a small orange-and-white-striped shack further along the shoreline near the far entrance to the bay. "Dave sells everything you need."

Russell's third-ever landing at the dock in front of Dave's Live Bait was comparable to his second. The door to the bait shop was propped open with a rock. Russell was greeted effusively by Dave

Burtnyk when he entered. "There's our pirate! Hoping I'd bump into you again. How's she goin', man?"

This was the second pirate reference to sail over Russell's head, so he ignored it. "Things are great, Dave. I'm falling in love with this place. I want to try fishing. I'm starting from scratch, so I need whatever rod and reel setup you think is best."

"Outstanding! Give a man a fish and you feed him for a day. Teach a man to fish, he starts drinking, calling into work sick, ignoring the wife and drops thirty grand on a fishing boat he can't afford after he gets fired and divorced. Always happy to help. Casting or spinning?"

"Don't know the difference. Walleye and musky. Speak to me as if speaking to a child."

"Well, you need a spinning rod and reel for walleye and small-mouth, a casting rod and reel for musky and big snakes. Can get pretty pricey. Why don't I set you up with everything you need for spinning, then lend you a musky rod?"

"Seriously?"

"Sure. I'm the rep for a half-dozen rod and reel manufacturers. I have sample gear in back I can cobble together for muskies. Let's get you going." Burtnyk selected a six-foot graphite rod from a rack, matched it with a sleek new spinning reel, then selected fishing line and additional accessories from the massive inventory at his disposal, neatly arranged on pegboard walls. "You know how to put line on a reel?"

"No idea."

"OK, this is ten-pound test braid. Open the package and I'll teach you."

Under Burtnyk's tutelage Russell loaded one hundred-sixty yards of fishing line onto the spool of his new spinning reel and learned the knot to secure a small clasp swivel to the end of the line. They were interrupted several times by customers buying minnows, worms and leeches, all cheerfully served and sent on their way by Burtnyk.

"Where do you get the minnows?" Russell asked after

watching Burtnyk fill a customer's bucket, scooping the minnows with a dip net from the aerated fiberglass trough running along one wall.

"From my traps. I lease eighteen land blocks from the Ministry, around five hundred square miles. Kamini is about in the center of it. I have minnow traps set in six small lakes and ponds at a time, then early morning I head into the bush and harvest a different set. You were lucky to catch me. I'm only at the shop one day a week. The rest of the days I'm out harvesting minnows and rotating my traps. Let me give you the grand tour."

An open door at the end of the trough led to the other half of the building housing three larger aerated troughs filled with minnows. Various wood-framed screening devices hung from the wall. A door at the rear opened to the gravel parking lot behind the shop.

"This is where the minnows go after I bring them in from the bush. We sort them by size with screens then move them over to retail as needed. I also sell to the fishing camps and other bait shops around Miskwa, so we fill bulk orders right here."

Burtnyk's cell phone gave a chirp. He glanced at it and grimaced. "Rat bastard!" he shouted, furiously typing a reply to the text he'd received.

"What's the matter?"

"My girlfriend Sheri just texted. She's out collecting leeches from a few ponds where she sets traps for me. One pond is near a lake where I set minnow traps yesterday afternoon. One of my competitors stumbled onto it last year, snooping around my territory because he's a lazy asshole. Twice when I went there, he'd beaten me to my traps and I only harvested a tenth of the minnows I should have. I know who it is. Operates out of Miskwa, uses a floatplane. Sheri just watched his plane flying low over the trees toward the lake, which means he's going in for a landing. Rat bastard!"

Dave made a phone call and after a few seconds left a message. "Faith, it's Dave. I have to leave the shop for a few hours.

Larry's at it again. Give me a holler back or just come over if you can fill in."

He turned to Russell. "Dang it. Faith Pearson—you met her, the schoolteacher—works here two days a week in summer. School got out Friday and she probably ran into Miskwa to shop and have her hair done. Grab your rod and gear, I'm going to have to kick you out and close up. The lake being poached is only thirty minutes away. If I hustle, I can get there and catch him in the act. Swing by tomorrow to pay for your gear, I'll have that musky rod ready for you."

Two fishing boats pulled up to the dock and two of the six fishermen in them walked up the ramp carrying four plastic minnow buckets. Dave eyed them through the open door. Russell could tell he was debating turning them away or staying ten more minutes to make what obviously was a nice sale.

"Dave, why don't I stay and run the shop while you're gone?" Russell said.

"Seriously? You're on vacation."

"Well, I've watched you fill minnow buckets, bet I can operate a cash register, and can't think of anything scheduled for this afternoon I would enjoy more. You're lending me a musky rod ... what goes around comes around."

Burtnyk thought for only a second. "OK, my man, you're on. Listen up." At the long, elevated minnow trough, Burtnyk pointed out how two interior walls divided it into three sections: small, medium and large minnows. Leeches and worms were in Styrofoam containers in the upright cooler. Prices for live bait were on a sheet by the cash register. Artificial lures and the accessories all had prices on the packages. If they pay with American money, there's the calculator, multiply the amount they give you by 1.25 and give them change in Canadian. He quickly explained how to use the credit card swipe device and cash register. "That's plenty enough to make you dangerous," Burtnyk said. "If you screw something up, who cares. You're a good man, Pirate. Be back as soon as I can." He rushed into the other room and out the back door to his pickup.

Russell slipped his expensive watch into his pocket, rolled up his sleeves and sold seven-dozen minnows, three-dozen leeches, four artificial lures and a handful of lead jigs to the Manitoban fishermen for a total of one hundred-seven dollars and forty cents. He ran the credit card through without a hitch. No sooner did they exit the shack than another boat landed. A friendly Minnesota couple with two young kids in tow entered and requested two-dozen minnows and a dozen worms.

"So where are the walleyes biting?" the husband asked Russell as he scooped minnows into the bucket.

"Afraid I'm no use to you there. New in town. Just helping out a friend who had to run an errand."

"Fair enough," the man said. He paid with an American twenty. Russell adjusted it to twenty-five dollars in his head before giving the man his change in Canadian currency.

There was a lull in customers, so Russell stepped outside and sat down in a plastic chair on a small deck beside the front door. His perch offered a stunning view of colorful Town Bay, alive with boats of all sizes crisscrossing in and out. Tourists and cottagers were headed to and from the marina, the fishing camp on the opposite point and the large municipal dock serving the Hudson's Bay store and other small businesses up the hill. Relaxing in his chair, he gazed across the idyllic scene as the temperature climbed into the seventies.

Russell looked up at the sky and became entranced studying the random collection of small cumulus clouds slowly floating by, so white and crisply outlined that they jumped from the rich blue background as if in 3-D. Had he ever studied, or even noticed, clouds in the sky over Chicago?

He caught the bald eagle out of the corner of his eye as it soared from the mainland behind him out across the entrance to the large bay. Passing on his right, Russell could see clearly the exquisite detail in the eagle's brilliant white head, unblinking golden eye and orange-yellow beak. As it reached the far point it turned and traced the shoreline of the bay from a height of thirty feet, curving over the cottage docks then the marina and municipal dock. Only rarely did it flap its enormous, brown-black wings as it glided on air currents from the gentle wind and continued its shoreline loop back toward the bait shop.

Several boats in the bay stopped, people pointing and looking upward, their eyes following the large, graceful bird. When the eagle approached the bait shop it glided downward and flew directly toward Russell so low he could see individual white feathers on its legs, wrinkles in its orange-yellow feet and each of its black, curved talons. Adjusting his gaze upward to the head, he and the eagle locked eyes. The bird passed so closely overhead he heard the soft whoosh of air as the eagle gave a flap of its wings, rose over the trees behind the bait shop and glided out of sight.

Russell was spellbound and didn't know if he had blinked, breathed or held a thought the entire time he witnessed the flight of the majestic creature. A calm washed over him instilling a sense of contentment unlike any he'd felt before. He stared straight ahead, motionless lest even his slightest movement would cause the warm sense of calm to disperse.

Russell closed his eyes. Everything was so clear, so simple ... so real here. Time seemed to travel at a different pace, if it had any relevance at all. In fact, just now, it had stopped. Suspending time sure gave one a chance to think clearly. What was he doing right now? He'd volunteered to work at a bait shop in Kamini, Ontario. Could anything be finer? Only a few days ago he was in his office, immersed in a multimillion-dollar advertising campaign, going berserk as usual, his mind nearly overrun by details and deadlines ... for what? To what end? It all seemed so crucially important to him at the time. Was it?

The engine on the big boat packed so much horsepower that as its menacing roar broke Russell's meditation and he opened his eyes, even he, a most novice boatman, thought it was traveling too fast. It ripped around the docks of the old fishing lodge on the far point and entered the bay with blinding speed. Numerous boats were cruising slowly along the bay's wide entrance, including a small sailboat and several kayaks, but rather than slow down, the sleek, sharply pointed vessel shot dangerously through them, veering aggressively left and right like a skier through a slalom course. One female kayaker threw up her hands and appeared to yell something as the boat raced by her tiny craft but the deep, thrumming roar of its engine erased her words.

Twenty yards from the bait shop's dock the driver throttled harshly back, causing an enormous wake to roil the floating dock so violently that the wood frame groaned while the iron hinges on the beams securing the dock to granite shrieked under the strain. Only after the series of rolling waves were dashed on shore and the dock ceased bobbing did the boat glide smoothly forward and land.

The fiberglass boat was long and low, with a metallic red finish accented by sleek black striping. The racecar-like cockpit housing the small steering wheel and throttle controls was wrapped in front by a low, curving windshield. At the stern rumbled a three hundred horsepower Mercury ProX3 outboard motor. A large electric trolling motor lay sideways mounted to the bow. The boat's registration number was in black on the side of the bow beneath it, a three-inch-tall decal reading IL 1206 ZW. An Illinois boat, Russell realized.

One man sat in the cockpit while two others rose from the contoured seats at the stern. One gave a gleeful hoot. All three wore black wraparound sunglasses and windbreakers. As the driver expertly sidled the boat into the center slip, the two men got out to tie up. The driver slipped on a Chicago Cubs baseball cap, grabbed three minnow buckets and the three scaled the ramp.

Russell returned inside the shop and stood behind the glass counter with its display of fishing reels. The three men dispersed as they entered, one approaching a pegboard wall holding boxes of artificial lures and another studying the contents of the live bait cooler through its glass door. The third man, the driver, placed the minnow buckets on the counter then removed his sunglasses and slid them onto the bill of his cap.

Russell's firm handled the advertising for a major American clothier. He took note of the man's finely detailed North Face windbreaker, expensive G-Star designer jeans and L.L. Bean duck boots. He pegged his age at early thirties.

Studying the reels in the display case, the man spoke without looking at Russell. "Three dozen medium and one dozen large, chief. Split the medium minnows between two buckets and put the large in the third. How much are they a dozen?"

"Six dollars for medium, seven for large," Russell said as he walked around the counter, placed the buckets on the end of the trough and began filling them with water.

"You gotta be kidding me. Six and seven bucks a dozen? That's armed robbery."

"And Richie, look at this," the man eyeing the lures said. "Ten bucks for a medium Shad Rap. What a rip off!"

"I don't set the prices," Russell said.

"No, of course not," Richie, the man in the Cubs cap, said. "Blame your boss."

"Realize, also, the prices are in Canadian currency," Russell said as he began scooping the minnows.

Richie spun and gave a goofy look to his buddies, who laughed, then he turned back to Russell. "Oh good, we drove all the way from Chicago to get an economics lesson from the bait shop guy. For what you charge, how about you tell us where the walleyes are biting, chief, give us some spots on a map?"

"Sorry, I'm new in town myself. Haven't been out fishing yet. Swing by later and talk to Dave, the owner. He'll be happy to give you some fishing spots."

Richie gave an exaggerated shake of his head. "Oh, I get it. I don't know anything, I just work here. Figures."

Russell refused to take the bait, as it were. Something was delightfully strange. The jibes bounced off. He didn't care what the men said or thought of him. He was as calm and relaxed as if he were asleep. He finished with the minnow buckets and asked if they needed anything else.

One of the men removed two-dozen leeches from the cooler and placed them on the counter. "That'll do it."

Russell stacked the Styrofoam containers in a paper bag. "Your total comes to forty-five dollars."

Richie gave a grunt and another theatrical headshake and handed over an American fifty.

Russell tapped on the calculator, figured the exchange amount and ran the sale through the cash register. "Your change is seventeen-fifty," he said, placing the cash in Richie's outstretched hand.

"Can't you give me change in American? I hate going home with this funny money. You must have American in the till."

"Sorry. I gave you the fair exchange rate for your fifty."

"Aw, so nice of you. Tell you what, chief. The boss is gone. How about you grow a pair and break a rule for once in your life?"

"How about you take your bait and scram, shit nuts?" Faith Pearson said as she entered from the adjacent room. "And when you fire up that big red shiny penis you drive to make up for the tiny one in your pants, how about you drive it slow as you leave the bay."

At first Russell hadn't recognized her. Faith's curly brown hair was now platinum blonde and cut short, the tips dyed pink and light blue. Faded jeans and black cami wrapped her slender body. She walked directly to Richie and on tippy toes put her face in his. "I saw your boat come in as I was walking down the hill. Are you crazy? You don't do seventy kilometers an hour through boat traffic. If the Ministry or OPP had an officer in the bay, you'd get a three hundred-dollar fine and be lucky they didn't take your stupid boat."

Richie and the two other men were speechless. Add Russell to the list. As the reference to his penis sunk in, along with recognition he was faltering in any attempt to respond to the exotic, upright, ferocious female pit bull before him, Richie's face flushed a rich crimson. He handed the bag to one of his buddies, grabbed the minnow buckets and stomped toward the door. He stopped to turn but again realized he could conjure no worthy retort.

Russell came from behind the counter to stand next to Faith in the center of the room. Through the open door they watched the boat leave the bay. It cruised slowly up the shoreline, exploding to full speed only as the bay merged into the main channel.

"Shit nuts," Russell said. "I like that one."

"Well you sure are a gentle soul. I came in the back door and was listening from the next room as that asshole was giving you a hard time about the prices. I'm sorry, I can't take crap like that from people. Comes from being a teacher, I guess. I love my students and most of them are great, but one thing you learn early is you have to be the boss. I need a cigarette. Let's go sit outside."

On the deck, Russell explained how he'd stopped to buy a fishing rod then offered to work the shop when Dave had to leave. Faith said she'd headed into Miskwa by boat in the morning to go to the gym, do some shopping and have her hair done. The gym reference made sense, thought Russell. Her slim, muscular body was athletically tapered and toned, like a gymnast's. She probably also did free weights at home.

Faith said she didn't get Dave's phone message until she returned and docked her boat at her slip at the marina. "I called him back. He said you were here and I told him I'd come over to relieve you. He nailed the poacher, by the way."

"He what? Confronted him? Duked it out?"

"No, silly. He crept along the shore with his deer rifle and shot a hole just below the waterline in each pontoon of the guy's plane. That'll make you take off in a hurry. Then he called the OPP ... Ontario Provincial Police. They already know who it is, just need proof. They'll check his plane, which he'll have to beach so it doesn't sink, and arrest him for poaching minnows."

"You folks seem to take matters into your own hands up here. I like that. Sort of a Wild West feel."

"Oh, it's a wild feeling of something."

"I like your hair very much, by the way. Almost didn't recognize you."

"Yeah, it's fun, eh? I have to wait for school to end before I can get a little wild."

"So you zoom up to Miskwa by boat like it's nothing? You don't ever get lost and hit a reef?"

Faith laughed. "No. If it's a nice day, even with the road open, I'd rather take my boat. It's fast. Quicker than driving."

"And you get to be on the river."

"Exactly."

They sat comfortably silent for a moment, soaking up the sun and watching the activity in the bay. Faith went inside and returned with two beers from the refrigerator in the side room. She asked Russell about his work and he told her he was in advertising. He asked how long she had lived in Kamini and found out she was born and raised there. Back and forth they filled in the details of their lives, childhoods, schooling, careers, failed marriages, grand memories and disappointments. Their conversation was effortless.

A boat containing three men pulled up to the dock. "You can take off if you want," Faith said. "I got this."

"I'd rather stay."

"Good."

Faith and Russell served the new customers, who needed fishing licenses in addition to bait. Dave had forgotten to mention selling licenses during his frenetic training of Russell, so Faith showed him the simple process by selling Russell his own while ringing up his earlier purchases. They returned to the deck and spent the afternoon chatting, laughing and waiting on customers.

Russell took his watch from his pocket to check the time. Just after five. He'd have to leave soon to meet Gribber at the Lodge. He told Faith and asked when she thought Dave would be returning.

"He's probably home taking a nap. I told him I'd stay and close up at seven. Go ahead, grab your new rod and take off in case Gribber's back early. He taking you fishing tomorrow?"

"No, I think he's guiding. I'll ask him about hiring a guide, though. I'm really pumped to give fishing a try."

"Well, if you're hot to trot, may I do the honors? It's a big deal, you know, your first time. I'm a Kamini girl, been fishing this river all my life. Not prone to getting up too early in summer, but for you, I might manage to get to the Lodge by, say, eight o'clock."

"Faith, that would be fabulous! Thank you so much. I can hardly wait."

"Meet you at the Lodge dock at eight, then." Her pretty smile flowed across her face into her lively, dark brown eyes. "I'll pack us lunch and bring everything else we need. You pack a swimsuit and towel. We'll fish around Little Sand in the morning, then after it gets nice and warm, I'm taking you up to Big Sand Beach."

Chapter 24

Russell landed at the Lodge dock only a few minutes before Gribber's arrival with his fishing party in one of the Lodge's elaborate aluminum fishing boats. Gribber spent a few moments engaged in lively chatter and backslapping with his guests before walking over to Russell.

"Ahoy, matey," Gribber said. "Had a nice day. My new party is strict catch and release. They just shoot photos of each fish, which is nice. I don't have any to clean and freeze for them. Let's boot it over to my place, and we'll get on our way to Miskwa."

Gribber praised Russell for his exemplary landing as they docked their boats at Morning Wood. "We need to stop at the Community Center real quick," he said as they hopped into Ramble. "A Ministry Officer called me earlier. She's coming into town to investigate the walleye poaching incident. I need to grab the key to a trailer and open it up for her."

The two men set out for Miskwa after Gribber had unlocked the trailer. He asked Russell for the highlights of his day. Russell recounted his meeting Annie, the tour and fine lunch, then his boat trip into town for gas and ultimately his stint as a volunteer employee of Dave's Live Bait. He left out the visit from Richie but did mention his encounter with the eagle.

"Lots of eagles on the river," Gribber said. "You'll see them nearly every day. This one today, when it circled back and flew over you, did it see you?"

"See me? Hell, we locked eyes."

"Did you feel anything? What did you do right after that?"

"I sort of went into a trance … then I meditated, I guess."

"Interesting."

"How about you?" Russell asked. "What's your story?"

"Well now, be careful. You ask an Indian his story, it could begin back five or six generations."

"You know, I was wondering about that, the term 'Indian.' It's not derogatory? Politically incorrect?"

"Matter of choice. I've never considered it offensive. If some native people do, particularly the younger generation, I understand. But realize, it's not a word coined by Columbus when he sailed to South America and perhaps was unsure about his whereabouts. That's a myth. A country named 'India' didn't exist at the time. A better theory concerns the Spanish holy man he had on board. The padre was impressed by the gentle nature of the native people and called them 'Los Ninos en Dios'—children of God. Or perhaps it was the Latin, 'Du Corpus in Deo'—body of God. At any rate, 'Indios' became the Spaniards' term for them, then as the word crept north to English speakers, it become 'Indian.' Hardly a term lacking in respect.

"Some educated white people who otherwise never give us a second thought object to the word, fine, use a different English word for us, if that makes you feel good. Plenty of Indian writers and scholars use it in both our countries. It was the folks in the US government who coined 'Native American,' not the Indians down in the States. 'Aboriginal' is another term trotted out by well-meaning white folk, but the Anishinabek Nation of Ontario—that's like our union—nixed it about six years ago. 'Ab' is the Latin prefix for 'not,' so it actually means 'not original.' I never liked 'aboriginal' anyway. Conjures up images of birch bark boomerangs.

"'Indigenous' flies, although it describes an awfully large group of people across the planet, and in Canada would include the Inuit and the Métis. 'Native' always works in a pinch, but the best way to show respect and steer clear of the PC police is to refer to Indians by their tribe. I'm Ojibwe, as opposed to Cree, Dakota, or, say, the Illinois, the tribe that inhabited the land around what is now Chicago."

"So, your last name, Dogrib, that's an Indian name?"

"No, a white man name, kind of a funny story. Indians don't use first and last names, that's a European thing. In the eighteen hundreds, the Canadian government insisted on giving every Indian an English first and last name. They were tired of trying to spell and pronounce ours, and thought 'real' names might help the heathens assimilate. While in his twenties, my great-great-grandfather stood in front of a white man with a book of English names to choose from. He riffled through the book and wrote down William Dogrib.

"His first name he picked because he knew a guy named William happened to be king of England at the time. Dogrib wasn't in the book, it was the English name for a far northwestern tribe, the Thlingchadinne, or Dog-Flank People. But he knew it, was fairly fluent in English, could spell it and was a trickster. The man looked at the last name and didn't realize it wasn't in the book."

"I find it remarkable you know so much detail about your ancestors," Russell said. "How is that?"

"The oral tradition of my people, of many indigenous people. My ancestors lived the traditional Ojibwe life longer than most. Some were involved in the fur trade with the French and British as it moved across Canada, early seventeen hundreds. It wasn't a terrible deal. They were paid in food and other goods, things that helped, wool blankets, flintlocks, steel knives. Alcohol was kind of a ticking time bomb, but the white fur traders weren't louts.

"What my people didn't see coming was the socioeconomic impact. The white man looked at beaver, mink, all game, as a product. This was a concept we didn't understand. Animals are our relatives, and Indians were always good stewards of their populations, of the whole environment.

"We also had no concept or word for 'property' as it relates to land, let alone private property. We are connected physically and spiritually to the land, and the land to us. So as the game diminished and trading posts became established, so did our reliance on money. It became difficult to live in the traditional way, hunting, fishing, gathering. It was adapt or starve."

As Gribber spoke, Russell absorbed his words while soaking in the kaleidoscopic scenery. The road snaked through the wilderness, exposing pristine snapshots of lakes, streams and vast sloughs, all defined by the rounded, rising and tumbling towers of gray and pink granite. *We are connected to the land, and the land to us,* Russell pondered. That would explain a lot of it. In Chicago, in any concrete jungle, the land was gone, for all intents and purposes. His isolation—self-prescribed though it were—was a comfortable shroud. He recalled staring out the window of his office overlooking Chicago and thinking the only truth, honesty and sanity he could feel in the world existed in the few inches of air surrounding him. Now, seated beside Gribber in his funky old car, gazing out at the fluid wilderness, he glimpsed that truth, honesty and sanity existed in grand supply, from a tiny Ontario bush town to the farthest reaches of the cosmos.

"So then came the government treaties and the reservations," Gribber said. "Indians were forced to live on reservation land, though some chose to break the white man's law and slip away. No one can hide and live in the woods like an Indian. My great-grandfather and grandmother on my father's side lived off reservation. You had to be careful, though. If caught, you went to jail.

"But it was the government schools that hurt most. Started with the Indian Act of 1876, forced all Indian children to go to schools funded by the government and run by Christian churches. Well, Indians were scattered across a country larger than the US, so for most it meant boarding schools. They created the schools as far from Indian populations as possible to minimize contact with family and tribe. And it wasn't like the kids were coming home for Christmas, or for spring break to fly to Florida.

"The goals were assimilation into Canadian society and conversion to Christianity. First thing that happened was all the kids were taught to speak English. Beatings with straps and paddles were common, and there was sexual abuse. Kids ran away. You're not just talking about speaking a new language. With the Indian, you're talking about trying to teach an entirely different way of thinking. That's what the framers of the law failed to realize. It wasn't the same as rounding up poor, white, rural Canadian kids and teaching them which one's the salad fork. It was like aliens arriving in spaceships and trying to turn the indigenous people into aliens. It's not going to happen.

"In one of the books about it, an Ojibwe writes how the first thing they did to him at the school was cut off his braids. Well, in Ojibwe culture, cutting off your braids is a sign of mourning, and the shorter you cut the braid, the closer the relative. His braids were cut off right at the scalp and he feared his mother had died. Not a great start to your first day."

"That's horrible," Russell said. "But learning to speak English, with the transformation taking place, wasn't that at least a positive thing?"

"Had it been taught as a second language, maybe. But speaking in your native tongue was banned. So the Ojibwe language, the languages of all the tribes, started to disappear. That's key. When a language disappears, there's no solace in the fact that the people are still around. A way of thinking disappears with it. That's when the people disappear, even though you still see them standing before you.

"I was lucky. My great-grandparents held onto the Ojibwe language and passed it down. My grandparents and parents spoke Ojibwe in their homes. I retained a lot of it, and help teach Ojibwe at the Blackdog reservation school in winter. Because speaking in your native tongue can restore more than just the language. What happened was the language ban broke the ancestral transfer of each tribe's heritage, belief system, religions. Some of the kids who came back to their reservations were like ghosts. No longer spoke the language, didn't think the same way anymore, but didn't see any sense in thinking like the white man after what they'd been through. They were in mental and spiritual limbo. Can you spell alcoholism?

"Of course, many did survive, even flourish. They'd meet people from other Indian nations, form networks, enter white society and become successful while retaining their heritage. My grandfather was a tribal elder and had become enamored with log building construction. After the reservation laws were loosened he and my grandmother bought property south of here, built a log home and farmed. My father worked all his life in the logging industry, became a foreman. Died a few years ago. My mom died when I was twelve, flu virus. I'm an only child.

"By the time I was born, it was the seventies and Indians were like, screw your rules, government. We were living on the family property near Fort Francis and the law was amended so Indian kids could go to public schools."

"I passed through Fort Frances at the border," Russell said. "Beautiful river."

"The Rainy. Nice enough place. When I was growing up there, half the days in summer it smelled like farts after everyone in town binged on chili. The smell from the pulp factory where my dad was a foreman."

"Was it rough in the public schools?" Russell asked. "I mean, prejudice, bad shit?"

"Wasn't bad, can only speak for myself. By the seventies, Indians were hip, at least to some. You know, the whole back-to-nature thing and the peace-love-harmony glow left over from the sixties. Plus, we'd started pushing back. AIM had started down in Minneapolis, activism was finally spreading across the US and Canada. If you gave me a hard time you didn't for long. I enjoyed high school. I was a good student and an athlete, played varsity football and ran track."

"What did you do after high school?"

"I received a full-boat scholarship to Dartmouth College. Majored in philosophy with a minor in Indian Studies, as it was called at the time. I think they call it Native American Studies now. Was on the track team."

"Philosophy," Russell said, while processing the fact that Gribber was an Ivy Leaguer. "Getting to know you, that makes sense."

"The study of the fundamental nature of how mankind mostly drives itself crazy."

They pulled up to a stop sign at the Trans-Canada Highway. Gribber crossed onto an asphalt road winding through the outskirts of Miskwa.

"So, you graduated college, then what?"

"Traveled around Canada, a lot of it. Worked on lobster and scallop boats off the coast of Nova Scotia. Spent two years in Montreal, met a woman, learned French, worked for a corporate event planning company. Spent a year in Paris at the Canadian Embassy, working in Bilateral Relations. Came back, headed west, bummed around BC. Worked road construction mostly. Spent a few years in Behchoko, Northwest Territories, on the northern tip of Great Slave Lake. Beautiful place, maybe twelve hundred people, mostly Dogrib tribe and some Métis. Worked as a fishing and hunting guide, tourism was really opening up.

"Stumbled onto Kamini thirteen years ago. Thought I was just passing through, but something about the place. So I bought the cottage. The couple that owned it had died, daughter lived in Vancouver and didn't use it much. Sat there abandoned for four years. I fixed it up, winterized it, felt like home."

"Sounds like you'd saved your money."

Gribber laughed. "It didn't cost much, but yes, I have a little money. Living your life should never be expensive."

Russell thought about his nine thousand dollar-a-month mortgage payment.

They drove down winding roads past small, well-kept homes, crossing old steel bridges across narrow stretches of the Lake of the Woods, skirting downtown Miskwa on their way to Miller's Landing.

"I've done too much of the talking," Gribber said. "How about you? What's your road to Kamini?"

"Grew up on a farm in central Illinois. Went to Northwestern, moved to Chicago, worked for a big advertising agency. Got married, eleven years, no kids … my wife is divorcing me. Anyway, another guy and I left to start our own agency. It's been successful. Ten years ago we won the Ontario Ministry of Tourism account and did all the US advertising for a number of years. That's how I knew about Kamini and the Lodge."

"Ontario—Friendly, Familiar, Foreign and Near," Gribber said.

Russell was astonished. "Yes, exactly, that was the tag line."

"We had the tourism brochures at the Lodge for people to take home. Aerial view of the Lodge on the cover, with that line. I remember it because I thought it was pretty good. Four simple words that convey a lot."

"I wrote them. Message has always been my thing."

"Well done. Your origin on a farm I could have guessed."

"How?"

"I've been guiding tourists for years. You're not a born city slicker. Plenty of them are nice, but the jerks you can spot when they walk down the dock. You're a country boy. You know what you don't know, aren't afraid to ask for help and automatically volunteer it. Sitting in my veranda with a bunch of bush townsfolk you'd just met, you fit right in, didn't put on airs, laughed when we gave you shit. You figured out how to land a boat in a snap, you've handled machinery. The fancy clothes you had on when we found you on the road didn't fit as well as the ragtag outfit I gave you afterward. That Cartier watch of yours is over the top, a badge. Hey look, this farm boy made it. But that's not the real you."

Russell sat silent for a moment. The watch was in his pocket. "What if I told you that was me until just a few days ago?"

"I said the real you. Seems like you're at a crossroads. You need a guide, but it isn't me. You'll learn who it is. You have a very receptive spirit sense. Remarkable, really. You're listening to eagles and fish converse and receiving messages from eagles when they fly overhead. The land, the water, the wind speak to you also, I've seen it. I'd say, welcome to Kamini. Gizhe Manidoo, the Creator, is pleased you're here."

Gribber turned off the road into the parking lot at Miller's Landing. Though it contained pickups of all makes and sizes, without bothering to look at license plates he pulled up to what he knew was Russell's red, shiny new Ford F250.

Chapter 25

Russell followed Gribber into downtown Miskwa, where they parked in a waterfront lot on Main Street. "A more bustling town than I expected," Russell said.

"Around fifteen thousand. Smallest city ever to win the Stanley Cup. The Miskwa Muskies, 1907. Very useful piece of trivia."

"Must be a clothing store in town? I need to buy a few things, if we have the time."

"Time is an illusion. Albert Einstein. Sure, McTaggart's, a block down from the electronics store."

The store sold iPhones, but the salesperson told Russell they couldn't acquire his phone number and plan. He purchased an inexpensive flip phone and pre-paid minutes instead. At McTaggart's, Gribber chatted with the owner while Russell bought a pair of hiking boots, socks, two flannel shirts, a sweatshirt, another pair of jeans and a lightweight nylon jacket.

"Rusty, you have a rain suit?" Gribber asked. "They sell good ones here. You'll need it eventually, either this year or next." Russell added a rain suit to his purchases. Near the cash register was a display of cheap digital watches. He selected a black one and tossed it on the counter.

They drove to Canadian Tire, where Gribber bought thirty bags of concrete mix. Russell noticed he used a personal debit card. As they stacked the eighty-pound bags into the bed of Russell's truck—its new plastic bed liner so pristine one could eat off it—minute amounts of gray, powdery material sifted from the sealed ends onto the bed liner. Russell took note with a furrowed brow and hoped there was a garden hose somewhere at the Lodge where he could rinse it off.

"Hey Russ," Gribber whispered.

"Yeah, Grib?"

"It's a fucking truck."

Russell laughed and shook his head. "Damn city slickers. What's the concrete for, anyway?"

"Setting posts for new boards for the hockey rink up at the reservation. Everything's rotted, needs to be torn out and replaced. Waiting for some funding help from the government but the request has been in for two years. The new posts are up there, some of the Kamini businesses chipped in and Wolf ran them up for me last Sunday. I'm taking Friday and the weekend off. Jam's going to help, see if we can't at least do the tear out and put the new posts in. The grant for lumber for the boards, we didn't hear anything this spring so that means wait another year. The kids will just have to practice pond hockey like last winter and play all their league games as the visiting team."

Russell drove Gribber back to his car when the bags were loaded. "Follow me back," Gribber said. "Instead of crossing the tracks and turning onto the road to the Lodge, you'll go straight, along the bay, past the marina to the building at the end of the point."

"The old log building?"

"That's it. Holst Point Lodge. We can unload the bags at my place tomorrow, if that works. Gang Green is lending me his store's pickup so Jam and I can drive it up to the rez on Friday. Right now, I owe you a beer or three. I'm taking you to the world famous Holst Point Pub."

Following Ramble down the Kamini road, Russell didn't know what to think about first. His yearning for Annie Chase remained a near-constant low rumbling but not in an overtly sexual sense. He hadn't undressed her in his mind or visualized making love to her. He was still too in awe and felt strangely beholden. What

Gribber said about his needing a guide, his spirit sense—there's something to think about when you're not concentrating on driving a twisting gravel road through the bush hauling over a ton of cement mix. The bags. Stupid to unload them just to load them back into another truck. Keep them in the truck. Friday he'd drive up to Blackdog and help with the posts. His thoughts shifted to his delightful afternoon with Faith, her crazy hair and spirited demeanor. He was going fishing tomorrow. Excellent.

The two vehicles rolled into the gravel parking lot carved into the bush behind Holst Point Lodge. To the right of the main entrance and restaurant, a long wing was river-facing guestrooms. To the left, the building jutted out into a large rectangular room with its own entrance. A faded wood sign above the door read Holst Point Pub.

Entering the pub was like walking from serene woods into an Old West take on the Cantina Scene from *Star Wars*. Russell glanced at his new digital watch. Eight o'clock and the place was roaring. Elton John's "Saturday Night" blared from a jukebox in one corner, while two young Ojibwe women danced in the small open space in front of it. People sat on pine log chairs or stood, clustered around pine tables, laughing and conversing. Smoking apparently was tolerated, drinking heartily encouraged. A large cedar-log bar ran prominently along the center of the rear wall displaying tiered shelves of spirits. Two bartenders were scurrying behind it shaking drinks, sliding beers down the bar to patrons and filling drink orders from the bustling servers. Two twelve-foot shuffleboard tables stretched along one wall, both hosting loud and contentious competitions.

"Local hangout," Gribber said into Russell's ear so he could be heard above the din. "Grab a menu if you're hungry. Have the walleye fish and chips. The Point's owned by Kamini Lodge, caters to the more economy minded tourists. A few guests wander over from the main Lodge but can enter only if they know the password."

"Pirate!" came a shout from a table near the center of the room. Dave Burtnyk motioned Russell and Gribber over. Russell recognized Lou LeBlanc and Jammer Mackay among the large group seated at the table. Chairs were slid and tables pushed together to make room for two more. Russell plunked down next to Burtnyk's girlfriend, Sheri, a cheerful, tattooed and pierced faux redhead in her late-thirties. On his other side sat a distinguished-looking older gentleman in a worn corduroy blazer smoking a cigarette and sporting a magnificent helmet of wavy, silver-gray hair.

"Well for fuck's sake, so you're the famous Pirate. Frank Dobbs," the man said, extending his hand. "I am the ghost ship Lollypop, the spirit of St. Louis, the keeper of the flame and the heart of Seoul, South Korea."

Russell shook his hand.

Dobbs pinned Russell with his eyes. "Did you know that if you stand on the end of the Holst Point dock at midnight on August seventeenth of each year, stare at the stars due north for fifteen seconds without blinking, then close your eyes, the impression you'll see from the dots of the brightest stars if connected by lines form the exact contour of the Great Wall of China from Panjiakou to The Dajing Gate, including the loop up to Dushikou?"

"I had no idea," Russell said.

"Craziest damn thing. Tell me there aren't people living underground. Now if you'll excuse me," Dobbs said, rising from his chair, "I have to go see a man about a horse."

A beer appeared in front of Russell and he drank it from the bottle like the rest of the crowd. He ordered fish and chips from a passing server. Much of the discussion at the table surrounded the previous night's events at Andriy Karpenko's landing, with townspeople not present coming over to ask questions of those who were. Gribber mentioned that the Ministry Officer assigned to the case was driving into town tonight and dropping by the pub to meet him. The conversation swung over to Dave Burtnyk's tale of adventure, shooting the pontoons of his minnow poacher's floatplane.

"Should have put one right up Larry's ass," LeBlanc said. "The moron has it coming."

"Who was this poacher?" Russell asked.

"Larry Dunsmore, a retired Miskwa realtor," Burtnyk said. "Got into the minnow business after he retired. Everyone thinks it's easy money. Bought some blocks way north of here, but the guy couldn't pull his dick out of a pail of lard. Tries to set traps and harvest using his floatplane, but when it's windy you get blown all over the place. You need to store a skiff on shore for all your lakes. Fifty other things you need to know to do it right. He's already been charged."

Russell's meal arrived and he began wolfing it down. Frank Dobbs had not returned. His chair was soon occupied by a tanned, muscular man in his forties wearing a battered fishing cap and sporting a large, drooping mustache. "Tony Carter," Gribber half-shouted to Russell from across the double table, pointing to the man. "Second best fishing guide in Kamini." The two shook hands.

"Dave was telling us how you've broken into the minnow business yourself," Sheri said to Russell. "I ran over to the shop at closing. You had a good afternoon. Rang up some big sales, you and Faith."

His mouth full of walleye, Russell limited his response to a muffled, "It was fun."

"Pirate, you look like you need another beer," Burtnyk said, scanning for a server. Russell noticed Gribber had about drained his tall cocktail glass. "Thanks Dave. Tell you what, I have to hit the can. I'll stop at the bar and get the next round."

Russell elbowed into the center of the bar next to Frank Dobbs holding court on a stool and talking to a haggard man in his late-fifties who was intent on something. The man was dressed like nearly everyone in the pub: blue jeans and flannel shirt, tattered sweatshirt or light down vest optional. Russell picked up on the man's flat, upper Midwest accent. Rural Minnesota or Wisconsin, take your pick. No doubt a Holst Point guest. The man was standing hunched in front of Dobbs and obviously had opted for an early start to his daily allocation of alcohol. "I'm telling you, Frank, it was the biggest smallmouth you've ever seen!" the man said, leering into Dobbs. "I didn't have a tape, but it had to be twenty inches. Been coming to Kamini eighteen years. Biggest bass I ever caught. Has to be a record!"

"Nonsense," Dobbs said with a dismissive wave of his cigarette. "Behind that wall is a storage room filled with a ton of dusty old stuff, including two smallmouth each over twenty-two inches."

"Are they mounted?"

"No, they're just holding hands."

The American was too drunk to get the joke. He muttered something and wandered off toward the other side of the room. Dobbs swiveled around to face Russell. "So, Pirate, what do you think of our little slice of Jupiter?"

"I love it, Frank."

"Well, be careful, grasshopper. Roach motel or Hotel California, either or."

The bartender came over and Russell ordered a round for the table. "Something special for Gribber. Do you make a fancy cocktail you know he likes?"

"Gribber doesn't drink, alcohol anyway. His drink is ginger ale with a splash of cranberry juice."

"Then make it a double splash." Russell noticed a drop in the volume of general revelry in the room and turned to look around.

A stout woman in an olive green police-like uniform with a black automatic pistol holstered to her belt and stern look on her face had entered the pub. She swiveled her head slowly as she walked toward the bar, silently surveying the scene across the large room. Beneath her western-style canvas hat emblazoned with a large gold badge, her long black hair was pulled tight in a ponytail. She walked up to Russell and Frank.

"Officer White, Ministry of Natural Resources. How is it that smoking is allowed in this establishment?"

"Kamini is a disorganized township," Dobbs said. "What establishment?"

"I assume you mean an Unorganized Township. I didn't realize that, so yes, you have leeway with certain rules, but still, I'll want to speak to the head of your Town Council at some point."

"Certainly, he's right over there," Dobbs said, pointing out Lou LeBlanc standing midway across the room. LeBlanc had placed a crumpled bar napkin atop Tony Carter's cap and was behind him attempting to light it but was encountering difficulty manipulating the paper matches.

Officer White gave the room another quick scan, shaking her head as she noted tobacco use at various tables. "I just don't understand why people smoke when they're so aware of the dangers."

Dobbs took a long, elegant drag from his Player's. "It makes us look like adults," he said as he exhaled.

Gribber rose from his chair and joined them by the bar. "Lydia," he said, smiling broadly as he placed a gentle hand on her elbow, "John Dogrib. We spoke on the phone. Thank you so much for coming. How was your trip? Were you able to access the trailer? I hope it meets with your approval."

White's face and rigid stance softened as quickly as an inner tube pierced by a Bowie knife. "Mr. Dogrib!" she gushed. "So pleased to meet you. Yes, the trailer is fine, thank you. I moved in and had some time to walk around. Kamini is beautiful."

"Tell me how I may be of service. I'm guiding tomorrow but can give you simple directions to Mr. Karpenko's property, or we could run over there now. I could begin telling you how we came to discover his gross malfeasance."

"That would be awesome, yes," Lydia said. Thrown by the word "malfeasance," she guessed it meant something bad and quickly recovered. "It's still light out. Let's go now and get started."

"After you, then," Gribber said, bowing and gallantly sweeping his left arm toward the exit.

By now all in the room were focused on Gribber and the attractive female Ministry Officer. Gribber pushed open the door and held it for Lydia to exit first. He followed close behind and just before letting the door swing shut, turned and gave the room a wink. The pub patrons burst into polite applause.

The Ministry SUV was parked outside the door. Gribber hopped in and Lydia drove up the hill toward town.

"Nice wheels," Gribber said.

"Not really. I've pleaded with the Ministry to transition to electric vehicles, but of course they claim budgetary restraints."

"Oh, that and getting less than two hundred kilometers on a full charge when it's thirty below, I suppose. Ontario's a big place. The time will come. Stay left around the bay and head out of town. It's about six kilometers."

Lydia snuck a glance at her handsome passenger. "From your English last name, I assume you are Thlingchadinne tribe?" She pronounced the difficult word perfectly.

"Ojibwe. The last name is a long story. First time to Kamini?"

"Yes. I've worked out of Miskwa. It's nice, but everyone at the Ministry says Kamini is special."

"That it is." Gribber told Lydia about his discovery of suspicious nets in Roughrock and how he and his friend Daryl—Jammer—had monitored Karpenko's activities. He described the confrontation between the townspeople and Karpenko but left out large amounts of detail. They'd suggested to Karpenko that he leave town, and he did so willingly.

"A bigger boat than I thought from the pictures," Lydia said as they exited the vehicle at the landing. "Anyone in town we can hire to haul it onto shore? The Ministry can auction it off from here."

"Sure, Jimmy Douglas is the big construction guy in town. He'd get it out and up on blocks for you. I'll give you his number. Come on aboard."

Gribber and Lydia stepped into *Keeper* and entered the cabin. Gribber showed Lydia the switch for the bilge pump and flipped it on but didn't turn on the overhead light. The hum of a small electric motor came from beneath the stern followed by the soft, steady splash of water pouring from the bilge hose into the bay.

The sun had just set but the moon and stars were taking over and the calm water in the bay glowed. Lydia felt comfortable and liked being alone with Gribber in the confined space with soft light filtering through the cabin windows. A fish jumped in the bay. The pump started sucking air and Gribber turned it off.

Back on shore, Lydia and Gribber checked out Karpenko's garage, various rusted remnants of equipment stashed around the grounds and the contents of his shack. "I'll run over to Surveys and Land Titles in Miskwa tomorrow to get the plat of the property," Lydia said. "Tear down the buildings, haul out the junk, and this is a nice piece of land. And I'd like to sit you down for a proper interview, also interview a few others who were involved. Start building The Ministry's case."

"Of course," Gribber said. They stood side-by-side, gazing out at the shimmering bay. "I get home from guiding tomorrow by six. Why don't you come over for dinner around seven? We could do the interview and perhaps go for a paddle in my canoe. This time of night on the river, so many of the spirits speak."

"Oh, I would love that, thank you. You're so right. There's something magical about a canoe ride."

Gribber lifted his gaze and spoke to the stars. "The white man roars across the middle of the lake in his motorboat and sees nothing. The Indian paddles quietly along the shoreline in his canoe and sees everything."

"That's ... that's beautiful. Is that saying one of yours?"

"My grandfather's. A tribal elder and very wise man. Now, unless there's anything else you can think of, perhaps we should head back."

Gribber gave Lydia the phone number for Jimmy Douglas, and as they entered town in the SUV, he pointed out the gravel road leading to his cottage. They said goodbye at Holst Point, Lydia thanking Gribber while clasping his hands and confirming that she'd see him at seven.

Gribber started toward the pub entrance then realized that if he drove home, got in his boat and headed over to Annie Chase's tonight, he wouldn't have to do so early tomorrow morning. Back at Morning Wood he slipped on a jacket, got into his boat, drove out of Gunn Lake past Town Bay, under the bridge, around the Lodge peninsula and landed at Annie's dock in Jackfish Bay.

Annie was reading by kerosene lamp on her veranda, and hearing his boat pull up ambled down to the dock.

"An urgent item concerning the Ministry of Natural Resources has just entered my surveillance," Gribber said. "Can I borrow your canoe?"

Annie smirked. "You know you can, you mangy mutt. Who's the unlucky girl?"

Chapter 26

Russell set the alarm on his bedside table for five so he could witness sunrise, but his eyes popped open a few minutes before it went off. He'd hung on at the pub until nearly midnight, mostly talking about fishing with Tony Carter, who proved a gracious and friendly fount of information. Russell dressed in the clothes he'd bought at McTaggert's, put on his new cheap watch then walked to the beach. A few guests were seated in folding canvas chairs scattered across it, some with coffee. All sat silently in the soft dawn light, attuned to the gentle, humbling ritual of watching the birth of a new day.

Beyond the beach a broad granite point jutted out forming the tip of the peninsula, separating the beach area from the boat docks around the other side. Russell saw it offered a supreme view of the river as it flowed north past small and large islands before curving out of sight several miles downstream. He found a comfortable perch in the low, rounded granite bluffs near the gently lapping water and sat down. Following Gribber's instructions, he sensed the wilderness awaken.

After about an hour, Russell didn't know how long, his head jerked up, as it does when one nods off during an airline flight. Except he knew he hadn't been dozing. For long periods he had stared at the view and thought of nothing, as still as a solar panel absorbing energy. He felt a powerful peace, infusing, altering his being, so palpable it felt like more than he could contain.

He walked up to the Lodge, bought a cup of coffee and strolled down to the docks. The guides were arriving. When he saw Gribber pulling in, a thought occurred to him. Russell went over to help tie up Gribber's boat. "Thanks for taking me to the Point last night, I think. You brought the Ministry under control?"

"Work in progress. Meant to talk to you about the cement mix last night but I got distracted. Was wondering if it could stay in your truck. That way I can back up the other truck to it first thing Friday and Jammer and I can transfer it."

"Leave it in my truck and I'll drive up with you Friday and help with the posts."

Gribber was standing in his boat and for the first time since making his acquaintance, Russell saw a startled look cross his face.

"Wow, you mean it? Well of course you do. That would be great. Thanks a lot."

"Let me tell you my new thought," Russell said. "The lumber. I'll buy it. Let's get it up there and build a proper hockey rink for the kids."

Hearing this, Gribber sat back down. "Russell ... I don't know what to say. With the hardware and other materials, it could be eight, ten grand."

Russell heard the figure but it had new context. "So no more than a French watch I own that tells me the same time as the fifteen-dollar watch I'm wearing now. Do you have all the tools we'll need? Maybe we should sit down and draw up a plan."

Gribber was still processing Russell's offer. He stepped out of his boat, and as he shook Russell's hand, placed his other hand on Russell's shoulder. "Thank you, my friend. We should hook up with Jammer. He's the builder. Talk it through and work up a materials list. I have something on tonight but I'll call him and set a time. Tomorrow night, probably."

"Let me know," Russell said.

The main dock was coming to life with jabbering guests carrying fishing rods.

"I should check in," Gribber said. "What's your plan for the day?"

"Faith Pearson is coming over in her boat at eight to take me fishing."

Gribber's eyes brightened. "Atta kid. Faith's an expert fisher-person. She'll teach you everything a guy needs to know. You're going to have a good time fishing, at the very least."

Russell accompanied Gribber to the guide's shack then continued on to the Lodge. The dining room would be open for breakfast and he was starving. He was back on the dock by eight with his new fishing rod and small tote bag packed with swimsuit and towel. The sun warm on his face, he took off his sweatshirt, tied it around his waist and slipped on sunglasses. A minute later Faith Pearson pulled up in her eighteen-foot G3 fishing boat.

"Holy smokes," Russell said as he reached for the impressive boat's gunwale and held it to the dock. "That's quite a ride."

"Worth more than the three years I spent with the jerk I married," Faith said. "At least I got something out of the deal. Tie up, I'll give you a quick lesson with that new rod of yours." Faith selected one of two rods mounted to a nifty rack system along the inside wall of her boat. She chose a curving lead weight from the top tray of an enormous tackle box, and together they walked to the end of the dock. "Clip the weight onto your swivel," she told him, "and I'll show you how to use a spinning reel."

In a matter of minutes Faith taught Russell how to loop the line on the forefinger of his right hand as he held the rod, open the bail of the reel with his left, lower the weight to the bottom, note the slack, turn the handle causing the bail to snap closed, and reel the weight to the surface. Faith pointed out how to lock the reel so it didn't rotate backward, adjust the drag, and a few things to watch for as the spinning bail returned the line to the spool. She then pronounced Russell ready to catch a fish.

Russell eased into a comfortable swivel seat and faced Faith as she started the motor. His guide for the day was wearing flip-flops, blue jeans and a cotton top underneath a lightweight hoodie. He was thrilled that they veered left when they pulled away from the dock and headed downstream, directly into the view he'd been contemplating earlier that morning. They were heading into a vast section of the river new to him. Virgin territory.

They didn't travel far before Faith slowed the boat at the start of a narrow channel along the backside of a large island within view of the Lodge. "Indian Island. Good current through here. Low reefs and humps off the two little rock islands at each end. Should be fish cruising along the entire channel. We'll drift with the current and jig it." Faith handed him a chartreuse jig tied to a leader. "Clip that onto your swivel."

She selected one of her rods with a bright pink jig ready to go. Russell watched as she took a minnow from the bucket and pushed the jig hook up through its head. She handed Russell another slick, wiggling minnow and after dropping it twice he did the same. She flipped on the electronic depth finder, cruising slowly while eyeing the device's screen and the small rock island ahead.

Faith turned off the engine. "OK, down we go. When you hit bottom, reel up the slack plus one more turn. We're at thirty-one feet and it's going to get shallower as we drift, so reel up to keep the jig just above the bottom. Jig it like this." She showed Russell how to jerk the rod tip up a few inches then let the lure drop back down. "Jig slow. If you feel a tug or anything that doesn't feel like the jig bouncing on the bottom, jerk the rod tip hard, to set the hook."

Russell was matching Faith's every move and only a few seconds after starting to jig, he felt life not his own transmitted from the jig through the line down the rod to his hand. The rod tip magically bent down and back up twice on its own. Russell felt the curious sensation and observed the rod motion with inert bewilderment.

"Set it!" Faith said.

Russell's first fish was a small walleye that Faith netted and swung over to his feet. She showed him how to slide his hand to collapse the sharp, spiny dorsal fin running along its back while picking it up. "Don't squeeze too hard," she told him. "That little thing won't squirm or fight back." She handed him a long-nose pliers and talked him through the process of removing the jig hook from the fish's mouth. "Pretty little guy. Too small to keep but your first fish, you have to take a picture."

Faith grabbed her cell phone. Russell held the small fish and smiled sheepishly while she took a few snaps. "Drop it back in. I netted it because it's your first and wanted to be sure you got it. From now on, a fish that size you can reel to the boat and lift in with your rod. I'll holler if it's a fish I think we should net."

"We can just take pictures of all the fish today," Russell said. "Fine with me."

"Me too. I packed some sandwiches, fruit, dessert and a bottle of wine for lunch."

Faith caught the next two fish, walleyes of comparable size. Russell was so focused on the sensations emanating from his jig that for the next fifteen minutes he barely spoke, staring at his rod tip like a little boy. Faith picked up on this with amusement. Kamini had stripped off the fancy varnish job on this one with record speed.

As Russell grew more comfortable with the process, he and Faith resumed their relaxed banter from the previous afternoon. They jigged in a few different spots along the channel and caught several larger walleyes. A fish hit Russell's jig particularly hard and for the first time he heard the whir of his reel's drag as the fish yanked out line even while he attempted to reel it in.

"That's a smallmouth bass!" Faith said immediately.

"How can you tell?" He had to concentrate on this one. The fish was fighting hard.

"The way it's fighting. Look, it's cruising away from the boat. Walleyes fight straight down. Bass and snakes, they go off on runs. Look how quick your rod tip's bending, bang bang bang. That's a smallmouth fight. If it starts heading for the surface, get ready to reel and pull back on the rod at the same time, because it's going to jump."

As if on cue, the fish erupted from the surface and flew a foot in the air, flapping its head furiously before splashing down. Russell brought the shiny brown bass to the side of the boat where Faith netted it. He dutifully followed her instruction to pick up the fish by sticking his thumb down its mouth and grasping it by the bottom jaw.

"Don't bass have teeth?"

"They do, but tiny. Now pick it up, curl the jaw back against your index finger and it won't move."

Russell removed the jig and held the fish proudly while Faith took a picture. "I can eyeball it at seventeen inches," she said. "That's a nice bass. Now say bye-bye." Russell slipped the fish back into the water where it disappeared in a flash.

For the rest of the morning Faith cruised north from Kamini into the ever-expanding portion of the river called Little Sand. Sparsely spaced cottages accessible only by boat appeared along the way, but as they boated further north the cottages dwindled in number until once again Russell viewed untamed Ontario wilderness in whichever direction he gazed.

Faith introduced Russell to spinning, removing their jigs and replacing them with lead weights and long leaders with a hook and colorful spinner blade at the ends used for trolling minnows. They continued to catch fish. Faith landed the first big walleye, which Russell taped at twenty-two inches, while Russell caught his first snake, an ephemerally hard-fighting northern pike that Faith referred to as a "hammer handle" due to its long albeit slender size.

They floated slowly around a point while jigging a narrow channel. Russell looked up and was surprised by the unfolding view of an immense stretch of shoreline many miles away.

"Reel up, minnow off, line locked, minnow bucket in," Faith said. "Welcome to Big Sand."

Big Sand Lake was a gigantic bay measuring seven miles across in whichever direction one chose to cross it. The few islands it contained were tucked along its shoreline.

"This is the midsummer hotspot for big walleyes. Doesn't get good until later in June, but it's swimming time, and lunch time, and wait'll you see the beach." Faith fired her boat to full speed and began racing across the large expanse of open water.

Looking straight off the bow, Russell saw they were angling toward a slender strip of light tan shoreline. As they closed to within a mile Russell realized the shoreline was a lengthy stretch of wilderness sand beach. Faith slowed the boat and toggled up the engine in such a fashion that as the bow hit the beach it glided smoothly up the sand and came to rest.

Russell removed his boots and socks, and from the storage compartments he and Faith removed a cooler, cloth bag, large quilt and Russell's tote. The beach ran nearly thirty feet up from the water toward the erratic forest line of spruce, birch, red and white pine. Faith spread out the quilt on the warm sand and arranged the cooler, cloth bag and Russell's tote along its edge.

"A swim before lunch," she announced, kicking off her flip-flops then slipping out of her jeans and top to reveal what Russell judged a wonderfully scant, black bikini. She turned her slender back to him and marched into the water as Russell dropped his jeans and boxers, grabbed his suit and pulled it on. He tossed his shirt and followed Faith into the cold, clear water.

Faith waded past her knees before diving and swimming a dozen strokes. Turning to face Russell as he approached the water, she could still stand on the soft, sandy bottom. "It's cold at first and then it isn't," she said.

Russell ran into the water toward Faith and dove. He swam to where she stood then both swam until neither could touch bottom. "You're right, the water's amazing," he said as the two faced each other, treading water. "Quite a shock at first, but then you adapt."

"Yeah, even middle of summer you get a little jolt when you jump in."

Russell rotated so he faced the beach. "This beach is incredible. It's as pretty as any tropical beach I've been to, but then you drop it down into the Canadian wilderness. It's like we're the only two people on the planet."

Faith took a few strokes toward Russell and put her hands on his shoulders. "Frozen in time," she said. "I've been coming here as long as I can remember. This was the big weekend party place when I was a teenager. Still is." Russell placed his hands on Faith's waist, both treading water with their legs.

Looking over Russell's shoulder, Faith spotted something she didn't like. "Poobah, boats coming in." Russell turned his head and spotted two boats, one very large, making a beeline for the beach.

"Cottagers," Faith said. "And maybe some fishermen. I didn't think anyone would be up here so early in the season."

"Too bad. I suppose it was too much to ask, having a lunch spot like this all to ourselves."

"Nonsense. Plan B. Back to the beach!" She let go of Russell and began swimming swiftly toward shore.

They loaded their things back into the boat. The large fiberglass cruiser approaching appeared to carry at least three adults, a gaggle of small children and a dog. "There's more than one beach on Big Sand," Faith said. "I'll show you my secret spot."

They slid the boat into the water and climbed in. Faith started the engine and rounded the boulder point at one end of the beach, entering a narrow channel between the mainland and an island blocking the view of the lake. She sent Russell to the bow to watch for submerged rocks, raising the engine partway each time he called out a boulder looming up from the bottom. When they entered a small cove, Russell spotted a stretch of pristine sand beach nearly hidden between two jagged stone bluffs. Faith landed at one end. They unloaded their things and again Faith spread out the quilt on the warm sand near the tree line.

"It just keeps getting better and better," Russell said. "This is fantastic."

"Mystery Beach. Tourists and most cottagers don't know it's here, and if they do, don't come in because of the rocks." Faith walked to the water's edge. "And you know the best thing about it?"

"What's that?"

Her back to Russell, Faith untied her bikini top and dropped it onto the smooth, firm sand at water's edge. Then she pulled the ties at each hip and did the same with her bikini bottom. She looked over her shoulder at Russell and winked. "It's a nude beach."

She ran into the water and dove.

Chapter 27

Cuddling naked with Faith on the quilt in the warm sun after their skinny dip and ensuing mad tango at water's edge, Russell stared up at the sky and held her closer. That Faith was taking him to a wilderness beach to seduce him did not enter his mind until he found himself tearing off his swimsuit to join her in the water. Nor had he thought to pack a condom, of which he made mention at some point. It had occurred to Faith, however. "Your guide told you she'd pack everything we need," she said laughing, racing back after nabbing one from her cloth bag. In addition to her comprehensive attention to detail, she showed herself to be a loud and inventive lover.

Russell breathed in the freshwater scent of Faith's hair. "This is better than perfect," he said, one hand gently massaging her scalp.

"Ooh, I'm so glad," she said, raising her head to stare into Russell's eyes. "No complaints from this girl. You're lucky. The sex on the beach season is a brief one up here. Another week and the black flies would have us racing for a monastery."

"I consider myself very lucky. This was my first time."

Faith gasped. "Ever?" She widened her eyes in mock astonishment. "You must watch a ton of porn. The good stuff, too, you know, some thought to lighting."

"You know exactly what I mean. First time on a beach."

"Oh, OK. Well, what are vacations for, if not to meet new people, try new things, eh?"

Faith sat up, dug into the cloth bag for a cigarette, lit it and stared at the water. As before, they were comfortable in silence.

She put out the cigarette in the sand after a few minutes, placed the butt in a zippered pouch, stood, and tied on her bikini.

"I don't know about you, but I'm starving," she said, looking down at Russell. "Put some clothes on, you creep, and let's eat lunch."

Lunch consisted of two well-adorned and delicious roast beef sandwiches and a fruit salad. Out of the cooler for dessert came two pieces of divine, wild blueberry pie Faith baked the previous evening. The two ate ravenously, washing it all down with more than half a bottle of chardonnay.

"White wine goes with everything, as far as I'm concerned," Faith said.

After lunch they lay in the sun, took another brief, nude swim and made love again, this time managing to make it all the way up to the quilt for a longer and gentler fulfillment. They briefly fell asleep. Late afternoon they loaded up the boat and headed toward Kamini, taking a different route through Little Sand so they could fish in a few more spots—with Faith hauling in a very large small-mouth—and Russell could see even more of the boundless beauty of the Winnipeg River.

They stopped to jig a hump in a channel Russell recognized a few miles from town.

"Look, eagles," Faith said. "Two of them in the tallest white pine at the top of that bluff. See them?"

Russell looked far down the opposite shoreline and spotted the white head of each eagle, the larger of the two perched on a dead limb at the top of the tree. Their only movement was their heads, smoothly swiveling left and right as they surveyed the land and water.

"Gribber says they're messengers," she told him. "It's an Ojibwe thing. Not all the time. Sometimes they're on the river just fishing and hunting like anyone else. But when they come over to you, or focus on you for more than a glance. It can be a sign, like there's an opportunity or awakening ahead. You're supposed to clear your mind. See if they bring a message."

"Gribber said something to me about this. I'm still not clear. A message from whom?"

"The Creator, you know." Faith swept her hand at the river and shoreline. "Whatever it was that put all this into motion."

Russell looked back at the eagles. Neither was paying attention to them. He felt a soft hit on his jig, set the hook and reeled in a small perch.

"That's the one we were looking for," Faith said. "I'm getting little nibbles too. Nothing tells you it's time to stop fishing like the start of a perch fest. Toss it back, lock and load, minnows in, let's call it a day." She caught Russell's eye and smiled. "A good day."

Russell released the fish, stored his rod in the holder and pulled in the minnow bucket. As he swiveled to face Faith, he heard the distinctive whoosh of wings in the air. He looked up and was startled by a large eagle landing on a branch at the top of a dead spruce near the boat. Looking back to the white pine on the bluff, Russell spotted only the one eagle perched farther down in the pine.

"Don't move, I want to get a picture," Faith whispered, slowly reaching for her phone.

Russell stared nearly straight up at the eagle towering above them as it adjusted its footing on the barren branch. Once set, it began scanning its new view, looking high over Faith, Russell and the boat. The eagle swiveled its head slowly left, right, then to center before snapping it sharply down to lock eyes with Russell. Russell stopped breathing and stared back as his mind went blank. Seconds later he heard a soft click from Faith's phone. The eagle broke Russell's stare, looked up, dropped from its perch and with great flapping of wings flew overhead, back to its mate. Faith followed it with her phone, taking more pictures.

"Ooh, I think I got some nice ones," she said, tapping at her phone. "I did. One where it's staring down almost right at me. Another as it dropped. I'll get these onto my computer and do some cropping, send them to you."

Russell decided to let Faith take the lead upon landing at the Lodge dock. So far, that was working out well. She said she needed to head home, tend to some baking duties and meet her friend Annie who was stopping by after work to pick up some plants she'd purchased for her in Miskwa. Would he like to meet up at the Holst Point Pub around nine?

"Yes, please," Russell said. "And by 'Annie,' you mean Annie Chase, I assume? I met her yesterday. She gave me a tour of the Lodge. Known her long?"

"Since the day she stepped off the train eleven years ago. She lived with me for two years right after my divorce, before she bought her cottage. Annie and I are best friends."

This news, with its potential consequences, did not startle Russell. He certainly hadn't any thoughts toward Annie Chase during the day. What he had was an extremely fresh awareness of several things he needed to ponder. He leaned over and kissed Faith.

"Thank you for a fabulous day. I'm going to curl up in bed in the fetal position for a few hours. That way I should be able to crawl to the Point by nine. See you there."

Chapter 28

Faith waved to Gribber, coming in with his fishing party, as she pulled away from the dock. Gribber landed and, carrying a two-pound walleye, walked whistling to his boat. He hopped in and raced to Morning Wood. There was much to do in preparation for his dinner guest. He showered, shaved, put on clean jeans and a tight black turtleneck. He made a Caesar salad with bacon bits, put baby potatoes in a pan of water, located a can of cream corn, and cleaned the walleye. He made himself a cup of tea.

Lydia White was pacing in her trailer in town, in a tizzy over what to wear for her dinner date. She wasn't able to get Gribber's stoically handsome face and graceful, sculpted body out of her mind. No, it wasn't a date, she told herself. It was Ministry business. She should be in uniform. Except that arriving in her crisp, starched uniform, gun or no gun, was certain to be a mood killer. Mood killer? Who was she kidding? She had said she needed to interview him. He invited her over for dinner because he was a gentleman. Still, they'd be breaking bread. She put on a pair of designer jeans and her hemp sandals. She had packed a blue halter top on the off chance she would be in a social setting. It was lined, offered support and matched her eyes. She put it on, but standing at the bedroom mirror realized it was a bit much. Or a bit too little. Over it she put on a white, long-sleeve cotton blouse she left unbuttoned and tied at the waist. It could be brisk later in the evening, in a canoe on the river.

What she might be served for dinner was also troubling her greatly. As she applied a touch of makeup and brushed out her long black hair, she regretted not telling Gribber she was vegan, but knew why. Her diet often was an issue with the scant number of boyfriends in her past. Tommy, who'd broken up with her a year ago, complained that her eating habits too often impacted his, though he had claimed the final straw was her criticism of him for wearing leather belts and work boots.

Tonight she would suck it up and eat whatever Gribber was serving. One meal wouldn't kill her. She could always bring up her veganism later on, if there was a later on. (Who was she kidding?) She only hoped he wasn't grilling burgers. She'd not eaten beef in years, and the thought turned her stomach. He was an Ojibwe fishing guide, so maybe he was cooking walleye. She'd never tasted walleye, didn't eat any type of fish, but it might prove palatable. She grabbed her briefcase, headed outside to the Tahoe and drove to Gribber's cottage.

Gribber greeted Lydia at the back door and asked if she wanted something to drink. Whatever he was having. Gribber made two ginger and cranberries and ushered her to the veranda. "The potatoes are on, I made a salad, the rest of the meal will take only ten minutes, so why don't we do the interview first? I asked my friend Annie Chase to swing by at seven. She's a key witness, that way you can kill two birds with one stone."

"Wonderful idea. Your cottage is beautiful. And the view." Lydia sat down on the chesterfield, removed her cell phone, interview forms and a pen from her briefcase and placed them on the coffee table. A boat pulled up to the dock and a moment later Annie Chase stepped into the veranda.

"Annie, this is Officer White. Officer, Annie Chase," Gribber said.

"Nice to meet you, Annie. Please, call me Lydia. Thanks for coming over. This shouldn't take long." Gribber placed two chairs so he and Annie could sit down facing Lydia.

"Nice shirt," Annie said to Gribber. "I never see you in turtlenecks. New?"

"I need to inform you I'm going to record this," Lydia said, looking down and fiddling with her phone. Annie took a good look at Lydia, glanced at Gribber, closed her eyes and shook her head. You whore, she mouthed to him.

The interview took only fifteen minutes, Lydia impressing both with the range and insightfulness of her questions. She finished making notes and asked them to read and sign their statements. Annie signed hers, stood, and shook Lydia's hand. "If that's all you need, I'll let you two go at it. So nice to meet you, Lydia." Annie looked hard at Gribber, crossed her eyes, pushed open the screen door and returned to her boat.

"What a nice person," Lydia said. "And gorgeous, my goodness."

"Runs the orphanage in Miskwa," Gribber said.

Lydia's pulse was racing when she knocked on Gribber's door, but his gentle demeanor and the familiarity of conducting investigative interviews had calmed her. She sat on a stool in the kitchen while they chatted and Gribber prepared dinner. He whipped minced garlic and spices into the egg batter before dipping the fillets then shaking them in a plastic bag filled with his secret-formula bread crumbs. As the fish began to cook in the hot oil and butter, the sumptuous smell made Lydia's mouth water.

They ate on the veranda, Gribber expressing great interest in Lydia's background and her work with the Ministry. He peppered her for details about her cases and reveled in her accounts of tracking and arresting poachers. "You provide a great service," he told her. "The Earth thanks you."

Lydia spoke as politely as she could between mouthfuls, for she was famished. That morning she'd gone to the Office of Surveys and Land Titles in Miskwa to research Andriy Karpenko's property, then to the OPP to acquire personal information on him from the Ontario and Manitoba police and government databases. Unable to locate anything even remotely resembling a vegan restaurant, lunch had been a plain salad at McDonald's.

Devouring her Caesar, she considered scraping the bacon bits off to the side but knew that would look weird. She'd never eaten bacon bits. They did give the salad a nice flavor. The walleye was beyond delicious. Gribber topped it with fresh lemon juice and after watching her inhale the first few bites suggested she add a dollop of cream corn to each mouthful. Potatoes were potatoes, and as a vegan Lydia had eaten barge loads of them, but the herbs, spices and still more bacon bits Gribber used in their preparation gave them a zesty, unique taste. She had seconds of everything.

Lydia insisted she help with the dishes, and as Gribber put away the final plate he suggested they go for a paddle in his canoe. At the dock, he put the canoe in the water and took the stern. Lydia proved a strong, able paddler in the bow. They paddled smoothly along the shoreline of Gunn Lake, following its contour around the granite points and into numerous bays. Silently they encountered still waters, ducks and ducklings, blue herons and the captivating, close-up view of granite, moss and timber shorelines gently pulsing in the rich contrast of low evening light.

As the sun began to set, they paddled to a small island that hosted only a few sprawling white pines. There they witnessed the transcendent arrival of twilight, sitting together in silence on a comfortable quilt of moss, tufted native grasses and white pine needles woven into the sloping granite shore. Gribber leaned back on his elbows and crossed his long legs. Doing the same, Lydia felt the warmth of her shoulder make contact with his. Did Gribber press his shoulder ever so slightly firmer against hers? she wondered. She wished he would take her hand, yearned to place her head on his broad shoulder.

"This magic moment," Gribber said softly, "when one realizes the boundless opportunities of life … yet senses the cursing brevity of mortal existence."

Lydia tilted her head closer to Gribber's and turned to look at him. Gribber smiled gently as his warm, brown eyes embraced hers. Their faces were mere inches apart. Lydia didn't know if she had inched closer to his nearly prostrate body or he toward hers, but she felt the warmth of contact running from her shoulder down to her hip. She thought Gribber might speak again, or make some kind of move, but didn't, instead holding her gaze in his boundless, mesmeric eyes. Seconds passed, then time seemed to dissolve altogether.

Lydia drew a deep breath then quick as a cat rolled over on top of Gribber and kissed him hard on the lips, her pulse racing from both frenzied desire and horrific fear he would push her away in astonishment. When instead he wrapped his arms around her and kissed back, adding a touch of tongue, Lydia clamped his head between her hands and kissed him so greedily that were she able to fit his whole face in her mouth, she would have.

At approximately the same time four miles downstream, Russell walked into the Holst Point Pub. Faith wasn't there. Greeted by calls of "Ahoy, Pirate," he sat down at a large table with a group which included Gord Fanson and Bruce Anderson and had been commandeered by Frank Dobbs. Russell was introduced to Jeanette Green, the postmistress, her husband Gang, manager of the Hudson's Bay store, and a flat-nosed, sharp-eyed older gentleman named White House Johnson. Seated next to Johnson, Russell felt compelled to inquire about his name.

"There be two of us in Kamini with last name of Johnson," White House said. "Both of us moved here around the same time, forty years ago. More than the townspeople could handle. I painted my house white."

"Versus ..."

"Red House Johnson. You might guess the color he painted his house."

"White House is the Johnson we allow to be seen in public," Dobbs said.

Faith arrived and joined them at the table. Conversation ranged from provincial politics to the new forest fire north of the English River to Frank Dobbs's theory that through genetic engineering he was capable of creating freshwater lobsters, thus ushering in a new industry certain to be a boon to the Kamini economy. "All I need is around one million bucks, enough for a minimal bio lab," Dobbs said. "Spectrophotometer, robotic reagent dispenser, follicle stimulating hormone centrifuge, thermal cycler and two, maybe three live lobsters. I have room for all of it in my shop. We could be harvesting lobsters in Gunn Lake in five years, for fuck's sake! Average age of a lobster at harvest is seven years, but I'm going to splice in a growth gene from a duck." Faith, sitting across the table from Russell, told Frank he could count on her for a quarter mill, looked at Russell and smiled.

Russell and Faith left the pub, hopped into their boats and raced the short distance to the Lodge. As they entered the cottage, Faith glanced left and right at the two bedrooms. "Oh boy, options," she said before slipping into the bathroom.

Russell stood in the front room and looked out at the river, shimmering with herringbone patterns in the moonlight. His computer sat on the small coffee table, and he realized that for thirty-six hours he'd completely forgotten about checking his emails. Or emailing his new cell phone number to his partner. Curiously, it was as if the modern world of Samuels Dean, of emails, cell phones, the Internet, existed somehow as relics of the past. Or at the very least, his past.

He considered checking his emails then thought, screw it. Faith had exited the bathroom. Russell found her in the second bedroom, engaged in some intriguing rearranging of the furniture.

Chapter 29

Russell awoke at five and heard Faith in the shower. It was her day to open the bait shop. As she was leaving, he told her he'd swing by after breakfast. He watched the sunrise at the granite point past the beach, then sat there for an hour longer before buying his coffee at the Lodge and heading down to the docks.

"Just called you as I was leaving Morning Wood, figured you'd be up," Gribber said as he tied up his boat.

"Oh wow … I walked out without my cell. That's a first."

"That's a good sign, is what that is. Only called to tell you, I spoke to Jam. He said swing by this afternoon around five. He's finishing up a new deck on a cabin in Pistol so he's nearby. You two can sit down and hammer out the details for the rink."

"You won't be there?"

"No, sorry. As soon as I'm off work, I'll have urgent matters to attend to with Officer White."

"I'll bet. Where does Jammer live? How do I get there?"

Gribber pointed straight across the channel to the bay on the opposite shoreline. "See the little channel in the center?"

Russell studied the shoreline. Dense shrubs and trees grew along the water's edge. Looking close through a narrow gap, he saw a stretch of treed shoreline further away.

"Hidden Lake. Big crappies in it. Jammer's houseboat, too. Be careful going in, stay in the middle, watch for rocks. The houseboat, you can't miss it."

After breakfast Russell succumbed to the duty of checking his emails. None were of importance. Nothing from Dan or anyone at the firm. Samuels Dean was humming along just fine without him. He fired off emails with his new cell number to Dan, Caroline Klein and Bill Carter, then spent an hour researching several topics. He returned to the docks, put on his lifejacket, and headed for the bait shop.

A boat was leaving from the dock as Russell pulled up. Faith, dressed in a light blue cami and shorts, was sunning on the deck. She ducked inside as he walked up and emerged holding a beautiful fishing rod and reel.

"This is from Dave," Faith said. "A really nice, seven-foot St. Croix Mojo. Heavy duty. This won't bend like your walleye rod when you hook your first musky. Really good reel, too, a Shimano. Dave put fifty-pound test on it."

Russell took the shiny, burnt red graphite fishing rod with sleek black reel in his right hand and fell in love with it. "Wow, does that ever feel nice."

"Dave said you can have it. His thank-you for helping out at the shop, I guess."

"Are you kidding me? He doesn't have to do that. What does a rig like this cost?"

"Retail, over five hundred, Canadian. That's a three hundred and fifty-dollar reel. Go buy a few musky lures, and we'll go down to the dock to try it out."

Between customers, Faith refined Russell's musky casting skills. Russell related his experience with Ralph Mailer on Pelican Lake, when the musky followed his lure.

"Follows are fun," Faith said. "Up here, you'll see a musky nearly every time you go out. Getting one on the line will happen fairly often, too."

It was decided that Russell needed to go all in: tackle box, an assortment of artificial lures, minnow bucket, net, plus all the various accouterments. Faith shopped the racks and bins for Russell, giving a running commentary on each item she selected for him as she rang it up.

Russell assisted Faith serving customers and by noon was hungry for lunch and eager to go fishing again.

Faith read his mind. "Why don't you buy a dozen minnows, go fishing, hit some of the walleye spots I showed you? You could also cast shorelines for bass with your spinning rod. First time you cast for muskies, you might want to wait until someone who knows how to handle a musky at the boat is with you."

"Sounds like good advice," Russell said. "I was told the musky I saw, which was huge, was a little one."

Faith gave him a kiss. "I'm here until seven. You want to come over for cocktails and dinner, say, seven fifteen?"

"Love to. I'm meeting with Jammer at five, not sure how long it'll take. Could be a couple hours."

"What are you cooking up with Jam?"

"I'm going to run up to the Blackdog reservation Friday, help Gribber with a hockey rink project this weekend. Jammer and I have some construction details to work out. My pickup comes in handy."

"OK, the Gribber factor, you have a truck, now it's making sense. Well are you ever a sweetie. Just doing burgers on the grill. Park your boat here, walk up the road behind the shop. Third street is Pine, house on the corner with a big deck in back. Call if you're running late."

Russell had again forgotten his phone. Faith jotted her number on the back of one of Dave Burtnyk's business cards. Russell boated back to the Lodge, ate lunch, grabbed his phone and spinning rod and went fishing. He missed Faith's camaraderie but testing his new fishing skills without supervision was exhilarating. He limited his range to the entrance of Little Sand and hit the spots Faith had shown him. Jigging he caught a walleye larger than he'd caught previously and lost a big bass at the boat.

Just before five, Russell was back in the main channel within site of the Lodge and railway bridge. He drove into the bay across from the Lodge and, raising his motor partway, putted slowly down the center of the slender channel into Hidden Lake. He hoped his meeting with Jammer wouldn't be a waste of time. He'd barely spoken to him since arriving in Kamini, but after observing the quiet, grinning young woodsman at Gribber's veranda and in the pub, Russell wasn't sure all the wiring in Jammer's brain was code. He wished Gribber were coming.

Hidden Lake was a large, nearly round bay. Much of its shoreline consisted of scrubby dogwood, sumac and serviceberry bushes growing tight to the water's edge. Russell spotted the houseboat anchored offshore near one of the lone stretches of granite shoreline. A well-used aluminum fishing boat was tied along one side of the narrow decking surrounding the structure. A small, single-engine floatplane was tied to a floating dock extension on the other. Russell headed for it.

The intricate detail of the houseboat's construction became apparent as Russell approached. Built atop three aluminum pontoons, the A-frame structure exhibited the intricate styling and flair of a full-scale German cuckoo clock. Both sides of the steeply pitched roof curved slightly inward and were shingled with foot-wide half-moons of rough cedar planking. A triangular window at the roof's peak was accented by an ornamental deck railing.

The exterior of the front and one visible side were made of horizontal cedar lap siding, except where interrupted by perfectly balanced medallions of curving, Tudor-style boards nailed over white stucco. Stained a variety of rich brown and gray hues, with light blue door and window trim, the houseboat looked like something inhabited by a wealthy, seafaring Hobbit or the hero of a Brothers Grimm fairy tale.

Jammer Mackay emerged through the front door as Russell docked. The meticulous detail and craftsmanship of the charmingly funky houseboat were even more impressive up close. "Jam, this is amazing. Coolest houseboat I've ever seen."

"Came out pretty good," Jammer said, offering a shy smile.

The interior was just as charming. Windows on all four sides made the space bright and feel large. The simple kitchen at the far end featured a sink, small propane refrigerator and stove, varnished oak cabinets and countertop. A slender, pine-log ladder was mounted to one wall accessing the loft bedroom that extended out over the kitchen and a portion of the living space. A small wood stove sat along the opposite wall, its black metal chimney running up through the sharply angled roof. "You just running on a pump and a hundred pound propane tank?" Russell asked.

"Yup. On the deck in back. Barbecue and shower too. Five-gallon jug under the sink. It don't drain into the river. Just a drop of biodegradable soap when I wash dishes. Dump it way up on shore when it fills up."

Russell scanned the room. "Ten by eighteen?"

Jammer grinned. "Pretty good. Beer?"

"Please."

Jammer gave Russell a beer from the fridge and grabbed an energy drink for himself. The two sat down on a slender, beautifully crafted oak-frame couch facing the stove. On the matching coffee table before them sat a file folder and several rolled-up plans. "So, a couple years ago I sketched out some plans for the rink to get a cost for the grant proposal. Need to ask you some stuff, I guess. I went with half-inch treated plywood to keep the cost down, three-quarter would be better."

"Go with three-quarter," Russell said. "What size are the posts?"

"Four-by-four. In concrete and tied in with the plywood, that's plenty. Posts spaced at eight feet."

"Wait a minute. So is lumber up here in inches and feet, not meters and, well, all that metric stuff?"

"No, we do lumber and building in feet and inches in Canada."

"Why is that?"

"Beats the hell outta me." Jammer took a sip of his energy drink.

"Well, doesn't matter, I guess. So, to make the boards sturdy, what do you see? Three horizontal two-by-fours on the outside of each plywood section, top, bottom and center?"

"That's one way, but if we got the budget, go with vertical studs every twelve inches. Would make the boards rock solid.

Horizontal two-by-fours as a cap railing along the top and as the base along the bottom."

"Great idea." Russell sipped his beer. "Setting the posts will be tricky. They have to rotate slightly in the corners, so the plywood can be screwed on flush."

Jammer raised his eyebrows and gave Russell a broad grin. "You saw that coming? I tried explaining that to Gribber, and he didn't know what I was talking about."

"And the rounded corners in general, what's the length and degree of curvature? Is there a standard in hockey?"

"I looked that up online. There is, and I can figure it out with a tape measure and string."

"Write down spray paint. As we measure, we spray marks every eight feet and spray the curves right into the dirt to help set the posts. Also, we need additional posts in the corners, don't you think? If we're bending plywood, we need something to screw to closer than every eight feet."

"Not if we're building mini-wall sections with studs." Jammer did a quick sketch on a pad and slid it in front of Russell. "Plus, the corners are where players give harder hits. Use carriage bolts with rounded heads instead of screws."

Russell studied the sketch. "Oh, of course. This is perfect. Don't know how we'll do the curving top rails and base boards, though."

"I got that figured out."

"Excellent, surprise me. The four straight sides at ninety degrees will be easy, the 3-4-5 string trick."

"Yup," Jammer said. "I used that for the deck I finished today."

The two men continued to talk through every element of the project, Jammer jotting down items under separate headers on a legal pad. Thirty-five minutes later, they were finished. *Jammer is damn good*, Russell thought.

"I'll clean up the list and get it on my computer tonight," Jammer said. "I use a good lumber yard in Miskwa. They'll have most of it. The rest we can get at Canadian Tire. I'll email the lumber and hardware order to my guy. Going to need a credit card number, or something."

"You got it," Russell said, reaching for his wallet. "Write down my phone number and email, also. Send me the Canadian Tire list tonight, and I'll go there tomorrow."

"Will do. I got a big flatbed trailer. Go and pick up all the lumber Saturday morning, ya think?"

"That will burn quite a bit of time. Will they deliver?"

"Yeah, but it's probably two hundred bucks up to Blackdog."

"Have it delivered. Friday afternoon."

"Got it." Jammer made a note then drained his energy drink. "So, you a builder? I was worried our meeting would be a waste of time, but this was great."

Russell chuckled softly, not at Jammer but at himself. "No, I'm not. Grew up on a farm."

"Oh, OK." Brown eyes dancing, Jammer gave Russell his lop-sided grin. "That explains how come you know so much. Good thing this went so quick. I gotta head up to the English River. You wanna come? Won't take long."

Russell didn't understand what he was being asked. "In your boat?"

"No, my plane. Gotta check out the new fire. I'm a spotter. When there's a fire in the area, one of us with a plane goes up every few days to monitor it. You send a report to the Ministry, get a little check at the end of the year, enough to cover your fuel."

Russell wasn't thrilled by the offer. He wasn't comfortable flying and barely tolerated the many flights he took aboard large commercial aircraft. He became especially antsy when having to board smaller commuter jets. "I think I'll pass. Meeting someone for dinner."

"You sure? Faith won't care. Ever been up in a plane over this country before? Pretty neat. You get an eagle's-eye view."

Russell paused to reconsider. The mesmerizing photo of the Lodge shot from a plane entered his mind. An eagle's-eye view. Then Faith's words—what are vacations for, if not to meet new people, try new things—entered also, as did something else. "Is that the reason you didn't join me for a beer?"

"Yup. No alcohol or hippy lettuce if I'm gonna be flying."

"Then let's go, buddy."

Approaching the plane, Russell suspected the old, bare-aluminum aircraft had been yellow at some point, the faded color still clinging to a few crevices and rivets. Jammer opened the metal door and directed Russell into the small, single backseat. There was evidence it had at one time been padded. He was thrilled to locate a threadbare seatbelt stuffed behind it.

Jammer untied the plane and standing on a pontoon reached in and turned a key on the small dashboard. He pulled the throttle knob out an inch then pushed a small metal plunger rod three times. Priming the engine, Russell noted, same as starting the old tractor on the farm. Jammer left the door open and walked to the front of the plane. "I checked the oil and gas and pumped out the pontoons just before you came. One's kind of a leaker, but only when you take off and land." With one foot on the deck and one on a pontoon, he pulled the nearest of the two propeller blades down until he felt piston compression and spun it. On his third hand bomb, the engine fired and rose to a smooth purr.

The plane immediately started pulling away. Jammer waited for the open door to come past before diving into the narrow pilot's seat. He slammed the door shut three times before it latched. Jammer pulled the joystick mounted to the floor into his crotch and tugged gently on the throttle knob, maneuvering the float rudder controls beneath each foot to angle the plane toward the east side of the bay.

"Been flying long?" Russell asked loudly, so he could be heard above the din of the engine. He already was well past the decision-re-evaluation stage.

"Eight years, maybe," Jammer said over his shoulder. "Bruce Anderson showed me. You know him, owns Great North. Sold me this plane, a 1955 Piper Cub. A real classic." The plane was cruising with moderate speed across the surface of the bay.

"Not, uh, too difficult to master, flying a simple plane such as this, I wouldn't think?" Russell said, his hands clenched tightly in his lap. There were no seat arms to clench.

"Nothin' to it. Just like riding a bike." Jammer paused long enough before extending the analogy that Russell discerned the line forthcoming had just popped into the young bush pilot's head. "Except when you get where you're going, your legs aren't tired!"

Without warning Jammer swerved sharply away from shore, so jostling Russell that his head banged the side of the curving metal wall. The nose of the plane pointed out toward the length of the bay. "Nice calm day, light wind from the west," Jammer said. "Good conditions for your first time. Taking off in big waves, that's when it gets hairy. You only flip one of these things once before you decide you'll never do that again."

"But you, you have a pilot's license?" Russell rubbed the side of his head while attempting to sound calm.

Jammer didn't immediately respond, staring intently at the few gauges before him. He pressed a button on the dashboard and pulled a lever at his feet while intermittently glancing at the view through the windshield. Finally, he turned his head sharply to reply to Russell, a look of mild confusion on his face. "You mean, like, a real one?"

Their conversation was cut short by the deafening roar of the engine as Jammer pulled the throttle wide open. As the plane rapidly gained speed, he pushed the joystick slowly away from him and in a matter of seconds Russell sensed the drag from the pontoons dissipate and that he was flying through the air.

As it broke free of the water, the plane accelerated on a mild ascent that Russell judged would cause them to crash into the approaching trees just below their tips. The plane soared upward more sharply and easily cleared the treetops. All at once the immense panorama of the wilderness surrounding Kamini was before them.

"Wow," Russell said.

"Yeah, amazing, ain't it? I get the same thrill every time."

Russell caught a glimpse of the massive green roof of the Lodge and surrounding golf course fairways flowing off its front before the plane veered to the north. Though seated behind Jammer, side windows curving just past his shoulders afforded Russell a clear view of the astounding scenery below. They flew in silence as the plane climbed to six hundred feet.

In only five minutes they were gliding over an enormous body of water. "Big Sand," Jammer called out. Russell looked down and saw the beautiful sand beach. Ten minutes later, they crossed another large expanse of water stretching east to west nearly as far as the eye could see. "The English River," Jammer announced, swerving slightly while dropping altitude. "The fire is just ahead."

Russell looked around Jammer's head and out the windshield. A dense gray fog covered portions of the forestland. "What caused it?"

"Lighting strike. Causes ninety-nine percent of the forest fires in Ontario. Nature being nature. The average is around seven hundred fires a year, I think I read."

"No people in danger?"

"Naw, no one down there. Bruce has guests at his fishing camp about twenty minutes west, but they're OK. You'd be lucky to fly over a human being between Big Sand and the Arctic Circle." Jammer flew closer to the ground and arced the plane in a wide oval around the burn area. "She's not doing much, just crawling along. Still pretty wet down there. A good hard rain will pretty much knock it out." Jammer leveled the plane, veered right and headed south.

As the plane skimmed gently onto the calm waters of Hidden Lake, Russell was disappointed the flight had been so brief. Jammer circled slowly around the houseboat, cut the engine then hopped out to tie up as the plane coasted alongside the dock. Russell got out, clasped Jammer by the shoulders and thanked him, confiding he wasn't comfortable flying, but the experience had completely erased his fear. It was true. As soon as the plane had cleared the trees that circled Hidden Lake, giving Russell an eagle's view, the peaceful calm he felt repeatedly since the start of his journey had blossomed from within him.

Russell checked the time as he got into his boat. He'd sold bait, gone fishing, worked out the plan for the hockey rink, been up to the English River and back, and still wouldn't be late for dinner.

Chapter 30

Russell and Faith relaxed after dinner with wine and conversation on her deck. They spent the night in Faith's cozy double bed, Russell rising quietly at five to witness the sunrise from the bait shop dock. Finishing up the breakfast dishes, he invited Faith to accompany him to Canadian Tire but she demurred, telling him that going to Miskwa was something one did only if unavoidable. Russell understood.

Friday morning broke gloomy, though the dark low clouds were predicted to give way to clear skies by afternoon. The clouds hid the sunrise and cast the river steely gray but from his granite perch, observing with eyes closed, the wilderness welcomed Russell all the same. An hour later he walked back to his cottage, kissed a drowsy Faith goodbye and drove to Morning Wood.

Parked next to Ramble was a Chevy Tahoe bearing the logo of the Ontario Ministry of Natural Resources and Forestry. Behind it was a large GMC pickup, its bed rammed with tools. Russell parked behind Ramble. He was greeted in the kitchen by Jammer and Gribber.

"Just serving up," Gribber said. He looked tired. He slid three plates of bacon, scrambled eggs and toast onto the kitchen table. Russell noticed a surfeit of bacon in the frying pan and more scrambled eggs in a bowl.

"We should have everything we need," Jammer said to Russell. "Gang Green gave us his pickup. Jimmy Douglas gave us a bunch of tools I went over and got last night."

"The paint and everything else is in the back of mine," Russell said. "What about the Ministry? I'm hoping the Tahoe and its convivial driver are part of the convoy to Blackdog?"

Gribber gave Russell a dirty look. "Take it easy on me, Pirate. I didn't get much sleep last night." He didn't look happy about it. The three ate in relative silence. Russell heard a clunk in the plumbing as the bathroom shower was turned off, followed by footsteps padding quickly across the center fireplace room to the bedroom. No one spoke of it.

They ate quickly. Russell and Jammer went outside followed by Gribber a minute later. Gribber hopped into the GMC pickup, and Russell was pleased when Jammer opted for the passenger seat of his F250. They talked about flying and fishing the entire fifty-minute drive north to the Blackdog Indian Reservation, Jammer regaling Russell with tales of ice fishing for lake trout in the uninhabited lakes surrounding Kamini. "Come up in winter," he said. "I'll take you."

The road crossed a bridge at the narrow waist of a large lake, and the two trucks entered the reservation. They drove past dozens of manufactured homes and side streets then arrived at a large and architecturally impressive school. Gribber led the way along a service road to the grassy field behind it. A group of Ojibwe teens were playing basketball on an asphalt court, circled by kids of varying ages. In the center of the field was the hockey rink, the boards surrounding it leaning or fully collapsed. At one end lay a large stack of new four-by-four posts and a Bobcat with bucket beside it.

As the three men exited the vehicles, the group from the basketball court walked over. "Boozhoo!" Gribber called to them. "Gimiigwechiwininim. Niminwendaan omaa aayaayeg." (Hello! I'm so glad to see you all. Thank you for being here.)

Russell had never heard the Ojibwe language spoken. It was blunt, beautiful and ancient-sounding, like Latin.

The group of youngsters approached smiling. Three children in the group, two girls and a round-faced, cherubic boy, ran up to Jammer. "Can we help you, Uncle Daryl?" the boy said. Jammer knelt on one knee and gave the boy a high-five.

"You sure can, Oscar, I need all the help I can get," he said, grinning at the boy. "You let us get unloaded, then you're going to have fun. You can help us knock stuff apart and break it."

With the group of Ojibwe youth assisting, the trucks were unloaded in minutes.

"How do you think we should do this?" Jammer asked Russell.

"I think you should be in charge," Russell said. "Tell us what to do."

Jammer divided the volunteers into small groups, each led by an older teen, and assigned each group a sledgehammer, crowbar and shovel. Removal of the old posts and boards was swift, the smaller children gleefully attacking their task of dragging the rotted posts and splintered lumber to a large burn pile at the edge of the field.

While Jammer and Gribber ran extension cords, set up sawhorses and began cutting the posts, Russell fired up the Bobcat and deftly graded the rink area. He ran swiftly in reverse with the bucket down, smoothing out the small humps in the ground and skimming off the heavy weed growth. Russell made short work of it, having done this many times when building a barn or new shed with his father on the farm.

Jammer and Russell began laying out the rink, hammering wood stakes into the ground and running Mason's string to outline the four sides. As soon as they defined the first posthole with a spray paint circle one of the teens began digging it. While Russell measured and painted more holes along the straight sides, Jammer measured and painted in the four curving corners. Posts were being set in concrete before noon.

When told lunch was ready, Gribber gave a whistle and led the crew into the school. It was a striking, newer building featuring a multi-level, gracefully curved design.

"Beautiful building," Russell said to Gribber as they walked a bright, locker-lined corridor toward the cafeteria.

"Just ten years old. The government did a nice job on this one, finally. It was badly overdue. The old school wasn't in as rough shape as the hockey rink, but it was close. So, you just keep screaming. Some Canadians gripe about the government supporting the indigenous populations like this, but very few on the reservation have any money beyond their welfare checks. Unemployment runs eighty percent. We're not a bunch of derelicts. People want to work, but where are the jobs for five hundred adults living up here on a reservation in the middle of the bush? Building tepees, living off the land, going back in time four hundred years? That beaver has left the bay."

"Eighty percent, good god," Russell said. "What's it going to take?"

"Well, it starts with schools like this, and great teachers, and the young generation you see now. In addition to regular curricula, we want these to kids learn to speak some Ojibwe, properly learn their heritage, customs and values. Then they need to get the hell off the reservations and go to work, or to college or trade schools, and contribute to society as proud Ojibwe, or Cree, Chippewa, Algonquin. Work across the province, develop their skills, maybe come back and start a business on their reservation. My people have a lot to offer Canada. But for Pete's sake, acknowledge the hole dug for us."

Russell grabbed a tray, went through the lunch line, and sat down with Jammer and Gribber at a table of Ojibwe youth, including the solidly built Robert Cameron, to whom Jammer had delegated crew leader status at the start of the day. "Wanted to thank you for the money for the rink," Cameron said to Russell. "It's really cool of you."

"Robert's one of the star hockey players in the league," Gribber said. "He's only fifteen but is a cinch to make Juniors next year."

Russell didn't know his gift had been publicized. "You're very welcome, Robert, it just seemed like … a good thing to do."

"My dad asked me to pass along his gratitude and thanks to you also," Robert added. "He's at a conference in Ottawa and is very sorry he can't meet you in person."

"His dad's the Chief," Gribber said.

Work on the new hockey rink continued at a rapid pace after lunch. The lumber delivery arrived and was swiftly unloaded. Russell and Gribber began cutting two-by-fours while Jammer supervised the youth in building the framed-and-studded plywood sections. By late afternoon, half the new boards were in place.

"This is outstanding," Gribber said, surveying the scene while he and the teen leaders packed up the tools. He looked at Russell. "I took Sunday off thinking Jammer and I would need the whole weekend just to set the posts."

"You didn't organize the volunteer crew?" Russell said.

"Nope. They organized themselves. They're just so damned excited about the new rink. So, Sunday morning, my friend, I'm going to pry you away from Ms. Pearson—I'll knock and close my eyes—and take you musky fishing. I heard Dave gave you a new rod. Time to see if you can snag a musky."

Russell chuckled, realizing that in Kamini, no doubt everyone knew everything about anything going on around town. "I'll clear my calendar."

"You guys take off," Gribber said to Russell and Jammer. "You can leave the other truck. I'm spending the night on the rez. I need a little 'me' time."

The conversation between Russell and Jammer focused solely on musky fishing during their drive back to Kamini. Jammer's boat was at Morning Wood, and as they pulled up they saw that the Ministry Tahoe was parked behind Ramble. Officer White had no doubt left to continue her investigation, then returned.

"Hoo, boy," Jammer said as he opened the passenger door. "Grib asked me to cook Lydia dinner. She's pretty much moved in. Then he said I should take her for a canoe ride, but I hope he was joking." The two agreed to meet at Russell's truck at the Lodge at seven in the morning.

Russell drove to his cottage, showered, and called Faith. They opted to meet for dinner in the casual Holst Point dining room. After dinner they went next door to the pub for a few hours before heading to Russell's cottage.

The next morning, following his meditation and breakfast, Russell walked to his truck and was surprised to see Jammer and

Annie Chase sitting on the open tailgate, chatting and drinking coffee.

"Good morning, Russell," Annie said brightly. She was dressed in jeans, work boots and flannel shirt, a well-worn leather tool belt around her waist. Most of her lavish hair was piled beneath a weathered Kamini Lodge fishing cap.

"Well good morning to you, too. You on crew with us today?"

"Absolutely. My day off. Everyone in town is talking about your amazing donation to the reservation. Thought I'd better come up and make sure you boys aren't building a square hockey rink."

"Annie's an ace builder," Jammer said. "You should see her outhouse."

Jammer hopped into the back seat while Annie climbed into the front. The three chatted nearly nonstop on their way to Blackdog, Annie and Jammer filling in Russell on over a hundred years of Kamini history. Despite having Annie seated beside him, Russell breathed, spoke and laughed without discomfort.

Russell parked alongside the pile of remaining building materials, and the three of them helped Gribber set up the work area. Gribber appeared well rested and his usual jovial self. The volunteer crew had grown, parents and other adults from the reservation introducing themselves and ready to lend a hand. Under Jammer's direction the brisk work on the hockey rink resumed. Annie and Russell worked with the volunteer crews building the remaining plywood sections. Gribber, Jammer and their crew carried a stack of two-by-sixteen planks into the school. An hour later they walked out with the curving top rails and base boards for the curved corners.

"Now I get it," Russell said. "The school has a wood shop."

"Wood, metal and leather," Gribber said. "A nice one. With a big industrial jigsaw." The final, curving sections of new boards were constructed and bolted to the posts. They fit perfectly.

One of the Ojibwe youth had been shooting photos for the reservation's website since the start of the project. He asked Russell, Gribber, Annie and Jammer to pose for a shot. They sat atop the boards while the young photographer took several photos, then more with all the youth volunteers fanned out around them, standing and kneeling.

Six twelve-foot galvanized steel pipes and two large rolls of chain link fencing were all that remained to be installed. "Been looking at that since we unloaded it," Gribber said. "Is that what I think it is?"

"Yup," Jammer said. "Pirate's idea. I told him the old rink didn't have them and none of the others did, but he had me order it anyway."

"I've been to enough Blackhawks games to know that most pucks leaving the rink fly out around the goal," Russell said.

"OK gang," Jammer called out to the volunteers, "grab the pipes and carry three of them to each end of the rink."

Two of the youngest teens picked up the first long pipe, but in their haste to start walking, misjudged its length. As they turned, one end struck the rear side panel of Russell's truck with a loud thump, leaving a dent and six-inch gash in the paint. The boys put down the pipe and stood paralyzed with alarm as everyone turned to look at Russell.

"We're sorry," one of the boys said softly. He stared at the ground and closed his eyes.

"Hey, it's OK," Russell said. He put a hand on the boy's shoulder. "It's just a truck. They get dinged up when you do real truck stuff with them. We wouldn't be almost finished without all of you. Just be careful now, walk slow while you carry that thing." Russell gave the boy a light pat on the bottom.

Holes were dug, concrete was mixed, and by four o'clock the completed rink featured twenty feet of ten-foot-high chain link fence rising up behind the boards at each end.

"Who's painted before?" Annie asked the students. Six raised their hands, including Emma, a tall and gregarious member of the group and goalie for the girl's team. Cans of white paint were opened and stirred. Annie put Emma in charge of the five other painters and showed them how to load a roller with paint, paint a large "W" on a four-foot section of the plywood, then paint the entire section. "You should be able to finish the first coat before supper," Annie said to the group, "then close up the paint and clean the rollers. Emma, the forecast is for rain late tomorrow afternoon, so watch the weather. The next nice spell, call your crew and give the boards a second coat."

Russell watched the painting of the boards with his back to the school, unaware that a crowd of people was approaching him from behind. When the painters put down their rollers and started walking with Annie toward him, he sensed something was afoot. He felt a tap on his shoulder and turned to see Gribber and the large group of Ojibwe students and adults standing before him. Two older teenage girls he didn't recognize were front and center, one holding a dark blue cardboard box. On it was the regal logo of the Hudson's Bay Corporation.

The young woman with the box stepped forward and presented it to him. "Mr. Dean, we wanted to give you a present from all of us, to thank you for the new hockey rink."

Russell hadn't yet set foot in the Hudson's Bay store in Kamini, but he knew from talking with Gang Green in the pub that the store sold dry goods, including all manner of clothing as well as the iconic, striped Hudson's Bay blankets. He smiled as a wave of gratitude swept over him. Perhaps they'd bought him a blanket, or shirt.

Russell lifted the lid on the box and swept away the tissue paper folded over its contents. He froze as he stared at the two most beautiful pieces of art he had ever seen. The pair of calf-high buckskin moccasins were brilliantly adorned with colorful beadwork, fringe and embroidered floral inlays of velvety fabric. Stunned, Russell set the box on the ground and marveled as he lifted a moccasin full length in each hand. "I'm guessing they don't sell these at the Bay in Kamini," he said to Gribber, who stood beside the two teens.

"Oh, no one sells those anywhere in the world. At least not until Emily and Star graduate next year and open up a store in

Miskwa. They're the two best native clothiers on the reservation, probably in the province, along with Star's mom. But when it comes to moccasins, they've taken it to a whole new level."

Oscar, who unlike the rest of the younger children had hung around both days to help in any way he could, piped up. "I followed you around yesterday morning until you left a big footprint in the dirt. That was my 'signment. I showed it to Robert, and he measured it."

Emily smiled. "They should fit you perfectly," she said.

"So, you made these in two days?" Russell said, blinking his eyes.

"It was good training for rush orders," Star said. "We didn't get much sleep last night."

Despite his rapid blinking, Russell's eyesight became so blurry he couldn't see. He didn't know the last time he cried. He couldn't remember because he'd been so young. As he slumped forward and bowed his head before the crowd, the tears poured out in such a torrent that he raised the magnificent moccasins up and away from his body so he wouldn't get them wet.

Chapter 31

Annie Chase was the first to comfort Russell, gently taking the moccasins from him, folding them carefully and returning them to the box. She hugged him close without speaking then Emily, Star and Gribber did the same. As Russell walked through the parting crowd toward his truck, he shook and slapped hands with the young volunteer crew. Each adult came forward to thank him.

Gribber gave Russell a handful of paper towels so he could dry his face. "You OK to drive?"

"Oh, I'll be fine," Russell said, smiling. "I don't think I've ever felt this good."

"I'll ride shotgun with you," Annie said.

Gribber and Jammer hopped into the GMC and led the way back to Kamini. Russell and Annie drove with the windows down, the fresh, pungent northern air swirling through the cab. As they crossed the bridge over the lake bordering the reservation, Annie studied the water then turned to Russell. "Well, you've packed quite a lot into your vacation so far. Your final days I suppose you'll want to relax. You've certainly earned it."

Russell was elated Annie chose to ride in his truck and that they were alone, a situation for which he was well prepared. "I'd like to tell you something," he said. "That night at Karpenko's landing, when I saw you for the first time. You were walking down the dock, then bent over, picked up my torch, and entered into the light. I saw your face and fell instantly, totally, impeccably, um …" Russell was grinning sheepishly. He looked quickly at Annie, who cocked her head with raised eyebrows.

"Go on," she said, a look of cautious bemusement on her face.

"… horrifically in lust with you. Lightning bolt to the gonads, May Day, May Day, all hands on deck. I thought my heart might explode. Damn near passed out."

Annie shrieked a laugh then sat bolt upright and stared straight ahead. She jerked her head to look at Russell, wanting to be certain she was making the right read. "Thank you for sharing. You should have said something. We have a fine hospital in Miskwa."

"Oh, hey, I'm better now, really," Russell said with a laugh. "But it was painful, let me tell you. Debilitating. I couldn't get you out of my mind."

"Well, I hope you didn't fantasize about me in private."

"Oh, God no. Couldn't do that. You were Zelda, Imperial Queen of the Canadian, I don't know, Queen of the Canadian Amazon."

"Oh good, a gentleman."

Both were silent for a second before erupting into laughter. His head lowered as it bobbed up and down, Russell drove onto the edge of the gravel road before swerving the truck back into the lane.

"Hey, watch the road there, Pirate. I said we have a hospital, but it's nearly two hours away."

"And what is it with everyone calling me Pirate? I've been meaning to ask someone."

"Well, if you don't know, I'm not going to tell you. Ask Gribber."

"Gribber …" Russell's thoughts raced back to their initial meeting. "Oh, of course, the eye patch. I'd completely forgotten. Duh."

"Not only that, he painted it black. You made a striking figure, this tall, chisel-chinned, broad-shouldered Dudley Do-Right with torn clothing, twigs in his hair and an enormous black patch over one eye. Look at it as an achievement. Not everyone in Kamini gets a nickname, and you got one in record time."

This time as they convulsed Russell kept his eyes on the road.

"So anyway," Russell said, wiping a tear from his eye, "if you'll indulge me further, I finally looked it up online. Did a search for 'love at first sight' but that led me to the good stuff, Cupid's Arrow, quotes from Socrates, 'the thunderbolt,' which is the Italians' name for it. Then articles referencing a lot of scientific studies. Turns out it's all chemicals in the brain." He looked at Annie. "Really, really *nice* chemicals."

"Dopamine, I'm sure, would be one."

"Yes, dopamine, serotonins, also epinephrine, that one's not so much fun. Kicks up your blood pressure and makes your heart race. All these chemicals and hormones flood your body from different areas of the brain. The glands in your hands open wide and your palms begin to sweat."

"Ooh, that's sexy. You know, I read something about it once, back in my *Cosmo*-reading days. As I recall, it can happen to anyone, seeing anyone, not just seeing a person who, I don't know, a majority of people would consider attractive."

"Yes, true. But what finally made me curious enough to research it was meeting Faith. Because I'm going to be honest with you, and you'll no doubt find this a huge relief … once I started seeing Faith, well, sorry darling, but I never gave you another thought."

Annie exploded with laughter. "Why that little hussy! Oh well, it's nothing new. I never stand a chance with men against Faith. She has an eighteen-foot G3."

"Yeah, that's an uphill battle. Anyway, I just felt this need to tell you. I hope you'll keep my little ephemeral lust fest private, if that's not asking too much. I know you two are best friends, and I'm sure Faith has filled you in about us."

"Oh, that you guys are seeing each other, everyone in town knows that. You just told me something in private, and I'll certainly honor your request. But also know, Faith didn't regale me with any of the spicy details about the two of you. But hey, we're girlfriends. I know she took you up to Big Sand to ink the deal."

"Oh, let me tell you, she crossed t's and dotted i's I never knew I had."

They shared another prolonged laughing spell.

"Now we just need to get Gribber sorted out," Annie said, her turn to wipe her eyes from laughing. "He's bitten off more than he can chew, or maybe it's a case of what he's bitten off chewing back. I'm worried about him."

"Yeah, what's going on? Officer White?"

"Yes, Lydia. He claims she jumped *his* bones, but you have to know Gribber like I know Gribber. As soon as they had sex, she took it as an invitation to move in with him. Unpacked all her clothes in the guest room. Apparently, she's not much in the kitchen. Gribber cooks for her constantly, walleye, ham, pork loins, a half-pound of bacon for breakfast. You'd think the poor girl had never consumed any protein in her life. She's eating him out of house and home."

"He did seem a little off when I was over there yesterday morning."

"He hid out on the rez last night just to take a break from her. Called me for about the fifth time asking what he should do. I told him he'd made his bed, etcetera. And Lydia may be mellowing, who knows. She interviewed Lou LeBlanc about the poaching and didn't give him any crap about the smoking in the pub. Gribber says she's finished her investigation, so I guess that means she heads back to Thunder Bay soon, maybe even tomorrow. Gribber's hoping tonight is their tender goodbye. You've seen Lydia. He says the sex is great, oops."

Russell was curious about Gribber and Annie's relationship but felt no right or compulsion to learn more than Annie was comfortable sharing. "You've obviously known Gribber a long time."

"Eleven years, since a few days after I arrived. He's impossible for a woman not to fall in love with. You talk about the thunderbolt. I may have hollered only one May Day, but it certainly struck me the first time I saw him. He's brilliant, and very kind, very loving. I wasn't terribly interested in men when I came to Kamini. I don't mean sexually, but I was sick of being hit on. We were friends for a few months, then I dove in. We were together for just over two years. I was living at Faith's for most of it, then I bought my cottage. He helped me fix it up and winterize it."

"Sounds like Gribber."

"Absolutely. He'll do anything for anybody." Annie paused before she spoke again, and for the first time Russell detected a note of melancholy in her voice. "But I guess sometimes you don't marry the person you fall in love with. Sometimes you love a person just as a friend." She turned her head away and looked out the open window.

"Well, he's certainly gone out of his way to help me," Russell said. "He's taking me musky fishing tomorrow."

Turning back, Annie's tone resumed its usual upbeat nature. "Oh, he adores you. And why not? You're a good man."

Russell was caught off guard by her unexpected appraisal. "I doubt you thought that after you hung up the phone following our discussion about my reservation at the Lodge."

"Oh, I just figured you were upset about being delayed."

"Please, be honest with me." Russell looked at Annie. "Tell me what you really thought."

Annie gave a wry smile. "Alright, I thought you were an asshole. In this business, you do run into them. And I thought OK, Mr. Dean is one of those guests where we want to ensure things go smoothly."

"You've asked me not to, but I again want to apologize, not only for me but on behalf of all Americans."

"Oh please, a huge majority of Yanks who stay with us are just the nicest people. Nationality doesn't have anything to do with it. The jerks, they're liable to come from any country, including Canada. Canadians can be the worst. When they get upset about something it's all very passive-aggressive. At least with Americans, and Germans, if they don't like something, they give you clean, pure shit right up front."

"Damn straight!" Russell said with a quick pound of the steering wheel. "You know where you stand!"

Both laughed then drove awhile in silence, Russell contemplating the words Annie had spoken, her offhand opinion that he was a good man.

As Pistol Lake came into view, the road from Blackdog intersected the Kamini road. Gribber and Jammer were long gone ahead of them, Russell choosing not to match Gribber's barreling speed. He pulled up to the stop sign and waited for a vehicle headed from Miskwa toward Kamini to pass. In silence, he and Annie observed Lydia White drive by in the Tahoe, pulling a large aluminum boat with full windshield, steering wheel and beefy Evinrude outboard. On the side of the boat was the badge-like logo of the Ontario Ministry of Natural Resources and Forestry.

"Aha," Annie said. "The plot thickens. It appears our Officer White is going to stay awhile and check fishing licenses. Which is a good thing. I don't recall the last time the Ministry monitored the fishing up here." She pulled out her phone. "I have to text Gribber. He'll be elated."

Once in town, Annie directed Russell down the narrow road between the Post Office and Hudson's Bay store leading to the mainland cottages on Jackfish Bay. They passed several driveways as the bay came into view then turned down one to Annie's cottage. "You and Faith want to come over for dinner?" she asked. "I can give her a call right now. Maybe chicken breasts and peppers on the grill. If you come, remember, Faith always brings some fantastic dessert."

"Would love nothing more."

Annie called Faith and dinner was set for seven. "Faith says she'll pick you up at the Lodge."

Back at his cottage, Russell set the box on the table in the front room, sat down on the couch and tried on his new moccasins. They indeed fit perfectly, the tall, elaborately paneled and embroidered upper leggings tying firmly over his jeans just below the knee. He stretched out his legs and gazed in awe of their primal, majestic beauty. Leaning back and looking out at the river, he felt better than ever in his life, except for several nagging thoughts left over from his conversation with Annie.

Confessing to his volcanic reaction after seeing her for the first time was a relief. But he had not shared everything about the thunderbolt he'd researched online, namely, its psychological causes. A person could immediately be attracted to another when the object of desire resembled someone the viewer loved in the past. More often, the person being severely smitten had suffered a loss of love and felt desperately, hopelessly alone.

Nor did he tell Annie that reading about the topic, it was with a pulse-jarring jolt he remembered something he had somehow forgotten, stuffed away or painted over, for whatever terrible, egotistical reasons. The thunderbolt on the landing at Pistol Lake was not the first ever to strike him. The first time he saw a woman and was helplessly overcome by tidal waves of chemicals unleashed by the brain was eleven years ago, in Minneapolis, when at the corporate offices of Life Time Fitness he was introduced to Cheryl.

The articles on the topic referencing studies made clear something else. Occasionally, love at first sight signaled love.

Chapter 32

As he sat on the stone ledge meditating to the Sunday sunrise, Russell again felt like an updated version of himself from the day before. He discarded the notion that he was there as a person, a body and mind separate from the wilderness swirling around him. He was not separate from anything, not the sun, water and wind, the mosses, grasses and trees, not even the warming granite shore formed billions of years ago by some ever-present, ongoing principle of creation.

He was at one with it.

Russell and Faith had spent a delightful evening at Annie's, feasting on quite a bit more than grilled chicken and peppers. After dinner the two women had taught him to play cribbage, a seductive card and board game that, while being beaten repeatedly by either Faith or Annie, he realized involved far more skill than the relatively simple rules implied. He finally achieved his first victory playing Annie after she was dealt one poor hand after another while Faith advised him on his choice of the two cards to place in the crib.

Faith was still in bed when Russell returned to the cottage from his meditation and a long, cleansing swim in the cool Ontario water. She wished him luck and rolled over to resume her sleep. He changed and walked down to the Lodge docks carrying his new tackle box and splendid musky rod.

Just after six-thirty, Gribber pulled up in his boat. "Sit your butt down and let's see what you have for musky lures."

Russell opened his tackle box and removed his four musky lures for Gribber's appraisal.

"A big Mepps Musky Killer," Gribber said. "Silver blade, good for sunny days later in summer when the water isn't as clear. A big plastic rattler, theory is the little steel balls inside mimic the vibrations made by schools of scared shitless baitfish because fish can sense distress vibrations. But this is interesting—muskies can't detect vibrations above a thousand hertz and most of the lures have been tested much higher. They catch fish, but I don't find them any better than non-rattlers. Two big Suicks, one orange and chartreuse and one painted to resemble the golden scales of a walleye. Put that one on. In clear water and sun, start with a lure that resembles the native baitfish."

Russell clipped the twelve-inch-long, wood-bodied lure to the steel leader at the end of his line. Gribber handed him a long-nose pliers. "Now bend down the barbs."

"Easier to remove the hook," Russell said.

"Exactly. Any lure without a solid body, just a big, barbed treble hook with a blade and some hair, like that Musky Killer, a big musky can inhale it. The lure is aptly named. It can get hooked way down in the throat or the fish slashes at it and hooks itself in the gills. You never want to be performing surgery on a musky, or big snake for that matter. Get it to the boat, get the hooks out, tape the length if it's big, and wish it bon voyage. Shoot a picture of your first and biggest."

"Man, there's a lot to this."

"There's a lot to life," Gribber said as he pulled away from the dock. He barely brought the boat to plane before stopping at the first casting spot, a small rock outcropping only forty yards off the tip of the Lodge peninsula.

"See if the ghost of Jingles is home," Gribber said.

"I'm afraid to ask."

"Ross McDonald, one of the great Kamini guides, hooked her in the seventies. Fifty-seven inches. The Canadian record until 1988, when a guy caught a fifty-eight incher in Georgian Bay on Lake Huron. Jingles is long gone but muskies still like this rock. Ross still lives in town. He's my partner every year for the musky tournament."

"Pro tournament?"

"No, local event, very informal, end of August. Wraps up with a banquet at Great North and bragging rights. The big pro tournament is the CanAm Walleye Tour. Three years ago, it added a stop in Kamini, coming up later in June. It's not one of the major stops but it'll attract thirty-some pros. Around a hundred thousand in total payouts. Jammer and I compete in it every year."

"How have you done?"

"We won it the first two years and finished second last year."

"Jeez, Grib, what happened to you last year?"

Gribber didn't respond.

They continued casting for muskies along weed beds and shorelines in the entrance to Little Sand. In Pistol Lake Narrows, Gribber had the first follow, a big musky that cruised like a torpedo behind his lure all the way to the boat but sat inert while Gribber dipped the tip of his rod six inches into the water and paraded the lure in front of the unexcitable fish by weaving it in a figure eight pattern. After a few seconds of observation, the musky turned and swam away.

"So that's the famous figure eight move," Russell said. "I've heard tell of it."

"You should probably do it at the end of every cast. In fact, why don't you, to get the hang of it? Can entice a strike after a follow. Sometimes a musky will follow deeper than you can see and after a figure eight surprise you by coming straight up to strike."

The two men spoke infrequently as they cruised deeper into Little Sand, Russell sensing that Gribber, like himself, was most content embracing in silence the tranquility the wilderness so effortlessly imparted.

Until Gribber caught the first musky.

"There's one," Gribber said with a grunt as he gave a tremendous jerk of his rod to set the hook. "Saw a flash of it. Decent." With his rod bending except when he lowered it to reclaim line to the reel, Gribber moved to the center of the boat while directing Russell to the stern. He brought the musky to the boat far quicker than Russell expected. "Hooked deeper than I like. Pay attention."

Sweeping his rod, Gribber brought the fish parallel to the boat so
its head was to the bow and tail to the stern. He kneeled, reached
over the gunwale, placed his wide-open left hand on the musky's
body just behind the head and held it snug to the side of the boat.
He put down the rod and grabbed the long-nose pliers from his
back pocket. "Get your left hand and forearm on her near the rear
dorsal fins and pin her body and tail against the boat."

"You're not going to net it?" Russell asked as he kneeled beside Gribber. Gribber wasn't even attempting to lift the large fish
from the water.

"No." With a few deft moves, Gribber extracted the lure. "Let
go and hand me the tape by the depth finder."

Gribber held the end of the tape at the tip of the musky's tail
while extending it to its snout. As he stared at the tape, the big
fish began gently weaving its tail and swimming toward the bow
of the boat. "Forty seven inches, rounding down a half. Watch her
go." The immense, dark silvery fish, its long body the diameter of
a man's thigh, swam faster past the bow then disappeared into the
depths.

"Holy smokes," Russell said. "That was worth the price of
admission."

Gribber grinned broadly as his eyes danced. "Get a musky to
the boat as quick as possible so it doesn't expend all its energy.
Keep it in the water. Get the hooks out, tape it if it lets you, then
say goodbye. The net is for extenuating circumstances. Now it's
your turn. Gotta get you at least a follow." Gribber studied the
sky. The sunny day was rapidly turning cloudy. "Put on that other
Suick, the brightly painted one." Russell changed lures and with
the pliers began bending down the barbs while Gribber drove
into a large bay.

Casting the next spot, a fish hit Russell's lure only seconds
after it splashed into the water. Both men could tell it was small
as he reeled it in, and Russell brought the fish quickly to the boat.
The fish had a dark back and dull white spotting on its grayish-
green sides. "Snake," he said.

"Correct. Twenty-two inches, maybe. Aggressive little guy, hitting a big Suick, I'll give him that." Gribber took out his pliers as the northern pike floated nearly motionless at the surface. "Only hooked by the rear treble. Swing it alongside for me."

Having rested briefly from fighting on its way to the boat, the northern attempted one final escape, slashing its tail to dive a foot deeper before its progress was halted by Russell's stiff new rod. Russell, for the first time, was disappointed by a fish he'd caught. Stupid snake. Wasting my time and Gribber's.

The musky emerged up through the dark water like a translucent vision. Opening wide its enormous mouth, it struck the northern dead center from beneath, clamping its jaws shut with such ferocity Russell thought it bit the smaller fish in half. The drag on Russell's reel gave a high-pitched shriek as the musky slashed its head violently, curled its body then dove with its prey toward bottom. Its broad crimson tail waved goodbye as in a blink it disappeared from sight.

Neither man spoke, Russell because he couldn't believe what he just saw and Gribber because he'd seen it dozens of times before. A struggling fish on the hook was perhaps the most enticing musky bait of all, sending distress vibrations through the water that attracted large predator fish. "Stick the end of the handle into your belly and start cranking," Gribber said. "Get her back up here as fast as you can."

The musky was having none of it.

"Tighten your drag," Gribber said.

Russell turned the star-shaped dial at the base of his reel one full rotation. By lifting the rod tip upward with all his might while the end of the rod handle dug painfully into his stomach, Russell finally was able to lift the huge fish from the bottom, reeling in the slack each time he managed to coerce it a few feet closer to the surface. Twice the musky made strong, sideways runs off the bow.

With the relatively puny northern clenched sideways in its mouth, the musky resembled a hammerhead shark as Russell finally brought it to the surface. Stepping slowly toward the bow he managed to drag the silvery, log-like monster parallel to the boat.

"You want a picture with it?" Gribber asked.

"Maybe practice that on the next one," Russell said. His stomach and both hands throbbed.

Gribber leaned down and with one stern jerk of the pliers ripped the treble hook from the northern pike's mouth.

"No need to be gentle," he said. "The snake is already dead."

Gribber stepped to retrieve the tape measure but the musky began cruising slowly forward, its mouth still clamped tight around the northern. It arced downward and swimming faster waved goodbye with its huge tail for a second time as the two men watched. "Say goodbye, sweetheart," Gribber said.

"Goodbye, sweetheart."

Both men sat down. "Heading to the bottom to finish its lunch," Gribber said, "and wonder what the hell that was all about. You did a good job with her. Mine was forty-seven inches, how big do you think that one was?"

"A bit bigger."

"I'm saying fifty-two. Not being generous in the least. Congratulations. That's the Holy Grail, a fifty-two inch musky. Some people come up here for years trying to get their fifty-two-incher."

"So it counts?"

"Of course it counts. You got it to the boat and I got it off. Sorry I couldn't tape it. Next time." Gribber studied the low, dark clouds looming closer from the northwest. "Storm coming in. Looks big. Bet I forgot to mention rain suits. Enough fun for one day."

The wind picked up. Russell spotted rolling whitecaps ahead as they veered into the main channel and aimed for the Lodge. The bow of the boat started hammering up and down as Gribber only slightly reduced speed. Approaching the Lodge they noticed a large boat towing another beneath the railway bridge. A smaller aluminum boat was cruising slowly bedside the boat being towed. Gribber headed past the Lodge and caught up with the boats.

Russell could see it was Jammer driving alongside the boat being towed. Lydia White sat in the driver's seat of the large boat doing the towing, her Ministry hat pulled down low on her head against the wind. The long, low, bright red fiberglass craft being towed, its sleek, black Mercury engine tilted out of the water, was the Illinois boat that a week earlier raced so menacingly through Town Bay before pulling up to the bait shop.

Jammer had spotted the Ministry boat towing another while casting for muskies near the entrance to Roughrock, and after a quick conversation with Lydia provided escort. Gribber pulled alongside the Illinois boat so it had escorts on both sides. Lydia looked back to check on the boat she was towing, spotted Gribber and gave him a nod. Gribber nodded and gave a salute back.

"Engine trouble, you think?" Russell shouted to Gribber.

"Don't think so," he replied with a puzzled look. "The passengers in the boat look a little … subdued."

The man in the rear contour seat closest to Gribber's boat was leaning back and staring dully ahead with one arm on the gunwale. The man in the seat on the other side, the one who had remarked on the high price of lures, was leaning slightly forward with both hands behind his back. Russell couldn't see much of Richie, who was sitting bent over on the floor of the boat. Only his head was visible. He was not wearing his Cubs baseball cap.

The entourage entered Town Bay and headed toward the marina docks. A black and white OPP van was parked next to the ramp. Two police officers walked briskly toward Lydia's boat as she pulled up. One helped Lydia tie up while the other began untying the tow rope and pulling the red boat to the dock. Gribber and Jammer parked their boats and with Russell got out.

When the red boat was tied, Lydia walked to it and addressed the two policemen in a firm voice. "Mathew Lebowski," she said, pointing to the man with his arm on the gunwale, "charged with possession of walleye outside size and limit restrictions." She pointed to the other seated man, his hands bound tightly behind his back with the stern rope. "Andrew Mason, charged with possession of walleye outside size and limit restrictions and resisting arrest." She turned and pointed to Richie, who sat doubled over on the floor of the boat with his hands handcuffed behind his back. A red welt was developing under one eye. "Richard Wilkins, charged with possession of walleye outside size and limit restrictions, resisting arrest, and assaulting an officer of the Ministry of Natural Resources and Forestry."

"Assaulting an officer?" Richie said, whining. "You kicked me in the balls!"

Richie didn't mention being struck in the face. On his knees with his eyes closed after being kicked in the groin, he never saw what Lydia hit him with. She had hit him on the cheek just below the eye socket with a short overhand right.

"Mr. Wilkins said some very naughty things to me after I asked to inspect the live well and boarded his boat," Lydia said to the officers. They were having difficulty stifling smiles as they stood in awe of the female Ministry Officer and the trio of serious law offenders she had collared single-handedly. "Then he grabbed me around the chest from behind and attempted to stop me in the performance of my duties." She turned to look at Richie. "Isn't that right, chief?"

Richie again found himself at a loss for words.

The three law officers huddled away from the boat and in hushed voices discussed how to proceed. "Do you want to follow us back to Miskwa to file the charges?" one police officer asked Lydia. "Or would you rather we take them in and store them overnight, because, you know, you've just been in a tense situation and maybe need time to wind down?"

Lydia gave him a knowing glance. "Exactly what I was thinking. Plus, there's a storm coming in. I need to deal with their boat and the fish. Toss them in a cell, get them on the judge's docket for sometime tomorrow—the day after, of course, is fine—and I'll come in first thing in the morning."

"You got it. Outstanding work, Officer White. See you tomorrow."

A light rain began to fall as the police officers placed handcuffs on two of the men, and with Lydia, escorted all three to the OPP van. She returned to her boat as the van pulled away.

"Can I help you?" Jammer asked. "Cuz from the look of that sky, any minute it's really going to open up."

"Sure, thanks." Lydia retrieved a camera and large measuring stick from her boat. "Shoot a photo of each fish as I measure it. That's a big help."

Lydia got into the red boat, dropped to her knees, placed the stick on the floor and reached into the vessel's live well. One by one she removed nearly two-dozen walleyes, from well below the size limit to well above it, holding each fish just above the stick to record its length as Jammer took a picture. Gently she released each fish into the river. When finished, she pulled the key from the ignition.

The rain increased in intensity.

"You wanna come over to the houseboat?" Jammer asked her. "A lot closer than Gribber's, and it's getting ready to pour. You said the other night you wanted to see it."

"Sounds great. Why don't you hop in my boat? I can run you back when it stops raining."

Jammer got into the Ministry boat and Lydia drove out of the bay, surging with whitecaps, headed toward Hidden Lake.

Gribber looked at Russell. "You're about to see your first big blow. You want to watch it from your cottage or hang out at Morning Wood? I have food, records and a cribbage board. Annie tells me you're a new convert."

"Let's go to your place."

Gribber untied his stern line then looked out at Lydia and Jammer in the Ministry boat, bouncing across the whitecaps as it disappeared around Holst Point.

"God, I love that boy," he said.

Chapter 33

It stormed through the night. The rain was a minor player compared to the frequent lightning that lit up the veranda at Morning Wood like giant, cosmic flash cameras while the pounding thunder and surging wind rattled its floor and timbers. Russell and Gribber played cribbage and snacked while listening to Gribber's extensive vinyl record collection. Gribber played dee-jay, blending album sides of Leonard Cohen, David Bowie, Joni Mitchell, White Stripes, sixties Neil Young and seventies Kinks.

Russell asked what would happen to Richie and his pals. The boat and everything in it were now property of the Ministry, Gribber explained. All would be sold at auction in the fall. Richie was in deep shit but might avoid jail time by pleading guilty and paying a hefty fine, as would the other two. The assault conviction would follow him to the States. Regardless of outcome, none would be allowed to set foot in Canada again.

Russell phoned Faith, who was riding out the storm at Annie's and was relieved he was safe at Gribber's. He spent the night in the guest room.

Russell's final five days in Kamini passed far too quickly for him. At his request, he and Faith slept only at his cottage so he could rise each day just before sunrise to meditate on his bluff. Faith knowingly did not offer accompaniment. Russell responded to emails in the mornings, and talked occasionally with Dan or Caroline at his office. Things were running smoothly without him. He fished alone and with Faith and one evening went musky hunting at the invitation of Jammer. Each had a follow and stared in smiling reverence at the two muskies that briefly showed themselves while electing not to hit their lures. Russell knew exactly what Jammer meant when he proclaimed their evening expedition a success.

One morning Russell's cell phone rang, and the caller identified himself as a reporter with the Miskwa daily newspaper. He'd gotten Russell's phone number from Gribber, whom he knew. He asked Russell about his donation of funds to the hockey rink and additional questions. He said the paper sent a photographer up to the reservation and from the photos the new rink looked terrific.

Russell spent an afternoon at Dave's Live Bait helping Faith and two extended evenings in the Holst Point Pub, during which time his nickname was shortened to "Rat" by way of greeting from Lou LeBlanc, after which "Pirate" and "Rat" became interchangeable. He gave a delightfully soused Frank Dobbs a lift home on his way back to the Lodge on the night Faith stayed home to bake and he'd driven his truck instead of his boat. Dobbs asked Russell if he'd like to come in for a drink and perhaps catch a glimpse of the albino Sasquatch or true Yeti—Dobbs couldn't be certain which—that often in the middle of night opened the wire suet feeder in his back yard and munched its contents. Russell declined, claiming a fear of both. Dobbs said they indeed were frightening, unpredictable creatures, and that he understood.

Thursday morning Russell returned from his sunrise meditation, sat on the bed beside Faith and told her that when he returned to Chicago he was going to meet with Cheryl to see if they could get back together. He wasn't far into his loosely memorized speech before she sat up and hugged him.

"Well, of course you should," Faith said. "Almost two weeks and you've never said boo about her, and almost nothing about your divorce. You've never bored me with sad tales of what a terrible marriage you had, or horrible person you married. A woman can sense these things. You love her. Well, all I know about her is, she's a lucky woman."

Russell put his arms around Faith and buried his head in her shoulder. "Thank you, so very much. But she wasn't lucky. I was an awful husband. Or turned into one, I guess. We had a wonderful marriage, at least for a while. Cheryl's from a small town, like me. She's so smart, so honest … so *authentic*. Not a bone of BS. I was the fortunate one when we married. But I lost track of what's important. I made her move into a giant house because a guy like me thinks he needs a giant house. It was the first time we ever fought. I put my foot down and made her do it." He lifted his head to look at Faith. "After that I was off and running."

Faith leaned back and smiled softly. "Then you go back and show Cheryl who you really are. You want to make amends to her, and I think that's the sweetest thing in the world. And don't overthink us. Did it ever dawn on you, you big lunk, that when we began this torrid affair, I knew you were from Chicago and were going home in two weeks?"

"The thought did cross my mind. But I'll tell you what you did. This sounds like a dumb cliché, but you reminded me what tenderness is, to give and receive. Made me realize how awful it is to be alone. And yes, I love her. I realize I love her more than I could ever know. And in large part, that's because of you."

"Aw, thank you sweetie. If you were single or I was lucky enough that Cheryl was a witch and you came up here for good, I'd clamp onto you tighter than I usually clamp onto you. Tell you what. I'll let you off the hook. Nighttime we should spend in our separate abodes. But I still want to hang out with you, you big knucklehead."

Russell gave Faith a peck on the cheek. "Why is everyone up here so smart?"

"Smart, hah. Come up and visit us sometime when Celsius does the tango with Fahrenheit at forty below zero. Now get out of my way so I can shower. Dave can't keep up with the demand for leeches, so Sheri has to set more traps this morning. I have to cover for her at the bait shop."

After Faith left, Russell sat with his computer and sent an email to Cheryl asking her to please come over to the house and meet with him on Sunday afternoon at four. He kept it brief, saying only that he wanted to discuss a few things concerning their divorce and would appreciate it if they could do it in person. Then he spent an hour typing out his thoughts about all the things he would say to her.

Russell ate breakfast in the Lodge dining room, then grabbed his spinning rod and tackle box and got into his boat to head over to the bait shop. Just before starting the engine, his attorney called him on his cell.

"Just a quick update," Bill Carter said. "The divorce hearing has been set for two p.m. on Tuesday, June twenty-fifth. Almost two weeks away, I realize, but what can I tell you? Summer has bloomed in Chicago. Everyone wants to get divorced."

"That's fine."

"Really? Aren't you the mellow vacationer. I was all prepared for you to be pissed off at me."

"I'll be back in plenty of time. It is what it is. Thanks."

Faith and Russell were finishing up with a bait shop customer later in the morning when Gribber pulled up in a Lodge boat with his fishing party, three twenty-something men from Kansas. He was dressed in jeans and his faux, souvenir-shop buckskin shirt. Accompanied by the three vacationers, Gribber gave Russell a stern look as he placed two minnow buckets on the edge of the minnow trough.

"Boozhoo Biidaapiwinini," Faith said. "What'll it be?"

"Four dozen medium," Gribber said.

"So, the fishing must be good if you had to come back for more minnows," Faith said as she filled the buckets with water.

"Oh, the fishing's been fantastic," one of the men said. "We weren't doing so hot our first three days. Then this morning, John here walked up and said he was our guide for our final day. He taught us this lucky Ojibwe phrase, and we've been pounding walleyes since the first spot he took us to."

"The great river has welcomed them," Gribber said. He turned and spoke to the three young men. "It can take several moons before one's soul aligns with its current."

Faith rang up the sale.

"Gimiigwechiwi'in," Gribber said with a nod as he paid for the minnows.

"Gimiigwechiwi'in gaye giin," Faith said.

She and Russell watched from the deck as the four men got into their boat. "What the hell was that all about?" Russell asked.

"Gribber doing his Indian guide routine. He gets bored. And it always brings a nice tip."

"What did you call him? Bidoppa-what?"

"Biidaapiwinini. It's his Ojibwe family name. His late grandfather gave it to him when he was a toddler."

"What does it mean?"

"One who enters with laughter."

"His grandfather must have been a very wise man."

"Must have been."

That evening in the pub, Gribber asked Russell how he was going to return his rental boat to Miller's Landing when both his boat and truck were at the Lodge. Russell hadn't given it a moment's thought. Gribber suggested they both drive their boats to Miskwa late tomorrow afternoon. After dropping off his rental, they could fish walleyes on the way back.

Russell was greeted on Friday morning after his meditation by a courier who assisted him in moving his belongings to a room in the Main Lodge. He found the room delightful: two double beds surrounded by four varnished walls of cedar log construction with a large window overlooking the river. The bathroom featured a black-and-white tile floor, beautiful antique sink, and claw foot bathtub.

Russell was sitting in his boat late that afternoon when Gribber returned with his new fishing party. Gribber accepted their boisterous thanks, then walked to his boat parked near Russell's. "How's your gas, Rat?"

"Oh god, not you, too. My gas is fine."

"Hey, before I forget. Did you ever get a thank you note from the kids on the reservation? They know they're supposed to send one."

Russell gave Gribber a blank stare. "No, how would I?"

"They know they can send mail to a guest at the Lodge. Should take only a day. Other guests have made donations before, slip me a few bucks if I'm guiding them and they get interested in the rez."

"I don't need a thank you note. They gave me the moccasins."

"Doesn't work that way. I don't lift a finger, it's all on them, but they know the rule. I'll check on it." Gribber got into his boat and they set out for Miller's Landing.

The weather had been cooler since the storm, with brief periods of rain, but that morning a warm southwest wind had ushered in clear skies. Gribber and Russell zoomed side-by-side across The Big Stretch then weaved their way toward The Dalles. Though they drove magnificent stretches of the river new to him, Russell had difficulty tapping into the serenity boating typically granted him. He had checked his emails before meeting Gribber and received no reply from Cheryl. Focusing on the glorious sky and water, the commanding shoreline bluffs and the sculptural evergreens, his concerns about the days ahead slowly were supplanted by peaceful acceptance. What will happen was what will happen.

They returned Russell's rental boat and fished their way back to Kamini. A few miles above The Dalles they dropped jigs and drifted down one side of a channel.

Russell checked the time. Not quite six-thirty. "So it takes only forty-some minutes to get to Miskwa," he said. "I was trying to pay attention, but right now I'm not sure I could direct us back to Kamini."

"Each time you swing a point, you aim for a spot on the horizon," Gribber said. "You memorize those. At night you navigate by knowing which dip in the tree line to head for. You'll get it. You'll be back."

"I know I have to come back, but that's about all I know for sure. I hope it's with Cheryl, but right now I'm not sure what that will take." Russell told Gribber about his conversation with Faith the previous morning then went into some detail about why Cheryl was divorcing him.

"Keep listening and watching," Gribber said, staring at his rod tip. "Keep your mind open to the messages. Your next pathway will come to you."

"From the eagles, right? They're the messengers?"

"They are, but the wind, the water, the forest, the creatures, all of nature and its elements speak lessons to us also. Reel up, I want to show you something."

Gribber drove to the headwaters of The Dalles and cut the motor. Converging shorelines forced the broad river into a bottleneck. The current, tightly contained, accelerated such that their boat was swept rapidly down one of two long, narrow channels edged by tall granite bluffs. At the bottom, the shorelines curved broadly apart. The boat slowed and drifted aimlessly. "Look up through The Dalles and tell me what you see," Gribber said.

Russell studied the view. "I can see the current, the ripples and whirlpools ... jagged bluffs, the trees. Blooming flowers near shore. It's beautiful ... serene."

"Serenity is present, yes, but what else? What are you really seeing? Look all around."

The now gentle current had swung the boat into a calm eddy near shore. Looking into the shallow, clear water, Russell saw vast schools of minnows swirling like dark cyclones across the river bottom. Dashes of burnt orange color drew his attention to crayfish, two of them peeking out from crevices in the submerged granite, one boldly exposed as it danced delicately across a smooth green slate of algae-covered stone. Along the shore, water beetles, hundreds, a thousand, skittered across the surface in flowing paisley patterns.

"Minnows, crayfish, water beetles ... the entire river is alive."

"So, what do we have here? What is truly present? You're the wordsmith. Don't think in terms of material things, think in terms of principles."

"Um, life, food ..."

"Food would be a thing."

"Beauty, harmony ... bounty."

"Oh, you're so close. I'll give you one hint. There are a lot of good fishing spots above and below The Dalles. Now look again, from the top of The Dalles to the view downstream. Take it all in then stop thinking and close your eyes. Listen for the wilderness to speak in spirit. Tell me the first word to enter your mind."

Russell gazed again from the top of The Dalles down to where the boat drifted, then past it to the rocky points and bays expanding outward downstream. He closed his eyes and cleared his mind of all thought, except he could not shake the image of The Dalles, two narrow, living, bountiful ... pipelines. The word came to him and he spoke. "Supply." Russell opened his eyes and looked at a smiling Gribber.

"There. That wasn't so hard. Perfect, effortless, constant supply. All the food every creature in the river needs, from the single-cell algae up to your five-foot musky, spring, summer, fall and winter. It's by design. Look at the bluffs we just floated past. Tell me what the trees can teach you."

Russell had become used to seeing trees—primarily birch, white and jack pine—growing from little more than crevices in the Shield granite. A dozen birch, young to mature, dotted the bluffs like mountain climbers clinging precariously to the sheer stone cliffs. "Adaptability. Perseverance. The will to live."

"Exactly. Principles. When you've had a setback, a big white pine toppled by a storm twenty years ago that simply curved the lead candle of its trunk toward the sun and is now enormous is a good thing to ponder." Gribber paused to take in the view, swiveling in his seat to witness three hundred and sixty degrees of Ontario wilderness. "Beauty, serenity, peace, and yes, hardship, all the principles of being, are taught by the wilderness. The love a mama wolf has for her pups as she nourishes, cleans, and teaches them. Love is instinctive, yet humans restrict it. Did you know that you can love everyone as effortlessly as you love your spouse or child? It's not easy. That takes work. I'm sure not perfect. But the wilderness shows us perfection in its design. The perfect system of supply in a river, a maple leaf's perfect symmetry. All here to teach and guide us down the right path."

Russell didn't realize he had closed his eyes as Gribber spoke. He opened them and with his fingertips wiped away moisture from his eyelashes. "I've never felt so hopeful and helpless as I feel right now."

"Then ask for help, guidance. You are connected to the wilderness and all it contains. You were created. The Creator knows you're here, knows you're troubled. Pathways lie before you. The principle behind pathways is choice of direction. Some pathways are known, safe, we take them every day. Other pathways, we hesitate out of fear of the unknown. But what if it's the right path?"

Gribber started the motor and drove downstream a short distance to the entrance to a bay. "This is a good spot. Let's drop jigs here."

Russell sat silent for a few minutes, his mind adrift with questions. "That morning you taught me the sunrise meditation, you do that for everyone you meet?" he said without looking up.

"No."

"Why me?"

"Because I sensed you could."

"But I didn't know I could."

"You're not the one who needs to know."

Russell pondered for a moment. "My guide that you referenced once, the guide you said I need, is me, isn't it?"

"Reading the signs bestowed by the Creator, yes," Gribber said. He jerked his right hand hard, setting his hook into a fish. "Now get the net. Got me one big walnut."

After releasing the large walleye, they worked their way downstream. They continued to catch fish, Russell thrilled when he caught his largest walleye yet, a twenty-seven-incher. Beaming, he held it while Gribber took a picture.

"Beautiful walnut," Gribber said as Russell slipped the fish back into the water.

"Evening fishing is the best. Walleyes feed at night. What you catch during the day are usually young numbskulls or if you get a big one, the fish didn't get its fill the night before. Next time you come up, we'll go fishing around eleven at night, troll floating Rapalas along shorelines and weed beds. The big walleyes are hungry and feeding in shallow water. That's the time to fish if you want to hook a real lunker."

Gribber dropped Russell at the Lodge, and he went up to his room to get ready for a going-away dinner in the dining room with Faith, Annie and Gribber, followed by drinks at the pub. Before walking out the door he checked his emails.

There was a reply from Cheryl. She would meet him at the house on Sunday at four.

Chapter 34

Russell awoke before sunrise on his final morning in Kamini. He splashed water on his face, dressed and sat down to put on his hiking boots but the thought came to him to put on his beautiful moccasins instead. Walking along the sand beach toward his sunrise spot, he wondered if the inspiriting energy flowing upward from his feet was of his own predilection. His footsteps made no sound as he hiked the terraced granite bluff. Waves splashed the shore in a gentle, rhythmic cadence. He sat down, cleansed his mind of thought—it was effortless now—and joined the creation of a new day.

After an hour of mediation, Russell walked to the Lodge to buy his cup of coffee. He stood in the Rotunda and looked out the window at the royal blue river. Though he felt humbled by its majesty, and during his morning meditation had asked the Creator for guidance, Russell was not at peace. The only conceivable pathway before him led back to his life in Chicago. He could not escape a sense of foreboding at facing Cheryl, at attempting to explain what he now understood and who he now was trying to be. There had to be another message for him, a most important message, a message not sent.

A message not sent until he learned a final lesson making him worthy of receipt.

Russell entered his room, removed his moccasins, packed them carefully, then carried his luggage to his truck. He had mentioned at dinner what time he would be leaving, and found Gribber, Faith and Annie sitting on the tailgate. Annie had his golf clubs. "Jason at the pro shop called me yesterday to ask if you were still around," she said. "Apparently your clubs didn't get much use."

"Blame the rascal standing next to you," Russell said as he hugged Gribber. "Thank you, my friend. You'll take good care of all my fishing equipment, I trust?"

"Already stashed in the shed at Morning Wood, awaiting your return."

Russell hugged Annie and saved his longest embrace for Faith.

"Give us a call sometime," Gribber said. "Let us know how you're doing."

With a wave, Russell climbed into his truck. Gribber put the golf clubs into the bed, closed the tailgate and gave it a slap. Russell turned the key and began the long drive home to Chicago.

He thought of nothing as he navigated the twisting gravel road toward Miskwa, gazing blankly at the lakes, streams and sloughs he passed. At Miskwa, he drove the Trans-Canada Highway several miles before turning south onto the highway to the US border. He slowed when he entered Fort Francis, joining the single-lane traffic bound for the US. He stared out at the hypnotic, swirling current of the Rainy River as his truck crossed the international bridge. When he pulled up to the US Customs kiosk, Russell sensed the familiar pangs of loneliness seeping into his consciousness. He stopped in International Falls, where he filled his tank, bought a cup of coffee, a few energy drinks, two sandwiches, beef jerky, cashews and a banana. He hadn't made a motel reservation.

As he barreled south through Minnesota, Russell witnessed the striking emergence of the wilderness in reverse. The looming granite bluffs along the highway diminished in size mile after mile as the Canadian Shield loosed its hold on the continent. The lakes lost their pink and gray granite shorelines as the stone receded from the water's edge. The pine, spruce and birch trees scattered farther and farther into the distance, as if in retreat.

Minnesota reverted to flat farmland, Russell judging the various crops off to a strong start as he drove past the miles of verdant fields. It was the final stretch of his journey in which he found any comfort. Traffic grew congested as he approached the cityscape of St. Paul and the towering Minneapolis skyline to the west. Re-emerging into the urban world, Russell's reservoir of serenity drained slowly from him like a dripping fluid from the bottom of his truck, staining the pavement past Milwaukee and marking his route up to the northern suburbs of Chicago. He arrived at his house shortly after midnight.

Russell went into the elaborate kitchen and opened a can of soup. Standing at the six-burner stove, he ate it from the pot as soon as it was warm. He climbed upstairs and got ready for bed, though he knew as his head hit the pillow that he would sleep only fitfully despite the exhaustion from his marathon drive. He drifted in and out of slumber and awoke for good at five. He put on his jeans, flannel shirt and hiking boots then walked down two flights of stairs to the lower level, through the game room and into the living room.

For the first time, the glistening kitchen at the far end of the huge space looked ridiculous to him. There was a full kitchen just upstairs. Russell exited the sliding glass door, crossed the flagstone patio past the swimming pool and descended the trail to the rocky shoreline of Lake Michigan below. The sun was beginning to rise.

The sunrise was pleasant, but it offered little of the rejuvenation Russell had felt during his morning meditations in Kamini. The horizon over which the glowing yellow-orange orb rose offered no perspective, only water extending as far as the eye could see. Instead of ducks, pelicans, hawks and eagles, early morning air traffic from the O'Hare and Midway airports dotted the sky. On his right, his neighbor's house loomed above the lake like the harsh, gray, cube-shaped monstrosity it was.

Russell's eyes scanned further down the shore. The helter-skelter collection of wood, brick and concrete structures transitioned from private homes to warehouses rising erratically in height, their jumbled forms ultimately merging into the distant downtown skyline. Breathing in through the nose, he found no hint of a wilderness scent. The wind was from the south. He smelled Chicago.

Twenty-four hours earlier, he was soaking in the wilderness air and listening to the birds while meditating in Kamini. Hiking up the path from the lake to his house, Kamini seemed a million miles away. He climbed the stairs to the house's ground level and sat on the leather sectional couch in the enormous main living room. He stared up at the vaulted ceiling then across to the glossy black Steinway grand piano that served no function beyond filling a tenth of the room as expensive sculpture. Russell remembered telling Cheryl when they bought it that he was keen to learn how to play. He dabbled at it for at most a week.

Now he should sell the Steinway. No. Now he should put it on a truck. Put it on a truck and drive it to Kamini. Drive it to Kamini and give it to Jammer. Give it to Jammer so later this winter when Jammer's houseboat was frozen tight into Hidden Lake, he and Jammer could haul it upside down across the ice. Laughing, and maybe a little drunk, they would break it into pieces and use it for firewood in Jammer's wood stove after a day of ice fishing. In addition to the firewood, Jammer would no doubt make good use of the wire strings and metal fittings, discover clever, artful uses for the eighty-eight keys. That's what he should do. Give it to someone who would use it.

Russell decided that in a little while he could see what was in the house for food. He could unpack. He could do laundry. He could trim his beard. Later, he could take a nap. There was plenty to do. But for now, he would sit alone in his gigantic, ludicrous house and wait for Cheryl to arrive at four.

Cheryl Carlson Dean also was thinking about the house. She'd not slept well during the night. She would have to leave her friend Jennifer's house in Naperville at three-thirty in the afternoon to get to the house in Forest Lake by four. She lay in bed and thought about Russell.

After being introduced to him at the corporate headquarters of Life Time Fitness, she was intrigued by his initially bashful, almost goofy demeanor. He was very attractive physically, but unlike other attractive men didn't flirt with her, make suggestive comments, ask her out for dinner, or even furtively glance at her breasts while speaking to her. As she drove him on a tour of Life Time health clubs, they bonded over their similar small town origins, he from Kaweena, Illinois and she from Park Rapids, Minnesota.

Russell's second day in town they spoke to each other as if friends since childhood. She was impressed by his creative mind but also by his common sense and upbeat demeanor. He flew into Minneapolis the following week for a few days to discuss details they could have handled with phone calls and emails. She asked him out for dinner after fine-tuning the new Samuels Dean marketing program one afternoon, taking him to a good Thai restaurant nearby. She ordered the appetizer and helped him select his main dish. He'd never eaten Thai.

When Cheryl dropped off Russell at his hotel after dinner, they looked at each other in the car and kissed. He told her he'd been thinking about her for a week, and she admitted the same. It said a lot to her when he didn't invite her up to his room. When the next night he didn't have to, she began to fall in love with him.

And it was love. One way she knew was she'd never felt that way about a man before.

For the next seven months they were together nearly every weekend. Both took days off from work and twice visited her parents at their home in Park Rapids. She flew to Chicago where they drove to Kaweena to meet his parents and spend three days on the lovely farm. Living and working in Minneapolis proved a good warm-up for Chicago, which she found a bustling, welcoming city. Just before the wedding they bought a three-bedroom house in the suburbs, and after moving in settled happily into married life. They agreed to wait to have children.

One of Cheryl's duties at Life Time Fitness was running the company's charitable donations program, and she was surprised to discover Samuels Dean had no such community outreach.

Creating the Samuels Dean Charitable Foundation became her full-time job and she relished every minute of it. Russell suggested Upward Youth as the name for the Foundation's primary program. It was perfect.

She liked Russell's partner and mentor Dan Samuels but found him a bit narrow-minded and overly driven. All he talked about was advertising, clients and sales numbers. Five years into the marriage, the firm had won multiple national and international awards, all resulting from Russell's creative mind. It seemed that nearly every month the firm picked up another major account. As the firm's income and profits ballooned, they hired streams of new employees and moved into lavish offices in the Willis Tower. Russell began working longer hours and spoke of little except work when they did spend time together.

As Cheryl lay in bed staring at the ceiling on this Sunday morning, she realized that in her passive, small town Minnesota manner, over the course of their sixth year of married life, she had quietly watched him grow apart from her. That's what made the second half of the marriage so painful—a slowly breaking heart.

Cheryl got out of bed and went to the kitchen in her pajamas to make coffee. While she sat at the kitchen table waiting for it to brew, Jennifer entered in her robe. She sat down across from Cheryl and looked her sternly in the eye. "I'm warning you," Jennifer said, "I've got Thorazine in the house, and I'll give you an injection if I have to." She was a registered nurse. At thirty-seven, she was a year older than Cheryl. Married and divorced twice, one of her bad marriages was her fault and the other wasn't.

"He just wants to talk a few things over about the divorce," Cheryl said. "That's all he said in his email."

"And there it is, what he didn't say. It's a setup, Cher. This is the scene where the self-centered husband gets on his knees and pleads for his precious wife to come back to him. Because his perfect world where he gets to do whatever he wants has been shattered. He needs his little blonde bombshell dressed in Versace and on his arm for the *Tribune* cameras at whatever gala."

"I'm not his little blonde bombshell."

"Well OK. But you are gorgeous and a real blonde, unlike all the other blondes in the photos. And me." Jennifer got up and came back to the table with two cups of coffee.

"And you know I don't care about dressing in Versace and all that other stuff in my closets," Cheryl said.

"Your closets at the house you mean, all ten of 'em." Jennifer took a slurp of coffee. "That house and everything in it epitomizes Russell. He shows what he thinks is love by giving you things only money can buy. The free stuff, like his time, his care, him, the really valuable stuff, he can't part with. He's never even shown any interest in the work of the Foundation, of helping the kids. You said so yourself."

Cheryl looked up and stared blankly out the small kitchen window. "It wasn't always like that."

"But it is now. Has been for years. You told me when you got pregnant you were worried about the type of father Russell would be."

"I said I was hoping that, when we had a child, he would spend more time at home! I wasn't worried about him being a good father."

"Same thing. He's an egotist, Cher. Fancy house, fancy cars, fancy watches, fancy clothes. You don't see it. It's like being married to an alcoholic. You enable him. You ignore the facts. You start to waste away alongside his stinking corpse. Trust me, I know."

Cheryl took a sip of coffee and rolled over Jennifer's words in her mind. She was right about the house. It was far too large for them and cost millions of dollars, but Russell had demanded they buy it. While touring it she asked why in the world a house needed another full kitchen in the walkout lower level. For entertaining in summer, Russell replied, serving food on the patio during pool parties with friends. Except these pool parties never materialized. The house became a showcase for after-parties of Samuels Dean corporate meetings, entertaining wealthy CEOs and their spouses whose companies spent millions of dollars in advertising with the firm. Cheryl couldn't think of a single time they'd had a simple dinner on the patio with a few of their friends. Then the one thing she always found a bit unusual about Russell came to mind.

He had no friends.

"He's going to tell you he'll change. Look for it. And he's going to tell you he'll do whatever it takes to save the marriage. Except people don't change, Cher. Certainly not men in their forties. You did the right thing filing for divorce. I'm proud of you. You saved yourself. You're still young, you're beautiful and smart, and you deserve a man who loves you more than he could ever know."

Cheryl blinked away tears and looked up at the ceiling.

By quarter to four, Russell had eaten, unpacked, done his laundry and trimmed his beard. He hadn't napped because he couldn't. All day he focused on all the things he wanted to say to Cheryl. The phone rang as he sat in the living room. The landline. A number few people knew and very few used. Russell reached for the sleek black handset on the marble table beside him. "Hello?"

"I tried calling your cell, but you didn't pick up."

"I lost it up in Canada. Long story." There was a pause before Cheryl spoke again.

"I'm not coming over. I'm sorry. Anything you need to discuss you can send in an email to my attorney. I think it's best if we not have any direct contact, phone, mail, even emails."

"Cheryl, listen to me, I need to …"

"Russell, please. Don't contact me again. We're getting a divorce. Then it's time we both move forward with our lives. Again, I'm sorry. Goodbye." She hung up.

The phone slipped from Russell's hand, and as he fell backward on the couch the walls of the giant house swayed then toppled as the enormous roof collapsed on top of him. The house continued to shudder inward as the walls and everything they contained imploded into a smaller and smaller sphere, closing tighter around him until all he possessed, the appliances and cabinetry, the furniture and clothes, the piano and vehicles compressed into a tiny, impenetrable world the size of a stone with him in the center.

In the evening as he prepared for bed, Russell knew of only three things he must do. First, go into the office tomorrow morning and speak with Dan. Second, phone Bill Carter to ask if his presence was required at the divorce hearing next week. Both were necessary because of the most crucial thing on the list: Get in his truck and return as quickly as possible to Kamini.

Good thing he'd done his laundry, he thought.

Chapter 35

Driving into downtown Chicago and going to work was as appealing to Russell as plunging a fishhook into his thumb. Still exhausted from his long drive, when his eyes popped open before sunrise, he hit the snooze button in his brain and slept until eight.

He dressed in jeans, plaid flannel shirt and hiking boots, passed his BMW and got into his truck. He realized he couldn't face the traffic on I-94 as he backed from his garage. Better to cruise the suburban route into the city. Driving along the lake, he merged onto the lakeshore highway. Traffic into downtown was slow. Russell stayed in the right lane, content to ramble along in his F250. He was in no hurry.

As he approached Grant Park, he realized that, though he had a view of the enormous downtown park complex from his office, he'd never been in any portion of it. He exited Lake Shore Drive and drove between Millennium Park and Maggie Daley Park. A large number of Chicagoans were out enjoying the massive green space on a beautiful June morning. Mothers and fathers wheeled their babies in strollers along curving, landscaped sidewalks. The soaring, stainless steel Jay Pritzker Pavilion served as backdrop for groups of inner-city youths who tossed baseballs and flung Frisbees all across the Great Lawn. He was surprised so many kids were up and outside so early, then realized that many of them probably didn't have lawns to play in.

Russell continued south and passed the exquisite Buckingham Fountain, attracting still more people to its elaborate aquatic display. Trees, greenery, water, open spaces. It wasn't wilderness but still eased him into a more tranquil state of mind. Chicago really was a magnificent city.

Russell had remained entombed in his suffocating shell for over an hour last night after Cheryl's phone call. When slowly he crawled out, all he held in his mind was her beautiful face. Plus the realization she was right. She had her own life to lead. He had no right to ask her to listen to him, to think he could somehow change her mind. He would instead have to accept that his sins would not be absolved. After the divorce, he needed to put it all behind him and move forward. Cheryl did such important work on the firm's behalf. At least the funding of the Samuels Dean Foundation offered him some small redemption. It truly impacted a large number of citizens in desperate need of help. Not all of Chicago emitted the beauty and harmony of Grant Park on a sunny June morning.

Cheryl's world was primarily on the Southside. It was there the Foundation devoted most of its resources and Cheryl much of her time, meeting with city council members, citizen groups and church leaders. Russell had been to the heart of the Southside exactly once: six years ago, accompanying Cheryl to the opening of a youth center and community garden made possible by a grant from the Foundation.

Driving with Cheryl on that Saturday morning from their new home in Lake Forest into the Southside, Russell was astonished the streets of his city connected the two. As they approached the new youth center they passed rows of small, two-story homes with tiny front yards packed tight side by side, some maintained in good repair while others were dilapidated eyesores. Junk and garbage littered their yards. Some were boarded up, stern warnings against trespassing posted on the front doors. Kids played in the streets and yielded ground to Russell's vehicle grudgingly and with attitude. He was driving a silver Cadillac Escalade in those days, and more than once the request was shouted by the youth to stop and give them a ride. Most just slapped its doors and side panels as it rolled by.

Russell, while stopped at a red light driving home later that afternoon, eyed the people milling about the street corners and sidewalks with apprehension. Particularly the younger males. Cheryl sensed his concern and told him to relax. The soul of the Southside was loving and good, she said. A lot of its residents were working hard with the mayor's office, the Foundation and other organizations to make the area a better place to live. She reminded him the homicide and overall crime rates were again down from the previous year.

True, the crime and homicide rates in Chicago had trended slightly downward over the six years since that community center opening. Yet the level of violence remained statistically alarming, thought Russell as he pulled his truck into his reserved spot in the Willis Tower garage. What was the cause of the cancer that had spread across one area of a vast city? The word "despair" came to Russell's mind. That was a good word for it. Despair caused by the principle tenets of the concrete jungle: poverty and unemployment, particularly trapping the young. Despair fomenting desperation leading to dropping out of school leading to teenage pregnancies, drugs, gangs and crime. Despair bolstered and sustained in some by the daily, limited view of the harsh, gray, unnatural environment surrounding them. Cheryl and the other players had their work cut out for them. That was a vicious cycle to attempt to break, if even possible.

The elevator doors opened to the 70th floor and Russell stepped out. Tyrell, the security guard, did a double take worthy of Morgan Freeman or Tom Hanks. "Mr. Dean!" he said finally, breaking into a startled grin. "Digging the beard, sir."

"Thank you, my good man." Russell extended his hand as he walked toward the stylish kiosk. Tyrell stood and shook it. "And from now on, please, call me Russell. You do an impeccable job and I appreciate the formality, but, well, knock it off. Especially the 'sir' shit."

"Yes sir, or … you got it, Russell." Tyrell pressed a button and the doors to Samuels Dean Advertising swung open.

Jessica stared in dreamy eyed wonderment at the tall, rugged lumberjack appearing suddenly before her. In addition to his full beard, Russell's hair hadn't been cut in over two weeks, rare for him. He passed her desk uttering a simple, "Good morning, Jessica," wondering how far he would go toward Dan's office before she recognized him.

Dan Samuels was on his phone facing the glass wall when Russell walked in. As he spun around in his chair, his blank expression somehow shifted blanker. "Sounds good, Robert," Samuels said. "We'll take a look and get right back to you." He hung up the phone. Turning his full attention to Russell, Samuels finally smiled, though his face couldn't disguise a degree of perplexity. "Welcome back, killer. This is a new look for you."

"Amazing what a sabbatical can do for a man. And I want to tell you how much I appreciate being left out of the loop while I was gone. It was humbling, in fact, to discover that the world of Samuels Dean can purr right along without me."

"So, are you planning to stick around today, or fire back up tomorrow? Looks like maybe you just got home."

"Dan, that's what I came to talk to you about. After I leave your office, I'm driving back to Canada. I need more time off. I know you think I'm built of stone, but the divorce has really thrown me for a loop. I'll be able to work from there. I'll have Internet and can do everything I do here through emails and phone calls. We can even conference. Just like the last two weeks."

A look of concern crossed Samuels's face. "But what about ESPN? It's going great, by the way, thanks for asking. We're moving into new phases of the campaign, so there's more writing to be done, the next generation of promo copy. Remember how you set it up, so it reflects breaking sports stories. There's not always a lot of time for rewrites and approvals. I know how you need to stay right on top of that stuff."

"It'll be fine ... turn all the writing over to the blonde Stanford kid. Who is it ... Corby, Adam Corby. Put him full time on the ESPN account."

"But you told me we were having trouble, hiring kids with fancy marketing degrees who couldn't write."

"Did I? Well, if I did, I certainly wasn't talking about Corby. I've mentored him. He's terribly gifted."

Samuels's furrowed brow relaxed a degree. "Well, if you say so."

"Besides, it was your decision to level off for awhile, not take on any new accounts after we landed ESPN. And a brilliant decision it was. I'll be as close as an email or phone call away." Russell gave his partner a smile and turned to leave.

"So how long are you going back to Canada for, you think?"

"Oh, I don't know. Couple of weeks, a month. You just be sure to stay in touch with me any time, for any reason. Caroline too, and any of the staffers."

Russell took the elevator back down to the garage and climbed into his truck. He'd loaded his luggage into the bed the night before. He needed a new phone, and drove several blocks around his phone carrier's outlet store without finding a parking spot. Traffic was jammed, so he decided screw it, his little flip phone worked well enough.

He phoned Bill Carter as he left the city. "I'm not able to make the hearing next week," Russell told Carter. "Is my presence required, or can you cover for me?"

"Jeez, it's preferred, but not required. I can cover for you, then email you a bunch of e-documents to sign."

"Do that."

He next phoned Mailer's Resort in Orr. Ralph happened to pick up. Yes, they had a vacancy that evening. Then he called Kamini Lodge.

The wonderful Grace at the front desk answered. "Pirate! So good to hear from you ... no, dang, we're fully booked. Can't think of a single resort that isn't full."

Russell thanked her, phoned Gribber, got his voicemail and left a message.

Russell pulled up behind Morning Wood just after four the next afternoon. Ramble was nowhere to be seen. He grabbed his luggage and went to the back door. It was unlocked, though Gribber hadn't left it unlocked for him. People in Kamini never locked their doors. Russell put his bags in the guest room and walked down to the river. Simply being back in Kamini—gazing at the river, smelling the air, hearing the birds calling from the woods—calmed his frazzled mind and gave him hope. He realized he could never leave.

Gribber's steed was tied to the dock. All of Russell's fishing gear was neatly arranged in the boat. A lifejacket lay on the driver's seat. There was a piece of paper folded in half tucked under the handle of his tackle box. Russell stepped into the boat and grabbed the note.

It read: "Welcome Home."

Chapter 36

Russell was in the kitchen seasoning steaks he'd dashed out to buy at the Bay when he heard Ramble pull up. Gribber entered and raised his eyebrows. Russell smiled and shrugged his shoulders. "So, you sure it's alright, me staying with you for a few weeks?" he asked. "The guest room is vacant?"

"Not only is it vacant but from now on, Morning Wood is men only."

"How is the lovely Lydia?"

"Lovely and in love. She's shacking up with Jammer. Houseboating up, I guess. And the great thing is, they have this goofy chemistry. She's crazy about him and I think the feeling is mutual. Jam taught her how to fish, and that's all they do after work. Until the sun goes down, that is."

"But how long will she be around? For Jammer, I mean?"

"Another Ministry Officer arrived a day after Lydia busted those Illinois fishermen. Tyler, I think his name is. There's supposed to be two officers in the boat when they patrol the fishing. That day we saw her towing the boat she'd jumped the gun. After Tyler arrived, Jammer said Lydia phoned and told her boss they should spend at least two weeks monitoring the river and he agreed. After that, I guess they figure it out." Gribber went outside to start the charcoal for the grill.

Russell donned his moccasins early the next morning and headed for the dock. Gribber was already there, sitting with legs crossed. Russell sat at the other end, and together they witnessed the sunrise. Russell closed his eyes when the day brightened. He did not ask the Creator for an answer to a question. He did not ask for guidance in finding his true pathway. Instead, from his heart burst forth something he'd been neglecting to express, something that dawned on him when he read Gribber's note. Something he couldn't believe he had missed all along: sincere, humble gratitude for friendships, for love and laughter, for the grace and beauty in the world, for his life so far and for the journey ahead. Gratitude, as his thoughts distilled to their core, for being a part of the grand design of creation. As his mind went blank, the leaves of the shoreline poplar trees rustled, and a warm, gentle breeze caressed Russell's cheek.

Russell washed the breakfast dishes after Gribber left for work, then put on shorts, sandals and t-shirt and drove Gribber's boat to the bait shop. Faith was sitting on the deck dressed much the same. She welcomed Russell with a broad smile and long embrace, and asked how he was doing. He gave her the rundown on his failed meeting with Cheryl, told her he was fine and that as long as he was in Kamini he could accept whatever the future held. They ran the busy bait shop together all morning, Russell surprised by the uptick in customers from a week before.

"We're into full-blown tourist season," Faith said when they found a few minutes on the deck. "Plus a lot of the cottagers are down with their kids. Just wait 'til this weekend. The pro walleye tournament is Saturday and Sunday. The pros arrive tomorrow and will be out scouting all day Friday. Best to stay off the river unless you want your boat cut in half by yahoo pros tearing across the water in boats that can hit sixty miles per hour, in Yank-speak."

Faith asked if he wanted to stay for lunch and Russell said he was thinking of eating at the Lodge. He should at least stop by to say hello to Annie. "Do that," Faith said. "She'll want to know how you're doing."

Russell docked at the Lodge and walked slowly up the pathway so he could witness the gradual unveiling of the historic structure. Grace greeted him warmly at the front desk. He asked if Annie was around and moments later she came smiling to the desk. Annie was wearing another elegant pantsuit and carrying a newspaper.

"Just stopped in for lunch," Russell said. "Wanted to say hi. Things didn't go as I'd planned in Chicago, but what else is new. But it's all right. I don't know what I'm going to do, only know this is where I need to do it."

"Then let's do lunch," Annie said. "I have something to show you."

They were seated at a corner table with a view of the golf course. After ordering, Annie placed the Saturday edition of the Miskwa newspaper in front of Russell. "You made the front page. A really neat article."

Russell picked up the paper. "Grand Gift Gratefully Received" read the headline, with the subhead, "Generous Lodge guest donates money and sweat for new Blackdog hockey rink." The article continued inside and included photos from both the paper's photographer and the reservation teen chronicling the rink's construction.

"Isn't that wonderful!" Russell said, breaking into a grin. "We all made the cover, you mean. That's a keeper, thank you. I can't wait to read it."

"It's good to see you," Annie said, "and good to see you so upbeat. Faith shared with me a bit of what you told her about your marriage situation. Don't be angry. She thinks the world of you. She was impressed you were so determined to try to make things right. I don't need to know any more, just want to let you know that you have good friends here, and we're all rooting for you."

"Thank you, Annie. Cheryl wouldn't see or talk to me, but you know what? That's OK. She has that right. We both need to move on. I'm done trying to control people and events."

After lunch, which Annie insisted was on the house, Russell decided to go fishing. He already missed it. He spent the rest of the afternoon casting with his spinning rod, catching and releasing smallmouth bass along reefs and rocky shorelines he judged good smallmouth habitat.

Russell spent time at his computer that evening on the veranda while Gribber read. On impulse, Russell typed "John Dogrib" into a search engine and pulled up a number of articles from the Miskwa newspaper and Canadian fishing sites. A listing near the bottom of the page caught his eye. He clicked and read until he came to the name John Dogrib at the end of the first paragraph.

"I have some bad news for you, Grib."

Gribber looked up from his book. "Be gentle with me."

"Last week a runner from Cornell University set a new Ivy League track record in the men's 800 meters. He beat the old record by just under a half-second. The old record was the longest standing track and field record in the league, set in 1996 by some guy from Dartmouth named John Dogrib."

Gribber went back to his book. "Records were made to be broken," he said softly. "At least it was beaten by a bellhop and not a bleepin' Harvard or Yale man."

When Russell fell asleep that night the gentle breeze carried the rich wilderness scent through the open bedroom window and the giant musky returned. Russell was standing in Gribber's boat looking out across a perfectly still body of water. The sun had just dipped below a distant horizon of finely serrated evergreen treetops. Slender ribbons of clouds in shades of pink, yellow, orange and indigo fanned out in layers from the horizon to high overhead. The vivid colors were projected across the entire expanse of water as it mirrored the sky.

The enormous fish was swimming just below the surface straight toward the boat, the V-shaped wake expanding outward from its head sending multicolored ripples across the glass. As it swam to within two feet of the boat, the musky raised its head above water and stared straight at him. Russell heard nothing. Then the earlier dream with the musky and eagle burst as a flash in his consciousness, and Russell sensed its meaning: At a moment of grave despair, a creature from one world did something selfless and extraordinary to help a creature from another.

Russell sat bolt upright in bed. Over the next ten seconds every puzzle piece dropped into place in a single, blistering download. He blinked his eyes and tried to keep up with the list of everything he must do from that moment forward. It was all there, he realized in astonishment, laid out before him like the carefully unpacked components of new Ikea furniture.

He leaped up, and in his boxers burst into Gribber's room. Gribber was asleep with his back toward him. Russell grabbed his shoulder and shook it. "Gribber, wake up. Wake up, I need to ask you something."

Gribber curled tighter into a ball and pulled the covers over his head. "I don't need to go to school today, mommy," he said, moaning.

Russell bent down, lifted the frame of Gribber's bed and let it drop. "Gribber, it's important."

"Hay Zeus Christo," Gribber said sternly as he rolled over and sat up in bed. He rubbed his eyes. "What the hell time is it?"

"No idea. Property. What's available? What does it cost? How do I buy it?"

Gribber stared blankly at Russell. "If you'll stop acting like a crazy man and go back to bed, I'll sell you this joint."

"Thank you, but property without a building. Just the land. Where I can build what I need to build."

Gribber twisted his face in a long yawn. "Well, Rat, I realize this is merely Canada, but we do have the Internet, and realtors, and currency, and only about five agents in Miskwa who specialize in cottage country real estate, from Lake of the Woods at the border all the way up to the English River."

"It has to be on the Winnipeg River. In or around Kamini."

Gribber scratched his neck. "That can be a little sparse. But check online, parcels pop up every few years. Talk to Lydia, come to think of it. Karpenko's landing in Pistol isn't on the market yet, but will be."

"The landing! Road access. Gribber, it's perfect. I could kiss you."

"Well, we need to hold hands first." Gribber laid back down and rolled over.

Russell went into the kitchen and made a pot of coffee. Glancing at the stove clock, he saw it was ten minutes to two. He ran over the components of his plan in his mind. There was much to think about, with more arriving every minute. He poured a cup of coffee and headed for the veranda.

Seated with his laptop on the chesterfield, he typed a variety of words into a search engine. He became even more excited as he scanned the pages and clicked websites. Colorado. Washington, DC. Minnesota. New York City. Of course. His idea was far from original and that was perhaps the best thing about it. There was precedent. Links, reviews, articles in newspapers, testimonials. Proof that it helped, proof that it worked.

He pulled up a Word document and began typing, recording websites, names, addresses, emails, phone numbers. After conducting the research, he opened a second document and began outlining his plan.

Gribber got up at five, came out to the veranda in his underwear and found Russell sitting on the chesterfield typing furiously on his laptop. Russell didn't hear him or sense his presence. Gribber watched Russell's fingers fly across the keyboard for a solid minute, wondering what in hell he was doing. "Have you been at your computer all night?" he asked finally.

"Yes," Russell said without stopping or looking up.

Gribber was silent for a moment. "What are you doing now, writing a novel? If I'm in it, you have to be sure to tell the reader how stoically handsome I am."

"I'm not writing a novel."

Gribber yawned, reached down and scratched his crotch. "You joining me for sunrise?"

"Knock yourself out. I'll watch it from here. Right now, I'm supposed to do this. Do you have a printer?"

"Used to. It stopped talking to my computer or my computer got mad at it, I forget which. If you need to print that tome, you can put it on a stick and do it at the FedEx in Miskwa."

"What day is it?"

"Thursday, I'm pretty sure."

"How long does it take first class mail to get from Kamini to Chicago?" Russell still hadn't looked up.

"There's an eternal question. I don't know, seven, eight days. Send it FedEx, get there before noon and you'd have it in Chicago tomorrow."

"Thank you." Russell realized he was being rude. He looked up at Gribber leaning against the wood frame of the veranda entrance. "I had my breakthrough last night. A message came to me. I figured out the meaning of my dream with the musky and the eagle."

"What, that the most important thing in life is to help people, even those from different worlds? I think you figured that out before last night, you just didn't realize it. Anyway, that's great. Take it step by step. Watch out for the odd landmine. You're presently in the material world, after all. And thank you."

"For what?"

"For confirming for me that the way I think this stuff works is the way this stuff actually works."

Gribber turned and walked back to his room, put on his bathrobe and headed to the dock to watch the sunrise.

Chapter 37

At seven-fifteen in the morning in Kamini—eight-fifteen in New York—Russell pulled up his contact page and placed a call. He asked to speak with the Executive Director, and to his delight the woman came on the line. He explained who he was, quickly described the Samuels Dean Charitable Foundation and began asking questions. The gracious and enthusiastic woman told him the story of their one hundred forty-four-year-old youth program. They spoke for nearly forty minutes.

The director of a similar program in Washington, DC wasn't available, but the media contact manager was equally helpful. Expressing his gratitude, Russell said goodbye and dove back into his program outline. He finished it just after ten-thirty.

Russell fired off an email to Chief Alfred Cameron at the Blackdog reservation, grabbed a memory stick from his computer bag and downloaded the document. He decided it would be best if he put on clothes before driving to Miskwa. At the FedEx outlet he printed out the proposal and proofread it. It was perfect. He stapled the six pages together and went to the service desk. Russell hesitated as he was about to recite Cheryl's name and address to the clerk.

Cheryl had made it clear he was not to contact her in any way. The only address he knew for her was the Foundation. Addressed to Cheryl, the FedEx envelope, like the mail, would land on the desk of Abby Washington, Cheryl's assistant. Abby would examine it, see it was from him and, assuming it was personal, deliver the unopened envelope to Cheryl. He couldn't be deceitful and give a false name as the sender. Cheryl would look at the label, see it was from him and if she stuck to her guns, toss it in the recycling bin.

Russell closed his eyes and cleared his mind. The solution came to him: Address it to Abby. Then she would open it, discard the envelope, and evaluate its contents regardless of the sender. She would see what it was and what it explained. Abby would do her job and pass it along to Cheryl as a straightforward proposal to the Foundation. After Cheryl began reading, it wouldn't matter that she would soon realize it was from him. He'd written it as a willing donor to the foundation with a killer lead sentence. There was a wonderful opportunity for the Foundation to expand its work with at-risk Chicago youth through an uplifting, empowering, proven program for which the funding already was in place. There was nothing personal in the proposal, not a word concerning their marriage and impending divorce. That was out of his hands. Russell gave the clerk Abby's name, the Foundation address, phone number and his name and Gribber's address as sender. Thirty dollars and fifteen cents, delivery guaranteed by three o'clock tomorrow afternoon.

When Gribber came home from guiding, Russell told him his idea and the project it entailed. They continued to discuss it over leftovers on the veranda, Gribber adding several insightful comments and suggestions. They dished up ice cream for dessert.

"If we have your new career sorted out," Gribber said, "I need to talk to you about something. I'd like you to be my partner for the walleye tournament this weekend."

Russell assumed Gribber was joking.

He wasn't. "Jammer's starting a new cottage on Muriel Lake, second one where it's his design and he's the general contractor. He's hired a crew including the top framer in the area, but only has him for eight days. So he's busting it through the weekend."

"What about one of the other guides? Surely Tony Carter would be a better choice."

"They all have to work. The Lodge, all the resorts are full. I get the days off to represent the town."

"Then what about your musky tournament partner? I forget his name."

"Ross McDonald. He turned me down. He'll fish muskies with me a few hours in evenings but said he's getting too old to spend two long days in a boat fishing walleyes."

"What about Faith, then? She's much more capable than I."

Gribber flashed his exasperation. "I'll be honest, I called her this morning and asked her. She said she'd rather spend her weekend sleeping late, baking and gardening. She said to ask you."

"You know I will. I just don't want to lose it for you."

"You'll do fine. The pros that show up know how to catch walleyes but don't know the river like I do. Besides, no matter where we finish, there's only one guy we have to beat. Erik Lindstrom, a Wisconsin pro and world-class jerk."

"Is he the guy who beat you and Jammer last year?"

"Indeed he is."

"What's his story?"

"Come with me to the pub tonight. Most of the pros are coming in today. They all stay at the Point. I'm sure Erik will be there. You'll learn all you need to know about him."

"Can't wait." Russell looked at his watch. "First I need to call Lydia and ask her about the landing property. She done with her patrolling for the day, you think?"

"Should be. But she and Jammer tend to ignore their phones after five o'clock. Just grab my steed and run over there. If they're not outside on the deck, though, you'd better knock. Loud."

Russell saw the Ministry boat tied to the front deck of the houseboat as he cruised into Hidden Lake. Jammer's boat was tied to the side opposite his plane, so Russell putted around to the back deck. Jammer was standing at the smoking barbecue grill and broke into a grin.

"Pirate!" he said, reaching for the bow rope. "I heard you were back."

"Can't get enough, my man. Lydia inside? Need to talk to her."

"She sure is. Just getting dressed from her swim." Jammer hollered through the kitchen window. "Lyd, you decent? Someone here to see you."

"Yeah. Is that Pirate? Tell him to come to the front."

"I'd invite you for dinner," Jammer whispered, "but I don't think I have enough."

"Not a problem," Russell said, turning to walk the narrow side deck to the front.

Lydia opened the door and invited Russell in. "You want something to drink?"

"I'm good, Lydia, thanks. I wanted to ask you about the Karpenko property in Pistol. Is it up for sale?"

"Not quite. Still going through the process. Soon, though. The Ministry will list it with an agent we use in Miskwa. It's pretty neat, over four acres. It includes those beautiful bluffs. Three hundred feet of shoreline."

"Feet, not meters?"

"We do property in feet in Canada."

"Why is that?"

"Beats the hell out of me. I also found out the property on either side, the entire rest of the bay, is Crown land."

"Crown land?"

"It's owned by the Queen of England. Well, the Ontario government controls it, but she sorta has first dibs. All it means is it's not for sale, can never be developed. It's a Canada thing. Eighty-seven percent of Ontario is Crown land."

Jammer hollered through the window from the deck. "Back bacon on your burger, babe?"

"Of course," Lydia hollered back. "And cheddar. Yum."

"So, it's a private bay? I'd like to buy it."

"I'll call my boss and tell him, ask him to let me know before it's listed. That's good for us, a quick sale, and the agent will like it because she won't have to drive up to shoot photos."

"You are fabulous, thank you." Russell almost grabbed Lydia and kissed her, but thought better of it.

"Don't you want to know about what it'll cost?" Lydia asked as they walked to the door.

"It doesn't matter what it costs." Russell went around to the back to speak with Jammer. "I hear you're starting on a new cottage. Good for you. What's your schedule look like after that? I might have something for you."

Chapter 38

Russell filled in Gribber about the landing property upon his return, and Gribber filled in Russell on the rules for the walleye tournament. Tomorrow was the scouting day, the participants zooming all over the river, hitting spots quickly while testing a variety of fishing techniques and baits. On Saturday, the tournament started at six a.m., a "shotgun start" from Holst Point. You fish as fast and furiously as possible, then return to the Point at noon to check in. You head out again, fish all afternoon and return to the Point no later than five-thirty.

Each boat contained two anglers. The maximum catch per boat each day was five walleyes. Three of the walleyes had to be within the Ontario slot size parameters for "keepers," converted from metric to fourteen to eighteen inches long. The goal was to catch three fish at or near the maximum eighteen-inch length, the fatter the better. Two fish could be larger than eighteen inches. These fish often decided which team won the tournament. Russell's twenty-seven incher from the week before was a fish that certainly would be kept during the tournament. But the boat that happened upon a real lunker or two, walleyes exceeding thirty inches, often came out on top.

At the end of each day, tournament officials measured and weighed the fish from each boat then released them. You kept your fish in your boat's live well and were penalized eight ounces if a fish was brought in dead. The team with the heaviest two-day total of walleyes was the winner.

Getting into Gribber's boat to head to the pub, Russell spied a number of strange insects clinging to its sides. He swept away several from the bench seat with his hand. The bugs were about an inch long, with translucent wings rising straight up from slender, yellowish bodies. What the hell were they?

"Mayflies," Gribber said. "Notorious for not keeping track of what month it is. Looks like we're getting a hatch. It's the warm weather that came in. Won't bode well for the fishing this weekend, their role in the chain is to be fish food. The fish will gorge on them at night for the next few days. Look out there."

Russell looked at the water surrounding the dock and saw mayflies in large numbers floating upright on the surface.

"Catching fish right off the bat in the morning will be crucial," Gribber said. "By afternoon it will be tough to get a fat and happy walleye to hit our bait."

Russell and Gribber passed the lighted parking area reserved for guests' boats and trailers as they walked from the Holst Point dock to the pub. The entire area sparkled like the Las Vegas Strip, filled with glossy, expensive fiberglass and aluminum fishing boats even more impressive than those Russell had ogled in the parking lot of Mailer's resort in Orr. Similar to pro stock cars, the boats were adorned with sponsors' names and logos, from fishing rod and reel companies to lure, boat and motor manufacturers. Each boat featured a large trolling motor mounted at the bow and monstrously large outboard engine at the stern.

Gribber appraised the boats. "I see the three big Ontario pros are here, Derek Reid, Luke Flintoft, Billy Coke. All good guys. Looks like a few others. A lot of Manitoba pros too. More boats from Minnesota than last year. That blue one is Steve Larson. He's one to watch out for. Nice guy though." At the top of the lot, parked with its trailer at an angle so other boats couldn't be parked next to it was a flashy red, black and silver nineteen-footer adorned with more sponsor decals than the others. "The great Erik Lindstrom," Gribber said.

Russell took in the sleek, long and low speedboat bearing a Wisconsin registration decal. It was packing a black, four hundred horsepower Mercury Verado outboard engine, as menacing as a giant Darth Vader helmet.

"Aren't we at a disadvantage?" Russell asked. "No offense, but these boats go a hell of a lot faster than yours. They must be able to cover a lot more territory, move faster from spot to spot."

"Jammer and I beat all of 'em two years in a row in my humble steed. Last year, Lindstrom got lucky. But don't worry. This year we're unveiling a secret weapon."

The pub was more crowded and boisterous than usual. A lot of faces Russell didn't recognize belonged to men sporting crisp shirts and caps embroidered with logos matching those from the boats outside. Gribber was welcomed to a table where they sat down with several Ontario and Minnesota pro fishermen.

"Great to see you, Grib," Derek Reid said. "Going to kick our bums again this weekend, or take it easy on us?"

"Who knows, Derek. We have a little mayfly hatch just to make it interesting."

"Saw that," Steve Larson said. "Ran into the same thing at the tournament on Red Lake two weeks ago. Sure made for slow fishing."

Two tables over, a large hatless man with blazing red hair and matching goatee was laughing too loudly at something. To his left sat a young man who, judging from his facial features and matching sponsor shirt, obviously was his son. To his right sat a second young man similarly attired but rail-thin with long, stringy black hair escaping from beneath a tattered baseball cap.

Gribber leaned over to Russell and pointed out the men with his eyes. "That's Erik Lindstrom with the goatee. His son, Dan, he's his fishing partner. The third guy with the cap I don't know. He came with them last year for the first time. Probably peels Erik's grapes."

Gribber drank his usual while Russell sipped a beer. Several of the other pros passed by the table to say hello to Gribber.

A few minutes later, Lindstrom came over carrying his drink. "Who let Cochise off the reservation?" he yelled so the whole room heard, too broad a smile on his face. "Good to see you Dogrib. How ya been?" He circled around to Gribber's chair and shook his hand.

"Erik, the pleasure is all yours." Gribber introduced Russell as his partner. "Didn't think you'd bother with this little sideshow four years in a row. No live TV coverage, just taping for one of their tournament specials. Do your sponsors even pay your entry fee for this one?"

"Oh, they pay, they pay. And I always come back to defend a title. So far, I won the opening tournament in May, since then a third and a fourth, so guess who's the current points leader? I average over a hundred grand in earnings most years. Now that I got this river figured out, I'm gonna be tough on you again, buddy." Lindstrom drained his glass and called over to the man with the stringy hair. "Sammy, go up to the bar and get me another screwdriver, will ya?" He turned back to Gribber. "The service in this rat hole stinks. And the drinks."

"Well Erik," Reid said, "always nice to see you in a gregarious mood. All I can say is, may the best man win."

"Best two fishermen, you mean," Lindstrom said. He glanced at Russell. "That's what it always comes down to." Flashing a fake smile, he returned to his table.

Russell finished his beer. He glanced at Gribber who nodded. Gribber wished everyone at the table good luck as they stood to go.

The sun had set beneath a cloudless sky by the time they docked at Morning Wood, the rising moon a soft spotlight across the water. Russell was mystified by what was taking place across the glassy surface as he tied up the boat. It appeared to be boiling, gently and erratically, in various portions around the dock and shoreline.

"Wait right here," Gribber said in an excited tone. He turned and ran up the path, returning in seconds with an old bamboo fly rod. "Schools of whitefish," he said. "Coming in from the deep water to feed on the mayflies. They're following them from the river bottom to the surface as they hatch. You only see this one or two nights a year." Gribber picked up a mayfly by the wings and slipped it onto the tiny hook on the end of the line. Pulling out line from the small reel, he waved the rod back and forth then sailed the bait out into the middle of the school.

"You never told me about whitefish," Russell said. "How come we never fish for them?"

"Very difficult to catch. Rarely hit a minnow or a lure. Small, soft mouths, they usually move slowly along the bottom sucking up grubs. In spring they move from the shallow bays and go way deep. Most people who come here to fish don't even know they're in the river."

"What do they taste like?"

"Heaven. Even better than walleye." Gribber continued making casts into the gently roiling water until he hooked one. Russell grabbed the net from the boat and deftly netted the eighteen inch-long fish. Compared to a walleye it looked prehistoric, with its small head and dull, bone-white scales.

Gribber put down the rod and kneeled at a corner of the dock. He pulled on a slender nylon rope secured to a cleat until a rectangular wire cage appeared at the surface. "Bring her here." Gribber removed the hook and dropped the fish through the spring-loaded plastic lid of the cage. He lowered the cage back into the water where it sank to the bottom. "One more for me then your turn." He soon hooked another whitefish, the same size as the first. Russell pulled up the cage and Gribber dropped the fish inside. He handed Russell the rod. "Just do what you saw me do."

Though it can take many hours of practice and even lessons to cast effectively with a fly rod, on his third attempt Russell hooked a fish after flailing the bait out only six feet from the dock. It was a larger whitefish, around two feet long. Gribber netted it and added it to the cage.

"Getting late and I'm tired," Gribber said. He placed his thumb over one nostril at a time as he leaned over the edge of the dock and blew his nose. "I can clean them tomorrow night, even Sunday after the tournament. Fish keep in a cage for several days. Let's get to bed. We have a big day tomorrow."

Gribber cooked breakfast the following morning while Russell made sandwiches and packed the cooler. Gribber had the sniffles and several times turned away from the stove to sneeze. "Damn summer cold," he said. "Rotten time for it." He asked Russell to fill one of the Thermoses with orange juice.

They ate quickly then grabbed their fishing equipment from the shed and headed to the boat. At the bait shop they bought minnows and leeches from Faith, who wished them luck with a kiss each. They drove to the marina, Russell assuming they needed gas. When they pulled up to a side dock, Russell spotted Richie's red, Illinois fishing boat. Gribber withdrew a key from his pocket. "Compliments of Lydia, bless her heart. We'll call her Red Rocket."

They transferred their fishing gear, then Gribber drove the sleek boat to the gas dock, filled the tank, and roared out toward Little Sand. Seated in the back, Russell closed his mouth and breathed through his nose. Richie's boat flew, literally taking his breath away. Gribber didn't throttle back until they were at the entrance to Big Sand. "We'll be hitting spots boom boom boom," Gribber said. "Get to the bottom, see what's there, then on to the next spot."

The two men jigged and trolled along shorelines and islands as well as underwater humps and bumps far off shore. Fishing was slow. Gribber handed Russell a pair of binoculars and assigned him the task of periodically monitoring the action of the other pro boats scattered across the immense body of water. None of the boats appeared to be catching many fish. More than once, Russell spied on the activity of another boat only to discover a pair of binoculars focused on them.

Bombing across the water from Big Sand to Roughrock, they fished at a frenetic pace. Gribber's congestion and sneezing worsened as the day progressed. In early afternoon they roared under the bridge and headed upstream, fishing all the way up to The Dalles with moderate success before heading home. "We should be fine," Gribber said as they tied up at Morning Wood. "The mayfly hatch will make for slow fishing, but I know a few late June spots the pros don't. Unless someone gets lucky and lands more than a few lunkers, I like our chances."

Gribber's face folded into a tight knot as he unleashed a violent sneeze.

Chapter 39

Cheryl Dean checked Abby Washington's desk for afternoon deliveries before heading home. Abby had taken the day off to prep for her son's high school graduation party. The UPS package she recognized as printer toner. The FedEx envelope, she realized as she examined it, was from ... Russell.

It was addressed to Abby. What was he thinking? That addressed to Abby, Abby would open it and seeing it was personal and meant for her boss, discard the envelope and hand the pages to her? Russell was a masterful writer, but words didn't exist in the English language that he could arrange in such an order as to change anything. To so slyly contact her, to try to draw her into some last-gasp plot to stop the divorce, after her explicit request on the phone!

Cheryl stared at the envelope in her hands. What was inside? Wait, rewind. How could she be feeling even the slightest temptation to open it? She closed her eyes and drew a long breath. To that she knew the answer.

A few small, tender slices of the love she felt for Russell doggedly remained. She could feel them at night when her thoughts turned to memories from their courtship and early years of marriage. Or whenever she faced the impending finality of Tuesday afternoon's hearing. Damn him, she thought. Damn the man who went away.

Slow, subtle torture. Face it, that's what it was ... what it is right now, staring at an unopened envelope. Six years on a gentle downward slope of listless isolation. She needed to keep that in mind. What was in the envelope? Apologies and promises.

Jennifer was right. To get through this stage in her life, it must become part of her past.

Cheryl had told the rest of the staff to knock off at four to get a jump on the weekend, so she was the last person in the office. On her way out the door, she stepped into the copy room and tossed the FedEx envelope from Russell into the large blue recycling bin.

Chapter 40

Gribber ate a light supper, then flooded his body with tea and lemon for the rest of the evening. He was in bed just after nine and Russell by ten. When they arose at four-thirty, Gribber's condition had worsened. He forced down a bowl of fruit without appetite while Russell packed their lunches and beverages. They stopped at the bait shop, open early for the tournament, and traded jabs with several other pros. At five-thirty they landed at Holst Point to check in for the six o'clock shotgun start to the tournament.

Russell was impressed by the transition of the ramshackle, century-old fishing lodge into a colorful sixth stop on the CanAm Pro Walleye Tour. Two long banners strung from poles marked both sides of the point. A large, furnished canvas tent served as tournament headquarters and media center. Just up from the docks stood a large stage featuring a backdrop of sponsor logos and large video screen. At one end stood a table of equipment where the fish were measured and weighed.

Gribber pulled Red Rocket into its assigned slip. The tournament camera crew was focused on defending champion Erik Lindstrom in his boat, barking orders to his son while they organized rods, tackle boxes and coolers. The third member of his team, Sammy, was nowhere to be seen.

Fifteen minutes before start time, three tournament officials spread out and inspected the live wells in each boat to ensure all were equipped for aeration and none contained fish. At the sound of the starter pistol, thirty-eight blazing, high-powered pro fishing boats with over ten thousand combined horsepower fired out in all directions with an ear-splitting roar. Gribber and Russell headed for The Dalles, stopping along the way to jig humps and troll a few channels.

Gribber caught the first walleye, netting it himself so Russell could keep fishing. Gribber had fashioned a quick, movable measuring device, a three-foot long strip of plywood with lines marking quarter-inches beginning at fourteen. Placing a fish with its mouth flush to one end resulted in a quick, accurate length assessment. The fish was just over seventeen inches. Gribber placed it in the live well.

They caught several more walleyes too small to measure, then Gribber caught a nice one. "Dang," Gribber said as he placed it on the measuring board. "Just over eighteen. We'll keep it in case it's one of our two largest."

"We don't weigh them as well?" Russell asked.

"No. When I narrow it down to our final five fish, if two are about the same length I can tell which one weighs more."

They continued upstream to The Dalles and fished different spots. Five other pros were fishing in the same vicinity and occasionally came close enough to Red Rocket to engage in friendly banter. All the walleyes being caught were small, so Gribber drove further upstream to a point swirling with current. Drifting with leeches on plain hooks, Russell caught a fat walleye measuring exactly eighteen inches and Gribber caught one just a quarter-inch shorter.

They landed at the Holst Point docks at a few minutes before noon to check in. Erik Lindstrom pulled in just ahead of them. He didn't look happy. He had spent the morning fishing in Little Sand, productive for him in previous years but not today.

Gribber raced Red Rocket to Big Sand after initialing the check-in clipboard. Jigging with leeches, they boated two more walleyes between seventeen and eighteen inches. Gribber checked his watch. "The walnuts here are all about the same size. We have our slot fish covered for the day. We're better off trying to snag a big one in Roughrock. We have time to hit the narrows and a secret spot before heading in."

Drifting in the current with leeches at the entrance to Roughrock, Gribber caught the first large fish of the day, measuring over twenty-six inches. The fish stopped biting shortly afterward. For the next four hours, no matter where they fished, they caught nothing but small walleyes and the odd perch. Gribber fished in silence, his sneezing now augmented by a hacking cough. He opened the lid to the live well just after five, selected the five keepers, and released the rest. He fired up Red Rocket and raced back to Holst Point for the Day One weigh-in.

Erik Lindstrom and his son pulled in last, Gribber noting they had rounded the point from Gunn Lake. Must have spent the afternoon fishing between Myrtle Rapids and the south end of Gunn, he surmised.

Two tournament officials carrying a large cooler filled with river water stepped into the boats one by one, removed the fish and carried them to the stage. Each fish was measured and placed in a plastic cradle atop an electronic scale, then the tournament announcer called out the length and weight into a handheld microphone. After the total weight was inputted into a laptop, the names on the screen slid up and down the leaderboard. The fish were returned to the cooler and released.

Each pro and his partner stepped onto the stage as their fish were measured and weighed. All the boats had five walleyes, but the weight totals varied greatly. Some of the pros failed to catch any fish exceeding eighteen inches. Luke Flintoft, one of the Ontario pros, held the lead until the five fish from Boat #6, Gribber and Russell, were weighed. Their five walleyes totaled seventeen pounds, five ounces. Before exiting the stage, Russell slapped Gribber on the back as they watched the name John Dogrib blink to the top of the leaderboard.

It remained on top during the weighing of the fish from the next four boats. Erik Lindstrom, as defending champion, was assigned Boat #1, meaning his catch would be weighed last. Lindstrom's first three walleyes were between sixteen and seventeen inches long, the fourth only a hair longer than fifteen.

Standing on the dock Russell and Gribber exchanged smiles. Several of the pros hooted as the stern-faced Lindstrom and his son stood on stage.

The hoots turned to silence when the final fish was removed from the cooler. It was a fat, thirty-two-inch lunker weighing thirteen pounds, ten ounces. As the weight of his fish were totaled, the name Erik Lindstrom blinked into first place with a four-ounce lead over Gribber and Russell after Day One. "Bastard!" Gribber said, muttering. "He stumbles onto the only lunker of the day. How does he do it?"

Annie and Faith were in the large crowd assembled to watch the weigh-in. As they approached Gribber and Russell, Annie flashed a look of concern. "You look terrible," she said to Gribber.

"Just a summer cold. All I need is sleep." Annie drew closer and placed the back of her hand on Gribber's forehead. "You're running a fever, Biidaapiwinini. You need chicken soup, tea and drugs. You haven't taken anything for it, have you?"

Gribber shrugged.

"Your place or mine?" Faith said to Annie.

"Mine." She gave Gribber a hard look. "You're staying at my place tonight. I have soup, tea and a couple different flu meds. You need to get into bed so Faith and I can take care of you. No argument, birdbrain. If you want a shot at winning this thing tomorrow, you'll do as I say."

Annie, Faith and Gribber climbed into Faith's boat.

"I'll grab his boat and meet you there," Russell said. Boats used by the pros during the tournament weren't allowed to leave the Holst Point dock after five-thirty, so Russell jogged the half mile to the marina, hopped into Gribber's steed and drove to Annie's.

Annie met him on the path from the dock and told him in hushed tones that Gribber was already crashed hard asleep in her guest bedroom. "Flu bug," she said. "Hopefully just a twenty-four hour. He had some soup and meds then passed out as soon as his head hit the pillow. Stay for a while. We were just fixing dinner."

They opened a bottle of wine after dinner and the three re-laxed on Annie's veranda, conversation and music interspersed with games of cribbage. Annie or Faith would occasionally check on Gribber, who awoke periodically and was served tea with honey. Russell was surprised when he glanced at his watch and saw it was ten forty-five. He thanked his hosts and rose to return to Morning Wood.

"We'll bring Gribber over to the Point at five-thirty tomor-row morning," Annie said.

"Thanks," Russell said. "I'll buy the bait and see you there."

As Russell stepped into Gribber's boat and clipped on his lifejacket, he realized he'd never driven a boat from Jackfish Bay to Gribber's at night. It was not a great concern. Though the night was partly cloudy, one could see a fair distance across the water. The shorelines were dark but visible. He started the boat, flipped on the running lights and drove out of Jackfish Bay.

Rounding the peninsula, the grand façade of the Lodge was an impressive, glowing sight, the lighted Rotunda visible through the large windows facing the river. Russell passed under the bridge and headed toward Holst Point, after which he would cross the entrance to Town Bay on his right. The channel would widen as he entered Gunn Lake. Morning Wood was a few miles down the mainland shore on the right, just before Big Island. Nothing to it.

With the moon high on his left Russell had a surprisingly clear view of Town Bay, the moonlight polishing the large ex-panse of gray-black water. He could see the outline of the marina's prominent roof. Just as he began to turn his head back, he saw movement.

It was a boat, coming out of the bay, not from the marina docks but from the municipal dock further down shore. It was on a course up the far side of the bay past the bait shop, meaning it would intersect with Russell's boat in perhaps thirty seconds. As it drew nearer Russell could see it was a small aluminum fishing boat with a lone driver. The boat had no running lights, or if it did, the driver had chosen not to turn them on. Russell slowed then came almost to a stop so the boat could pull out of the bay safely ahead of him.

As the driver veered into Gunn Lake, the moonlight cast directly onto the side of the boat and Russell saw the words "Miller's Marina Rental" flicker briefly. He also got a look at the driver, not precise details so much as a softly glowing outline view. A slender man, long, straggly dark hair flying back beneath a baseball cap. The man turned his head to study the boat with running lights that had slowed to allow him to pass. Russell caught a moonlit glimpse of the man's face and recognized him from Thursday night at the Pub.

It was Erik Lindstrom's third man, Sammy. But what, Russell wondered, was Sammy doing heading away from town into Gunn Lake at eleven at night? It took only a second for the answer to come to him.

Sammy was going fishing.

Russell let Sammy's boat put a hundred yards between them before throttling up to full speed. He could just make out the dark outline of Sammy's back. Was he turning his head around, watching? Nearby on the right was the first cottage on Gunn, with a floating aluminum boathouse. Russell drove toward the boathouse at full speed then slowed as if to land. He peered out to locate Sammy's boat, barely visible, a small dark shape slinking away in the distance.

Russell flipped off his running lights, throttled up to full speed and took off in pursuit. Absent the halo glare of the green and red running lights emitted from the bow, it was easier to see across the water at night. Sammy was headed straight down the length of Gunn, staying left of Big Island, the most direct route to where that branch of the river funneled to a single channel before swinging left and roaming six miles up to Myrtle Rapids. Russell judged the speed of Gribber's steed was greater than that of the rental boat, so slowed enough to keep Sammy only a distant, dark blur. Studying the outlines of the distant shorelines ahead, Russell found the pronounced dip in the black tree line marking the channel to Myrtle Rapids. Sammy was headed straight for it.

About a mile before Myrtle, Sammy slowed down. The clouds were gone and the view across the water was becoming brighter. The wide channel had narrowed. Russell slowed and veered left to stay closer to the granite-and-timber shoreline. It was dark there, the tall pines offering shade from the angled moonlight. Russell shut off his motor to see if Sammy had shut off his. He hadn't. It purred softly as Sammy approached a broadly rounded point ahead. The sound from Sammy's motor would make it impossible for Sammy to hear his, so Russell putted stealthily up the dark, opposite shoreline until he was only forty yards behind.

The wind had died, the water glass-calm. Russell shut off his motor. Sammy had slipped his boat into neutral. Russell could tell he was fiddling with a fishing rod and above the soft purr of the motor heard the distinct rattle of a tackle box being opened and closed amplified across the still water. Sammy lowered his rod, slipped the motor into reverse, opened the bail on his reel, and jerking his wrist as if jigging, let out line. *Must be trolling a floating lure*, Russell thought. He heard the sharp click of Sammy's bail as it closed.

After trolling a mere sixty feet Sammy caught a fish. When he let out an animated, "Yeah, baby!" it sounded like he was sitting in Russell's boat. The fish obviously was fighting hard, for it took over five minutes for Sammy to bring it to the boat. Russell watched as Sammy netted the fish, astonished at how clearly he could see the activity. It was a big net. Sammy put his rod down and lifted the net into the boat with both hands. The big net contained a very big fish. Sammy leaned over and placed the fish in the boat's live well then began trolling again, heading further up the shore. Just before the boat disappeared around the point Sammy hooked another fish.

Russell wondered how many fish he was after. Two? Three? The answer became apparent when after another long tussle Sammy netted the fish and placed it in the live well. The rod disappeared into the boat. Sammy sat down, gunned the engine, and drove in a sweeping curve back toward Gunn Lake. With a thump in his chest, Russell realized that for a few seconds Sammy would be aiming directly for him, before straightening out to shoot down the middle of the channel. Russell turned the key to start his motor, threw it into reverse while toggling it up partway and backed even closer into the dense shadows of the shoreline. He only hoped the water near shore didn't contain barely submerged boulders.

Russell cut the motor and dropped to the floor in a ball as Sammy's boat turned slowly in an arc toward his. He heard Sammy's boat roar past. Raising his head, he saw the boat zooming away across the softly glowing water. Sammy wasn't looking back.

Russell resumed following in stealth mode. Sammy steered toward the left shoreline as he sped under the power lines marking the entrance into Gunn, then veered into Lost Bay. Russell watched the outline of Sammy and his boat as it slowed before disappearing around a small granite point at the start of the bay. Was he going to fish? Would he go deeper into the bay? Russell knew he couldn't follow. When Sammy drove out, he'd be spotted.

Russell headed for the base of the point and pulled in tight to shore where he wouldn't be seen. No sooner did he arrive and cut the motor than he heard Sammy's idling motor revving up. The rental boat shot out around from the other side of the point and headed toward town, Sammy focused straight ahead.

Russell cruised slowly around the point and entered a small bay. It was crescent-shaped and less than seventy feet across. Most of its shoreline was granite except for the brushy center where Russell could just make out a small weed bed off shore. What the hell was Sammy doing in here?

Scanning the water, Russell almost missed the plastic boat bumper floating near the weed bed. He almost missed it because unlike virtually every lost bumper on the river, it wasn't white. Russell brought the boat in closer and saw the bumper was painted brown, the color of a deadhead. He slipped the motor into neutral. As the boat sidled up to the bumper he reached down and snatched it from the water.

There was a slender nylon rope tied to one end. Russell began reeling in the slack hand-over-hand until he felt weight. He continued pulling up the rope, knowing what he would find tied to the other end.

Chapter 41

Russell stopped for bait and arrived at the Holst Point docks at five-twenty. Adrenaline blasted him wildly awake even though he was running on only three hours of sleep. When Annie, Gribber and Faith pulled up, he crouched beside their boat and explained his night's activities in hushed tones. The three sat in wide-eyed silence, segueing to gasps and finally into deep-throated laughter.

"Brilliant play," Gribber said, a fiery twinkle returning to his eyes. "You've made the acquaintance of the spirit Nanabozho. He's a trickster. That's exactly what he would have suggested to me." Gribber took over the conversation, hatching a plot involving Annie and Faith. Both had the day off.

At the firing of the six o'clock starter gun, the flashy boats again blasted off in all directions. Gribber was on the mend, his body healed by sleep, his head dried up from flu medicine and his devilish grin restored. As he shot Red Rocket into Little Sand, he kept looking back at Russell and shaking his head in amusement.

They didn't travel far. After three minutes, Gribber pulled up smack in the middle of a large expanse of water that stretched outward through the distant islands like tentacles of an octopus. "Chartreuse jigs with minnows," he said. Three other pro boats stopped with them in the same general area but began fishing much closer to the surrounding shorelines.

Gribber glanced at the depth finder. "Seventy feet deep all across here, but there's a shallow hump, very small. The other pros don't know about it, it's not on their maps. Twenty years ago, a Ministry boat spent a month charting the depths of the river and they missed it. Been keeping it in my back pocket for to-day." Gribber's head was on a swivel, triangulating two distinctive shoreline treetops with a distant cottage roof while flickering his eyes to the screen. "Right here. Eighteen feet. Down."

Standing, both men dropped their baits to the bottom. "Mayfly hatch peaked yesterday," Gribber said. "The walleyes have been gorging themselves all night. That's why your friend Sammy had such good luck trolling a floater last night, big walleyes were cruising the surface. As the sun rises, they move deeper. All but the biggest are full. If we're going to catch a lunker, it's going to be now."

Russell felt his jig hit bottom but as he reeled up the slack the jig didn't budge. He jerked his rod violently upward, then froze as he held the sharply curved rod before him. Was it a fish or did he just set his jig hard into boulders on the bottom? Both men studied his rod tip. Nothing was happening. Gribber was holding the boat stationary against the gentle current with the trolling motor. Russell's line disappeared straight down into the water. "I think I'm hung up," Russell said.

"Reel in a few cranks," Gribber said, continuing to jig. Russell did so, which only lowered the tip of his bending rod closer to the water's surface. He tried to lift his rod. It felt like his jig was set in a barrel of concrete. Then his reel's drag gave a single tick as he watched the point where his line entered the water zigzag a few inches toward the boat.

"Fish," Russell said.

It took over ten minutes to get the lunker to the surface. Every time Russell reclaimed a few feet of line, the walleye took it back with short, powerful dives. When finally it appeared from the black depths, for a second Russell was astonished by how small it was—about ten inches long, bizarrely short but fat. Then as it emerged fully from beneath the boat, he realized he was viewing only the top of its head.

Gribber dropped the walleye net and grabbed the larger one. Both were silent as he netted the enormous golden walleye and immediately placed it in the live well. "Thirty-four inches, at least," Gribber said. "Could be a three-footer. Between catching this fish and your cold, black heart, you may well have won us the tournament."

"Ignoring the fact I never would have known to fish here, thanks."

They hit more spots in Little and Big Sand before noon and caught three additional walleyes in the seventeen- to eighteen-inch range. Red Rocket shot back to Holst Point to check in. Gribber wanted to be there when Erik Lindstrom arrived.

Lindstrom and his son Dan pulled up to the docks shortly after them, Gribber noting their arrival via the main channel from The Big Stretch. So they'd been fishing spots between here and The Dalles. Lindstrom displayed a wide smile to the TV camera crew taping his arrival.

Lindstrom caught Gribber's eye and bellowed at him from across the docks. "I was surprised to see you head for Sand this morning. You'd think a local Indian guide would know the river. You should have followed me. The big ones are upstream. We hammered them this morning. And you know it's gonna shut down again this afternoon. With what we've caught, this tournament could be over."

"Probably right," Gribber shouted back, shaking his head. "We couldn't even find the perch. And you know what they say … two fish in the bush are worth one in the boat."

Lindstrom leaned back, a puzzled look on his face. Finally, he shook his head and laughed. "Whatever you say, Cochise. We'll see you at the weigh-in—show you what lunker Kamini walleyes look like."

"Can't wait," Russell hollered.

Gribber initialed the check-in sheet, fired up Red Rocket and again headed downstream. Lindstrom had been correct about one thing: The fishing would be slow all afternoon. Racing between Little Sand, Big Sand and Roughrock they endured stretches of over an hour without catching a fish. Trolling near Big Sand

Beach, Gribber finally nailed a big walleye he didn't waste time measuring.

Upriver, Erik Lindstrom and son Dan were scuffling. Their morning catch was decent, far better than Saturday's. They had a twenty-five incher, two fat walleyes in the eighteen-inch range and two over sixteen. But by afternoon the incessantly sunny skies were scattering the walleyes deeper, their appetites completely shut down from the river's bounty of mayflies. Catching a lunker would be highly improbable.

Lindstrom considered his options. He would prefer to win the tournament without having to again take from his reserve stock in the cage. It sure was nice to have insurance, though. Yesterday he and Dan had swooped into Lost Bay before weigh-in to grab the thirty-two-inch lunker Sammy had caught Friday night, along with an eighteen-incher. Without grabbing the lunker their day would have been a disaster. With it, they nursed a four-ounce lead.

Gribber couldn't be trusted. No doubt he and his partner caught some walleyes this morning. Perhaps they'd gotten lucky and nailed a lunker. If he and Dan boated no more big fish between now and five o'clock, it might be wise to hit the cage and grab the eighteen-incher plus both of Sammy's fresh lunkers from last night. That would ensure a tournament win plus rub it in the faces of Gribber and the rest of the pros at weigh-in.

Lindstrom returned to the waters above The Dalles for the afternoon session. From there it was quick to Myrtle Rapids, the fishing spots below, and access into Lost Bay. They would again need to be careful not to be seen by another pro as they popped quickly in and out of Lost. Lost was a shallow musky bay. It might look suspicious.

At four o'clock Lindstrom told his son to lock and load. The fishing was dead. If they headed down Myrtle Rapids and into Gunn now, there would be little risk of being seen as they ducked into the bay. After they deposited the three fish from the cage into their live well, they could fish a few more spots in Gunn then race back to Holst Point for the five-thirty weigh-in.

"Look for other boats," Lindstrom said to Dan as they aimed toward the entrance to Lost Bay.

There were none—pro boats, at least. As they approached the bay, however, both men eyeballed the two attractive women in a sharp-looking G3 casting for muskies along the shoreline above the entrance. Dan placed two fingers into his mouth and fired off a wolf whistle that shrieked above the deep roar of the engine. The women turned, smiled and waved. The slender one with the short, weird hair dressed in a tank top and bikini bottom did a little shimmy.

Lindstrom coasted into the small crescent bay and swung the big boat sideways next to the bumper. Dan began pulling in the line. As the wire cage emerged he held it with its flat bottom barely in the water. Lindstrom flipped open the top of the boat's live well then bent over to remove the fish from the cage.

The human mind is a peculiar thing, hardly a novel statement never before expressed. All experience it, a moment when the eyes perceive something wholly unexpected. The image forwarded to the brain magically morphs into that which is desired to be seen—until the brain sternly commands explanation be found for the impossible incongruity between expectation and sensory perception. This is the moment, deep inside the cranium, when all hell breaks loose.

Lindstrom's brain was operating under the premise there would be three fish in the cage, the two lunkers Sammy caught last night, plus the eighteen-incher from Friday. Lindstrom looked down at the three fish resting placidly in a few inches of water on the bottom of the cage. The initial impulse fired from his brain stated, so far so good …

Except they were dead! Even a tiny walleye barely large enough to strike a lure has acquired shiny gold color to its scales. One of the fish had tipped on its side, displaying a dull, silvery white flank, the color of a dead walleye. The other two didn't look so good, either. Lindstrom's mind raced to the realm of mathematics: three times eight equaled twenty-four, the number of ounces he and Dan would be penalized for three dead fish at weigh-in.

A shot of warm assurance flowed next from his brain ... leave the dead eighteen-incher. Some in their live well were nearly as large. Two dead lunkers, those were fine. Sixteen ounces deducted from their total should still win the tournament. After all, they were about to add some twenty-six pounds of walleye to their live well.

This calming thought vanished when replaced by the jarring realization that ... the walleyes had shrunk! The largest fish Lindstrom gazed down at was twenty-four inches, perhaps, the others smaller ... where were the two, thirty-inch-plus lunkers Sammy texted he'd caught last night? Fish don't die then shrink! None of this made any sense, he thought. Wait ... that damn Sammy! *He* had screwed up, grossly overestimating the size of the two walleyes he'd caught. Or lied about it. But why would he lie?

"What the hell?" Lindstrom said, his mind still racing madly in every direction except toward the inexorable truth. He thrust his arms into the cage and grabbed one of the fish with both hands. It responded by wriggling vigorously. It was very much alive. He removed the fish and for the first time examined it closely. His eyes transmitted these facts to his brain: short, small head. Tiny mouth. Soft, silvery, two-inch-long dorsal fin centered on the back instead of the spiny, black dorsal fin of a walleye ...

The wildly careening carrousel of incomprehensible facts scorching Lindstrom's brain cartwheeled in splinters outward to the ether as the full truth flooded his mind like a sixty-foot tsunami.

Their cage contained three whitefish.

"Dad," Dan said softly.

"Shut up!" Lindstrom said with a snarl, still holding the whitefish in his hands. The fish was staring dumbly at him.

"Dad," Dan repeated, "look." Lindstrom looked at his son crouched beside him and saw he was staring neither at him nor the fish. Dan's head was cranked over his shoulder, his eyes focused on the small granite point barely forty feet away.

Still holding the whitefish, Lindstrom stood and turned to face the point. The two women from the G3 had landed quietly on the other side and were standing on it. A video camera obscured the face of the tall woman; all he could see was swales of long, auburn hair. The slender one with the crazy hair was holding a camera, a good one, with a telephoto lens.

A soft click, click, click was all that broke the resounding silence.

"Smile for the birdie, shit nuts," the pixie said as she lowered her camera. "These photos will look great on the tournament website. And the video is Facebook gold!"

Chapter 42

"Well I never been much at admitting things, that's why it's all so hard to say ..." erupted from Gribber's cell phone, the full-tilt galloping start to The Guess Who's "Star Baby" that served as his ring tone. He and Russell were fishing deep water along the backside of Indian Island, within view of the Lodge. He continued jigging while answering. It was Annie.

"Bubba One and Bubba Two just pulled out of Lost. We got all of it. They were a little muddled ... Lindstrom picked up one of the whitefish and stared at it like a monkey holding a Rubik's Cube. They dumped the fish, sank the cage and took off across Gunn toward town."

"Copy that, bravo bravo," Gribber said. He turned to Russell. "Lock and load."

Erik Lindstrom had said nothing to the women on the point. The thought flashed to him to attempt to seize their camcorder and camera, but he knew it wouldn't solve anything. One of the other pros had found the cage. He was caught. It wasn't quite four-thirty. He could drop off Dan at one of the docks in Town Bay just a short hike to the Point. Dan could sneak into the lot, grab Sammy, his pickup and trailer, and meet him at the public boat launch in Pistol Lake. Trailer the boat and beat it out of town without having to face the tournament officials, the film crew, the other pros and the townspeople at weigh-in. Not that it would change anything.

His professional fishing career was over.

Not slowing as he entered Town Bay, Lindstrom aimed for an empty cottage dock and started shouting instructions to Dan.

He paused when a swift red boat shot around the point from the other direction, spotted his boat and veered toward it.

Gribber.

Lindstrom slowed his boat to a troll as he approached the dock.

"Good afternoon, Erik," Gribber said as he motored alongside. "You're a little early for weigh-in, and the Point docks are around the corner."

Lindstrom said nothing.

"Slip 'er into neutral, there, champ, and let's chat about the situation."

Lindstrom hesitated, then shifted his boat into neutral.

Gribber stood, placed both hands on the gunwale of Lindstrom's boat and leaned over Lindstrom seated in the cockpit. "Here's how it's going to work, you big, dumb, ugly, cheating son of a bitch. Seems to me like you're heading for any dock except the Point's. What's the plan, drop off your son then load the boat in Pistol?"

Lindstrom stared straight ahead.

"Good," Gribber said. "You do that. We'll tell the tournament director the reason for your absence at the weigh-in, but the evidence won't be made public until tomorrow. Should give you just enough time to get back to your cave before the bomb hits."

Lindstrom spoke without looking at Gribber. "Sixty thousand."

Gribber raised his eyebrows. "Sixty thousand what?"

"US dollars. I can write you a check for thirty right now. Get you the other thirty in a week."

Gribber looked up at the sky, considering the offer. "Ninety thousand," he said. "Enough to cover my partner."

"Alright," Lindstrom said. "That much, I'll have to sell one of my boats. Just give me a couple weeks."

Gribber rose from hovering over Lindstrom. "Stand up, Erik. Look me in the eye and shake on it."

Lindstrom stood, turned and extended his hand. Gribber grasped it firmly, then squeezed so hard Lindstrom squealed and crashed to his knees.

"No." Gribber sat down, shifted into forward and roared away.

Nearly every resident of Kamini was present at Holst Point as the colorful boats raced in for the weigh-in. Crowding the docks with many more on shore, they erupted into cheers as Gribber and Russell coasted into their slip.

The crowd applauded each team as they took the stage for weigh-in. As the fish were measured and weighed, the pro's names again flipped and flashed up and down the leader board. Steve Larson, the Minnesotan, rose to the top when his catch, including a monster, thirty-five-and-a-half-incher, vaulted him up from seventh place.

"Wow," Gribber said as he stood in front of Red Rocket with Russell. "Forgot to mention, there's an extra five grand for biggest fish of the tournament. In all the excitement, I never measured yours. Keep your fingers crossed, it's going to be close."

Two officials entered Red Rocket and placed the five fish from the live well into the cooler. A gasp arose from the people packed around the slip as Russell's walleye was removed. Gribber and Russell took the stage.

The tournament announcer called out the weight and length of each fish as it was entered into the computer before being flashed to the video screen. "Two pounds one ounce at seventeen and one-half inches. Two pounds three ounces at seventeen and three-quarter inches. Two pounds five ounces at eighteen inches." The crowd erupted into cheers when it saw the size of Gribber's big fish. "Eight pounds ten ounces at twenty-seven and one-half inches!" called out the announcer, his voice booming louder through the speakers any time a large fish was unveiled.

As two men lifted Russell's fish from the bin to the table, the rowdy onlookers fell into stunned silence. "Measure her carefully, Roy, this is important," the announcer said. The man nodded as he measured the length, then both men lifted the enormous walleye onto the scale. Roy confirmed the weight and length to the announcer who took a deep breath before turning back to face the crowd. "Ladies and gentlemen, both measurements are right on the nose." He cranked up his voice to full boom. "Weight, twenty pounds. Length … thirty-six inches."

Gribber and Russell were again on stage thirty minutes later, accepting the winner's trophy and a check in the amount of $35,640. The crowd roared as a second check for $5,000 was presented to Russell. A photographer from the Miskwa newspaper shot photos of the two as they raised their trophy. Steve Larson finished second, Billy Coke third. Word spread quickly through the crowd: Erik Lindstrom had been disqualified due to a rules violation.

It was nearly eight before Gribber and Russell hopped into Gribber's steed. Russell was in a delighted daze, his voice raspy from answering questions about landing his lunker. "About the money," Russell said. "I'd like to donate my half and the five grand to the reservation."

Gribber looked at him and smiled. "Thank you, my friend. That makes it perfect. My half goes to the Kamini Community Fund."

The two boated out of Town Bay and around Holst Point to meet up with Annie and Faith for a celebratory prime rib dinner at the Lodge. After the waiter popped the cork on a bottle of champagne, Faith suggested they combine to propose a toast. "To native scalawags and wandering pirates," Faith said, raising her glass.

"To big fish and bigger friendships," Annie said, raising hers.

"To the wind, the water, the whitefish, the moon and the stars," Gribber said, holding his glass high.

Russell smiled warmly at his friends and raised his glass.

"To Kamini."

As Russell spoke the words a deep rumble of thunder shook the cavernous dining room.

"Now you did it," Gribber said, gazing up at the creaking log trusses arching high overhead. "Sounds like we're in for another blow."

Chapter 43

Abby Washington walked through the open door to Cheryl Dean's office and placed her mail on her desk. "Here you go. Quite a bit, even for a Monday morning."

"Thank you, Abby."

"Did we make a donation for a hockey rink on an Indian reservation in Ontario?"

Cheryl gave a chuckle. "Not that I'm aware, no."

"Well, I read the start of the letter and put it on top. Has what looks like a newspaper article with it."

Curious, Cheryl reached for the letter and removed the paper clip securing the folded newsprint.

On Sunday afternoon eight days earlier, Robert Cameron sat down at his kitchen table to write the letter. Gribber had phoned him the day before. He was right, thought Robert. Moccasins or no moccasins, he knew the rule. A thank-you letter—handwritten—was to be sent to every person or organization donating money to the reservation. If it was a youth project, the responsibility fell on him. It's too late to mail the letter to the Lodge, Gribber told him. Russell Dean had checked out and was driving home to Chicago. He was a partner in an advertising agency there. Figure the rest out, Gribber said.

Robert opened the family laptop and did a search for "russell dean advertising chicago." There. Samuels Dean Advertising. Flashy website ... list of clients, list of awards, Meet Your Team ... bingo. A photo of Mr. Dean in a killer suit sitting in a sweet office. Wow, did he ever look funny in a suit and without the beard. Clicking on "Contact Samuels Dean" two options appeared, one for the advertising agency and another for the Samuels Dean Charitable Foundation. Robert clicked on the Foundation and started reading. Founded ten years ago. Actively engaged in providing youth programs, facilities and aid to families in Chicago. And Ontario, thought Robert, if Mr. Dean happened along. So, the money had come from him through his foundation.

The site gave the name "Cheryl Dean" as the foundation's Executive Director. Must be Mr. Dean's wife. When writing a thank you letter to a charitable foundation, send it to the Executive Director, reasoned Robert. Mr. Dean would be sure to see it as well. He clicked on the name "Cheryl Dean." Her picture appeared with her bio. Wow. Blonde and smoking hot. Way to go, Mr. Dean! Robert jotted down the Foundation's address, took out a piece of First Nations letterhead, and began writing the letter.

When he finished, Robert remembered the article on the hockey rink from yesterday's Miskwa newspaper. Mr. Dean probably never saw it. That would be nice to include with the letter. His mom bought three copies since he was in one of the pictures. He clipped the article and included it with the letter, addressed the envelope and added postage to the US. It wouldn't go out until tomorrow but should get to Ms. Dean in about a week. Done.

Cheryl began reading the letter, hand-written in a sleek, artistic style.

> *Dear Ms. Dean,*
>
> *On behalf of all residents of the Blackdog First Nations Band of Ojibwe I would like to thank you for your foundation's generous donation of funds to build our new hockey rink. It came out perfect! All of us hockey players on the reservation figured we'd be going another year without the money to build a new one. Now we have the best rink in the league!*
>
> *To us it is more than a new hockey rink. It gives all of us a sense of pride and achievement. And we know that starting this winter we will be able to play home*

*games so our families and friends can watch. This means
a lot to us.*

*It was great to meet Mr. Dean and help him and his
friends build the rink. He was so nice and patient and we
all learned a lot from him. We hope he will come visit us
again soon. Or maybe this winter when he can watch us
play hockey and skate on his beautiful rink!*

Thank you again for your generous gift.

                                Sincerely,

                                Robert Cameron

Utterly perplexed, Cheryl unfolded the newspaper article. "Gracious Gift Gratefully Received" read the headline. "Generous Lodge guest donates money and sweat for new Blackdog hockey rink." Below it was a photograph of four smiling, woodsy looking adults, three men and a woman, their arms on each other's shoulders, sitting on the boards of a hockey rink in a field carved into an evergreen wilderness. A large group of Native American—Native Canadian?—young people stood or knelt in rows in front of them, like a sports team photo. Cheryl's eyes darted back to the dark-haired, handsome lumberjack with the full beard.

It was Russell.

Cheryl read the article. Russell's donation was over ten thousand dollars. On the second page there were three more photos, one of Ojibwe adults and teens during construction and another of the painted, pristine rink after completion. It was the final photo that riveted her gaze. Shot from behind a crowd, it was of Russell standing, his head bowed as if in prayer. His arms were raised outward, each hand holding a calf-length moccasin. His face portrayed a gentle smile and overwhelming sense of peace. She noted one more thing.

He appeared to be weeping.

Cheryl stood and walked to Abby Washington's reception desk. "The recycling," she said. "Do you know if the cleaners took it on Saturday?"

"Not sure. They do if it's full."

Cheryl discovered that the bin was half full. Beneath a few sheets of paper she saw the FedEx envelope from Russell. She removed it, returned to her office and closed the door. Cheryl poured over Russell's proposal to the Foundation for the next thirty minutes. It was beautifully written, expertly outlined, and compelling in its premise: the creation of a summer camp for underprivileged Chicago youth on a wilderness river in Ontario.

Four structures: a main lodge with one bedroom, bathroom, camp kitchen and large screened dining and activity area; two adjacent cottages with bunk beds, showers, composting toilets and a private bedroom for camp counselors; and one large storage shed. One cottage would house ten boys, the other ten girls. The male and female counselors would be young adults from the nearby Blackdog Ojibwe Indian reservation, hired and trained to the camp counselor standards of the Ontario provincial government. Unemployment among youth on the reservation age sixteen to twenty-two was over eighty percent. The program would provide positive benefit to these young people as well.

Every time a question popped into Cheryl's mind, it was answered within a few sentences. The camp could begin operations in mid-July next year and provide five sessions. In following years ten sessions would begin in June after school was out and conclude late August. Twenty campers would board the camp bus on Saturday afternoons. The bus would have two drivers and two camp counselors with reclining seats for sleeping so that it arrived at the camp at eight a.m. on Sunday. On Friday afternoons, the bus would return the campers to Chicago and pick up the next group of campers on Saturday.

Primary camp activities would be swimming, canoeing, fishing, hiking, camping and archery. Additional activities would include shelter building, woodcarving, wildlife tracking and identification, foraging for edible and medicinal plants, birdcall identification, fire making and nightly campfires with songs and storytelling. One activity Cheryl thought particularly clever was that each camper would make a pair of buckskin moccasins to take home at the end of their session. Always, emphasis would be placed on nature and environmental studies and awareness.

There would be no electronic devices at the camp. Cell phones would be turned in when campers arrived and returned to them upon departure.

Russell included a contact page of organizations providing similar youth wilderness experiences in other cities, as well as Wingate and Thriving Roots in Chicago. Cheryl knew the heads of both fine organizations and also knew that demand far exceeded supply. The positive, life-changing benefits of these programs to inner-city youth were made readily apparent in Russell's brief synopsis of testimonials and studies.

The final page was a breakdown of the costs. "Camp Kamini" had an estimated start-up cost of $970,000 US currency, to be donated by Russell Dean. The annual sustaining cost of $215,000 was to be paid by the Foundation through private and corporate donations raised by Russell Dean. Any shortfalls in the annual budget would be covered by Russell Dean.

Cheryl leaned back in her chair, her mouth agape. This was thrilling, astonishing ... brilliant. You didn't get proposals like this every day. Then she asked herself a question: What would she do were she to receive a similar proposal from a new private benefactor? Or a donation of over one million dollars for general use? The answer was obvious.

Without hesitation, Cheryl called Russell's cell. He certainly would have a new one by now. It rang as before, six rings then went to message. She hung up and called his office. "Jessica, hi, it's Cheryl, is Russell in?"

"Hi Cheryl, no ... he was, briefly, last week. Monday, I think. But he went back up to Canada."

"Do you have a new phone number for him? I'm not sure his old number works."

She gave Cheryl the new number.

Cheryl dialed it but after a series of beeps heard the message, "We're sorry, but the phone number you have dialed is either not in service or the system is experiencing technical problems."

Good grief, Cheryl thought. The newspaper article mentioned Russell had been a guest at the Kamini Lodge. She did a computer search and pulled up the Lodge's web site. For a moment, Cheryl sat transfixed as a photo of an astonishing, Canadian wilderness castle flooded her screen. She found the Lodge's phone number and dialed it.

"Good morning, Kamini Lodge, Grace speaking, how can I help you?"

"Hello, I'd like to speak to a guest of the Lodge, Russell Dean."

"I'm sorry, Pirate, er, Mr. Dean is not a current guest of the Lodge. I know he's in town though."

Did she just say pirate? "Well, do you know how I can reach him? It's important. I have his cell number, but calls aren't going through."

"No, a big fir went down last night in the storm, took out a support cable on the cell tower and it shut down. There's a crew on it. Not sure when it will be fixed." Grace thought for a moment. Rat was staying with Gribber. Was it OK to tell this woman that?

"Hold please," Grace said. "I'm going to transfer you."

Cheryl stared at Russell's proposal on her desk. A rich female voice came on the line.

"Good morning and thank you for calling Kamini Lodge. My name is Annie. How may I assist you?"

Chapter 44

The storm was still raging early Monday morning, the river furious with whitecaps while the rain pounded the roof of Morning Wood like sticks on a thousand Indian drums. Russell rolled over and grabbed a few more hours of sleep. Sunrise had been canceled.

When he awoke, the wind and rain were lessening but dark clouds lingered. He found Gribber in the kitchen cooking breakfast. "So, the power is still on but cell service is out," Gribber informed him. "My satellite Internet just kicked back in. Radar shows clearing around ten. I'll be shoving off around nine-thirty. What's your plan today?"

"Meeting with Chief Cameron up at the reservation at three to discuss hiring counselors for the camp. Other than that, read my emails, do some more planning work." Russell checked his emails while they ate. He clicked first on the one from Lydia White. "Yes! The landing property is ready for sale. Ninety-two thousand. Lydia sent me the name of the agent in Miskwa. She's expecting my call."

"Sounds about right," Gribber said. "Offer ninety thousand cash, you'll snatch it up. That's what, seventy thousand in Hawaiian money? Congratulations. Nice piece of property. If you want to call the agent, the landlines are probably working. Faith has one."

Russell drove to Faith's house after breakfast and found her gleefully up to her elbows in pastry dough. He called the agent and set a meeting for eleven-thirty. Back at Morning Wood, he transferred money from the cash account at his brokerage into his personal checking. The money was jointly Cheryl's, he realized, but that easily could be reconciled in the divorce settlement. They had over three million dollars of equity in their home. The market was good; it would sell quickly. Even after compensating Cheryl for this initial Camp Kamini expense, half the cash proceeds from the house sale would more than cover the camp's creation and first year operating expense.

At ten-thirty Russell drove to his meeting with the agent, Sally McBride. He'd grabbed his wallet, checkbook and passport, but as was becoming more the norm, forgot his flip phone.

The initial steps to the property purchase took only an hour. Russell admired the view of sprawling Lake of the Woods through the large window of McBride's tidy Miskwa real estate office. His offer was accepted and down payment made. McBride saw no reason she couldn't arrange the close on the property for later in the week.

Russell ate lunch at a good Greek restaurant on Main Street, bought socks at McTaggart's and kicked around Miskwa for another hour before driving up to the Blackdog reservation. He was greeted warmly by Chief Cameron in front of the band headquarters building.

"The elders and I are excited about your proposal," Cameron said. "I've already talked to several of the young people, and word has spread through the community. I don't think there'll be any problem getting your camp enthusiastic counselors."

Russell and Cameron sat for several hours in the band headquarters discussing the project. Counselors would work a long week, so they decided the camp would rely on a rotation of six. Cameron said he'd arrange it so those showing the best aptitude for the work would help prepare future counselors. Russell proposed a weekly salary for counselors that from his research he judged generous.

"That works," Cameron said.

Canadian Red Cross training courses teaching the required lifesaving and first aid skills were available year-round in Miskwa.

"Transportation?" Cameron asked.

In addition to paying for the training, Russell said that he would provide the reservation with a vehicle for camp-related use.

"Make it a crew cab pickup," Cameron said. "Those things are handy to have around."

Cameron pointed out that it could be used to transport new counselors and their gear to and from the reservation when camp was in session. In addition, the reservation could supply all the materials for teepees. Have the campers build a few traditional Ojibwe teepees and spend some nights in them.

"Great idea," Russell said. The pickup he had in mind was parked outside.

Both men had long lists of notes and action items when their meeting concluded.

"Hungry?" Cameron asked. "My wife Mary is making walleye tonight."

"My favorite," Russell said.

Cameron's cheerful wife, Mary, welcomed Russell into their home. Robert joined them for dinner. The four discussed the camp programs further as they ate fried walleye, wild rice and green beans.

"There should be a Rite of Passage," Mary said. "On Thursday nights, before the kids go home. A large fire, with drumming. The counselors could dress in native Ojibwe clothing, if you'd like. A ceremony where, one by one, each camper is acknowledged as family with the wilderness. Where they are told that what they have seen, heard, touched and smelled are now forever part of them. That the lessons they have learned from the wilderness can help guide them for the rest of their lives."

"That's brilliant," was all Russell could say.

Driving back to Kamini, Russell turned onto the narrow gravel road leading to the landing in Pistol Lake. He stopped and surveyed the property soon to be his. After Karpenko's shack was removed, there would be ample room for the main lodge building. The two cottages providing sleeping quarters could be nestled into the woods farther up from shore. The existing garage, he realized, wasn't in bad shape and could serve as storage space for camp equipment, with some improvements.

He walked to the water's edge. The rounded gravel comprising the center third of the shoreline transitioned to a white sand bottom stretching out as far as Russell could see—a beautiful sand beach. Though a stiff breeze fluttered the poplar and birch leaves, the water showed only ripples. The bay offered shelter from the wind.

On his right, terraced granite bluffs rose thirty feet high, speckled with moss and dabbed with tenacious birch and pine. Beyond the shack to his left, the dense forest rose gradually from the gently rounded granite shore. He made a mental note: create miles of winding pathways through the woods. The Queen certainly wouldn't mind.

Karpenko's fishing boat was gone. Russell examined the dock. It was in decent shape, supported by timber pylons driven into the soft, sandy bottom. It would suffice for next year. It could be replaced by a floating dock at some point in the future.

The future, Russell thought. He gazed across the property and envisioned Camp Kamini, the kids swimming at the sand beach, building a tepee in a clearing, discovering the plants and creatures and magic hidden in the forest, paddling canoes loaded with gear as they disappeared around the point en route to their next wilderness adventure.

Calls from the birds in the forest echoed across the bay as the sun began to set over the far shore. Russell gazed at the dappled water as it reflected the twinkling pinks and golds. He knew that, though he would possess this slice of wilderness by virtue of human law, he would never truly own it. The wilderness owned him. He closed his eyes and uttered a soft thank-you, aware that the grand future to unfold from this land could never have originated from his mind alone.

As he turned onto the gravel drive to Morning Wood, Russell checked the time and was surprised the evening had passed so quickly. It was nearly ten. The cottage was dark and empty, and the soft moonlight on the dock revealed that Gribber's boat was gone. Must be at the pub.

Russell switched on a light in the veranda and spotted his forgotten flip phone on the coffee table. Silly little thing, he thought to himself as he picked it up. Horrendous for reading or typing texts and as for emails, why bother. Good thing he no longer needed to set alarms, for that too was a convoluted chore. He looked at the small screen and saw he had messages. Three were from Gribber. The earliest was from his attorney, Bill Carter. He played it.

"Russell, it's Bill, it's uh, one o'clock. Hey, I just got a call from Cheryl's attorney. Damnedest thing … Cheryl has instructed her to postpone tomorrow's divorce hearing. She couldn't tell me anything more, so I don't know what the hell this is all about. Soon as I find out, I'll let you know. Later, bye."

As Russell stared at the river, the phone rang in his hand.

"Rat hole, you went off without your phone again," Gribber said. "Service was restored just after noon. Where the hell are you, Morning Wood?"

Russell was thrown off guard for a moment. It was the first time ever he heard Gribber sound a bit … angry. "Yes."

"Well good for you. Get your ass to the pub, *now*." Gribber hung up.

Russell dutifully climbed back into his truck and drove to Holst Point. Walking into the pub he spotted the usual suspects at their usual large, double table near the center of the room: Gribber, Jammer, Lydia, Faith and Lou LeBlanc facing him and the sides or backs of Wolf Graf, Dave Burtnyk, Sheri, Frank Dobbs, Annie Chase and Tony Carter, who was standing. Engrossed in boisterous, cross-table conversations, no one seemed to give any notice to his arrival. He grabbed an empty chair from another table and carried it over.

"Thanks, I think I *will* sit down," Carter said, snatching the chair from him. Carter began dragging it to the end of the table, revealing the slender back of a blonde woman Russell had not seen seated.

Cheryl Dean twisted her head around, looked up at Russell and grinned. "Hiya, Pirate," she said cheerfully. "Whatcha drinkin'?"

As noted previously, the human mind is a peculiar thing, hardly a novel statement never before expressed. So thoroughly out of context was Cheryl's presence in the Holst Point Pub in Kamini, Ontario that Russell's mind went as blank as the screen of his drowned cell phone. Involuntarily his mouth dropped open, he ceased breathing and lost the ability to speak. "What ..." Russell said finally, but could form no additional words.

"Not this routine again," Gribber said.

Russell scanned the faces around the table. Conversation had ceased and all were staring at him. He looked back to Cheryl. She was dressed in blue jeans and a flannel shirt. Still, it was not possible she was there. It was not possible that Cheryl was there in the pub seated between Annie Chase and Frank Dobbs.

"How ..."

Unable to hold their silence any longer the entire table burst into laughter.

"A two o'clock flight from Chicago to Winnipeg," Annie said. "Then she rented a car."

"Pretty drive," Cheryl said. "Only three hours."

"We've been here nearly two, waiting for you," Faith said. "Cheryl's a hoot. We're going to keep her and throw you back."

"Hey now," Cheryl said to Faith, "I told you I'm from a small resort town in the central Minnesota lake district. For two summers I worked in a bar a lot like this. Same kind of friendly folk." Turning back to Russell her face turned serious. "But now, I must confess, I have found a new love." She picked up the tall glass containing ice and amber liquid in front of her and marveled at it. "Rye and ginger ale. Who knew?"

"Take a seat, Rat," LeBlanc said, standing. "I gotta shove off. Some of us only drink every night but Mondays."

Russell sat down in the vacant chair across from Cheryl. She looked at him evenly but with a trace of a smile. "I want you to know that I'm blown away by your proposal for the youth camp," she said. "I started explaining it to your friends, why I was here, but they know all about it."

Russell glanced at Gribber, who looked up at the ceiling.

"Anyway," Cheryl said, "plenty of time to talk about things. That incredible Lodge is booked full, but my new pal Annie, here, is putting me up in her guest room. I've seen only the bit of the river on the boat ride from Annie's to Holst Point, but already I want to stay longer than I'd planned."

"Just wait," Russell and everyone else at the table said.

"And I want to go fishing!" Cheryl said. "Maybe with you, Faith, if the local pros are too busy?" She nodded to a fresh copy of the Miskwa newspaper lying on the table. The front page featured a photo of Gribber and Russell holding their tournament trophy.

"Tomorrow is good," Faith said.

"You fish?" Russell asked.

Cheryl looked at him and rolled her eyes. "I believe I just said I'm from a small resort town in the central Minnesota lake district. You've been there, remember?"

"Sometimes, Herr Pirate," Graf said, "in a moment of rising fortune, it is wisest to smile and say nothing."

"And as I was saying to *you*, my angel," Dobbs said, turning in his chair and taking Cheryl's hands in his, "before being interrupted by all this nugatory nonsense ... Did you know that if you stand on the end of the Holst Point dock at midnight on August seventeenth of each year, stare at the stars due north for fifteen seconds without blinking, then close your eyes ..."

Epilogue

For the first time in the nearly five months he'd known him, Russell sensed that Gribber, standing like a rock on the button of the curling sheet, was nervous. *Raise your head*, Russell thought. *Smile, even. At least look like you're not about to pass out.*

Gribber showed a few timid signs of life, lifting his head and emerging from what appeared to be a trance. He patted the beaded Ojibwe necklace flowing across his chest worn in lieu of a tie with his navy blue suit. Adjusting his footing ever so slightly, he was fortunate that on a mild October afternoon inside the Kamini curling rink, he was standing in the center of rings painted on concrete and not an actual sheet of ice. Wearing native Ojibwe moccasins, in his stupor he might have slipped and fallen right on his can.

Over one hundred people seated in folding chairs looked at Gribber, Jammer and another man standing at the end of the long, hangar-type building attached to the Kamini Community Center. Twenty round banquet tables filled the periphery of the three-sheet curling rink.

Neil Young's "Heart of Gold" began playing through two portable speakers. All heads turned when the door at the other end opened. Faith entered dressed in moccasins and a sleeveless beige dress. She held a small bouquet of native, fall-blooming flowers. Smiling softly, she walked down the center aisle to the end of the rink then pivoted to face the crowd. All in attendance again turned in their chairs to focus on the open door to the Community Center.

Annie Chase entered on the arm of her father.

She wore a dress similar to Faith's except accented by colorful beadwork along the v-neckline. The dress hung below the knee, just covering the tops of ornate, calf-high moccasins. Her hair was piled in billowy clouds held in place by a slender, beaded buckskin headband and artfully infused with white, yellow and pink blossoms matching those in Faith's bouquet.

Staring only at Gribber, the warmth in her beaming smile would have melted ice in January.

Cheryl gave a soft gasp and squeezed Russell's hand as Annie passed their row. Russell stared as transfixed as the first time he saw her, entering into the light at Karpenko's landing. With the exception of Cheryl, Annie Chase was the most beautiful bride he had ever seen.

The loud, unbridled reception that followed would be Kamini's biggest party of the year and the guests were determined it should last. After dinner, Russell and Cheryl caught up on news around town since their August visit. They congratulated Lydia on her appointment as Director of the new, six-officer Ministry office in Miskwa. She and Jammer would live in the houseboat until the river froze, then move into a house they'd rented in Miskwa for winter.

Both noticed Faith and Wolf seated together with the bride and groom at dinner. While chatting in a large group, Russell asked Faith by way of an inquisitive look if they were a couple. Her quick smile and nod of her head told him they were, and that it was good.

Chesterfield Potato kicked off an evening of dancing with a sure-footed cover version of Bachman Turner Overdrive's "You Ain't Seen Nothin' Yet." Their courageously tattooed and pierced current drummer appeared to be a devoted biker in his sixties, at least, but he knew his way around a drum kit. For the first time Russell heard Jammer play guitar. The best man was superb. Russell steadfastly avoided dancing, being poor at it, but happily gave Cheryl his hand as she dragged him onto the dance floor.

Russell and Cheryl located the bride and groom to say good-night before heading back to their room at the Lodge.

"So, the scoop for tomorrow," Gribber said. "Five-thirty, you two plus Faith and Wolf at my place ... our place ... one of our places, for a quick dinner then musky fishing. Supposed to be a beautiful day, maybe the last mild one of fall."

"Perfect," Cheryl said. "Russell and I aren't flying back until Monday."

Cheryl had remained in town for three days after stunning Russell with her presence at the Holst Point Pub, ample time for Kamini to claim a portion of her soul. Back in Chicago, whether during her morning commute, in meetings or preparing for bed, from over nine hundred miles away this abridged part of her beamed constant, soft assurance that she magically was now alive in two places at once. Russell had stayed for five days longer, leaving Kamini after closing on the landing property and meeting with Jammer at the future camp site. Arriving back in Chicago, the first thing he and Cheryl did was sell the house.

Dinner at Morning Wood the following day featured cubed walleye appetizers, hearty beef stew and Faith's blueberry pie. Wolf excused himself from the fishing and, with a kiss to Faith, drove back to his resort to deal with a persistently leaky roof on one of the guest cottages. Rain was forecast for tomorrow.

"Girls boat, boy's boat," Annie announced as they headed to the dock. Cheryl, Faith and Annie climbed into Faith's G3 while Russell and Gribber untied his trusty steed.

"Just bang around Gunn?" Gribber asked.

"Sure," Annie said. "Sunset is so early now. We'll be ice fishing before you know it."

The two boats headed across Gunn Lake, hopscotching from shoreline to shoreline as the group casted for muskies off various weed beds and reefs. Cheryl and Faith took turns using Faith's rod, Faith patiently tutoring Cheryl on the finer points of musky casting. Gribber and Russell ducked around the backside of Big Island where Russell caught a hard-fighting, forty-six-inch musky.

Emerging around the far end of the island, Gribber spotted the women casting in the narrows under the power lines and drove over to check in.

"Cheryl had a musky follow and caught a huge snake!" Annie shouted as they approached. "She's a natural."

Russell beamed at his wife who smiled back.

"Thought we'd run into Lost Bay," Gribber said. "Hit a few of the spots down to the end. Plenty of room for two boats."

"We're going to put the rods away and cruise up through Myrtle to The Dalles and back," Annie said. "Cheryl's never seen that part of the river."

"Besides, our boat features cocktails," Faith said, lifting a red plastic cup from one of the drink holders. "We want to putt the prettiest stretches and gab about the hopelessness of men."

"A cunning plan, ladies, but remember, the eagles are my spies," Gribber said. "Meet you back at the ranch." Gribber throttled up to full speed and headed into Lost Bay.

The water of the great river was turning colder, as if welcoming the impending gray skies and snow flurries of November. The big northern pike had returned to the shallow bays from their summer deep water haunts to join the muskies. Casting toward shore as well as into the wide, shallow channel, both men had pulse-pounding follows from big fish.

"So how is condo living treating you two?" Gribber asked as he paused to change lures.

"The only way to go," Russell said. "Cozy two-bedroom, nothing fancy, it's quick to Cheryl's office, and I walk ten blocks to mine. Turn the second bedroom into a nursery, the doctor says there's no reason not to expect a normal pregnancy this time. Probably buy a small house after that."

"So, your business partner bought into the new plan?"

"Oh, Dan hesitated, but already sees it's working out. I was always the creative idea man, so nothing's really changed. I just don't mother hen the process anymore. It frees up a lot of my time to spend on the camp. Still, Cheryl and I have a new rule: home from work by five-thirty, and no working on weekends."

"I swung by the camp last week," Gribber said. "It looks great. Jammer and crew are killing it."

"Should be ready to go this July. The funding has been even easier than I thought. I sit down and explain the camp, and corporations jump at the chance to support it. Cheryl and I will live at the camp full time in summer. I'll be Camp Director, and Cheryl can run the rest of the Foundation business from there."

Gribber started the boat and drove deeper into the bay before pulling up to a large weed bed.

"I told you last night, but your wedding was beautiful," Russell said as the two men resumed casting.

"Long overdue," Gribber said. "Your little odyssey helped me quite a bit, you know. You're not the only guy lucky enough to find his true love then be really stupid about it."

"How late did the reception go?"

"Annie and I left at two-thirty. For all we know, it's still going." The large orange sun was low on the horizon, visible through a tall veil of cirrus clouds. "Getting late. Lock and load, we'll zoom to the end, toss our final casts around Pirate's Reef."

Gribber hooked a small musky off the sand and boulder shoreline at the end of the bay, and brought it in quickly. He removed the lure and studied the fish as it recovered beside the boat. "Around thirty-six inches, one of the two or three males that hang around the female claiming this territory. Be fun to find her. Keep casting as we move toward the reef."

After casting thirty more yards of shoreline, Gribber approached Pirate's Reef and cut the motor. The sun had just dipped below a distant horizon of finely serrated evergreen treetops. Slender ribbons of clouds in shades of pink, yellow, orange and indigo fanned out in layers from the horizon to high overhead. The vivid colors were projected across the entire expanse of water as it mirrored the sky.

As Gribber finished a retrieve, Russell put down his rod and stood, waiting, staring out at the still water.

The enormous musky was swimming just below the surface straight toward the boat, the V-shaped wake expanding outward from its head sending multicolored ripples across the glass. As it swam to within two feet of the boat the musky raised its head above water and stared straight at Russell. Neither man spoke, Gribber because he had never seen a musky so large and Russell because he had.

Russell stared into the musky's eyes as his every thought vanished. After a moment he blinked twice and turned to look at Gribber. The musky lowered its head and began swimming slowly until its body was parallel to the boat.

"Friend of yours?" Gribber asked, feeling as if witnessing a dream.

"We've met, yes. She wants to show you something."

Gribber didn't understand.

"The tape," Russell said.

The fish was motionless beside the boat. Gribber picked up the tape measure. He leaned over the fish, pulled out the end from the rounded casing and held it above the tip of the musky's tale. Spreading his arms nearly as wide as he could, he extended the tape to the end of its snout and locked it with his thumb. He stood and studied the number emerging from the casing.

"Sixty inches," he said softly. "Five feet."

The musky slowly waved its tail and swam along the surface back to its lair surrounding Pirate's Reef. Angling toward the river bottom, it dissolved into the water like a ghost.

The lilting, echoing calls of birds in the marsh and vast forest beyond were the only sounds as the two men stood enveloped by the glowing twilight. Finally, Gribber spoke. "What did she tell you?"

Russell lifted his head to gaze at the tapestry of colors blended across water and sky. "She told me she has ruled these waters for a very long time and won't remain in her present state much longer. She told me it was nice to see me. She told me the false fish we splash into the water look ridiculous." Russell turned, looked at Gribber and smiled.

"Then she reminded me to always get up just before sunrise for as long as I am lucky enough to be in Kamini."

Acknowledgments

My warmest thanks to Margaret Noodin, Anishinaabe poet and Professor of English and American Indian Studies at the University of Wisconsin-Milwaukee and Director of the Electa Quinney Institute for American Indian Education. Margaret cheerfully served as Ojibwe cultural advisor to the novel, ensuring that my representation of Ojibwe fishing guide John Dogrib and depictions of Ojibwe history, culture and lore were accurate. She also provided the translations from English into Ojibwe and wrote the Ojibwe prayer that appears in the book. I was honored that she created and granted the Ojibwe name, "Biidaapiwinini," to Mr. Dogrib, no trifling matter. Miigwech!

Scott Walker, a marvelous writer and novelist, served as my Guernica editor and made my first time through this trepidatious experience breezy and fun. Scott, your suggestions, edits and astute literary judgment improved the novel throughout. Thank you, my friend.

To Michael Mirolla, Publisher and Editor-in-Chief of Guernica Editions, thank you for judging my work worthy of being published by your prestigious company.

About the Author

DON ENGEBRETSON grew up in Deephaven, Minnesota, but it was summers spent at the family cottage in Minaki, Ontario that shaped his character. At a young age, Don learned to swim, water-ski, fish and drive a boat, all the while relishing his tender, seasonal friendships with Canadian cottage kids. Sure, in his teenage years, his cooler, better-educated and infinitely more rambunctious Canadian peers led him resolutely astray, often to disastrous ends, but usually Don had it coming. Don began writing about gardening in 1990 and soon was writing for national magazines and newspapers across the US. He is a five-time winner of the Garden Globe Award from Garden Communicators International. In 2019 he wrote this, his debut novel, inspired by his decades of summers in Ontario. He and his Canadian-born partner of fourteen years, Karen, reside in winter at his home in Nevada and in summer at her cottage in Minaki, where they dated as teenagers.

Contact and keep up with Don at donengebretson.com.